A DREAM COME TRUE

"I didn't realize how much I've missed you," Ty admitted.

His voice struck a chord inside Cammie, and she gazed at him with unknowing longing written all over her face. Any skills she possessed as an actress fled with the need to be with the man she loved—and had always loved, at some level. Ty's swift intake of breath said he didn't mistake the signs, but he still hesitated.

"Cammie . . . ?" he asked uncertainly.

"Aren't you going to kiss me?" she heard herself ask from far, far away.

He smothered a sound of disbelief. "Yes," he said.

Putting action to words, he leaned forward. She could feel the heat of his skin through his shirt, and her hands eased their way up his chest.

She waited, suspended in helpless anticipation. She'd yearned for this since the night they'd made love so long ago, and even before that, when she'd been an adolescent awash in unrealized dreams, hungry for love and affection and the sensation of his touch. . . .

Also by Janelle Taylor:

ANYTHING FOR LOVE
BY CANDLELIGHT
CHASE THE WIND
DEFIANT HEARTS
DESTINY MINE
DESTINY'S TEMPTRESS
FIRST LOVE, WILD LOVE
FOLLOW THE WIND
FORTUNE'S FLAMES
GOLDEN TORMENT
KISS OF THE NIGHT WIND
LAKOTA WINDS
THE LAST VIKING QUEEN
LOVE ME WITH FURY
MIDNIGHT SECRETS
PASSIONS WILD AND FREE
PROMISE ME FOREVER
SWEET, SAVAGE HEART
TAKING CHANCES
WHISPERED KISSES
WILD IS MY LOVE
WILD WINDS

The *Moondust and Madness* Series:
MOONDUST AND MADNESS
STARDUST AND SHADOWS
STARLIGHT AND SPLENDOR
MOONBEAMS AND MAGIC

The *Savage Ecstasy* Series:
SAVAGE ECSTASY
DEFIANT ECSTASY
FORBIDDEN ECSTASY
BRAZEN ECSTASY
TENDER ECSTASY
STOLEN ECSTASY
BITTERSWEET ECSTASY
FOREVER ECSTASY
SAVAGE CONQUEST

SOMEDAY SOON

JANELLE TAYLOR

Zebra Books
Kensington Publishing Corp.
http://www.zebrabooks.com

ZEBRA BOOKS are published by

Kensington Publishing Corp.
850 Third Avenue
New York, NY 10022

First Printing: January, 1999
10 9 8 7 6 5 4 3 2 1

Printed in the United States of America

CHAPTER ONE

If fate were a woman, I wouldn't be in this situation, Cammie Merrill thought. *I'd be my own boss and my ex-husband would have no power over me. In fact,* I'd *be the boss and he'd be my slave. No, better yet, I'd be the boss and he would live on another planet . . .*

But the truth was, Paul Merrill stood right in front of her, arms folded over his chest, ankles negligently crossed in front of him as he leaned against the edge of his desk. It was a pose meant to relax her, but Cammie knew better than to let down her guard in front of him. She'd had four years of marriage to learn the true merit of the man, and she knew his summoning her today did not bode well.

"Sit down, Camilla," he urged, extending an arm toward one of the club chairs nestled against the wall.

"Thanks, I'd rather stand."

His lips tightened briefly, then he shrugged. "You know the show's going in a new direction," he began. "We're trimming a few of the lesser characters and focusing on the original cast. They're the lifeblood of *Cherry Blossom Lane,* and let's face it, Donna Jenkins isn't one of them."

Cammie met his gaze, desperately trying to get her suddenly banging heart to slow down. She didn't want to feel this way. She didn't want Paul to know how much he was devastating her. "I got you this job," she reminded him quietly. "And now you're firing me?"

The tips of his ears reddened. "It's not up to me! Donna Jenkins has been around for three seasons already, and frankly, she's about used up. Maybe if you'd created a more memorable character, things would have been different."

Cammie's lips parted in anger and disbelief. Before she could respond, however, Paul hurriedly jumped in again. "I know you tried hard. It just didn't work."

She regarded him coolly. Didn't work? He knew, as well as she did, that she'd taken a walk-on part and turned it into a living, breathing woman who'd touched the hearts and minds of a sympathetic public. Donna Jenkins, her role on the nighttime drama, *Cherry Blossom Lane,* was a woman whose search for love had invariably led her into the arms of the wrong men, men who used her as a stepping-stone for their own ambitions. As a parallel for her own life, it couldn't be more accurate.

"Now, I know what you're thinking," Paul said, spreading his hands. "But I had nothing to do with this. Everyone loves you here, but in a few weeks, when we film the finale, Donna Jenkins is kaput."

"All right."

His brows lifted in surprise. He did not expect her capitulation. "That's it?"

"What do you want me to do, Paul? Beg you to keep me on?"

"Come on, Camilla, relax. Don't be that way."

"What way?" Cammie was too upset to meekly turn tail and run.

"I know you didn't want me here," he sputtered. "I know you're thinking I'm behind this. But you know, it wasn't entirely because of your famous family that I landed this job. People know me in this town. I've got a reputation."

Cammie almost laughed aloud. She'd reluctantly helped him get hired on *Cherry Blossom Lane* only because he'd begged and pleaded and threatened her during the whole course of their marriage. But power was an addiction for Paul, and as soon as he was on staff, he set out to worm his way up the executive ladder. He'd succeeded, too, and had risen from minor underling to co-executive producer in less than three years.

But regardless of his assertion that she belonged to a "famous" family, she'd won her role by sheer talent and determination. Her famous family was really her step-family, and for reasons she didn't like dwelling on, she was no longer in contact with any of them. Just thinking about them sent a frisson of discomfort down her spine.

With an effort, she pushed those thoughts aside and kept her focus on her ex-husband. "Well, I guess that's all we have to say to each other."

"I may not be long with the show, either, as it happens," Paul said a bit reflectively.

"Hmmm." His future didn't really interest her.

Or so she thought, until he added, "I've been talking to some of the right people, and the Connellys have asked me to come on board."

The Connellys? Cammie's jaw nearly dropped, but before her shock could register, she gritted her teeth together and let her face register only mild interest. The Connellys were one of the hottest production teams going in Hollywood these days. If Paul were actually telling the truth . . .

Suddenly Cammie was angry, really angry. It wasn't fair that he'd up and decided to get rid of her. *And then to brag about his own continued success!* It was unconscionable.

"You're a real piece of work, Paul Merrill," she told him flatly. "You make certain I'm fired, then you have the audacity to tell me that you've got a better job on the line. Well, if you think I'm going to congratulate you, you're mistaken."

"Look, I've got other issues here, Camilla," he declared. "Don't insult me."

"Other issues!" she sputtered. "You took my job from me, and you know it. Worse yet, you don't even care."

"It's not like that. Just—relax."

"Stop telling me to relax, and stop calling me Camilla. You know I hate it."

His sigh was long-suffering, as if she were just too, too impossible to deal with. "You're always jumping to conclusions."

"Oh, am I? You mean, you didn't just fire me?"

"That's not the issue I wanted to talk to you about today."

She shook her head in utter disbelief. "Are you kidding? Forgive me, Paul, but it's all that's on my mind!"

"Come on, give me a chance to explain," he demanded crossly.

"Like you've given me such a chance?" she responded, her voice filled with sad irony.

That, at least, seemed to penetrate. Paul looked away for a moment, but he recovered with more speed than the situation warranted. Throwing her a quick, assessing look she couldn't quite read, he revealed, "I've got something else in mind for you."

"Oh, thanks very much."

"No, this is good. Great, actually." He pinched his lower lip together with his thumb and forefinger, a habit denoting intense concentration.

Still reeling from his earlier news, she shook her head. She didn't want to hear any more.

"Believe me, your part was written out on *Cherry Blossom* without any influence from me. The show's got a bold new direction. You've been scheduled to die at the season finale for a long time."

Cammie refused to acknowledge that she'd heard rumors to that effect. Rumors abounded on the set. There was a certain paranoia about being "let go" at all times in an industry where one pretty face could be substituted so easily for another.

"Well, it's fact," Paul said into the silence. He gave her

another look as he dropped into his desk chair, propping his ankles on the polished mahogany finish as if it were a secondhand reject. "Okay, I pushed the powers-that-be and had you bumped out a little sooner than originally scheduled. No big deal. And it leaves you free to try other things."

"Don't do me any favors, Paul!"

"The finale's fabulous. Judith and Becca are both accused of your murder. It's going to be fabulous. The ratings will soar!" His eyes actually misted over. Paul Merrill was ready to swoon with delight.

"I'm happy for you," Cammie murmured sardonically.

"Don't get snippy. I told you I've got something for you, and I do. It's big." He slid her a sideways smile. His expression warred between excitement and a certain hesitancy, as if he knew his pending news wasn't as wonderful as he would like her to believe.

Cammie braced herself. "What is it?" she asked, certain the other shoe was about to drop.

"Just a film role, that's all."

"Oh, sure."

"A co-starring role."

"Paul . . ." she warned. She'd heard that line a million times before. Half the time "co-star" meant minor character left on the cutting-room floor.

He waved her skepticism aside. "This is the opportunity of a lifetime!"

Cammie couldn't believe his theatrics. Around the set she and Paul had made a practice of ignoring each other, elevating it to near art form, and suddenly here they were, talking as if they were almost friends. She knew better than to trust him. She'd been down that road before.

"Paul—that you can get me fired, then try and make me believe you've done me a *favor!*" Cammie inhaled deeply. "Words truly fail me."

"You're not listening. I've got you a film, for God's sake. That's what I was talking to the Connellys about! Summer Solstice Productions, Camilla! Do you hear me?"

"Summer Solstice?" Cammie repeated blankly. Summer Solstice was the name of James and Nora Connelly's production company, and its string of successes was already legendary.

"Production starts next fall. This property's red hot and ready to roll. *And they want you!*" he finished triumphantly, holding his arms out as if she should want to jump into them.

Cammie didn't know what to think. She was still furious with him, but he seemed completely serious. A Summer Solstice film? Unbelievable. James and Nora Connelly were a young husband and wife team whose string of modest successes and last winter's huge blockbuster film had shot them from obscurity to fame and fortune. They were the newest rage. Hollywood's current golden couple. Everyone who was anybody tried to curry their favors.

Cammie didn't believe Paul. She couldn't. "They want me to screen test," she corrected. "I've got an audition, not a part."

"No, they want *you.*" He dropped his feet to the floor and leaned over the desk.

"What's the catch?"

"You hurt me, Cammie. You really do."

"You just fired me, Paul," she pointed out sardonically. "Who's hurt whom?"

"Oh, Cammie . . ." Paul sighed hugely and shook his head, but Cammie held firm. The way he was acting told her there was more going on here than met the eye, but to rail further against his letting her go wouldn't accomplish anything. Moreover, she sensed that it was water under the bridge. Paul and *Cherry Blossom Lane* were the past and had been for a while, it appeared, even though she'd been the last to know.

"All right, I'll bite. So, what's this fabulous role?" she asked into the gathering silence.

"Well . . ." He steepled his fingers together on the desk, staring at them as if they held all of life's mysteries within their grasp. Cammie suspected he was searching for the right way to lure her into the trap. "You're being considered for the female lead in a romantic drama."

Cammie didn't move a muscle. She was certain she was dreaming. The female lead? Impossible! Supporting role, maybe. But even that was an outside chance at best.

When she didn't comment, Paul clucked his tongue. "Here, you think the worst of me, but who do you think it was that talked Nora and Jim into using you? Who do you think that was, huh? Yours truly. Good old Paul. That's who got you the audition."

"Audition," she repeated, catching him out. Her hopes sank and she dared to breathe again. She'd been right. An audition meant you were in a cattle call with about ten thousand other hopefuls.

Paul waved that aside. "Aren't you listening? Right now you're their first choice."

"No."

"Yes!"

"How?" she blurted out, furious with herself for the rising hope she couldn't quite tamp down. If she didn't watch out, it would suffocate her. "How can I be their first choice? They don't even know me! No one knows me outside of television! How would James and Nora Connelly even consider a nobody like me? You're lying to me."

"I am not! You've got an audition on Friday. Because of me," he reminded her tightly. "And a lot of thanks I get."

"Paul!" Cammie shook her head.

"The role's tailor made for you. Young woman trying to make it in the world meets guy, falls in love, gets pregnant, guy leaves her, she has the baby, then they get together in the end."

"Now, there's an original plot."

"That's just your part. The basic story is about a guy who loses everything to greed, then fights his way back to the top, redeeming himself along the way."

"Are you for real, Paul?"

"Why do you doubt me so much? Here . . ."

He reached into a drawer and sailed a copy of a screenplay across his desk. It slipped over the edge and fluttered to the floor. Cammie picked it up.

"*Rock Bottom,*" she murmured, checking out the title.

"Read it tonight. It's good."

That little light of hope still flickered somewhere inside her; she just couldn't quite extinguish it. Sighing, Cammie gave in. "What are you up to, Paul? Do I have to strip naked and mud wrestle or something? No, I don't want to know." She held up her hand as he started to answer. "Whatever it is, it's no good. I'm not gullible anymore, Paul."

"Read the damn screenplay! See for yourself."

"I will read it."

"Good."

"Good," she repeated tersely, staring at him.

Silence stretched between them. She watched Paul pinch his lower lip once again.

"You're working yourself up to tell me something more," Cammie guessed.

"There is something . . ." he admitted, grimacing a bit.

Cammie, who'd perched on the edge of her chair to collect the screenplay, now flopped back into the chair. "I don't want to hear it!"

"Now, don't get all huffy."

She simply snorted her disgust, crossed her arms over her chest and tried to forget how much of a worm Paul Merrill was. What a jerk! He loved raising her hopes just to crush them back down.

"It's not that bad. You don't have to do anything on camera you might object to, within reason, of course. Nora and James just want you to help sign your co-star."

"What does that mean?" she asked cautiously.

"They're having a little get-together Friday night. At their house in Brentwood. We could go."

Cammie stared. Things were moving way too fast. Was there any chance Paul was on the level? Summer Solstice wanted *her*? As far as she knew, the Connellys only chose from Hollywood's A-List of stars—which Cammie definitely was not on.

Did I say A-List? I'm not even in the same alphabet!

"Cammie?"

With an effort she shook herself out of her reverie. "Help sign my co-star?" she asked, remembering the request tagged on to this startling bit of news. "I don't understand. I don't have any clout with anyone."

"Well, that's not quite true."

"Who?" But before her lips could change from the "o" of her question, the answer sizzled across her brain: the Stovalls. Her famous stepfamily.

"If they want Samuel Stovall, they can certainly pick up the phone themselves," Cammie stated tightly, referring to her ex-stepfather. Samuel was a Hollywood icon, and one of the most selfish men Cammie ever had the misfortune to meet.

"It's not Samuel they want," Paul said slowly, his eyes closely watching her face.

Cammie sat perfectly still; her brain strangely frozen. Some part of her had known this was where Paul had been headed from the moment he'd brought up her connection to the Stovalls. There was another actor in the Stovall family, and it was thinking of him that made Cammie squirm and feel heat invade her cheeks.

"No," she said in a low voice.

Paul nodded solemnly.

"No . . ." she whispered again, not believing what had to be true.

"Tyler Stovall," he said aloud.

Tyler Stovall . . . Hearing his name again after all these years had the power to turn Cammie's insides to liquid. He was her worst mistake—more dire than the one she'd made by marrying Paul—and the thought of him still held so much power that for a moment Cammie couldn't speak. Finding her voice with an effort, she said, "He's been missing for ten years."

"You can find him," he said with certainty.

Cammie's aqua eyes gazed at him in disbelief. "Are you crazy? *Tyler Stovall?* Was this your idea? For God's sake, Paul. You're unbelievable!"

"It's not that big of a deal."

"Not that big of a deal!"

"You know him," Paul pointed out tautly. "Better than anyone."

"Not true! I haven't been close to him in years—even before he disappeared. You know that! For heaven's sake, no one's sure if he's even alive!"

"Oh, he's alive."

"How do you know?"

"It stands to reason. If he were dead, the whole world would know it. That kind of news travels like lightning. No, he's hiding out somewhere. Cammie, it's Paul you're talking to, remember? We've discussed this. You and I both know that, for whatever reason, he packed it in, left Hollywood and chose to live the life of a recluse in some podunk part of the world where no one can recognize him. But whatever sent him away is long over now," Paul rationalized. "It's time he came back."

"Easy for you to say, Paul! We don't know what happened to him. No one does but Tyler!"

"Look, I'm just being realistic. Nora and James want Tyler for this picture. It would be a great comeback film for him. They're willing to use you if you can get him."

"Otherwise, any number of starlets will do," she stated with a certain amount of bitterness.

He spread his hands. "I didn't make the rules in this town."

"No, but you sure know how to play by them!"

"Camilla, come on. You can reach him. I know you can."

"I don't have any idea where he is!"

Paul made a face, as if Tyler Stovall's disappearance had been perpetrated just to annoy him personally. "No one does. The guy's a damn *ghost.* But you could find out. His family would talk to you. Hell, they're your family, too."

"Not anymore!"

"Well, they were once. Come on, Cammie. You know what I'm saying. This could be the biggest thing you'll ever see."

Her legs shaking from outrage, Cammie strode over to the desk, glaring down at her ex-husband. He straightened in his chair and smoothed back his thinning hair. He'd once been very good-looking, but now he sported that well-fed, too-many-steaks-and-martinis look, and his natural appeal had all but vanished. She wondered anew what she'd ever seen in him. "I won't do it."

"You're slitting your own throat."

"My prerogative."

"Look, somebody's going to find him. If you don't do it, someone else will. Nora and James really want him, and they're willing to pay a lot. Someone with less scruples than yourself will get the job done, and your role will go to an actress with less credentials and talent, but who'll play the game. That's the way it always is."

"Your cynicism has rotted your soul, Paul."

He half-laughed. "I don't have a soul left, Cammie. I sold it years ago. You should take a lesson."

"I'd rather die a painful, humiliating, grisly death."

"That's what the death of your career will feel like."

"Go to hell, Paul." She strode toward the door, feeling slightly sick and definitely depressed.

"Think about it, Cammie. Friday night. At the Connellys' Brentwood home."

She glanced back, so infuriated she could hardly see. And the worst of it was that Paul was right! Just because she possessed more morals and ethics than most of the dwellers around these parts didn't mean it would turn her into a success. And that made her all the angrier. She wanted to call him filthy, low-down dirty names, and when he lifted his brows in challenge, she had to fight down the bile bubbling in the back of her throat.

"Fate *is* a man," she muttered through clenched teeth, and was gratified at least to witness his look of total incomprehension before she slammed the door to his office behind her, closing his wretched visage from her sight.

Maybe it was because she never spoke of it. Maybe it was because Tyler's father, Samuel Stovall, had been married so many times that some of his ex-wives, and certainly his ex-stepdaughters, were forgotten memories. Or maybe it was because Tyler had been gone for so many years and that she, Cammie, refused to think about him.

Or maybe it was remembering how close they'd once been . . .

Shivering in the bright L.A. sunshine, Cammie climbed into her blue BMW and headed outside the studio, waving to the guard at the gate for one of the last times. With a pang, she thought about the job on *Cherry Blossom Lane* that was about to end. A new chapter of her life was beginning.

Tyler Stovall . . .

Waiting at a red light, Cammie closed her eyes for a moment. Thinking about him wouldn't do. Not now. Not ever. She wanted her association with the Stovalls to be a forgotten memory in this community. It was just too bad Paul knew so much about her history.

But he didn't know about Tyler and her. Not all of it. Tyler, himself, might not remember that last fateful night they'd shared together, for he'd been too unhappy, too destroyed, and too drunk for it to be a complete memory.

At least that's what she told herself.

Oh, Cammie, she thought for about the billionth time. *How could you have?*

Punching out a number on her cellular phone, Cammie weaved her way toward the Hollywood Freeway. Teri, the receptionist for her agent, Susannah Coburn, put her on hold without checking who was on the line. Knowing how busy Susannah could be, Cammie hung up. She would call Susannah later. Right now, she just wanted to get home.

Tyler Stovall . . .

She'd adored him as a teenager, and when he'd gone on to megafame, becoming an icon in the acting profession in six short years, she'd nearly fallen into a coma of delight. All those other girls might salivate over him, but Tyler was her big brother.

Sort of.

Tyler, for mysterious reasons no one seemed to understand, had disappeared ten years earlier. There was speculation he was dead, ill, or dying. People thought he'd run off with some woman he didn't want the press to know about. While a Hollywood celebrity, he'd been hounded by paparazzi in the usual fashion and had been known to politely, but firmly, run them off his property. Once, if one could believe everything they read, he'd actually come at a trespasser while riding on his lawn mower. Tyler had simply pushed the man and his invasive camera into the water of a pond located on his property. Incensed, the interloper had sued him—and lost. He had been trespassing, after all, and no one looked favorably on the viciousness of celebrity stalkers in the first place.

Glancing in the rearview mirror, Cammie encountered her own blue-green, anxious eyes. That anxiety was for a lot of reasons, not least the matter of *her* one night with Tyler. She'd never forgotten him; he probably didn't remember. But if she should encounter him again . . . then, what? How could she ever explain that sleeping with him while he was under the influence had just happened, the result of some unfulfilled love and need that had suddenly taken over her common sense.

No! She could never try to find him now. However remote her chance of success might be, she couldn't face him again. She couldn't face herself.

You called Paul a coward, but you're *the coward.*

Pressing her foot to the accelerator, she headed up the on-ramp to the freeway, desperately in need of speed to help her outrun her memories. But once trapped in the afternoon traffic, speed eluded her, and her jumbled thoughts and fears surged to the forefront of her brain.

The soft touch of his kisses, his sinewy limbs surrounding her, the sweet thrill of his uneven breaths feathering her skin, the strength of his possession . . . to this day the recollections made her shudder and squirm with humiliation, although another part of herself was still so very susceptible! She hated thinking about their night together, yet it crept into her dreams even to this day. She wished she could forget the feel of his strong body pressed against her softer form, his lips possessively demanding her response, her own body eagerly responding.

Unbidden, a squeak of protest rose to her lips. She shook herself to get rid of the feelings, wishing she were free of the past.

And though she should be glad that he'd been dead drunk at the time and probably didn't remember a thing, she still couldn't help wishing he'd been sober enough to realize what he was doing. Maybe then he would not have reached for her, and maybe then she would have been able to resist . . .

She hadn't been in contact with Tyler since that night, and though she'd wondered about his later disappearance, she'd been aware Tyler had been suffering some kind of major emotional trauma the night she'd slept with him. He'd been distraught and seeking comfort—and she'd been there. It was just too bad she hadn't relied on her normal common sense and had succumbed instead to hot desire.

Ah, well, Cammie thought resignedly. Such were the mistakes nightmares were made of.

How did Paul expect her to find Tyler anyway? There was no doubt in Cammie's mind that Tyler's overbearing, egocentric father, Samuel Stovall, had raised heaven and earth looking for him. Why hadn't Paul contacted the great Samuel Stovall himself?

Wrinkling her nose in distaste, Cammie considered the Hollywood legend who'd sired Tyler. Sam Stovall was still a recognized leading man, though with the meteoric rise of Tyler's fame, his had certainly taken a backseat. And though it was true that Samuel's A-List stature had slipped a few degrees after Tyler's disappearance, he still was a fairly weighty name in town. He would certainly have a better chance and more resources for finding his son.

Maybe he even knew where Tyler was.

Cammie had lost contact with both Tyler and Sam when Sam divorced her mother. Samuel had moved on to a new wife—his fourth at last count—and Cammie's mother had slipped into deep depression, followed by a losing battle with cancer. Cammie, who'd never much liked her adulterous stepfather in the first place, Hollywood legend or no, blamed Samuel for contributing to her mother's death. Unwarranted, perhaps, but it was how she'd always felt, and she had been unable to ever completely recognize his innocence in the matter.

Tyler, on the other hand, held her heart within his grasp—had he but known it. Cammie dreamed of him long after he was a forgotten part of her life, and when she married Paul, it was simply as a substitute for the man who'd disappeared from her life and the world at large.

Oh, she hadn't known it at the time, of course. She'd made herself believe she loved Paul. Twenty-four years old with no family to rely on, the young Cammie had been entranced by Paul's quick wit and good looks. Paul had found Cammie at an audition and had promptly fallen in love. At least that's what he told her, and what she'd once believed. And when he met Cammie's mother, Claire, just before her death, he professed himself in love all over again. He flattered Claire, who responded like a wilted flower to water. When Paul asked Cammie to marry him, Claire clasped her daughter's hands within her own and begged her to say yes.

It was one of those moments etched in Cammie's memory. Her mother's dark blue eyes full of hope as she stared at her uncertain daughter. "Cammie, it's a once-in-a-lifetime chance. This man loves you. Don't marry someone who doesn't love you. Paul is right for you, I can feel it. Do you feel it?"

"Y-y-ess," Cammie struggled. She felt *something.* Was it love? She really hoped so.

"Marry him. Please."

If Cammie had known then how truly ill her mother was at that point, she might have hesitated, might have realized that Claire's desire for her daughter's marriage was based on her own need as a mother to have everything tied up neatly and done with before she died.

But she hadn't known. Nor had she realized her mother was truly on her deathbed. Though cancer had spread throughout her body, Claire's beauty remained, fooling Cammie into believing her mother's immortality.

"Are you going to marry Paul?" Claire beseeched her daughter, a now constant litany.

"Yes," Cammie told her.

"Good . . ." Claire's lashes fluttered. "I haven't made a mistake, have I? About Paul? You do love him, don't you?"

Cammie couldn't bear to air her own fears. She simply swallowed and nodded.

"You'll do fine. You're stronger than I am."

"Mom, please . . ." Cammie squeezed her mother's hand, sensing she was struggling hard.

"I'll tell you a secret." Her voice lowered. "I only loved one man, but he's a cheat. Sam . . ."

"Mom, don't—"

"No, listen. Listen . . ." She took several shallow, unsteady breaths. "I didn't understand when I was your age. Family's the most important thing. I thought love was everything. Romance, you know. But it turned out I just loved illusions. Your father never wanted to marry me, and he left us both, but Sam . . ."

"I know, I know. It's okay," Cammie assured her. "When you're better, we'll plan a wedding."

"Don't wait too long."

"I won't." Cammie just wanted to change the subject.

"Family is everything. It's all we have, in the end. And you need to have a baby, Camilla. Someone to love." She relaxed her grip on Cammie's hands, falling into a troubled sleep.

Three days later, she simply didn't wake up and suddenly

Cammie was standing at her gravesite, Paul by her side, wondering what to do. Her mother's death filled her with enormous grief. Claire had been Cammie's only true family and it seemed impossible that she was gone forever.

And it hadn't helped that Sam Stovall appeared at the ceremony. He murmured condolences, but Cammie couldn't look at him. Maybe her anger and blame were misguided. She didn't care. It just hurt too much. Tyler was already long gone. He'd disappeared soon after Cammie's night with him, and no one knew how to reach him.

Cammie married Paul soon afterward, abiding by her pledge to her mother. Then ironically, within the first few months of her marriage, she learned she was pregnant—Claire's other wish for her. Cammie had barely adjusted to the news when she miscarried. In those sad hours that followed, while she coped with this next unexpected loss, she learned another unpalatable truth: Paul might have professed his love for her, but he truly only cared about himself. He couldn't understand Cammie's melancholia.

"We'll have another kid. Better later anyway," he told her, checking his watch as if every moment counted in his busy, busy life. His impatience made her cover up her misery, and she pretended that it didn't matter.

But she learned that ambition was his true mistress; Cammie didn't even run a close second. She miscarried again, and Paul shrugged it off. Then, a few years later, she miscarried once more, and Paul grew even more callous and less empathetic, if that were possible. He couldn't understand her feelings, labeling them as some kind of weird "female phobia."

That's when she left him and focused on her career.

She was happier without Paul. She struggled, waiting tables and heading for audition after audition. She thought of Tyler often, wondering where he was, how he was, and though she believed Sam might know, she would rather walk on hot coals than contact him.

She was running out of money, literally scraping pennies to make enough for rent, when she got her break: *Cherry*

Blossom Lane was looking for a new character, Donna Jenkins, whose road to true love would be a rocky one, to say the least. Cammie beat out a slew of other would-be Donnas, her own pain in the romance department so real and raw that it translated onto her screen test. They loved her. They hired her, and she spent a blissful three seasons with the nighttime drama, thinking her luck had finally changed. Even with Paul on board, she seemed secure in her position. Now, of course, that was over.

Family . . . the only thing of value.

Her mother's words floated across her conscience again, almost forgotten until this moment of introspective pain.

Family . . .

Signaling for the next off-ramp, she considered her life to date, realizing with a sad smile that she wished she'd gotten pregnant all those years ago when she and Tyler Stovall had made love.

He awakened with a jerk, nearly rolling off the narrow couch onto the stone floor. In the semidarkness, he blinked, trying to orient himself. Across the room the television flickered noiselessly, an anomaly of the electronic age set in the fir and river rock wall of shelves that marched up the west end of the cabin. Squinting at the late-night host, Tyler Stovall blindly reached a hand for the remote control, sending magazines and papers flying in his search. Swearing good-naturedly, he finally discovered the rectangular object, clicking off the familiar face on the screen. Yawning, he stretched, and vaguely remembered the uneasy dream he'd been having. *Cammie Pendleton.*

Without a stitch on.

Ty shook his head in a mixture of disgust and amazement. What time was it? Ten o'clock? Eleven? He'd come in from chopping wood as the light was fading and had simply flopped down on the couch to relax before dinner. Well, he'd relaxed himself right through to bedtime, it appeared, although now he didn't feel the least bit sleepy.

Scratching his beard, he grimaced, pulling at some of the stiff, curling hairs. He needed a serious shave. He looked a bit like the hermit he was, and even his hair was too long, brushing the back of his collar and then some.

Frowning, he rolled to his feet, wondering where that thought had come from. His appearance had scarcely changed in ten years. In this Canadian border town, the locals simply knew him as Jerry, and for as long as they could remember, he'd looked just the same.

And he'd liked it that way. Tyler Stovall was dead and buried, as far as he was concerned; he was Jerry Mercer, no one else.

Still, he felt restless, and muttering an oath no one else could hear, he headed up the rough-hewn wooden stairs to the loft where his computer sat. He could chop wood, fish, even farm, with the rest of the locals, but he also wrote screenplays in his spare time. Or, at least, he attempted to. Why, he wasn't certain. Maybe it was because his mother had once been a screenwriter. Maybe it was because it was something he could do all on his own. He never turned in any of his work. Apart from the obvious problem that surfacing with his real name would blow his cover, he wasn't that eager to share some of his innermost thoughts with the world.

Which was why it was so incredibly ridiculous that he wrote screenplays. It wasn't something any sane human being did unless they were planning to turn them into films. And films were one of the most blatant, overt types of art there were. If he was so religious about keeping his whereabouts a secret, why did he choose to write something that was so obvious?

Growling at his own foibles, Ty glanced at the computer screen. A touch of the finger dissipated the screen saver of flying toasters and left him with the scene he'd been fooling around with before he went out to chop wood. It hadn't changed for the better, of course, and frustration gnawed at him.

Glancing outside, his gaze traced the glittering lights

across the bay reflected in the water. Dark shapes of clouds scudded by, obscuring the stars. As Ty watched, they moved lower, rolling in and covering the water with thick fog until the lights he'd seen just moments before were deadened and extinguished.

With a feeling of unreality, he trudged back downstairs to the tiny alcove of a kitchen, tucked beneath the loft. Heating some soup, he gazed at the notes he'd left himself all over the counter. The place smelled of emptiness. Once, it had been a cozy den, a refuge he'd sorely needed. Now, it seemed almost foreign.

For no good reason, he thought again of Cammie. Clothes on, this time, thank you very much! A skinny stick of a girl with thick, reddish curls and a smart little temper to match. He'd watched her grow into a lovely, slightly awkward, completely ingenuous teenager and had been amused by her sisterly adoration.

Still, everything had ended badly. His fault, he realized now, though at the time his own self-involvement and blind belief in his father had kept him from seeing the truth. Time had taken care of that, he thought bitterly. Since Gayle's death he'd had to face a lot of things about his father. Any last vestige of hero worship had disappeared at that moment, and when he'd surfaced from his drunken binge and taken stock, he hadn't liked what he'd seen in himself, either.

Cammie . . .

Ty shook his head and pulled on his beard some more. He wondered what she was doing now. Once in a while he received word of Hollywood doings, but Bruce, his one and only source, wasn't exactly on the inside track. Which was just as well, Ty could admit, since he really wanted nothing to do with that whole shallow, saccharine scene anyway. The trouble was, he'd really enjoyed acting. It had been his calling, his "magic," his true talent. Other forces had driven him away, however, and, in truth, he hadn't been able to handle all the bullshit that went with the job.

So, here he was, ten years older and a little bit wiser. Was he happier? He couldn't really say.

Staring through the window at the heavens, he thought about life. There was a misery inside his chest: betrayal. But over the years it had lost power. Still, it kept him a recluse. He never, never wanted to go back.

His lips curved ironically. *Lucky for me, no one really wants me to come back, either. I've been forgotten, just like I wanted.*

With that somewhat disturbing thought haunting the corners of his mind, Ty headed upstairs to his computer, pushing memories of his previous life aside. Recollections of Cammie were harder to ignore; they seemed to have infected his soul. And for some strange reason he thought of her, well . . . *sexually!* Off and on over the years, he'd been assailed by fragments of memory where he and Cammie made love with wild abandon. Only it wasn't true memory. Good God, no! It couldn't be. He'd never touched her. She'd been like a little sister to him, and he'd never even fantasized about her.

Except in his dreams. And those dreams sometimes awakened him with a start.

Like tonight, while he'd been napping. She'd entered silkily into his thoughts and desires, and the next thing he knew he awakened, confused and aroused.

And that ticked him off. At himself. What the hell was the matter with him anyway?

"You need a woman, my friend," he growled to the empty room.

You've got a woman. Missy. If you care to see her again.

Ty muttered a sound of disgust. One of his local girlfriends, his last, was probably still available, even though he hadn't seen her in months. But he'd only used her to salve his loneliness, and in the end, he couldn't keep up the charade. Missy deserved more. And though it generally didn't bother him to have everyone believe he was Jerry Mercer, hearing that name whispered in his ear at the height of passion was the sincerest, biggest, turn-off he'd ever encountered.

He just couldn't do it anymore. So, female companionship was out.

Barring a woman, he needed a stiff drink, and Tyler, sensing in some restless part of himself that somehow he needed something more, snatched up a long-necked beer from the fridge and headed back to his computer to lose himself for a little while longer in work.

CHAPTER TWO

"I know you're carrying Cole's child," Cammie choked out, her gaze on the glamorous blonde with limpid blue eyes who stood haughtily in the center of the crowded cocktail party, her full-length white gown hugging every sensuous curve. "And I know he thinks he loves you. But he loves me. He'll figure it out in the end."

The other woman clutched her flute of champagne, fingers tightening around the stem until it snapped in two. Cammie gazed at the remnants of the glass in horror as she felt camera one zoom in on her face.

"You're a pathetic loser, Donna," was the blonde's throaty reply. Out of camera range, she squeezed a packet of "blood." Red fluid oozed over her fingers. Cammie's gaze riveted to the woman's bloodstained hands, and the camera swiveled to catch the gory mess as it dripped onto the beautiful white evening dress. "One take only" had been the order from the director, although there were two more copies of the Bob Mackie rip-off waiting in the wings, just in case. "You'll never have Cole. You'll never have a child. You don't even have a life."

Cammie gazed helplessly at the other woman's triumphant face.

"Cut. That's a print!" Gary, this episode's director, called.

Cammie stood still on her mark for another moment, feeling slightly disoriented. Fridays were film days. No more rehearsals. And though she'd practiced all week for this scene it held more power today than she'd expected.

You'll never have a child. You don't even have a life.

"Cammie?" Gary looked at her inquiringly. He'd always been friendly to her, and like the rest of the cast and crew, had been especially kind since the news had broken that she was to be "let go."

"I'm fine. I've just got a lot on my mind," she murmured, hurrying to the dressing room she shared with the glamorous blonde, Jenny, who was new to the show and already making a huge splash. Cammie might have expected twinges of jealousy, but Jenny had turned out to be as sweet and caring in real life as her character was mean and manipulative on the show.

"You okay?" Jenny asked, her eyes filled with concern.

In the mirror, Cammie caught sight of Jenny's reflection next to her own. Two women, so unlike, yet not so apart in age. Cammie was auburn-haired with serious blue-green eyes which seemed almost too large for her face; Jenny was a streaked blonde with smaller eyes and a sensuous demeanor that played well opposite Cammie's understated elegance. Cammie had hoped that she and Jenny might become fast friends, but her subsequent dismissal had turned that hope into an impossibility.

"I've got an appointment with my doctor after this," Cammie revealed.

"Your doctor?"

"My gynecologist." Cammie made a face.

"Don't you just hate it?" Jenny commented, and Cammie smiled an agreement. "See you Monday?"

"I'll be here." She had a few more episodes to film before her stint on *Cherry Blossom Lane* was officially over.

Then she would be jobless, unless Paul's bizarre plans for her to co-star in *Rock Bottom* actually materialized. She couldn't imagine that happening, and she couldn't imagine herself actually searching for Tyler Stovall! More pressing, she hadn't even agreed to go with Paul to the Connellys tonight.

Sighing, Cammie changed from her costume into street clothes, collected her purse and headed to her BMW. Ten minutes later, she was off the studio lot and on her way to Dr. Crawley's office. It was still early afternoon; her scenes had been run first. Punching out Susannah's number on her cell phone, she was surprised and delighted when she was put straight through.

"Why aren't you busy on a Friday afternoon?" Cammie asked her agent, a smile in her voice. "Losing clients?"

Susannah snorted. "I wish. How do I get these no-talent losers all the time? Someone's sending them my way, and believe me, it's a nightmare."

"Hah." Since the irrepressible Susannah Coburn's client list was growing into a Who's Who of up-and-comers, Cammie couldn't feel too sorry for her. "I'm on my way to Dr. Crawley's."

"I hate going to the gynecologist," Susannah echoed Jenny's sentiments.

"Don't we all," Cammie sighed.

"You sound exhausted, hon. Don't tell me you're still on the fence about tonight. I'll be there, too, remember."

"Why can't I go with you? You know how I feel about Paul."

"You can go with me," Susannah said, repeating the same plan she and Cammie had discussed since the moment Cammie had revealed Paul's plan. "But this is Paul's show, for the time being, so I think we should be nice."

"I don't feel like being nice."

Susannah clucked her tongue. "I'm stopping by your apartment first and bringing a bottle of champagne."

"Susannah . . ."

"Shhh. No protests. Remember, this is all *good* news. Fabulous. The ultra-best."

"Sure," Cammie said with a noticeable lack of enthusiasm.

"Oh, stop that. I promise I'll be there lickety-split, as soon as I get off work. This is a celebration, my dear! You're embarking on a new career!"

Hanging up the receiver, Cammie eased off the freeway in the direction of Dr. Crawley's offices. She wasn't certain she was mentally ready for Susannah's bubbling excitement over the news that Cammie might be slated for a Summer Solstice film. As for the party later this evening, she couldn't picture herself there at all.

Still, she would be a fool if she didn't at least show up at the Connellys. Nothing was set in stone.

Dr. Crawley's office building was of the red-tiled roof, stucco-finish, Spanish-style variety, so popular in southern California. Purple bougainvillea filled the flower beds, and Cammie's shoulder brushed against a full blossom as she passed. The receptionist gazed at her wordlessly, brows lifted in inquiry, as Cammie closed the wrought-iron hinged entry door behind her.

"I'm here to see Dr. Crawley," she said.

"Fill out this form and take a seat."

Cammie obediently accepted the clipboard she was presented with each time she visited the doctor. She filled out the blanks in the same order, marking a "3" in the spot for the amount of miscarriages. Bothered, she reminded herself that this was why she'd asked for the tissue scraping last time she'd seen her gynecologist.

A few minutes later, Cammie was escorted to Dr. Crawley's inner office, a tiny, bookshelf-lined affair which smelled more like a library than a clinic. Taking a seat in a wingback chair, Cammie inhaled a deep breath, her thoughts drifting from the present. For better or worse, she was still focused on Tyler Stovall; she had been ever since Paul had introduced him into their conversation. And though Cammie told herself she was a fool, her brain kept spinning rapidly ahead, making plans even while she vowed she would never—never ever!—consider seeking him out. Susannah had kept fairly silent on that particular subject—unusually silent, Cammie felt—and that was a blessing. Cammie didn't need any coercion. She didn't need to even contemplate the possibility, but there was no denying the seed of the idea germinating inside her imagination.

Don't be an idiot, she told herself for about the billionth time. *You won't be able to find him, and it would be disaster even if you could. If Summer Solstice wants you, they'll take you regardless of Tyler Stovall.*

"Don't be naive," she whispered aloud, shaking her head, her own thoughts putting her on edge.

When Dr. Crawley entered, she was dressed in a black pantsuit, briefcase in hand. Cammie had caught her on her way home.

"Am I late?" Cammie asked, aghast. She hadn't rechecked her appointment time.

"No, no, it's just Friday afternoon." Dr. Crawley smiled. "I'm just planning to leave early, but not until after seeing you."

"We could have rescheduled for a more convenient time."

"I wanted to see you, Cammie."

Behind their wire-rimmed glasses, Dr. Crawley's eyes assessed Cammie with solemn seriousness and what could only be described as compassion. Alarmed, Cammie sat up a little straighter in her chair. "Why? Is something wrong? The tissue scraping, it's not—cancerous, is it?" she choked out, a dagger of fear shooting straight to her heart.

"No, it's not cancer."

"Oh, good!" Her shoulders slumped in relief.

But when the doctor hesitated, Cammie's anxiety thermometer started heading for the red again. "You have a condition called endometriosis," Dr. Crawley informed her after a long moment. "Have you ever heard of it?"

Endometriosis? Fragments of information tugged at her

memory. "Umm . . . no, well . . . maybe . . ." Cammie struggled to pull herself together. "Is it some kind of problem with the uterus?"

The doctor nodded, leaned a hip on her desk, then folded her hands together, much like a professor in a classroom about to embark on a long lecture. A no-nonsense woman of thirty-five who had four children of her own—ages six, eight, ten, and twelve respectively—Dr. Crawley was the most sympathetic gynecologist Cammie had ever encountered, and one of the best as well. Cammie inadvertently braced herself for what was to come.

"Last time we met, you were worrying about your chances of ever bearing children, based upon your three miscarriages," Dr. Crawley reminded her. "In endometriosis, there's a tightening of the uterus, some scarring perhaps, and it makes the whole process more difficult."

Cammie silently digested this information. Slowly, she asked, "Are you saying I'll never have children?"

"I'm saying that's a possibility. Often, the problems increase over time."

"I—see." Cammie didn't like the sound of that at all.

"There can be a lot of pain associated with endometriosis, but it appears you haven't experienced too much discomfort at this point."

Cammie shook her head. She felt fine most of the time. This appointment was supposed to have been a routine follow-up. She'd never seriously believed something might show up in her tissue sample.

"There's likely to be progression of the disease, however, and sooner or later, you may need surgery."

"Surgery?" Cammie repeated faintly. "A—a hysterectomy?" Cammie's voice was so soft, it was as if she'd mouthed the terrible word.

"Not always. Endometriosis is very individual specific. We'll wait and watch."

Cammie nodded. Dr. Crawley talked on, but the lecture became a long buzz inside Cammie's brain. Words floated to the surface: ". . . endometrial tissue from the wall of the uterus . . . sloughed off . . . created blockage . . . scarring . . . pain and bleeding . . . the suspected culprit in twenty-five to fifty percent of all infertile women . . ."

Into this discourse, Cammie blurted out, "But what if I wanted to have a child right now, before it worsens? Could I?"

"It's not impossible. Just because you haven't had a full-term birth yet doesn't mean it can't happen. We could remove some of that scarring and see if that helps. It may or may not affect your chances." Dr. Crawley cleared her throat. "Your most crucial enemy is time. As the disease progresses, your chances of conception and full-term birth are reduced."

Cammie rubbed her face with her hands. Family. So simple for most of the world; so impossible for her.

"There is some scarring around your right fallopian tube. Surgery could help. It wouldn't be any more serious than a tube-tying, as far as I can tell. Outpatient surgery."

"Will it make a difference?"

"It sometimes can," was the unsatisfactory reply. Doctors hated to be pinned down when a patient's hopes and dreams depended on the answer.

A long silence ensued where Cammie had nothing to say. She needed to think over this information in solitude. "I'll get back to you on it," she told the doctor as she stumbled to her feet. She couldn't stay here any longer. She just wanted to be alone, and with that urgent thought in mind, she hurried from Dr. Crawley's offices to her car and then home, to her apartment.

The only other car in her lot was a nondescript cream-colored sedan with a man seated behind the wheel. It was parked at the far end of the building, away from the stairs. Cammie scarcely glanced in its direction, then hurried upstairs to the sanctity of her one-bedroom unit, locking the door behind her.

Susannah was coming with champagne.

Having no wish to celebrate, Cammie nevertheless felt the urge for something to do, some measure of comfort.

Pouring herself a half a glass of white wine, Cammie stared at the chilled Chardonnay glistening in the goblet. Picking up the glass, she walked to her small balcony with its rather ugly view of Los Angeles buildings that blocked the skyline. Instead of drinking the wine, she merely held the glass between her palms, lost in her own thoughts, thoughts which kept circling back to the realization that she might never have a child.

Might never?

The truth was, it was darn near assured that she would remain childless. Apart from the obvious medical problems, there was no man in her life, and none on the horizon, for that matter. Artificial insemination held no interest for her. Just thinking about it made her shudder.

Don't knock it, she chastised herself as she tipped back her glass and let the chilled fluid cool her throat. *If you could be assured of a full-term birth, wouldn't you try?*

The wine was so cold, droplets of condensation ran down the curve of the stemmed glass. She watched one solitary drip work its way downward and closed her eyes, feeling suddenly so alone and miserable that her knees actually trembled. Before she fell apart completely, she sank into one of the wrought-iron swing chairs on her balcony. A glass-topped table sat between the two chairs and Cammie set her goblet down with unsteady fingers. A swelling pain threatened to consume her.

Okay. It was time to regroup. She'd accepted that she'd been let go from the show, and, truthfully, it hadn't been a complete and utter surprise. Though she hated to admit that Paul could be right about anything, she had suspected her character's days were numbered. The rumblings around the set usually had some merit. She should be glad she'd lasted as long as she had. Three years could be a lifetime in television.

And though Paul's manipulations were despicable, she could see how they'd come about. She was one of the few people who'd been close to Tyler Stovall. Even Tyler's father, Sam, had not enjoyed as warm a relationship as

Cammie had with Ty. True, it had been years ago, but it was fresh in her memory—Tyler had been her only sibling, step or otherwise. To her, he was a big brother.

Liar! Cammie shook her head, unable to convince herself of that untruth even now. She'd harbored feelings for Tyler that were unsisterly to the extreme. The truth was, Tyler was no blood relation. He'd entered her life when she was an impressionable teen, hung around for several years, then gone on to a life of fame and fortune before his mysterious exit. But while he'd been within Cammie's family circle, she'd learned to love him like a brother and more. Not that he'd known when they were teenagers. Goodness, no! She'd dreamed and fantasized about him, but when they were together, she pretended that she was his little sister because that's what he wanted. He liked having her around, or at least she thought he did. He never seemed to mind, anyway, and though other girls were always calling him, and though he went out with them now and again—much to Cammie's dismay!—he apparently never cared enough about any of them, for he didn't ever try to further a relationship. She'd taken this as a good sign. Someday maybe they could be together, she'd decided in her girlish fantasies. It just had to be the right time.

The right time.

As her thoughts touched on their one night together, Cammie grabbed her glass, swept in a gulp of wine, then choked and sputtered as it trickled down the wrong pipe. How had she let that happen? What was *wrong* with her! Even after all these years, even after an ill-fated marriage and some years of growth, Cammie still could look back on the night they'd spent in each other's arms and feel humiliation.

He'd never really known what had happened. She'd shown up during a time when he was unhappy and alcohol-impaired to the extreme. She'd wanted to talk, to reconnect, but it hadn't happened that way. His despondency had somehow transferred itself to her and when he reached for her, his breath sweet with scotch, his hands strong, his body taut with need—well, she hadn't exactly resisted the attraction!

She'd left before he'd awakened, and though she'd tortured herself with the memories of that night, she wasn't deluded enough to believe it would mean anything to him even if there were the small chance he would remember it. No, much better to let that memory stay buried and dead.

Shuddering a little, Cammie set down her goblet with deliberation. Her blood stirred even recalling those long-ago moments in his arms—and yet she'd been just part of one drunken evening!

Hugging herself closely, she watched afternoon sunlight slant through the glittering liquid remaining inside her stemmed glass. She ached for the "could have beens" she'd never quite realized.

Tyler, Tyler, Tyler . . .

He'd walked into Cammie's life at her worst period of adolescent awkwardness. She wore braces through ninth grade and was certain everyone stared at her. She was gawky and brainy and all but ignored by the popular crowd at her private school until her mother married the famous, and infamous, Samuel Stovall.

Cammie's mother, Claire Pendleton, had lived on the fringes of Beverly Hills most of her life. She'd done modeling in her youth and had been wooed and won by Cammie's father, only to be left in the lurch with no wedding, no husband, and no money. After Cammie's birth, Claire went back to modeling and was successful enough—with the aid of Cammie's father's pittance of child support—to exist and finally prosper. When Cammie was old enough, Claire enrolled her in a modestly prestigious private elementary school. Cammie made friends fairly quickly, but when junior high and high school hit, she discovered her own awkwardness.

She took acting classes to get over her shyness and discovered a serious desire for the craft. She made friends in the theater department; kids interested in what she was interested in. She was fairly happy. She dreamed of a career in acting when she finished school.

Claire was doing an outdoor shoot on Catalina Island when Samuel Stovall first encountered her. He was driving around the island in a Jeep on a beautiful sunny afternoon and he spotted Claire standing in the midst of wind and rock and sea. Within months she became his third wife—and Cammie his first stepchild. He'd sired a string of biological children he seemed relatively unconcerned with, however, and when Cammie and Claire moved in with him, it was to learn that one of his sons, Tyler, was part of the arrangement.

Tyler's mother, Nanette Stovall, had relinquished him as a result of the Stovalls' divorce settlement. Word on the street was that she'd amassed a cool two million as a result, but Cammie, who knew Nanette, thought that must be no more than gossip. Nanette loved Tyler and from comments Tyler made, Cammie suspected it was more likely a case of a teenage boy wanting to live with his father and Nanette unhappily giving in to the arrangement. Whatever the truth of it, Tyler resided in the bedroom next to Cammie's and became her stepbrother.

Word spread at school with the speed of a wind-driven brush fire. Cammie was Sam Stovall's stepdaughter! Suddenly, she was popular. Kids invited themselves over who'd heretofore never shown her an inkling of interest.

And then the girls spied Tyler.

He practically had to fend them off with a sword. Cammie watched this with a mixture of pride and dismay. She was proud he was her stepbrother—and dismayed that every girl wanted him. They hung on his every word, like he was the celebrity he would one day become. Tyler was clearly uncomfortable with this adoration, but he managed to stay fairly polite about it.

It was then that Cammie recognized her own feelings for Tyler. She tried to deny them, but her reaction to her so-called friends' attention to him made her rethink those feelings. Tyler was dark-haired, slow-talking, with expressive, thick-lashed gray eyes and a way of staring into a feminine soul that drove any clear thought from the poor girl's brain. He resembled his father, but there was an uncaring edge to Sam Stovall that his son luckily did not possess. Sam could be thoughtlessly cruel; Tyler was thoughtfully kind. Of course, that was only when it suited him. If Cammie, or anyone else, unduly annoyed him, he could certainly act like a jerky older brother. But he had moments of tenderness, where he understood things about Cammie that she couldn't even voice herself, and for that she loved him. Adored him. And began fantasizing about him.

Tyler graduated from high school three years earlier than Cammie. He attended UCLA and also picked up small acting jobs and TV commercials. It didn't hurt him that he was Sam Stovall's son; Tyler was the first to admit it. But when he was chosen for the supporting actor in a small-budget film that just happened to become the sleeper of the season, Tyler's success as an actor suddenly owed more to ability than nepotism.

He still lived with Sam most summers during those first few years. Sometimes he took summer classes, sometimes he worked doing odd jobs around the studios. Cammie's schoolgirl crush grew into out-and-out adoration. She followed him everywhere, and if he guessed why, he never let on.

She watched him date other girls, counting the minutes until he returned home. Luckily, he never brought them to his father's house; Cammie knew, because she always waited up.

She could still recall the way he looked at her one night when he discovered his "little sister" half-asleep on the couch, the TV silently flickering away across the room, a bowl of cold popcorn and a soda can on the table beside the couch, testament to her lonely vigil.

"You don't have to, you know," he told her, seating himself on the end of the couch so that she had to tuck her knees in or her bare toes would have actually touched his leg.

"Don't have to what?"

"Wait up. I can take care of myself."

"I know that."

"Then why do you do it?" he wanted to know, gazing at her in that penetrating way she'd come to both love and fear. When Tyler wanted answers, there was nothing to do but tell the truth.

Still, he made her so nervous! She had to fight to keep from chewing on her nails. "I'm not waiting up. I'm watching TV."

He flicked a glance at the screen. "What are you watching?"

Cammie had no idea. A black-and-white horror movie of some kind had appeared after the last program, and she'd paid no attention. "I don't know, I fell asleep."

"Ahhh . . ."

He said it so knowingly that it bugged her. "I was watching Letterman, okay? I didn't pay attention to what came next!"

"Well, Letterman must have quit the network because you're on a local channel."

"Oh, fine! I switched the channel first! What's the big deal?"

"You don't have to wait up," he repeated, picking up her feet and putting them on his lap, absentmindedly massaging her soles.

It was something he'd done upon more than one occasion during the years they'd been stepbrother and -sister. Tyler radiated physicality. He liked touching and being touched, not necessarily sexually, though she didn't doubt he liked that, too! But it was more than that. A way to connect and say, "I like being with you." His father was that way, too. He hugged everyone he met whether he liked them or not. For Sam, it was a way of saying, "Aren't we all just such great friends?" whether he felt the sentiment or not. Just part of the Hollywood bullshit, Cammie suspected. But Tyler's manner of touching was truer and full of unspoken loyalty.

Except that it played havoc with Cammie's fluttering emotions. Deliberately she pulled her feet from his warm embrace. Sensing the unspoken rejection, Tyler got up from the couch. That wasn't what she wanted! She hadn't meant for him to leave. She just couldn't handle his warm fingers on her nervous flesh.

But she couldn't tell him *that!* Instead, she blurted out, "Where are you going?"

"To bed. It's late."

"Don't go yet."

He stretched and yawned. "I'm done in."

"Stay and watch a little more with me."

"You're crazy," he murmured, but he sat back down again, carefully avoiding her curled up feet.

She was sorry she'd reacted to his touch, but how could she ever tell him she was afraid of herself? That every time he looked at her, her heart flipped over? That sometimes when she saw him pull off his shirt, the temptation to run her fingers over his strong, smooth muscles was almost more than she could bear?

Tyler found the remote and clicked through a bunch of shows until he landed on a late-night comedy revue. He laughed at some of the jokes, but Cammie could scarcely break a smile. She was so nervous that it felt as if moving might somehow give away her true feelings. When had it happened? This complete obsession with Tyler. It hadn't been that way in the beginning.

"What are you going to do after graduation?" he suddenly asked, flicking her a look. The room was dark except for the light from the television screen, but she could still see the way he peered intently at her.

"I don't know. Go to college. Maybe—UCLA—or I don't know, a community college nearby."

"You still interested in acting?"

It was embarrassing to admit. Tyler was the one beginning to be successful in that tough field. She felt like a groupie. Nodding jerkily, Cammie fought to think of something to say, some way to legitimize her desire so it wouldn't seem like she was just copying him.

"I could get Dad to introduce you to some people. He knows everybody."

"Oh, I don't know . . ." Cammie murmured. She could have kicked herself for how many times she'd stated that phrase this night. It sounded like she didn't have a brain in her head!

"It's always been who you know. It hasn't changed," he told her with an ironic smile that spoke volumes about his own loathing of the way things were. Still, neither of them could deny that being a Stovall opened some doors.

Cammie could think of nothing to say. Her brain just shut down again.

Eventually Tyler got to his feet again. "Well, good night," he said. And then he surprised her by leaning down and planting a kiss on her forehead. Cammie squeaked in protest; she couldn't help herself. He appeared not to notice, but long after he'd gone to bed she lay on the couch, staring at the ceiling, her forehead tingling with the memory of that platonic kiss.

Maybe things would have turned out as Tyler had predicted. Maybe Sam would have shown her around and helped her learn the ropes of Hollywood. Instead, shortly before graduation, Cammie raced home from school early, bubbling over with enthusiasm because Tyler had dropped by to tell her he'd been signed for a feature film and to congratulate her on her coming graduation day.

But the news was brutally knocked from her head because as Cammie ran down the hall to her mother's bedroom and threw open the door, she discovered Sam Stovall in bed with a beautiful starlet.

"Cammie!" Sam bellowed.

But it was too late. Cammie gasped in shock and skid to a halt. The bleached blonde atop Sam Stovall ceased riding him for all she was worth and collapsed, cringing, against his chest. Sam yelled, his face turning purple. Cammie backed out of the room and into the hallway. Her legs quivered. Her head thundered. She staggered downstairs and slowly remembered that her mother had told her she had a job in San Diego that would possibly keep her overnight. Sam had chosen the time to have an affair in their own home.

One of the few times she'd actually skipped class led to the worst few hours of her young life.

Sam, after hustling his lovely paramour home, sat Cammie down for a long talk. He didn't expect her to lie for him; he knew she would tell her mother the truth. What he *did* expect was for her to understand. Unbelievable! How could she ever understand anyone's infidelity? She wasn't made that way.

Nevertheless, Sam sat across from her at the dining-room table and explained in his own weird way that he should not be expected to live up to Cammie's standards. "That isn't the way it is here," he said, as if the speech were well rehearsed. Based on his succession of ex-wives, it probably was, too. "There's a certain amount of temptation that can't be ignored. Call it a case of too much availability. A man like me can't be that perfect," he added with his trademark smile. Sure, he was self-deprecating, but Cammie didn't believe him one bit.

"A man like you?" she asked through stiff lips.

"I'm a romantic icon to millions of women. Sometimes I stray." He lifted his palms in surrender to his weakness. "Your mother understands."

"My mother *knows?*"

"Did you think it was the first time?"

His blatant disregard for the sanctity of marriage hit something inside Cammie. "I think you're disgusting!" she bit out. "I hope my mom divorces you!"

"She won't." He started losing interest in the conversation. If Cammie wasn't going to believe his lines, then there was no reason to continue.

"She will, if I have anything to say about it!" Cammie declared.

"Your mother loves me too much," Sam responded matter-of-factly, as if he'd weighed all the angles and found he always came out on top. "I'd be more likely to divorce her."

"Then do it," Cammie stated through quivering lips.

He gazed at her blandly. "I just might."

Swallowing hard, Cammie suddenly saw a terrible trap yawning in front of her. Sam didn't care about Claire. He was bored with her. "If you hurt her, I'll never forgive you," she whispered.

"Oh, Camilla . . ." He clucked his tongue at her naïveté.

She ran from the room—smack dab into Tyler's broad chest.

"What?" he asked, concerned.

"Your father's a bastard!" she choked out. "A cheat. A lying, horrible bastard."

Tyler gazed from her tear-stained face to his father's stern visage. "What's going on?"

And that's when the other shoe dropped. "Claire and I are divorcing," he said. "Cammie didn't want to hear it."

"What?" Cammie gaped at him.

"I'm seeing someone else," Sam added.

Tyler shook his head as if he were struggling to keep up with the conversation himself.

"I've offered Claire an ample settlement—a king's ransom—but she's holding out for more."

"You're a liar!" Cammie breathed in shock.

"I'll probably have to give her the house, too." He gazed in mock pity at Cammie. "I'm sorry, Camilla, but she's no different from the rest."

Cammie gazed up at Tyler, who still held her in the grip of his two hands. "You believe him?" she asked.

"My mother was different," Tyler told his father in a cold voice.

Sam's lips tightened. "Well, yes, she was. Nanette was a special case."

"My mother's different, too!" Cammie cried out.

Sam kept his eyes on Tyler. "You know the truth, Son. You heard us."

"Heard what?" Cammie asked.

Tyler didn't want to say anything. He hesitated, his jaw working.

"Heard *what?*" Cammie demanded, silently willing Tyler to refute his father's claim, begging him with all the power of her soul and spirit for him to pick her side.

"Tell her, Son."

"I heard them fighting, that's all," Ty clipped out, his jaw rock hard.

"And . . . ?" Sam pressed. "What were we fighting about?"

Cammie kept her eyes trained on Tyler's gray ones, as if by merely staring at him she could keep him from saying something terrible, something truthful, something she didn't want to hear.

He swallowed. "Money."

"Money?" Cammie repeated blankly. "What are you saying? You think my mother wants this divorce? You think she wants *money?*"

Tyler shook his head. "I don't know. They were fighting, that's all. If they want out, let them."

"You're *condoning* this?"

"It's their lives, isn't it?" Tyler pointed out, struggling to make her see another view.

It was as if he'd poisoned her thoughts, tainted her love and belief. She gazed at him with all the revulsion of suddenly coming upon a snake gorging itself on a live, helpless creature. "You're just like *him!*" she blurted, then raced from the house, running full tilt until her lungs nearly burst and her throat ached, raw and painful. Then she threw herself on the grass of a tiny parklike area sandwiched between the several beautiful homes at the end of their street. Her fists clenched around grass blades. Her jaw ached from the effort of squeezing it tight. Her eyes burned hot.

Tyler found her. "Cammie, get up," he murmured with a certain amount of sympathy.

"Drop dead."

"You're making too much of this."

"Am I?" She lifted tear-drenched eyes to his.

He looked almost as unhappy as she felt. He said with perfectly horrible reason, "If they want a divorce, it's not up to us."

"But my mother doesn't want a divorce!"

"How do you know?"

"*I* know."

"Cammie, it looks like she married Dad for the money and prestige. When she was raising you alone, she was having trouble making ends meet. And she wanted to be somebody special instead of a model who was at the end of her career."

"Is that what he told you? Or, did you come up with it all on your own?" Cammie demanded bitterly.

"It's the way it is."

"My mother loves your father."

"Maybe. But your mother loves a certain lifestyle, too. The kind that money can buy."

"The kind that your father's money can buy?"

He didn't answer, and she hated him for his reasoning. It was so like Sam! Jumping up, she glared at him, her hands clenched at her sides. Throwing herself against his hard chest, she pounded her fists on his arms and shoulders and back, any piece of flesh within the arc of her swing. Cammie carried on in silent fury, and for a while Tyler simply let her. Eventually, he clasped her wrists and held her at bay. She could see the empathy in his eyes, and it hurt right down to her soul.

"I'm sorry you were ever my stepbrother! You're just as shallow and self-centered as he is! Let go of me!"

"I'm sorry, too," he muttered, though he meant it in a far different way.

Cammie's chest heaved. He released his grip on her and they stared each other down. She knew she was at a crossroads that could change her life, but she reacted on pure emotion, running away from him as if he were the devil himself.

Cammie could not bring herself to tell her mother of the events of that afternoon. She knew Sam's description of her character was a lie. In the end, it scarcely mattered, for their marriage broke up soon after; Claire discovered the signs of her husband's continued indiscretions on her own.

Tyler and Cammie's familial relationship ended that terrible day. Though they spoke to each other, it was only out of politeness. He continued on his path to fame and fortune and Cammie went off to college, and apart from that last memorable night in Ty's arms years later, Cammie had stayed away from the Stovall clan as a whole. The only person among them whom she would even consider contacting now was Tyler's real mother, Nanette. The antithesis of Claire, Nanette was boisterous and strong and had told Sam Stovall where he could stick it—or so the story went.

Samuel and Tyler had suffered a falling out as well. Was it over Tyler's skyrocketing career, the destruction of Sam's marriage to Claire, or something else? Cammie had no way of knowing, and though rumors abounded, no one seemed to really know. Like Ty's subsequent disappearance, it remained a mystery.

Climbing to her feet, she headed back inside the apartment, cheered by its tiny spaces filled with natural wicker furniture, bright watercolors and a healthy collection of books. It was a haven. All hers. And though she was currently unemployed, she could afford the rent for a while with her bit of savings even if she went without work for several months. Setting her empty wineglass on the counter, she returned to the balcony for a few more moments of reflection before she decided if she were really going to the Connellys with her unscrupulous ex-husband.

Below, in the parking lot, Susannah's newly minted green VW bug screeched to a halt beside the cream-colored sedan. Was that man still sitting inside it? Cammie wondered idly as Susannah, curly hair bouncing wildly against her shoulders, dashed for the outdoor stairs.

"Yoo hoo!" Susannah called as soon as she hit the upper landing. She banged loudly on the door.

"Coming!"

Cammie hurried to unlock the door and hug her friend as Susannah burst into the apartment. "I'm sitting out on the deck," Cammie said, inclining her head in the direction from which she'd just come.

"Here's the bubbly." Susannah waved a bottle of Dom Perignon in front of Cammie's nose, and Cammie didn't have the heart to tell her she was in no mood for champagne and fun.

"My God, Cammie. You're blessed, my dear. Blessed!"

"That remains to be seen."

"*Rock Bottom* is every actor's dream. Your role's small, but really good. Everyone's been talking about it, and now it's yours!"

"It's not like you to get so excited about a project that hasn't a snowball's chance in hell of succeeding," Cammie said to her.

"Pessimism, pessimism. But you know your ex . . ." She waved a hand in the air. "He's a louse and a whole lot of things we don't have to go into, but he's dropped the world in your lap. You've got to thank him for that!"

"Susannah!"

She held up her hands, warding off any further protests. "I know what you're going to say, but, kiddo, this'll set you up for life! You can find Tyler Stovall, if anybody can."

"Oh, sure."

"You can!"

"Finding Ty is the only reason they want me at all."

"So what? It's an open door. Walk through it. Wait a minute, I've got to uncork this bottle." She began untwisting the wire top with urgent fingers.

Cammie stared at her friend. Susannah always looked out for her best interests and her advice was generally sound. She knew the ins and outs of Hollywood better than anyone, and Cammie was lucky to have her as an agent and friend. But Susannah was over the top on this one.

"You know the person to contact is the man himself, Tyler's daddy-o."

"Samuel!" Very simply and very loudly, Cammie said, "No."

"No?" Susannah stopped in midtwist.

"I'm not going to talk to Samuel Stovall. Nothing on earth could make me try."

"Even if it led you to Tyler?"

"Susannah, I'm not interested. I can't be. I have to face facts: I'm not co-starring in *Rock Bottom.* It's not in the cards."

"Have you read the script yet?" Susannah lifted her brows. Cammie had purposely put off reading the screenplay from start to finish, afraid somehow that would make her decide the wrong way.

"Most of it," she admitted, her voice quavering with the doubts she so desperately wished weren't there.

"Then, Cammie . . ."

Fervently, shaking her head, Cammie declared, "Oh, pour the champagne, for pete's sake. I'll celebrate with you, but I can't talk about this anymore. It makes me crazy!"

Susannah scrounged in Cammie's cupboards until she found some more wine goblets. Champagne flutes weren't part of Cammie's glassware repertoire. Pouring them each a glass, Susannah held hers up in a toast, daring Cammie silently to do the same.

"You're going to the party," Susannah said. "You know you are."

Cammie rolled her eyes. Susannah had her number. Nodding, she said, "Paul left a message on my answering machine. I just don't want to call him back."

As if on cue, the phone started ringing. Since Susannah was nearest to it, Cammie indicated that she should do the honors. After a brief "hello," and with her gaze firmly fixed on Cammie, Susannah said brightly, "Oh, yes, Paul, she'll be ready. She's just dying to go, you know her. Can't wait. She even bought herself a new gown."

"Susannah!" Cammie hissed, to which her friend just waved her aside.

"Seven P.M. She'll be red hot and rollin'." Hanging up, Susannah fought back a Cheshire cat smile.

"You are no friend," Cammie declared.

Laughing, Susannah clinked her goblet against Cammie's. "The best one you're ever gonna have, hon! And you know it! Now, find something to wear in that closet of yours that looks new and expensive. We'll finish the champagne, then I've got to get going and change, too. This is going to be fun, Cammie. Fun!"

"Fun," Cammie repeated with a grimace, sensing she was about to make one of the worst mistakes of her life.

CHAPTER THREE

Cammie's hands clasped together tightly in her lap as Paul drove his purring Mercedes along the curve of the Connellys' circular driveway. Ground lights diffused illumination beneath their mushroomlike caps and spilled in roundish beams on the manicured grounds. A palm tree was up-lit, its fronds lifted by a breeze to gently fan the air. The house itself was white stucco with arched, wrought-iron pane windows set into thick walls. Red tiles spilled over a massive roof. Cammie couldn't even guess at the home's square footage—approaching ten thousand at least.

If you've got it, flaunt it, she thought with a hard swallow. Success wasn't something to be shy about, apparently; the Connellys sure didn't hide their light under a barrel.

Paul whistled as he brought his car to a halt and a uniformed valet stepped forward to usher them toward the front steps. "Is this great, or what?" he asked with a grin.

"Intimidating, that's for sure."

"Oh, don't be a spoilsport. You're impressed, just like I am."

"I didn't say I wasn't impressed." Being impressed and being intimidated were two separate things, though Paul obviously wasn't interested in the distinction.

As she stepped from the Mercedes and drew her thin floral wrap around her arms, she asked herself, *Why am I here? Am I crazy? How did I let Paul and Susannah talk me into this?*

"Man, what a spread." Paul couldn't get over it. Smoothing his bow tie, he crooked his arm for Cammie to take hold. Between his browbeating and Susannah's pleading, she'd reluctantly allowed herself to attend the Connellys' social gathering. A part of her—the part that had known better from the start—trembled with apprehension. Why hadn't she listened to her own vow to stay out of this whole deal? When had she buckled?

The answer was *Rock Bottom* itself. It was the best screenplay she'd read in a long, long time. The story wasn't just good; it was fantastic. Emotion leapt off the page from both the male and female leads.

Opportunity of a lifetime . . . a script to die for . . . something that comes along once in a blue moon, if you're lucky . . . a role other actresses would sell their soul over . . .

Susannah had not listened to her protests. "You have to do this. You have to try!" she'd insisted. "This is so good it positively hurts!"

"Susannah, you don't understand," Cammie had responded with a hard shake of her head.

Susannah threw her arms wide. "Then, make me. Explain to me, so that I *do* understand. Make it crystal clear why you would cut your own throat, so to speak. I mean, Cammie, nobody gets this kind of chance. Nobody!"

"Somebody does."

"Okay, sure. People with clout. The famous and the rich. And you know who else? The *lucky*. That's where you fit in. You're so lucky!"

Cammie could only stare at her. With her medical problems, she felt far from lucky. But Susannah knew nothing about her visit with Dr. Crawley; Cammie hadn't had a chance to tell her yet. Later, when Susannah was over her ecstasy concerning this screenplay opportunity, Cammie could confide the truth. For now, though, everything else had fled Susannah's normally sensible brain.

"You can find Tyler. I know you can."

"I will not contact Samuel Stovall!"

"Okay, okay. There's bound to be another way. What about Tyler's mother? You've always said you like her."

"I haven't talked to Nanette in years."

"Well . . . ?" Susannah lifted a hand in question, challenging Cammie to take the obvious route.

"I don't want to find Ty!" Cammie burst out.

"Well, why not?" she demanded.

"I just don't, okay? And why does everybody have this confidence in me when he's been missing nearly a decade! I'm no investigator. I don't get it."

"You have connections. Sam Stovall was your stepfather whether you like it or not."

Cammie pursed her lips and shook her head with finality.

Susannah, who understood only part of Cammie's aversion to the man, stated doggedly, "You could contact any member of Tyler's family by virtue of the fact you were once his stepsister."

"It's not that simple."

"Maybe it's time it was. I'm just saying, it's possible."

"Samuel Stovall hurt my mother, and me, and even Ty. He wasn't fair. I told you before: I caught him in bed with another woman when he was still married to my mom."

Susannah winced. "I know, I know. Just a sec . . ." She refilled their glasses.

"This is no celebration," Cammie warned her as Susannah pressed the goblet in her hand.

"Come on," Susannah urged, dragging Cammie by the hand back to the balcony and plopping her in a chair. Yanking her own chair close, perched on its edge, Susannah gazed straight into Cammie's blue-green eyes. Girl-talk was coming. Cammie could feel it. "Tell me why it's so impossible for you to do this one itsy-bitsy little chore. So, Samuel's a jerk. You like Tyler, don't you? Wouldn't you just love to see him again? Find out what he's been doing? Picture it, my dear! You showing up on Tyler Stovall's doorstep. It's too perfect."

Cammie had revealed some of her darkest memories to Susannah over the years, though she'd kept the secret of her one-night tryst with Tyler to herself. That was for her alone to know. She couldn't trust a single soul with that hurtful little tale.

"I can't face Samuel Stovall. And even if I could, what would I say? 'Hey, I know we've never really liked each other that much, but do you know where Ty is? Finding him would really help me get a part in a movie. Oh, and, by the way, it would be great for Ty, too, so you see, I'm not being selfish or anything.' I couldn't say that to Nanette, either."

"Kiddo, I see your point. I really do. But there are other ways to put it."

"Oh, yeah? How?"

She shrugged. "I don't know exactly. You could express concern for Ty. You've been thinking about him. A lot's changed."

Cammie snorted. "And then when it comes out I've been chosen to co-star with Tyler in a new film? What do you think either of Ty's parents would think about that? And then of course there's Ty himself!"

"Well, Sam Stovall would understand that motivation better than anyone. He's the master of self-promotion and manipulation, especially when it benefits him."

"Truer words were never spoken."

"Another glass?" Susannah asked, holding up her empty goblet. Cammie put her hand over the top of her glass, feeling the effects already and certain she needed to keep her wits about her. "Ty could be just waiting for someone to reach out to him and bring him back," Susannah observed, her voice trailing after her as she went to refill her glass.

"You don't know Tyler Stovall," Cammie pointed out dryly.

"Well, tell me about him, then," she called.

Cammie waited for Susannah to return, her own memories tumbling over one another, long-ago feelings flooding through her veins. For years she'd tried to convince herself that what she'd felt for Ty was puppy love and adoration, but she wondered if she'd been wrong. Whatever she'd experienced, its power remained true and strong. She couldn't even talk about the man without feeling something. It didn't seem to matter how much time had passed.

But when Susannah reseated herself, Cammie hesitated, not entirely sure she wanted to tread this particular path. There were stones and potholes and dangerous curves ahead. Carefully, she said, "Tyler's a lot like Sam, but not totally. He's certainly not as selfish. Maybe he's more like Nanette that way."

"Tell me about her."

"Nanette had—has—depth," Cammie said, smiling faintly. Though she hadn't seen Tyler's mother in years, it couldn't fade her memory of the vibrant woman. Nanette might not be a current part of the Hollywood scene, but she'd been a screenwriter in her younger days—until marriage to Samuel stifled her creative urges. "People don't remember her too much, at least not as much as they remember Sam's other exes. Even my mother's more noteworthy as a Hollywood anecdote than Nanette is," Cammie admitted ironically.

"But Nanette is Tyler's real mother."

Cammie nodded. "Maybe if he'd kept acting she'd be more in the spotlight today. Probably not, though, because she never cared for all the hoopla. And anytime Samuel tried to impress her with who he knew and all that, she just looked exceedingly bored. I do remember that!" Cammie added on a half-laugh. "My mother loved Nanette. She truly did. I think Nanette pitied my mother for making the same mistake she did." She shrugged. "It's kind of hard to tell after all this time."

"And Sam Stovall never appreciated either of them," Susannah said in her pithy way.

"Amen." Cammie cocked her head. "You know what's weird? I married a man a lot like Sam!"

"You made a mistake. Honey, it's all right." Susannah patted her knee. "But it's over now, and you can still benefit from it."

"You just don't quit, do you?" Cammie protested with affection.

"Never. Tell me more."

"Well, Ty was a great big brother. I cared a lot about him."

"You loved him," Susannah said, watching Cammie closely.

"Well, yes. As a brother."

"Uh huh."

Cammie was fairly certain she resented Susannah's carefully neutral tone. Her friend was humoring her a little, but trying not to show it. "But when I walked in on Sam and his lover, I flipped out. And it seemed like Ty took his dad's side. Maybe he didn't, I don't know. But it felt that way at the time, and I got really upset. I yelled at both of them. Sam tried to act like it was no big deal. Infidelity should be accepted and understood, et cetera, et cetera—given his position and all."

Susannah made a choking sound.

"Exactly," Cammie agreed, heartened by this bit of understanding. "Anyway, Ty and I had a falling out at that time and never spoke again."

"Never?"

Since this was a blatant lie, Cammie couldn't help hesitating. But she couldn't tell Susannah the truth, either. "Our brother and sister relationship was over after that," she compromised. "Completely over. In any case, it's not likely he'd want to see me now. I'm about the last person on earth. And I could never ask him for a favor."

"You're not asking for a favor. You're giving him one!"

"He won't see it that way."

"How do you know?"

"I just know."

"No, you don't." Susannah examined her half-filled drink. "Tyler Stovall's been gone a long time. What's the harm in looking him up?"

You have no idea! Cammie thought.

"I'm certainly no expert, but it sounds to me like you've got a lot of unresolved issues to deal with concerning him and his father."

"It was a long time ago," Cammie disagreed. She didn't want to hear this. She didn't want Susannah touching her innermost nerves where Ty was concerned. It was a tender spot. A weakness she instinctively knew was dangerous to her.

"It's not just the screenplay, is it? It's something else."

"I just told you, we had a falling out."

Susannah wrinkled her nose and narrowed her eyes at her friend. She was ten years Cammie's senior, single by choice, and full of wisdom about Hollywood specifically and life as a whole. Sometimes her ability to read Cammie was quite disconcerting, to say the least. Cammie didn't need for Susannah to become all wise and knowing right now, especially when it came to Ty.

"You're afraid to see him again," she said now, arching one brow, daring Cammie to deny it.

"No! Yes! I don't want to see him."

"Why not?"

"I just told you!"

Susannah swore in very unladylike fashion, then grinned as if she knew some inner joke that only she could truly appreciate. "All right, have it your way. However, I'm not giving up on this. But for now, I've got to get going. Time's a-passing. *I've* got to find something to wear." She eyed with approval the diaphanous rose gown Cammie had donned. "You look fabulous, my dear. I'm going to have a tough time upstaging you."

"Oh, sure." Cammie eyed her friend with affection. "You're so—you."

Susannah laughed. "Your problem is that you're fighting your way through something that happened between you and Tyler Stovall years ago. Give that up and everything else will fall into place. You'll see what I mean."

"Don't count on it."

Now, however, as she reluctantly took her ex's arm, she called herself all sorts of names, "hypocrite" being at the top of her list. She'd made the mistake of listening to Susannah and now things seemed almost possible.

The trouble was: the lead role in *Rock Bottom*, Joe Marks, *was* Tyler Stovall in spades. He was meant to play that part, and she wouldn't be surprised if the screenwriter had used him as his role model when he'd dreamed up the central character. Tyler needed to play the part of Joe Marks, and now that the vision was in her head, Cammie couldn't see anyone else in the lead. She felt sick and excited and overwhelmed all at once. Someone needed to find Tyler and show him the script.

If you don't do it, someone else will.

Paul's words of yesterday still rang true. Cammie hated the position she was in, yet a part of her felt revved up and ready. Charged. Poised on the brink.

It was a downright dangerous way to feel.

"Look at this tile work," Paul muttered. Circles of blushing pink Mexican tile complemented fountains and lush groupings of flowers, red bougainvillea, and vanilla oleander prime among the bunches. Birds of paradise stuck straight up as if they were on alert, and jade trees and palms kept a vigil along with them.

Paul rang the bell. Cammie's hand slipped away, but he grabbed it back again, tucking it inside the crook of his arm and holding her fingers tight with his other hand. She knew, then, that whatever he'd said, he needed her more than he was admitting. Was it because she'd been related to Ty? Probably. It killed her to think how she was letting herself be used.

A maid in a black uniform opened the door and music and loud voices drifted from the back of the sprawling stucco ranch. Cammie's heart leapt to her throat, beating wildly as she recognized Hollywood luminaries on every front. She was awestruck. No wonder Susannah had said she was going to the party come hell or high water.

If this is the Connellys' idea of a little gathering at their house, I'm in way over my head.

Swallowing, she managed to keep one foot traveling in front of the other. Sam and Claire had never hosted these kind of events, but then Cammie had always suspected that Sam was outrageously cheap. Either that, or he simply couldn't be bothered. He liked others waiting on him. He wanted to be wined and dined, not the other way around.

Lord, she was being uncharitable. With an effort she forgot her feelings for her ex-stepdad and concentrated instead upon the incredible crowd and the lavish, linen-swathed tables of catered food and ice sculptures.

Even Paul, still hovering beside her, was struck speechless. And when Nora Connelly herself walked over to join them, hands outstretched for a double handshake with Cammie, a squeak of fear squeezed out of Paul's throat. Cammie just gazed at her host, calling on her acting skills to get her through this odd and exciting moment.

"Cammie, isn't it?" Nora asked. She smiled, and suddenly she seemed more human, as if she wasn't one of the most sought-after producers of the last few years. She wore a plain black sheath and her hair swung straight and dark brown to her chin. More businesslike than elegant, she radiated confidence and power, and Cammie envied her apparent strength and success.

"Yes."

"Paul told us about you. He was rather insistent." Nora threw him a sideways glance.

"I—I—know Cammie's the best." Paul's voice was unnaturally high.

"He said you were a fine actress." Nora was gracious.

Cammie swallowed. "He said I was Tyler Stovall's stepsister."

Nora's brows lifted in surprise at her candor. "That, too," she admitted.

"I don't know what to say," Cammie began to disabuse her, but Paul broke in quickly.

"This is perfect! Just perfect! It's like a story in itself. She can go find him and bring him back."

"And it will be next year's true life drama," Nora agreed with a certain amount of irony. At that moment James Connelly detached himself from a blond woman and joined his dark-haired wife. With silvery, wavy hair and wire-rimmed glasses, he looked more like an art critic than a successful producer. He introduced himself to Cammie and tried, unsuccessfully, to politely ignore Paul. It became very clear to Cammie that Paul was not as tight with the Connellys as he would have her believe. He'd brought them an idea—a package, really, which included Ty's ex-stepsister—and they'd been intrigued enough to give him the green light.

Cammie picked up all the vibes in an instant. She was thinking of how to get past this polite chitchat with both James and Nora and tell them the truth about her feelings, when Susannah rushed up, her usually wild hair clipped back in a severe bun that, coupled with her flowing skirt and hoop earrings, made her look a little like a gypsy. "Hello, hello," she breathed in an excited rush to the Connellys. Her fingers gripped Cammie's arm so tightly it hurt.

"The upstaging's going just fine," Cammie said in an undertone, grinning. When Susannah didn't immediately respond, Cammie shot her a confused look. Susannah's gaze was focused past their hosts to the other side of the tiled atrium. Her breath caught and her grip tightened. Cammie followed her gaze and her own eyes widened as she locked on to the object of Susannah's distress.

"Oh, my God!" she whispered. Her gut felt knocked to the wall. Samuel Stovall, in all his splendor, stood with his arm around Felicia, his latest wife. He was blathering away about something, nearly obscured from Cammie's line of vision by an ice sculpture of Zeus.

She shrank backward automatically. She'd spent all these years within the same industry and had never actually crossed his path. It hadn't been a problem. His stature in this community was many rungs above her own. It had taken *Rock Bottom,* an A-List property, and her connection to Sam himself, to throw them together.

But then, why was she here? Why had she been approached for this mission if Ty's own father were available? It didn't make any sense.

Whatever the case, there was one unshakable fact: She wanted nothing to do with Samuel Stovall.

As if feeling her thoughts, Sam glanced around at that very moment, his eyes meeting Cammie's the millisecond before she could look away. Throat dry, she turned as if to run, but Susannah was there, still hanging on to her for dear life.

"Susannah," Cammie muttered beneath her breath.

"I know. It gets worse," she whispered back.

"What do you mean?"

"He wants to talk to you about—about—" She laughed a bit hysterically. "Finding Ty!"

"What?"

"Apparently he's been trying to contact Tyler for years. He's never succeeded. He wants you to try."

"I don't believe this!"

"Believe it," Susannah murmured, sucking in another breath.

To Cammie's dismay, Samuel Stovall unpeeled his wife's clinging hands and strode across the room toward where Cammie, Paul, Susannah and the Connellys had formed a small grouping. Instantly Cammie was struck by the way he moved, so like his son. Enormous, ground-devouring strides brought him nearer, making him seem bigger than life even without all the folderol that came as a part of his many film successes.

And he looked like Ty. An older, more urbane version with hair silvered at the temples and eyes Ty's same gray color, but colder, far, far colder.

Seeing him again filled her with longing for Ty. It came out of left field, this deep, treacherous ache. No matter how many years passed, how many suns set and lives changed, Cammie yearned to be with Ty again in a purely feminine way. She seemed to have no control over it, and Sam brought all those feelings to the surface, making Cammie resent him all the more.

"Long time no see," Sam said, reaching out to hug Cammie even while she stiffened into a board. Whether he noticed, she couldn't say. It was automatic on her part. "I understand you've been chosen for the role of Vanessa, so to speak."

"I know I'm being considered for it," she said, trying to be noncommittal.

"It's a little more than that," Paul expelled eagerly. "Cammie's everyone's first choice."

Samuel gazed at him as if he were a noxious worm. "And you are her agent?"

"I'm her agent," Susannah pointed out. She reached for a third glass of champagne as the waiter cruised by, her hand shaking a bit. No one seemed to be feeling secure.

"I'm her husband," Paul said. At Cammie's inadvertent gasp of protest, he amended, "Her ex-husband. But we work together."

"Mmmm . . ." Sam had lost interest.

Cammie, for her part, just wanted to be out of this situation once and for all. But Nora and James were enthusiastic about the project, and as soon as Samuel showed some interest, they were all over the topic. Cammie couldn't slip away, and in truth, their perspective on the story was worth its weight in gold—if she were ever going to screentest, that is, which she was fairly certain she had no interest in.

Or, did she?

Ten minutes later, she murmured an excuse and hurried off to find a ladies' room. She discovered a private one through a bedroom that afforded her some much needed space.

Staring at her reflection in the mirror, she almost laughed hysterically at the apprehension in her aqua eyes. Her hair was a riot, too. Naturally curly, her shoulder-length tresses were particularly untamed this evening, the small globe lights surrounding the mirror picking up streaks of fiery red in her dark auburn locks. She felt as wild as she looked. She wanted to just go home and cry.

Oh, Ty, what am I going to do? I want to see you so badly again. Where are you? Are you happy? I'd give anything to relive the past and be together with you again.

I'm afraid I still love you. I'm afraid I always will.

Ty, what, what, what, am I going to do?

Reading over his last words, Ty snorted in disgust. Hitting the exit program icon, the computer screen automatically asked, "Save changes to document?" to which he emphatically pressed his finger on the "No" button.

Rising from his chair, he headed downstairs from his loft to gaze at the water outside his back windows. Why did he persist in writing this screenplay when he knew he would never even attempt to turn it into a film?

Catharsis, he thought. His past life felt very close tonight. Gazing through the window at the twinkling stars in a deep velvet sky, he recognized his vague melancholia as being related to his work on the screenplay.

Strange feelings were possessing him. Thoughts that hadn't entered his head during all these past ten years. Struggling to define his emotional state, he finally settled on one word: *longing*. He was consumed with longing for something he couldn't name.

Surprised, Ty snorted again, disdaining his foolishness. Shrugging off the feeling with an effort, he trudged back up the stairs to his computer and the work that filled his idle hours.

CHAPTER FOUR

". . . I feel totally crazy. This isn't going to work. Call it desperation, but I know I'm heading for serious trouble." Cammie hesitated, watching the stretch of freeway ahead of her disappear beneath her tires. She held her cell phone in her right hand. She hadn't expected Susannah to be in the office on a Saturday. Still, she'd felt compelled to express her feelings on her agent's answering machine. "I don't know what I'm going to say to her when, and if, I see her. If you happen to come back anytime soon and find you're brimming over with advice, call my cell. I'll be on the road a while longer. Nanette doesn't live just around the corner."

Cammie hung up, frowning a bit at the task she'd laid out for herself. Samuel Stovall might not know where his son was, but Nanette probably did. She was, after all, Ty's real mother, and though Ty and Samuel had suffered some kind of falling out, Cammie believed Nanette's relationship with her son was still intact. At least she hadn't heard word to the contrary.

Lost in thought, she jumped when her cellular phone

trilled on the console beside her. "Susannah?" she demanded into the receiver before the caller could respond.

"You got it, hon. How ya doin'?"

Cammie swallowed at the unexpected tenderness in Susannah's tone. She'd managed to relate her medical problems to her friend a few days after the Connellys' party. Typically, Susannah had reached out her arms and hugged her like a mother bear and Cammie had fought back sudden, stinging tears at this measure of her friend's empathy.

"You might get a baby yet, y'know," she'd soothed. "Don't worry."

Cammie had quickly changed the subject, unable to talk about that any more than she was about her relationship with Tyler. Now, she said to her agent and friend, "Do you really think this is a good idea? I feel kind of like a marionette, like I'm letting someone pull my strings."

"Someone like Samuel Stovall?"

"And Paul," Cammie agreed.

"Do this for yourself, Cammie. You deserve it."

Cammie wrinkled her nose. "For better or worse, I'm on my way. I guess there's nothing to do now but wait and see what Nanette has to say . . ."

The cream-colored, dirt-smudged sedan threaded itself behind the blue BMW as smooth as oil. The man at the wheel counted on his current client to be so immersed in herself that she wouldn't notice. Anyway, she was pretty busy yakking away on the cellular, an important extension of the arm in this damn city. He didn't expect her to look in her rearview anytime this century. Most people didn't.

And who would notice him anyway? He knew, from years in the investigation business, that people tended to look right through him, even if he were to smile and try to catch their eye, which he seldom, if ever, did. It was a curse and a blessing, and now, as Orren Wesson followed one—

he quickly checked his crumpled listing on the seat beside him—*Camilla Pendleton Merrill*—he decided he didn't much care as long as the pay was right.

And the pay *was* right. His client had no trouble in that direction. Still, it seemed a silly roundabout way to find the information he wanted, especially since Orren had already provided it, but then, people *were* silly, in Orren's experience. Phenomenally silly.

Now, the break-in he'd been asked to negotiate was more serious stuff, and made a lot more sense. Orren had handled the whole affair in his normal, careful, unremarkable way, gathering the necessary data *tout suite* before leaving like the wind, in a soft puff and sigh. When the unfortunate, burgled homeowner returned, it was to a carefully orchestrated mess of papers that might fool him as to what was being sought—at least for a while. Even the dullest dullard might actually figure it out in the long run. That, too, had been Orren's experience.

But this client had paid plenty for that little bit of breaking and entering, too. Oh, yes. Then the knuckle-brained fool had asked that Orren begin following—he checked the name once again, committing it hard to memory—*Camilla!*—before he put Orren's hard-won information to use.

Shaking his head ironically, Orren watched his current quarry set down her cellular phone and begin driving with more determination. Checking the traffic on either side—L.A. could be such a quagmire of stupid drivers—he touched a toe to the accelerator and settled in after her.

She was heading south today, so it didn't look as if she were on her way to any acting job. He'd hung around her parking lot enough to get an idea of what her habits were, and though she'd actually looked at him one night, he'd been smugly certain she had no idea that he was watching her. Why should she? He, in fact, couldn't figure out what the big deal was with tailing her.

Still, this was his job, and he was exceptionally good at it. Just the plain truth, folks. No need to brag. With careful expertise, he let a couple of cars slot themselves between his sedan and his quarry's BMW. He smiled without much humor. No, he wouldn't lose *Camilla* unless the damn San Andreas fault broke open and swallowed him and most of the city into its volcanic depths before they were all swept out to the beautiful blue Pacific.

He was just that good.

Nanette Stovall's career as a Hollywood screenwriter had been truncated when she'd married Samuel Stovall, but Cammie seemed to recall a few minor successes after the fact. Still, somewhere during that period she'd chucked the whole kit and caboodle for a life of solitude and serenity. Now she lived on a dusty ranch in Orange County, tucked beneath the foothills of the Sierra Nevadas, and like her son, she'd renounced practically everything from the glittery life she'd once led. Luckily, Nanette's address wasn't a secret; her exit hadn't been shrouded in mystery as Ty's was. She'd just grown tired of the whole scene and so had found a way to make herself happy without fame sitting outside her doorstep like an unwelcome guest.

As Cammie drove along the dirt track that wound its way to Nanette's front porch, she swallowed back a clamor of renewed trepidation. She'd liked Ty's mother, and Nanette had seemed to enjoy her company, too. She would probably be glad to reacquaint herself with the girl she'd treated as a surrogate daughter.

But that didn't mean she'd appreciate Cammie digging into her son's life.

Dust billowed skyward from Cammie's tires, turning her blue BMW a kind of dirty gray. Sagebrush and brown field grass flanked the track like sentinels, meeting all guests first, and as Cammie stepped from the car, she stretched her back and wondered if she were on a fool's errand.

From somewhere behind the sprawling home a dog set to baying, followed quickly by two more canine voices. The symphony filled the air. Cammie's arrival was heralded with a passion.

Great, she thought. She hoped Nanette was in the mood for company.

Cammie had one dust-covered pump on the porch's top step when the front door flew open and a rail-thin woman with a braid of silvery hair lying across her shoulder frowned down at her as if she were some noxious insect. Sharp eyes very much like her son's searched Cammie's face.

"I'm not interested in buying anything," she declared, by way of introduction, "and if it's religion you're peddling, I've got my own, thank you very much."

"Hello, Nanette," Cammie greeted her, smiling. A thrill of remembered pleasure ran through her. Ty's mother had always been a character. She'd never let Sam Stovall's loud barking kow her. She could hold her own with the best of them.

Seeing her again was a delight Cammie hadn't expected to feel. She'd been colorful before; now she was an institution.

"Do I know you?" Nanette demanded, her frown deepening.

"It's Cammie. I–I used to be Ty's stepsister when my mom was married to Samuel. It's been a few years."

"Cammie, of course!" she chortled in delight, throwing her arms wide. "I won't say, 'My, how you've grown up.' That's obvious! My girl, I'm so glad to see you again. I always liked you."

Nanette's openness touched a chord within Cammie. Hugging Nanette back, Cammie cleared her throat, feeling emotion nearly choke her. It was difficult to answer.

"So, what are you doing here?" Nanette asked as she ushered Cammie into her living room.

"I'm just—reconnecting," she struggled to say, then covered up with a gasp of delight at the rustic interior of the house.

"You like it?" Nanette asked with pride, folding her arms over her chest.

"I love it," Cammie admitted honestly.

"It's ranch-tacky. I couldn't help myself."

Nanette had pulled out all the stops, from a wool blanket woven with images of cowboy hats and lariats hung along one wall, to a wagon-wheel coffee table, to a massive gray stone fireplace big enough to practically stand inside.

Nanette herself wore denim jeans, cowboy boots, and a gray corduroy overshirt with three buttons at the throat, all of which were open. She exuded a kind of raw sensuality mixed with hominess that hit Cammie's soul hard.

I love you, she thought. *You're all the family I have . . .*

A moment later she chased that fantasy away. She and Nanette were practically strangers.

"So, what's happening?" Nanette asked, shooing Cammie to a corner of the couch. The cushions, too, were a brown print in Native American designs splashed with red and ochre and tan. "Have you seen Tyler?"

Cammie's mouth dropped in shock. Was the woman a mind reader? "Ty! Well, no. He's been gone so long."

"Oh, yeah. I know." She waved a hand at Cammie. "But I thought *you'd* probably seen him."

"Why would you think that?"

"Because he cared so much about you. I figured by now you would have seen each other at least once."

"Cared about me?" Cammie repeated, feeling like the conversation was galloping out of control. "I—we—it was never that close. I haven't seen him since before he left."

She cocked her head, and Cammie realized she reminded her of a bird. Full of energy and quickness, Nanette seemed timeless and bursting with life. It was impossible to picture her either with Samuel Stovall or living the life of a screenwriter. She fit here on this ranch.

Maybe Ty fit better wherever he was, too, she thought with a new slant of insight.

"You do know where Tyler is, though, don't you?" Nanette asked, eyeing her.

"No." Cammie was honest. "In fact, that's why I'm here. I'd like to—contact him again. It sounds like you might know where he is, though."

"Of course."

Cammie's brows lifted at Nanette's candidness. "Could you—tell me?"

She considered thoughtfully and carefully. After a moment, she said, "Well, now, I'm not certain I should. If you don't already know, maybe it's for a reason. I'm sorry, but I have a pledge to keep to Tyler, you know."

"I understand," Cammie murmured, disappointed.

"Although I believe he wouldn't care if *you* knew. But I'd have to ask him first. And no matter what, we can't let Samuel know, for certain."

She acted as if Cammie were privy to some inside information. Stepping gingerly through the conversation, Cammie asked, "Ty doesn't want his father to know where he is?"

"Heavens, no!" She clucked her tongue and shook her head. "You really don't know anything, do you? I'm surprised, really. I mean, he loved you so much."

"Who? *Ty?*" She almost laughed out loud at the ridiculousness of it.

"Well, of course, dear. Surely you knew that."

Cammie shook her head. She was about to argue, but then her scattered wits returned. "Well, we were sister and brother once, sort of. I see what you mean." She was reading more into Nanette's words than she ever should. *And it's all because you want it to be true!* she chided herself.

Nanette smiled with secret knowledge. "It was a little more than that, wasn't it? I visited a lot back then, you know. Samuel wished I would just go away and never return, but Ty was—and is—my son. I love him," she added simply. "And I remember things."

Cammie didn't know how to tell her that she'd gotten this particular memory wrong, so she said instead, "I haven't even spoken to Ty since before he left. Why doesn't he want his father to know where he is?"

"Oh, because Samuel would just blab to the world, if it suited him. He doesn't care a whit about Ty, or anyone else for that matter, except himself. Does that sound bitter?" She shrugged, uncaring. "It's just God's honest truth. Ty learned that a bit late, unfortunately. He had a falling out with Samuel just before he left town."

"Do you know what about?" Cammie couldn't help asking.

"He never really said. But he was adamant that Samuel not know where he'd gone."

"I see . . ." Cammie murmured, though she really didn't. She'd always thought some great unhappiness had sent Tyler away. Her one night with him was a strong memory, and she recalled that he'd been full of some secret sorrow. At least it had seemed to her, though she'd certainly been swamped by a lot of sensations that night and probably couldn't be trusted to know exactly what had been going on. For her, that whole night and their loving union had been pure joy, a culmination of all her desires and needs. She'd made love to him for all she was worth. She hadn't known how much she loved him until that moment. But in all honesty, it hadn't been the same for Tyler. He'd barely known whom he was with, had probably forgotten it by the next morning, and, anyway, his lovemaking had possessed a desperate edge to it, as if he were a man drowning in misery, clinging to her—any willing woman—as a last lifeline.

He'd hardly been in love with her, as Nanette wanted to suggest. She was nothing to him. She knew it in her heart, though it was painful to admit.

"I can't betray his confidence," Nanette went on. "I may be in trouble just admitting I know where he is. Those jackass newspaper people wouldn't leave me alone for the longest time after Tyler disappeared. I mean, they just kept coming and coming. Finally, I met them on the porch with my shotgun and hounds."

"You're kidding." She nearly laughed aloud at the mental picture of Nanette Stovall holding the press at bay like a scene out of the wild, wild west.

She sniffed in disgust. "They ran for their lives, the miserable rats. And then I got a call from the sheriff himself. It seems they complained about my actions. Well, I told him that if I kept getting harassed by them, I'd take matters into my own hands and damn the consequences."

"What did the sheriff say?"

Nanette's eyes twinkled in remembered merriment. "He suggested I call *him* the next time those ferrets showed up. He was the law, and I didn't want to get in trouble with the law, did I? I said, 'Frankly, my dear, I don't give a damn,' which went over like a lead balloon. I did end up calling him next time they showed up, though, and the sheriff came out and shooed them away. It was all very official, but it worked. I've been left alone pretty much ever since." She paused. "What made you decide to find Ty now?"

"No special reason," Cammie fibbed. "I just want to see him again. I'm glad to know that he's alive and well, at least."

"Don't tell his father I'm in contact with him, will you?"

"I don't talk to Sam Stovall."

"That's my girl," Nanette said with a grin. "I didn't think you'd spill a secret. Would you like some lemonade? I squeeze it myself."

"I'd love some."

"Sit tight, I'll be right back."

She disappeared toward the rear of the house and what Cammie guessed was the kitchen. Cammie exhaled on a long sigh, unaware until that moment that she'd been holding her breath. Nanette had certainly given her a lot to think about, and though she knew Tyler's mother wasn't about to just hand over his address, she believed that she could garner the woman's trust and eventually pry the information out of her.

You're terrible, she told herself. *You care about Nanette and Tyler. What do you think you're doing?*

Cammie couldn't really answer. Digging inside herself, she came up with an answer she hated to believe. The truth was, she wanted to see Ty again because she wanted to examine her feelings. Forget the screenplay, though it was made for him. Forget the fact that Summer Solstice Productions *et al.* wanted him. Forget that Samuel Stovall himself wished to reconnect with his son.

She wanted him for her. For herself.

You're a fool, Cammie Merrill.

"Here you go," Nanette said, placing a tray on the wagon-wheel coffee table which held two frosted glasses of lemonade.

Cammie examined her motives uncomfortably. She wanted to see Ty again, but was she really planning on using the excuse of *Rock Bottom* as an intro? He wouldn't thank her for it, even though the part was perfect for him. More than likely he'd throw her out on her ear if, and when, she appeared on his doorstep. But wasn't that better than betraying the truth? That she loved him still, and that she needed to see him again?

Good grief. It was all so complicated. And yet she could admit now that she was intrigued beyond all reason. There was no going back. She wanted to see Tyler again. She wanted to feast her eyes on him and talk to him and be with him again—if only as a good friend.

Feeling a little like a Judas, Cammie sipped Nanette's lemonade and wondered how in the world she could pry Ty's whereabouts from her. Cammie would never give over the information to Ty's father; Nanette could be assured of that. Cammie only wanted it for herself.

"You seem pretty far removed from a screenwriter now," Cammie observed. "When did you quit?"

"Oh, years ago. It all started to kind of pale, if you know what I mean. I always hoped Ty would follow in my footsteps, he was so good with words. But he took after Sam, I guess, although I think he was a much better actor than his father ever thought of being." She smiled. "Maybe I'm biased.

"I wouldn't trade my life now for what it was then," she went on. "Living on the ranch is perfect. I sometimes wonder what took me so long to figure it all out." She frowned. "Didn't I hear you were working in television?"

"I've been on a nighttime drama, *Cherry Blossom Lane,* for three seasons. Do you know it?"

Nanette shook her head.

"It's basically a glorified soap opera, but it's been really terrific."

"You say that as if it's over," was Nanette's sage observation.

"It is. My ex-husband decreed it so, although maybe my character's days were done anyway." Cammie went on to explain her trials and tribulations with Paul. "Maybe things happen for the best," she finished, thinking how ironic it was that she should be echoing Paul's words.

"So, what are your current plans?"

Cammie hesitated. "I'm guess I'm kind of trying to figure that out."

Nanette's gaze turned reflective as she looked past Cammie and out the window to the dry April day beyond. "That's what happened to Tyler. He was at a crossroads and had to make a choice."

"A crossroads?" Cammie asked tentatively.

"He was facing some ugly truths in his life. A woman he trusted hit him with a paternity suit. It was all a lie. Tyler was trying to prove that when she committed suicide."

"Suicide!"

"There was more to the story. Tyler didn't want to talk about it, and I've never really understood all the ramifications, but somehow Samuel got involved and . . ." She spread her hands in lieu of finishing her thought. "Anyway, it was a mess."

For the first time Cammie understood Ty's long-ago sorrow. No wonder. "Did he love her? The woman?" she couldn't help but ask, though it hurt inside to even voice the worry.

Nanette's gaze softened. "Didn't I just tell you that he loved you?"

"Yes, but that's not true."

"Yes, it is."

"Did he ever say that to you? Did he say, 'I love Cammie'?"

"Well, not in so many words, but I always knew."

Cammie didn't respond. She suspected that, for all her outward show of toughness, Nanette was a romantic at heart.

"And you love him, too," Nanette compounded the problem.

She was thrumming taut nerves even Cammie couldn't touch. "My mother loved Samuel Stovall even though he treated her like she was an object. I think you've got us confused."

"I'm sorry about your mom. She was a lovely person."

"She was," Cammie agreed, her throat tight once again.

"I can't give you Tyler's address until I've talked to him," Nanette said.

"I know."

"I'm not sure what he'll say. If he'll agree, you understand."

"Yes."

"But you do want to see him?"

Cammie inhaled carefully. Her pulse beat light and fast at the realization that she was nearer her goal than she'd ever expected to be. "Yes. Yes, I do."

"And if he says no?" she suggested softly.

Suddenly, Cammie saw a yawning chasm, a pitfall, a terrible trap. Tyler could never know she wanted to see him! It would give him too much power. She had to surprise him, if she wanted to see him. She couldn't have Nanette test the waters if there was any chance Tyler would say no.

And he *would* say no; she was certain of that. Urgently, she reached for Nanette's hand. "Don't tell him I was here. I couldn't bear to have it be that—that—things went from bad to worse, you know what I mean?'' she pleaded. ''Let him have his privacy. I don't know what I was thinking.''

''He could say yes,'' Nanette pointed out, but her voice lacked the conviction Cammie needed to hear.

Snatching up her purse, she leapt to her feet. ''Please, no. I've got some issues to work out. I'd love to talk to him, but no, no . . .'' She shook her head. ''Just—no, okay?''

Nanette's understanding smile nearly broke Cammie's control, but at least she stopped trying to change Cammie's mind. ''Sit down a minute,'' she said, and while Cammie perched anxiously on the edge of the sofa, she steered the conversation away from the tricky subject of her son and talked instead about how she'd enjoyed living on the ranch with her horses, dogs, and small herd of cattle, letting the moment slip by. Cammie sent up a silent prayer of thanks for her understanding, and as she hugged Nanette good-bye, promising to keep in closer contact, she also sent a prayer to Tyler:

I hope these last years have been good to you. I hope that, unlike me, you've found some peace and happiness in the interval that we've been apart. And wherever you are, I hope you think kindly of me. As ridiculous as it sounds, I can't help still loving you and I don't expect to get over you. If I'm going to find you, it'll be on my own because that's just the way it has to be. I love you, Tyler, and someday I'll find the courage to tell you as much.

As she drove back toward Los Angeles and her own environs, she noticed a pale, flesh-colored sedan in her side mirror. Adjusting the rearview, she idly wondered if the driver of the vehicle could be going to the same area of town she was. Subliminally, she'd noticed him behind her for quite a long spell.

Moments later, she forgot that as the Chevy sedan slipped off the next freeway exit and disappeared from view. Tired, but feeling more settled and focused than she had in weeks, Cammie drove back to her apartment to make plans for her next move. There were other members of Ty's family who might know where he lived. Or maybe some cast mate from his last film, *Escape From Eden,* had been privy to that information.

Somewhere, somehow, someday . . . Cammie was certain to succeed.

Standing on the main street that ran through Bayrock, British Columbia, Tyler rubbed his bearded jaw and squinted through the curl of smoke from the older man's cigarette. The hazy, nicotine-lousy stuff stung Ty's eyes, flung as it was straight at him by the errant breeze.

"Ya got a nice piece of property over there," the man told him, gesturing in the general direction of east where some of Ty's real estate holdings lay. "How much ya want fer it?"

Too much, Tyler almost told him, certain he was about to blast the elderly farmer's suspenders right off his dungarees. The property was waterfront, valuable, and better suited to the tourist trade than for anything it might grow. Tyler hated to sell it, but it was time to move on. He'd been here far too long already.

"Check with my realtor," Tyler said, as a means to duck out of this dilemma gracefully. "She's got the figures."

"You must have some idea." He threw down his cigarette and squished it onto the sidewalk.

"You might not like what I'd tell you," he admitted. He'd learned from his years in this no-nonsense town to speak the truth, a quality he'd never really treasured during his years in Hollywood, but one he demanded of himself and others now.

He glanced down the street and toward that section that still lay as farmland, but would, with the inexorable passage of time, become more of the rustic tourist village that Bayrock was surely changing to. He'd bought the ten acres when he'd first arrived; his cabin and other pieces of property had come later, when he'd determined he would settle here.

At first he'd been afraid to be seen around Bayrock; his face was too well known, in Canada as well as the U.S., and a huge chunk of the rest of the world, too. So, he'd lived in the old farmhouse on the far edge of the property, fighting iffy electricity and poorly insulated walls for years before he'd dared to buy the cabin right on the edge of town. Of course, Bayrock wasn't exactly a bustling metropolis. Perched on the southern corner of British Columbia, its view of Washington State across the bay was almost a mirror of itself: a smattering of small resorts, local shops and restaurants, twinkling lights, and lots of sky. He'd landed here by chance, having fled the confines of Los Angeles in fury and disgust. No more fame. No more "yes men" with their hands out and their whining demands. No more nothing.

Of course there were other reasons he'd left—reasons he still didn't want to think about. Mostly he'd gone to save his soul. He'd been too young for that kind of notoriety, and though, at the time, he'd thought himself tough and capable, he now realized with the benefit of hindsight that he'd been naive and uncertain and just plain lucky. And having a famous father hadn't helped his maturity.

Not that Samuel was any model of maturity himself, Ty reminded himself with an angry sting of remembrance. But he shut his mind to those memories. He'd also learned to live in the here and now and forget the past.

Well, most of the time, he thought, recalling with a grimace his uncharacteristic wallowing the other night. But he was okay now. Back on track.

And it was just as well that he was away from Samuel for good. Dear old dad had been the root cause of much of Tyler's pain, and only now, after ten years of exile, was Tyler willing to even refer to him as "my father" without adding the requisite "the bastard" he normally tacked on.

"How much?" the farmer insisted, his chin jutting.

"Five hundred thousand," Tyler told him.

"Geez—oh, God—wha'd'ya take me fer? I ain't no rube!" the man sputtered in pure disbelief.

Tyler nodded kindly. "I know it sounds steep. Talk to my realtor," he suggested again.

"Not on your life, sonny!" He stalked away in a huff, leaving Ty to regard him with a certain amount of amusement.

The man had accosted him as soon as he'd stepped outside the cabin. Tyler had tried to avoid him; a part of him still worried that every stranger was some sort of autograph hound or celebrity seeker. But it had turned out he'd only been a potential buyer. Someone who knew Tyler by sight only because of the property he owned. There was irony in there somewhere, he supposed. But then this old guy looked as if he might find television a new-fangled contraption.

As the farmer moved off, shaking his head and muttering, he threw back one last baleful glance in Tyler's direction, as if he'd just met up with the biggest fool on the planet. Maybe he had, Tyler thought with a sigh. He doubted anyone around these parts would buy his property for its listed price.

Maybe that's why you've got it so high. You just can't bear to leave.

With a self-deprecating snort, Tyler traipsed back inside the two-bedroom cabin whose floors and walls were built entirely of fir. Thick beams spanned the ceiling, and area rugs in Native American prints skimmed the floor. It was rustic and comfortable and its view was of rippled water and shivering aspens. The loft was his office. A computer desk he'd had specially built was curved beneath a round window which looked across the water. Some days he just sat and stared through that oversize porthole at the edge of the United States. He felt dislocated sometimes. It still was a pang that caught him unawares at the strangest times. Loneliness could steal over you without warning, and in those times, sometimes, he reached for the nearest bottle of scotch and let it burn into his unhappy soul.

But those were the rare moments—even rarer with each passing year. He did *not* miss all the hoopla surrounding his acting career, though he did miss acting itself. He'd been naturally good; even he could admit that paradoxical truth. It was just too bad he hadn't been able to just be an actor. An idol, a role model, a "pretty" cover boy. Good God. It had been enough to make his stomach turn. One day he'd actually seen his face smiling from the cover of some teen magazine with the caption: Tyler Stovall's Thirteen Tips for Great Kissing!

What the hell was that all about? he'd wondered when he'd gotten over the first blush of humiliation. He'd called his publicist and demanded to know how the magazine had gotten his picture and okay to do the story. The picture was paparazzi produced, of course; the article written by one of the magazine's editors with allusions to some of Tyler's kissing scenes in various movies.

The whole thing had needled him. And when he'd wrapped that final movie, prophetically titled *Escape From Eden,* he'd gotten served that suit from Gayle and that had been the final straw. Well, at least he'd thought it had been. It was tragic how wrong he'd been, especially when he believed her death could have been avoided . . .

But that, as it turned out, hadn't been his issue at all. Still, with hardly a look back, he'd packed a small overnight case and simply disappeared.

No one had noticed at first. Why should they? He hadn't had anyone in particular to report to, and only after three weeks of complete and utter silence from him did his manager, agent, and publicist break into his apartment to find out if he was still alive. The news broke while he was in the Chicago airport. By that time he'd dyed his hair gray and grown a mustache, also streaked with silver, and, equipped with a pair of sunglasses and a slight hunch, no one had paid a whole lot of attention to him. He bought a three-hundred-dollar car from a kid off the street—probably hot as lava—and drove to Canada, eventually landing in Bayrock. In those days, the only person he contacted at all was his stockbroker, a personal friend from high school who understood Tyler's need for privacy and kept an oath of loyalty they'd sworn together as boys. Bruce handled all of Tyler's investments and, through some smart maneuvers and lucky breaks, had managed to give his reclusive client a healthy income so that Tyler, who'd made a ton of money before his disappearance, would never have to work another day in his life if he didn't want to. Of course, Bruce worked for a company who listed Samuel Tyler Stovall (his real name) as one of their clients, and once in a while some new, eager-beaver employee thought about asking questions. But the only address available at the office was Bruce's own. Without Bruce, there was no link to Tyler, and Bruce, being a bachelor, was in no danger of having another member of his family rat out his buddy. Bruce got a kick out of all the machinations to keep Tyler's whereabouts secret. Every so often he would visit Tyler in Bayrock and they would spend a weekend sailing, drinking, fishing, and generally catching up.

Those weekends were tough for Ty. It was after them that his loneliness and longing arose like a beast attempting to overtake him. He wanted a normal life. He wanted a woman. And although he did not want children—Gayle's selfish heartlessness and greed had cured him of that!—the thought of a wife whom he could love and hold and trust was an impossible dream that he cherished in his deepest heart of hearts. Of course, it would never happen. No woman who knew his true identity looked at him as Tyler Stovall, the person. He was TYLER STOVALL, THE ACTOR for now and always. And though he'd brushed through a couple of relationships in Bayrock, the last being Missy Grant, he'd never been able to tell his "dates" that he wasn't really just a Tyler Stovall lookalike, and that had bothered him even more. His fake ID read Jerry Mercer, the name of the character he'd played in his first film, a bit of trivia known to only the most avid Tyler Stovall fan. No one in Bayrock had ever made the connection.

Tyler did call his mother now and again. Nanette was a voice of reason. She didn't understand his antipathy toward

Samuel, but she was glad for it all the same. This they shared in common.

Thinking about his father depressed Ty, so he headed back inside to the computer and the half-printed hard copy of his screenplay. Not surprisingly, his story had turned out to be a semiautobiographical account of a child whose famous, successful, and somewhat tyrannical screen-legend father influenced his life more through his personal indiscretions and multitude of marriages than his acting prowess. Ty hadn't planned for it to turn out that way, but every time he read it over he had to admit it rang with truth and pain. He didn't expect to ever sell it; the story was too personal. Yet, it was good. He knew it would be snatched up if he ever chose to put it on the market because, he could admit, his screenwriting skill was top drawer. Add that to the subject of his story—yours truly—and the property was golden.

But he could never sell it. Never. It was just another of those paradoxes of life he seemed to find every time he turned around.

Suddenly, he wanted to talk to his mother. Urgently. Reaching for the phone, he was surprised when it rang beneath his hand.

"Hello?"

"Check your e-mail," a fuzzy male voice told him, before hanging up.

Bruce. Calling from his car phone. Ty had to smile. His stockbroker pal really got off on this cloak-and-dagger stuff.

Forgoing his call to Nanette, Ty sat down at the computer, signed onto his internet carrier and waited to be connected. His thoughts were random. Bruce seldom called him because he didn't trust anyone. Ty thought he was overreacting. It had been ten years, for pete's sake, and his whereabouts hadn't been discovered yet. Sure, there was always the chance, and even Ty himself felt the pressure to move on, but it didn't seem feasible that there was a serious threat out there. If anyone were to find him, he believed it would be just dumb luck. Some tourist stumbling across him in Bayrock and blabbing to the world, but luckily that hadn't happened, and with each passing day it was even less likely.

Still . . .

Bruce's missive popped up on the screen:

Bad news. Someone broke into my house. Nothing taken, but papers strewn all over the place. Your address was right there. Anyone could have written it down. It was under your name without the Samuel part. Sorry.

Ty stared at the words, absorbing them. A fluke. Not real. Any normal correspondence would have come to him under Tyler Stovall because he'd dropped his first name years earlier. For protection, Bruce kept most of Ty's financial records under Samuel T. Stovall, so even the most prying eyes would naturally assume it was Tyler's father, but at his home he'd had the address listed under Tyler Stovall.

Would any garden-variety burglar pay any attention? Not a chance.

Still . . .

Ty sent an e-mail back as fast as his fingers could fly across the keyboard:

Looks like it's time to move. Send nothing more. I'll let you know where I land. It could be awhile.

With a feeling of unreality, Ty scratched at his beard again. He wanted to shave the damn thing off, but now was not the time. Weariness invaded every pore and he flopped down on the couch, his mind traveling at the speed of light.

Why do you care? he asked himself. *Why don't you just let the world find you?*

He couldn't answer himself and eventually exhaustion took over and he fell into a troubled sleep.

Cammie poured herself a cup of decaffeinated coffee and tried to keep her eyes open. She'd interviewed several of Tyler's other half-brothers and -sisters to no avail. No one knew, or really cared, what had happened to him. They were all involved in their own lives, and she was left feeling like a complete failure as an investigator.

Though Nanette had never actually told Cammie where Ty lived, there was the understanding between them that she might eventually reveal his whereabouts. Cammie wasn't certain she could wait until Nanette had a change of heart, and she refused to let Tyler's mother tip her hand, so to speak. That would ruin everything.

Nanette had called and chatted with Cammie a few times since their meeting. She truly believed there was some unrequited love between Cammie and Ty that just needed to be addressed. Hah! Cammie might feel that way, but Tyler surely didn't. But Nanette would have none of it. She was certain—and there was no way Cammie could convince her otherwise—that Tyler held some deep, abiding love for her and that he was just waiting for her to reach out to him.

Cammie knew she was wrong, but there seemed no way to convince Nanette of that truth, no matter how hard she tried. In fact, the more she protested, the more entrenched Nanette became in her belief. It made Cammie shudder inside to think what she might actually say to Ty if and when she got hold of him.

But she had to put those uneasy thoughts out of her head for the time being. Tomorrow she planned to approach several of the cast and crew who'd worked on *Escape From Eden.* Though it was a long shot, she figured maybe one of them had some insight to where he'd gone. If that didn't pan out, she would have to wait and hope that Nanette would help her.

The phone rang as Cammie was watching the sunset from her back deck and perusing the paper. Reluctantly she got up to answer it.

"Camilla, the producers want you back on the set tomorrow to redo some of the scenes for the final episode next month," Paul jumped right in without preamble. "They're changing the ending again. Had any luck with finding Tyler Stovall?'' he asked in the next breath.

''No.''

''No, what?''

''No, I haven't had any luck finding Ty. And I'll be there tomorrow bright and early to finish off Donna Jenkins,'' she related. She was pleased to be able to send the character she'd played the last three years off. She missed working on the show. ''How's she going to die anyway?''

''This version is that someone's going to lock her in a room and asphyxiate her.''

''Nice,'' Cammie said with a grimace.

''This is strictly hush-hush. We're all signing contracts to the effect that we won't give away the surprise.''

''My lips are sealed.''

''Dr. Moran finds her, so it leaves room for her to be resurrected,'' Paul added. ''That's always good.''

Dr. Moran—affectionately known as Dr. Moron around the set—was the show's most egocentric character. He was played by a British actor with a flair for comedy, and just thinking about leaving everything she'd grown so comfortable with sent another wave of nostalgia cascading over Cammie.

She hung up as quickly as possible, unwilling to talk to her ex any longer than need be. She'd just settled back into her swinging chair when the doorbell buzzed.

Muttering a frustrated oath, Cammie went to answer the summons. She peered through the peephole.

Samuel Stovall stood impatiently outside.

Cammie couldn't prevent a choked gasp. *Oh, no,* she thought. *What does he want?*

Reluctantly, she opened the door. Her ex-stepfather had never come to see her before, so it had to have something to do with either Ty, or *Rock Bottom,* or both. Whatever the case, it wouldn't be pleasant. Her heart plummeted to her toes.

''Hello, Samuel,'' she greeted him with just the right inflection of surprise.

"Camilla." He inclined his head.

She suddenly remembered he'd always addressed her by her full name—a name she loathed. Her mother had named her after camellias, but it had always sounded stuffy and out-of-date to her ears. Paul, being a bit stuffy and out-of-date himself, was the only other person who refused to use her nickname.

"What brings you to my neighborhood?" she asked lightly, stepping back and therefore silently inviting him inside.

He strode across the threshold, casting a disparaging glance around her small, homey living room and kitchen. Cammie followed his gaze. It wasn't grand by a long shot, but it was all hers and she resented his tacit disapproval.

"I was wondering how you're coming with Tyler," he said.

"Isn't everyone?" At his frown, she said, "Paul just called and asked me the same thing. I hope this project isn't hanging on my success, because I don't have the faintest idea where to start looking. Have you tried private investigators?"

"Yes," was the shocking answer.

Cammie gaped at him. "Truly?"

"Well, of course I have. He's my son!"

His arrogance never ceased to amaze her. "But he's a grown man. An adult. If he wanted people to know where he was, he'd tell them."

"Is that your stand, then?"

"What do you mean?" Cammie asked.

"You're not actively looking for him?"

"Oh. No . . . I don't know. I've asked around, but nobody seems to know anything."

"I've asked around as well," Samuel said. He stood feet apart, challengingly, as if he were about to do battle with her. Cammie gazed at him and could reluctantly admit he was still a very good-looking man. His hair had silvered, but it looked as thick and lush as it had been in his youth, and his eyes, in that fantastic shade of gray he'd passed on to Ty, were still his most attractive feature. He was lean and tough, and though Cammie guessed his age to be near sixty, he could easily pass for midforties.

"Well, then you must know how difficult it is to find him."

"I do," he admitted, rubbing his jaw in a curiously nervous way, as if he were struggling through this conversation as much as she was.

Then he glanced up at Cammie, pinning her with those famous eyes. "I do, because I've been searching for him for a long time. I know where he is, Camilla. And I want you to go find him for me!"

CHAPTER FIVE

"What?" Cammie's lips parted in surprise. "You know where Tyler is?"

"I've known for a while," Samuel admitted. "I didn't want to reveal that I knew because I'd hoped you would find him for me."

Cammie gazed at him in confusion. "I don't understand."

"Tyler doesn't want to see me," he explained tersely. "I've thought it all out. It has to be someone else who approaches him."

"You knew all along? How did you know all along?"

"I have—had—an investigator." Samuel waved a hand in the air as if he were physically brushing aside an annoying insect. "What matters is that you go after him."

"Everyone's been pushing me to find him, and you knew all along," Cammie murmured in disbelief.

"I haven't told anyone else that I know where he is. Tyler wouldn't want that."

"Why haven't you contacted him yourself?" Cammie demanded.

"As I said, he doesn't want to see me."

"He doesn't want to see me, either! I bet he doesn't want to see anyone!"

"It's time for him to get over this and come back," Samuel declared stiffly. "He needs someone like you to convince him, that's all."

"Someone like me." She was furious and hurt and she couldn't even say why. "What does that mean?"

"Nanette seems to feel that Tyler feels something for you that's more than—"

"Nanette!" Cammie interrupted. "You've talked to Nanette?"

"I've talked to her for years," he admitted through his teeth, "for all the good it's done. Oh, don't go thinking she's the one who told me where Tyler is. She'd rather boil in oil first, and I don't even think she knows for certain. She didn't tell you, did she?"

"No." Cammie was terse. Her head reeled with all this new information. She couldn't trust this conversation at all. He could be lying to her, just to get her to blurt out something. No wonder Nanette had refused to say anything. Samuel Stovall was sly and tricky.

"Well, if she doesn't know yet, she won't learn from me," he declared, fuming. "But this role is perfect for Tyler. He's got to come back. I want him back, and I want him to take this part."

Bully for you! Cammie could not believe the man's arrogance.

"But if *I* suggest anything to him, it won't work," Sam continued bitterly. "I'm not fool enough to think he's learned any sense since he's been gone. He won't listen to me, but he might listen to you."

Cammie had heard enough. "Samuel, I'm through being everyone's patsy. If you want him, get him yourself!"

"It's not that simple, Camilla." His mouth turned down at the corners. Samuel Stovall was not a man who liked to be thwarted. Shooting her a swift glance, he revealed, "He's living in a little town called Bayrock in British Columbia, Canada. My sources tell me it's small enough that you could probably just run across him."

"Your sources." Cammie was ironic.

"Just go find him. Here . . ." He pulled a business card out of his pocket and held it out to her. "It's my travel agent. She'll get you a flight to Vancouver and you can go from there. I'll pay for everything, of course."

Cammie stared down at the gold-embossed card. Her hand automatically collected it, but then she just held it blindly in front of her. Too much information, too fast. And Samuel Stovall was not to be believed! As the messages sank into her brain, her chest began heaving as if she were at the end of a grueling marathon. She felt used and spent.

"No," she told him, attempting to push his business card back at him, but Samuel refused to accept it. With quivering fingers, she set the small white missive on her kitchen counter. "I wouldn't take your money if I were dying of thirst and it would buy me a drink of water. Don't count on me to do your dirty work. If you want Ty, go get him yourself!"

"You're making a mistake," he warned through lips that scarcely moved.

"Probably."

Heading toward the door, he glanced over his shoulder. Anger and frustration were evident in every twitch of his muscles. "You'll do it," he said calmly. "Not because *I* want you to, because *you* want to. And what have you got to lose anyway?"

Cammie would have loved to scream and yell and tell him to go to hell, but his words rang with ugly truths. How he knew her so well, she could only guess. Maybe she was much more obvious than she wanted to believe.

"Be sure and take a copy of *Rock Bottom* with you when you go," his voice trailed after him, the words hanging in the air long after Cammie's door had closed behind him.

* * *

Orren Wesson was half through a Subway pastrami sandwich when the yellow cab turned into his quarry's apartment parking lot and parked in one of the reserved spaces. A heavyset driver consulted an address book before trudging for the stairs. Chewing thoughtfully, Orren wondered if this might be the beginning of an expected journey. Why he had to keep following her remained a mystery to him, but his client was nothing if not thorough. The man wanted to know that she'd taken the trip to British Columbia, and he wanted Orren to follow.

So be it. And it was certainly a break from tailing oversexed, underloved husbands, or bored, neglected housewives meeting lovers on their lunch hours and carefully orchestrated weekend trysts.

Setting down the sandwich on its wrapper, he waited. Within moments, Cammie appeared with the taxi driver who carried her one, soft black overnight bag.

Orren waited until the cab had backed out of its spot and turned right at the street in front of the building. Twisting the ignition, he eased out behind it. If she were heading for Bayrock, she sure as heck was traveling light.

He lay back a long way, and noticed her head turn around a couple of times, as if she were looking for someone. Her surreptitious movements convinced him she was indeed on her way to find the missing Tyler Stovall, and she didn't want anyone to know. Fine. He could keep the information to himself for a while. His current client gave him a long leash.

And if he lost her, so what? He could pick her up at the other end.

With one hand, Orren picked up his half-eaten sandwich as he settled in for the ride.

The miles sped by beneath the wheels of her rented red compact as Cammie tore up I-5 from Seattle toward the

Canadian border. She was angry. Angry at herself and the fates and most of all Samuel Stovall. She'd refused his plan, even refused to fly into Vancouver, a city closer to Bayrock than Seattle. She'd ranted and railed and made a pretty big stink about the whole plan—and then she'd gone and done what he'd expected.

Fool, she berated herself, pressing on the accelerator in her fury. Moments later, she retreated from the gas. What was the point of getting a speeding ticket over a petty burst of emotion?

But her motivations bothered her. She was such a sucker when it came to Ty!

Glancing in the rearview mirror for about the millionth time, she could only see the faint images of cars behind her. She'd sped away from the pack she'd been engulfed in, and now was amid a new grouping. Traffic flowed full and freely on this stretch of I-5, but it was growing less congested the farther she pulled away from the Seattle environs.

For three days she'd stewed over the information Samuel had given her. Was it real? Could it be trusted? She'd considered calling Nanette and asking for verification, but then she feared Ty's mother might head straight for the telephone and warn her son.

And Cammie didn't want that. She wanted to see Ty on her terms, and now that she knew Samuel possessed his address, well, the hourglass was running out.

So, here she was. Doing exactly as she'd sworn she wouldn't. But call it a failsafe or just plain stupidity, she'd elected not to bring *Rock Bottom* with her.

Roaring past a huge semi, she glanced at the driver and received a toothy, appreciative grin in return. Cammie managed a smile in return, then shifted her concentration to the road in front of her once more. What did she think this was really going to get her? Ty was bound to have a fit when she invaded his privacy. And just because she'd purposely left the script on her bedroom nightstand didn't mean she was being noble. Her motives weren't *that* pure!

Ty could easily think Cammie had simply been scatter-brained, should the truth ever come out. It would be the flimsiest excuse of all. Still, toting *Rock Bottom* along with her would only aggravate her own misgivings about this trip. She was questioning her sanity already, and at least this way she could be honest enough with herself to admit that seeing Ty was for herself, pure and simple. He might not like it any better than being approached with a screen-play, but if he believed she'd come after him to better her chances professionally she had no prayer of connection at all.

Night had fallen. Cammie squinted at the flickering red taillights ahead of her. She wasn't certain how long it would take her to reach Bayrock. She had a map, but she hadn't glanced at it yet. She wouldn't until she was past the Canadian border patrol. She had too much filling her head already.

The day after Sam's revelation was the day she'd been called in to the set to "finish off" her character on *Cherry Blossom Lane.* At first Cammie felt she'd done a terrible job. She'd moved through the scenes by rote, her thoughts far removed from the trials and tribulations of the soon-to-be "late" Donna Jenkins. Luckily, no one had complained. The director gave her lots of time to get the feel of things again, since she'd been away from the job for nearly a month. It probably didn't hurt that her character was supposed to be at the end of her rope. Donna *would* act like an automaton, a feeling Cammie could certainly relate to these days.

And the main and final scene was short anyway. It had been little more than Cammie standing in a windowless room with the sound of gas hissing through a vent. She'd stood in frozen shock and muttered almost soundlessly, "Carbon monoxide."

So went the asphyxiation death of Donna Jenkins, may she rest in peace.

Cammie had left the studio feeling strangely uplifted, as if a burden had been taken off her shoulders. Though she'd lost the role, she was on the road to new adventures where anything could happen. Literally speaking, she was on the road to Bayrock, British Columbia, and Tyler Stovall.

Her heartbeat quickened in spite of her intentions to keep things in perspective. Optimism was her enemy. Her upcoming meeting with Ty was bound to be anything but pleasant. Still, a hopeful, girlish part of herself wouldn't quite believe what her rational adult self was telling her: Tyler Stovall was more likely to throw her out on the street than welcome her with open arms.

Oh, well . . .

The only person who had an inkling of her plans was Susannah, whom Cammie had phoned before she left. "I'll be gone for a while," Cammie had revealed. "Don't let anyone know my whereabouts."

"Whereabouts? What whereabouts?" Susannah responded, all innocence.

"I mean it. I don't want anyone to know where I am."

"You mean, like Samuel Stovall? Cammie, he's bound to guess."

"If he pesters you, tell him you don't know."

"Sure, and will he believe me?"

"It doesn't matter what he believes. Just don't confirm anything."

"Your wish is my command," she answered with ill-repressed delight.

Susannah was quietly thrilled about Cammie's decision. Of course, she didn't know that Cammie had purposely left the screenplay at home. And though Susannah's motivations were pure—she only wanted the best for Cammie—they weren't in line with Cammie's own.

After a few mundane questions that nevertheless sent Cammie's pulse into overdrive, as if she were some highly dangerous criminal, the border patrol waved her through without incident. Driving a bit farther north, Cammie exited the freeway and pulled into the well-lit parking lot of a McDonald's to examine the map. Bayrock was just a bit east on the north side of a small bay that separated the U.S. from Canada. It appeared that Canadians could look across at Washingtonians and vice versa.

Trepidation filled her soul. She rubbed her tired eyes and seriously considered turning right around, tail between her legs and driving all the way back to Seattle, maybe even Los Angeles. She tried to imagine what her first meeting with Ty would be like—and failed completely.

But she could sure remember the last one. She'd been depressed about the way things had ended between them. Though she'd tried to blame it all on the deterioration of Claire's marriage to Sam, she'd known at some level that it was her relationship with Ty himself that she'd wanted to restore. It had also been at the time when Claire's illness, an aggressive pancreatic cancer, was just beginning to develop. Claire kept the facts of her approaching death from her only daughter, and Cammie had believed her mother's growing frailty derived from her ill-fated love for Samuel Stovall. In truth, it was probably already too late to do much more than wait out the inevitable, but Cammie, at the time, was ignorant of the facts. That unhappy truth still hung in the stars, so Cammie fretted over her mother's well-being, which she believed depended upon Ty's father. This, then, was the excuse she gave herself for turning up unexpectedly on Tyler's doorstep.

She had a heck of a time getting past the gate of his home, the same property where he'd driven the paparazzi into the lake on his riding mower. But fate was with her, for after ringing and ringing him from the gate buzzer to no avail, she slammed a foot against the wrought-iron fencing in frustration and the darn thing swung inward as if pulled open by ghostly hands.

The latch hadn't quite caught from the last visitor, a stroke of luck that seemed to herald positive things. Cammie had chosen to think of it that way at the time, though, as it turned out, Tyler wouldn't feel the same way . . .

So, armed only with the knowledge that "blood was thicker than water," even if theirs wasn't strictly the same type, Cammie drove up the slate drive to the rear of the house where Tyler's black Land Rover sat outside the garage. She parked beside it, swallowed back her rising misgivings and strode with forced determination to the back door.

No answer once again. Any normal person would have given up right then and there, assuming that Tyler was simply not at home. But having come this far, Cammie wasn't willing to admit defeat, and when she twisted the knob, she learned it was, as the gate had been, open to the world.

"Ty?" she called, her voice a bit quiet as she was intimidated by the silence. "Ty?"

Soft music filtered from somewhere upstairs. Cammie crossed the gleaming white tile floor of the kitchen to a hallway through a butler's pantry. She'd never been to Ty's house before, and if she'd stopped to think about it, she would have said it was beautiful, but rather impersonal and cold. There was little of Tyler Stovall in it.

But that night her nerves were jangled, her senses attuned only to her mission. She followed the sound of the music, her hand sliding along the highly glossed cherry rail as she climbed the curving, gray-carpeted stairs to an upper gallery. "Ty?"

Toward the back of the house, emanating from behind a set of double doors, one of which was slightly ajar, the music swelled outward in loud crescendo, a classical instrumental she assumed was emanating from a bedroom stereo system. Was Ty actually listening to that cacophony? Or taking a shower? Or *with someone?*

She hesitated, nervous as a fawn. "Ty?" she ventured one more time, grimacing against the expected fury she would invoke should he find her sneaking through his house.

The groan wafting suddenly from his room sounded like a cry of pain. Instantly, Cammie shed her inhibitions and scurried into his room, skidding to a stop at the end of his bed at the sight she encountered.

Tyler Stovall, flat on his back, spread-eagled and completely nude.

She clapped a hand to her mouth to suppress a giggle, glancing away automatically, embarrassed for both of them. The music raged on, and Cammie, spying the stereo and desperate for something to do, quickly dialed down the volume by at least a score of decibels.

There was instantly an almost deafening silence, and with her ears suddenly free of bombardment, other senses took over, specifically her ability to smell. And the most redolent aroma in the room was the scent of bourbon, or possibly scotch.

Ty was dead drunk.

A second later, he whispered thickly, "Wha's goin' on?"

"Ty?" she answered uneasily, afraid to glance in his direction again. His male splendor was firmly, indelibly, etched across her mind, and she was finding it hard to think.

A rustling behind her. "Cammie?"

His second groan made her turn inadvertently—to find he'd flipped onto his stomach, a strong line above tight buttocks outlining the difference between what was tan and what wasn't.

She couldn't help staring. It wasn't that she hadn't caught glimpses of him naked when they were living in the same house, but that had been years earlier when she'd been an impressionable teenager who felt she ought to scream and gag when confronted with the bare essentials of the opposite sex. Ty had merely put up with her sophomoric behavior in those days, maybe even been a little amused by it. Then, when she was old enough to stop acting like an eleven-year-old, she made certain, as did Ty, that those glimpses were a thing of the past.

But now, confronted with Ty the full-grown male, who was clearly under the influence of serious alcohol imbibition, Cammie couldn't tear her gaze away. His back was broad and lean; she could make out the muscles near his shoulder blades, and when he moved, they in turn shifted like well-oiled machines. His legs were highly muscled as well, dusted with dark hair, his thighs and calves strong and infinitely interesting to feminine eyes. Tight muscles also defined his buttocks, but her eyes skittered away from too longing a look. Her face flushed in embarrassment, and she turned her back to him once again, her arms crossed around her abdomen.

Cammie, how could you!

"Are you okay?" she asked. "I heard you groan and I thought you needed help." More rustling from the bed. This time she bit her lip and remained focused on the stereo and the bank of windows to the east where the glimmering tiny lake lay. It was truly more pond-size, but she could well imagine the fury and indignation of the paparazzi who'd been nudged into its depths after he'd been caught trespassing.

Good for Ty, she thought, smiling to herself.

A bit of swearing followed, then stumbling footsteps. "Whad're you doing here?" he demanded.

Cammie shot a glance at him. He stood teetering at the end of the bed, running one unsteady hand through his dark, slightly wet mane. If he recognized his nudity, he did nothing to rectify the situation.

Well, if he can be that bold, so can I, she decided with false bravery, twisting slowly on her heel to face him.

"I came to see you." Wetting her lips, she added lightly, "Although I didn't expect to see all of you."

That seemed to finally penetrate. Ty glanced downward, took in his nudity, emitted a grunt that could have meant anything, then staggered around the bed to the bathroom. She realized he'd made his way to his walk-in closet. While she waited anxiously, wondering if she should check to see if he was still awake, she heard the ring of metal hangers, disturbed by Ty's undoubtedly rough pawing through them. A moment later he came back into view, a black terry-cloth robe cinched around his waist.

He'd taken a shower earlier and had collapsed on the bed without dressing, she realized, concentrating now on his wet hair, which continually flopped forward, slapping his eyes. Without the distraction of his naked body, she could bring her rollicking pulse under control and take stock of the situation. How much alcohol he'd consumed was anyone's guess. Why, was another. Whatever the case, he was decidedly unsteady on his feet, and she had to resist the urge to help him back to the bed.

Once again, he pushed his hair from his eyes, but it was a curiously sensual gesture that brought a strange feeling to the pit of Cammie's stomach. What the hell was wrong with her? She wasn't prone to flights of fancy about men. Certainly not sexual ones! And this was Ty, her *stepbrother!*

Oh, sure, her truth-telling brain reminded her. *He's your brother like Samuel Stovall's your father.*

Pushing back the offending strands of overly long hair, Ty pinned her with a glower from thickly lashed gray eyes. "You're not invited," he said succinctly.

"I know. I let myself in. I wanted to—I had to see you."

"Yeah?" One hand reached blindly for the wall, which was several steps out of arm's length.

Cammie stepped forward automatically, but a darker frown shot in her direction stopped her in her tracks. He managed, although it took some effort, to stumble closer to the wall, then he leaned against it for support.

"The gate wasn't latched," she explained.

"The gate wasn't latched?" he repeated, struggling to keep up with the conversation.

"No, I pushed it open. It looked closed, though."

"Damn my father's chauffeur! Never gets it right."

"I locked it behind me," Cammie assured him. "I tested it before I walked to the house."

"Why're you here?" He sounded more puzzled than angry.

"Actually, it's your father I wanted to talk about," Cammie admitted, linking her hands in front of herself. She still could scarcely look at Ty, though he was decently clothed now. The beauty of his male body was still emblazoned across her mind, and no matter how she tried to clear her head, it just kept superimposing itself over any decent thoughts she possessed.

"What?" Ty asked, rubbing a hand across his face.

"Well, maybe it's about my mother, really. She's miserable. Heartsick. And though I think it's a blessing in disguise that they divorced, it's really tough on her, and I just wish things were better, y'know?" she asked, sounding pathetic even to her own ears.

"Better?" He emitted a bark of laughter. "Are you serious?" he asked, as if she were incredibly slow on the uptake.

Cammie flushed. She didn't think she could bear his ridicule. "Your father didn't waste any time getting remarried," she said bitterly. "I don't care. But I'd like to ease my mother's pain somehow. I know it's crazy, but I thought Samuel might be willing to help. He loved her once, and I don't believe he hates her now, or wishes her anything but the best."

"He doesn't give a damn," Ty grated unexpectedly, his mouth flattening in fury and pain. "He doesn't give a *damn!*"

"What do you mean?"

"Don't you get it? He's Samuel Stovall. A heartless, vicious bastard who deserves a place in hell."

She was stunned by his vituperative rage. It was so unlike the Ty she thought she knew. "What's he done?" she asked.

"He kills things." The look that crossed his face was one of pure misery. Shaking his head, as if to clear it, he mumbled so softly she could scarcely understand him, "His egomania kills everything."

"Ty, you're scaring me. What're you talking about?"

"Nothing." He turned away, lost his balance and groped for the edge of the bed, half sitting on the end of it. Attempting to get up again, he merely slipped and slid some more, eventually giving up with a groan and flopping onto the cover.

Disturbed, Cammie couldn't get his words out of her mind, especially when he flung his arm across his eyes, retreating into a foggy misery that even buckets of booze hadn't been able to help.

"Don't try to tell me anything. I'm not wrong," he said. "God, I wish it were yesterday . . ."

"Did something happen?" Cammie couldn't help asking. She felt useless, hovering nearby like a mother bear.

She saw his jaw tighten. Throwing an arm over the edge of the bed, he recovered a fifth of scotch, its contents alarmingly low.

"Ty, you don't need that," she whispered.

"Don't I?"

She collected the bottle from nerveless fingers, his arm falling limply to the ground. Her efforts were useless. In her opinion, he'd consumed enough already to sink a battleship.

"Whatever it is, I'm sure it'll be better in the morning."

"Oh, sure." His laugh was more a hiccup. "Better in the morning," he repeated, rolling the words around on his tongue as if checking their flavor. "I'm sick. Sick of everything and everyone."

This last part was barely more than a mumble, and Cammie had to lean closer to catch it. "What?"

Tyler gazed at her from beneath his lids. The arch of his throat caught Cammie's attention, and though she didn't want to, she felt those treacherous stirrings of emotion within her. She stared at him, swallowed, and hoped what she was feeling didn't reflect on her face.

He closed his eyes and sighed, his lips twisting. The tempo of his breath was fast and uneven—ragged, really, as if he, too, were fighting deep, strong feelings and losing the battle.

"Go 'way," he said, waving an arm at her. This time his arm flopped over his chest, but not before his fingers grazed her breasts in the loose movement. He didn't seem to notice, whereas her knees had begun a ridiculous trembling she couldn't correct.

"Can I help?" she asked, aware that her voice sounded unusually husky.

His eyes were half closed. With devastating results, he reached forward and collected a curl of her auburn hair between his thumb and forefinger, twisting the silky strands together. "Yes," he said succinctly.

Swallowing, Cammie drew an unsteady breath. She knew she shouldn't be here, but she was unable to make herself leave. "Can I get you anything?"

"Get me anything? Do I look like I need something?"

"Maybe a cold shower and a cup of coffee," she said on a half-laugh.

Tyler didn't immediately answer her, and she belatedly realized that he'd fallen asleep. His hips were on the end of the bed, his legs slackening so it looked as if he were in very real danger of slipping off the bed entirely. Cammie hesitated, chewing on her lower lip, wondering what to do. Eventually she settled for leaning close to his ear and whispering loudly, "Tyler? Ty? You're going to fall off the bed. Wake up or you'll be on the floor!"

He murmured something and turned his head so that his face was within a hair's breadth of hers. She stared at the shape of his aquiline nose and the long lashes that lay so dark and spiky against his skin. He was so familiar to her, and yet such a stranger. Of their own volition, her fingers reached out and caressed his strong jaw.

His hand shot up and gripped her wrist. Cammie gasped in surprise, then her eyes widened in consternation as she realized he was dragging her to him, closer and closer.

"Ty?" she whispered uncertainly.

"C'mere," he murmured. "Mmmm, you smell good."

"I don't think—"

But her words were lost beneath the touch of his mouth to hers. Hungry. Wanton. Seeking comfort and relief. She understood the phrase "I just melted" with new clarity, as it felt as if her bones dissolved right there and then.

For the longest time, though it was mere seconds, she stood in frozen indecision. *No, no, no!* He was in the grip of some devastating emotion, brought on by God knew what, and it was clear he blamed his father at some level for his current pain. Or, maybe it was all jumbled together. Whatever the case, he certainly wasn't thinking clearly and she would be a complete and utter fool to give in to her own desires.

But her desires were raging out of control. The brush of his lips had set up some deep, pounding response within her that she couldn't control. Her whole body seemed to be throbbing and quivering, and no amount of rationalization could change the fact that his very touch was robbing her of every bit of self-control.

"Ty," she murmured uncertainly. His head lay against the spread, his mouth tipped forward in silent, inexorable invitation.

She leaned forward. Their breaths mingled: hers shallow and fast, his laced with the sweet and pungent scent of scotch. Tentatively, she touched her lips to his, dimly conscious that she was setting the course for disaster. But Ty wasn't interested in delicacy, shyness, or drawing out the moment of discovery. He reached for her openly, with male fervor, and though she had the power to resist his advances, she didn't. Instead, she breathed in the musky scent of alcohol and Ty's own unique aroma, a subtly masculine scent with just a hint of muskiness and a touch of the spicy odor of his aftershave. Its intoxication was complete. She was lost to sensation, and when his tongue found hers, she simply relaxed against him, following him onto the bed. Rather than slide off the bed, Ty instantly wound himself around her until they were a tangle of arms and legs and heartbeats. He might have been impaired by liquor, but his instincts were right on, and when he suddenly lay atop her, his masculine angles fitting oh so perfectly against her feminine curves, Cammie had a moment of conscience.

"Ty," she protested faintly, her heart galloping wildly, her blood singing in her veins.

"Don't . . . say no," he begged.

"I only wanted to help."

But it was a lie, she realized distantly, succumbing to his

persuasive lips and grinding hips. It was sweet, delicious desire with just a touch of sin, for she knew she was the one in the wrong. What he thought, what he felt, was under the influence of liquor, but she was completely sober. She *should* say no. She *should* stop this insanity right now, but when his hand caressed her breast through her sweater, she simply gave in, her arms and legs going limp, her body his to do with as he pleased.

"Ty," she murmured, her mouth searching his hair-roughened jawline for his lips.

His body moved restlessly, pinning her down, holding her captive though she had no will to resist. He kissed her ear and hair and chin, drawing lower, his hands fumbling with her sweater, drawing it up over her breasts. Through her bra she could feel a tense, spasmodic kneading, and she heard his groan of desire.

"I want you," he muttered.

"Yes . . . yes . . ."

She struggled to help him pull off the sweater, and when his mouth went to her bra, suckling her nipple through the thin, lacy material, she arched in involuntary surrender, her fingers twining through his hair.

"Ty!" she gulped. She'd never felt anything like it! She'd never been all that interested in sex, had thought she might be slightly frigid, so dismal was her seriousness in searching for love and physical desire. But now she knew that was wrong. One touch and she was suddenly ravenous.

Unclasping her bra, he removed it with a minimum of fuss. Some distant part of herself clinically questioned his experience. Unlike herself, Ty was no wide-eyed innocent, and though the thought pricked at her conscience, she was too far gone to consider what that might really mean.

His palm brushed her nipples, but his hungry mouth moved lower, his tongue tracing the waistband of her slacks and leaving a wet line on her abdomen that set her shivering. She realized, belatedly, that he'd drawn down the zipper and unbuttoned the tab. Next, he maneuvered them over her hips until she lay on the bed in only a lacy wisp of panties and the cover of his warm body.

One last moment of conscience assailed her. "Ty?" she whispered, her breath catching a bit.

"Don't," he said, answering the feeling, not the word.

And when he thrust off his robe with a muscular twist, then removed the last wisp of her clothing, her hands eagerly helped him. No longer just a willing slave, she became an active participant because she loved him, *wanted* him, couldn't bear to wait one more moment for him!

Later, of course, she would suffer terrible remorse and guilt, since she'd been the one who'd truly made the decision. She couldn't really blame Ty; she could have escaped at any moment. Cammie had been forced to face the fact that she was entirely at fault, and though a part of her wished she had listened to her conscience instead of her rampant emotions, another part was glad, deep down, that she'd at least had one shining moment with the man she loved.

But during those heated moments, she listened only to her anxious, flooded senses, and when they were lying together, naked and hungry, and she felt the tip of his manhood seeking her inner sweetness, all she wanted to do was hurry the moment, lest it be snatched away from her. Grasping his buttocks, she answered the unspoken question. A heartbeat later, he entered her more forcefully than she'd expected, for she was a stranger to sex, a stranger to romance in general, and she gasped in pain and surprise.

Clutching his shoulders, Cammie fought back tiny, shocked tears. But then his kisses rained over her neck and face, and she clung to him tightly, a dim part of herself realizing that her body was responding to his rhythmic, loving thrusts in spite of herself. With a knowledge and eagerness she found both astounding and slightly appalling and dangerously thrilling, all at the same time, she let herself feel the ecstasy of the primeval dance.

It was over much, much too soon. Cammie had just

found her own rhythm when Ty suddenly stiffened and groaned, flooding her with his male essence, before collapsing against her in total oblivion.

She lay there, counting her heartbeats, or maybe his, since their pulses thundered together as one. Burying her face against his warm neck, she mouthed, "I love you" silently into his flesh. Tears closed her throat. The bittersweet knowledge that this would not be what he needed and desired when they both awakened kept her anxious for long, lonely hours.

At length, and with an effort, she squirmed from beneath his weight, clutching up her scattered clothes, momentarily frozen at the sight of her stockings mixed up with his forgotten robe, an intimate union with poignant echoes of what she'd just experienced.

Turning back, she gazed lovingly down at him, but he was lost to the deep coma of too much alcohol. Running fingers down his cheek, she was relieved to see him flinch. Whatever amount of liquor he'd ingested, it wasn't enough to do serious harm.

"Ty?" she whispered into the darkness.

"Gayle?" he answered back, sounding frighteningly sober.

Gayle?

She wanted to scream with betrayal, but instead her rational mind took over. It was a dream. Nothing.

And when his breathing returned to the rhythm of deep sleep, she knew he wouldn't remember calling out "Gayle" in the wee hours of the morning.

He might not remember any of it.

Regret rushed over her in a cold wave. She shouldn't have allowed it. She *shouldn't* have? What could she have been thinking? Good Lord, she'd practically jumped on him and begged him to make love to her!

Cammie raced from the room, yanking on her clothes with such hurried disregard that she heard her panties rip, and there was a definite sound of threads breaking when she yanked her chenille navy turtleneck sweater over her head.

By the time she was in her car she was half sobbing, furious with herself. Whatever was she going to do? What could she say to him? Oh, Lord, it was such a disaster, and she was embarrassed to the tips of her toes.

But, she thought, grinding her teeth together, *I wouldn't change a minute of it!*

Reaching home, she locked herself in her apartment and sat up all night thinking about Tyler Stovall. She loved him; she was in no doubt. She would not have been so reckless, so heedless and rash if it weren't for loving him. That, she understood completely.

And she thought of her mother, how Claire had usually turned a blind eye to each and every one of Sam's conquests because she couldn't bear to face the truth. Now, Claire was suffering for her weak decision, and she, Cammie, had just made another fatal mistake with Sam's son! Could Ty be much different from his father? Especially in an industry where "sleeping one's way to the top" was so common that it was joked about among starlets seeking to make their way. Ty would be an attractive name on anyone's dance card. What chance did she, little sister Cammie, have of him ever taking her seriously or giving her his heart?

None. And she knew for a fact that she wouldn't be able to settle for less.

In a haze of self-doubt and misery, she waited for him to call and discuss what had occurred between them. When he didn't, she grew angry with him. It was easier than blaming herself so much, but then sanity prevailed and she knew the buck stopped with her: Camilla Pendleton Stovall.

It was no one's fault but her own.

Did he even remember? she asked herself. Could he? A part of her hoped it was all a dim dream, an imagined night of sensual images; another part wanted him to know it was her and to call her and tell her he loved her!

And then he was gone. Kaput. Off the map. Samuel Stovall never visited Claire and she slowly wasted away. Cammie met Paul and ended up marrying a man she didn't truly love. Oh, at the time, she fooled herself into believing he was the man for her, but now, with the benefit of hindsight, she could honestly say she'd lied to herself about her feelings because she'd been on the run from her love for Ty. She'd wanted to believe her infatuation with him was over, that she didn't care about him a lick. She wanted to outrun her past mistakes, as if anyone ever truly could.

So, here she was, on a fool's errand if there ever was one, and she knew for a fact, though it was difficult to admit her failings to herself, that she was still susceptible, still a little in love, still a little hopeful that something, something wonderful, might happen between them.

Still hoping for that someday, Cammie?

Closing her eyes, she inhaled a long, healing breath. "Okey dokey," she muttered, turning the nose of the small car in the general direction of east and silently invoking help from the heavens to guide her and ease her way.

With a grunt of exertion, Tyler slammed the heavy box down on the hardwood floor, convinced it was full of cement instead of books. It had been a hell of a day. Packing was a necessary evil that garnered all his energy and attention and frustrated him in the bargain. He didn't want to leave, and he was thoroughly annoyed that he was being forced to.

Could Bruce be wrong? he asked himself for the thousandth time that day. Break-ins occurred all the time. Thievery was as common as California sunshine, and there was no reason to panic just because Bruce's abode had suddenly been selected by some enterprising small-time crook.

Except nothing was stolen.

Strapping thick tape around the box, Tyler glanced up to view his efforts. It hardly looked as if he'd begun! A neat stack of eight boxes stood to one side of the fireplace, partially blocking the view of the bay, and tiny shreds of cardboard and packing paper dusted the slate floor, the only other evidence of this all-afternoon chore.

He flopped onto the sofa, ran his hands through his overly long hair, scratched the hated beard one more time, and sighed deeply, a reflection of his all-encompassing weariness. He just didn't want to go.

Glancing toward the loft, Ty considered e-mailing Bruce back and learning a little more. He didn't buy into his friend's paranoia.

With a feeling of facing his destiny, Ty picked up the telephone and dialed a number from long-term memory. Three rings in, a harsh, familiar male voice answered impatiently. "Hello?"

Samuel Stovall. Ty hadn't spoken to him in ten years.

Ty opened his mouth to speak, but then a vision crossed his mind: a woman's body broken and bleeding, eyes open blankly, limbs akimbo in the total abandonment of death.

Slamming down the phone, he was shocked and angered to realize he was trembling all over. It wasn't even a real memory. Just something his overactive imagination conjured up whenever he thought about Gayle.

And you only think about her when you think about him!

Ty jumped to his feet, his jaw set so hard that his teeth and muscles ached. To hell with it. Tonight he wasn't willing to sit around and bemoan his fate. He wanted action. He wanted excitement.

He wanted a woman.

Dialing the phone, this time with the aid of a small address book whose pages were pitifully empty, Ty put a call into his sometime girlfriend, Missy.

"Hi, there," a pleasantly seductive voice answered. "You've reached Missy and Janine. Don't forget to leave your number or we won't be able to call you back. 'Bye now."

Ty gently replaced the receiver, inordinately relieved that Missy hadn't been home. Her voice on the answering machine had chilled the urge to be with a woman—at least *that* woman, he admitted with painful self-honesty. He really wasn't attracted to her and seeing her for his own selfish interests would only complicate matters and make them worse, even if it would have been their last hurrah together.

Missy Grant. Sweet, simple, and nice, but without a goal beyond filling out the *TV Guide* crossword and making her deadbeat ex-husband pay child support. She'd become entranced with Ty's resemblance to, "that actor guy who disappeared. Sam Stovall's son. Remember him?" Ty had initially avoided her, afraid she would make the connection, but had subsequently learned he had no fear of that with Missy. She would never believe she'd met the genuine article.

Why he'd started seeing her was self-evident: loneliness. And he'd kept on for quite some time, desperately needing her uncomplicated lovemaking. But her lack of ambition and education had eventually taken their toll, and he'd been unable to connect with her on any other level than plain old sex.

Their relationship, such as it was, dwindled to an occasional restless night together. Even that had disappeared over the past year.

Now, with her voice still echoing in his ears, Ty mentally kicked himself for his own neediness.

The telephone rang almost beneath his hand. Fearing the previous call he'd made had somehow been found out even though his number was blocked, Ty picked up the receiver with trepidation.

"Hello?"

"Jerry!" a voice boomed. "Come on down to the rodeo. Got a longneck with your name on it, buddy. We're all bored to death. Come on."

Ty swallowed. *Jerry*. His alias hit him with almost physical force. How ironic. A longneck beer with *his* name on it? He almost laughed aloud.

"Hey, Corky. Can't make it tonight." *Maybe not ever again,* he thought with a pang.

"Ahhh, come on. I know what you're thinking, but you're safe with us, buddy. Missy isn't even working tonight."

That his few friends knew of his disinterest in the waitress made Ty feel like a true heel. He couldn't wait to get off the phone, and he growled out some excuses over Corky's rising protests, slamming down the receiver again and yanking the cord from the wall.

He hated himself. He flat out hated himself.

Ten seconds of churning indecision and he made a dangerously reckless choice. Bourbon. Straight. No long-neck beer or prissy glass of wine. He wanted to be drunk. Dead drunk.

Pouring himself a healthy dose, he prayed for sweet oblivion. The packing and moving could wait one more day. Tonight, he wanted a different kind of escape.

So, she would find Tyler Stovall just strolling down the street, huh? No problem. It was only pitch dark and the place looked as if it had rolled up and sneaked away when no one was looking. Down the way Cammie could make out a smattering of lights—a couple of restaurants and quaint pubs along the waterfront. The streets, however, were practically deserted.

Sitting inside her rental, she shivered. April might be here, but winter hadn't lost its grip on this little corner of the world yet. As she climbed from the driver's seat, a car passed her, a Buick or a Chevy, late-model sedan.

She barely flicked it a look. Ty had owned a black Land Rover in his previous life. She couldn't believe he'd changed that much!

Hunching her shoulders against the cold, she walked into a shingled building whose sign, an oval wooden plaque which sported a painted picture of the black-and-white

Canada goose, greeted her with the inscription: Welcome Friends and Strangers Alike. The Goosedown Inn.

The lobby floor was plank boards dotted with scattered braided rugs in bright colors. Tiny wooden Canada geese with red ribbons around their necks covered the window-sills and three-legged tables. They were for sale with a vengeance, but beneath the fluted lights, themselves replicas from a bygone era, the geese sparkled with familiar, country luster, and Cammie smiled at them happily, as if they were friends.

"Eight ninety-five," the lady at the desk beneath the wooden stairway said with a smile. "Lovely, aren't they?"

"Absolutely." Cammie picked up the nearest and paid for her purchase, feeling slightly sheepish for being such a tourist.

"They spend a lot of time on your side of the border, don't they? Heading south for the winter and all that. They're coming back now, but in November they fill the skies on their way to the U.S."

"A mass exodus, huh?"

She gazed at Cammie, seeming a bit confused. "I guess so."

"I mean they're all leaving at the same time."

"Oh, yes, ma'am. Were you looking for dinner or a room?"

"Maybe both." Cammie glanced through the wide archway that led to the dining room. "I'm—kind of looking—waiting for a friend," she stumbled, not sure how to continue. "A male friend."

"Would he be alone?" she asked. "We've had a few couples tonight, but that's it."

"Oh, I don't know. I think he'd be alone. But I'm not sure he even got the message to meet here," she lied. She hated tricking the unsuspecting woman who was genuinely friendly and helpful.

"What's he look like?"

"Ummm . . ." Cammie went blank. "He's about six feet

tall," she said slowly. "Dark hair. Gray eyes. Thirty-six years old. Gee, I don't know, I haven't seen him in a long time."

"Is he a tourist, or a local?"

"A local, I think. Actually, he looks a lot like that actor," she added, wondering if she were stepping over the line. "Tyler Stovall."

"Oh, you know Jerry?" The woman smiled at Cammie as if their friendship had hit a new level.

"Jerry . . . yeah . . ." Cammie murmured uncertainly.

"Good gravy, he hasn't been at the inn for quite a long while. Kinda keeps to himself, y'know."

Cammie's heart leapt erratically, clamoring wildly inside her chest. Hope was making her crazy. "He's kind of a loner," she agreed.

"I'm surprised he even has friends. I mean, don't take this wrong or anything, but he can be a real piece of work, y'know what I mean."

"I think so."

"So short with people. 'Course when he smiles, all's forgiven. He's sure got Missy Grant in a state. Oh, you know about her, don't ya?" Cammie could only shake her head. "I'm sorry. You aren't—*that way*—are you?"

"No, no." Cammie's pulse returned to near normal levels. Unwelcome news, but expected, if she'd thought about it.

"Oh, good. Not that they're seeing each other right now. I mean, she'd like to still be close, but he's difficult that way. Right?" She gazed at Cammie, trying to figure out if she'd revealed too much.

"Right," Cammie agreed. "How long has he been here exactly? In Bayrock?"

"Oh, years and years. Maybe ten or fifteen? I don't know. You want to call him? He might not have remembered he was supposed to meet you."

"I—don't have his number," she admitted. "You don't happen to know his address, do you?"

"Why, he's right down the street. But if you're wanting

dinner, you'd better come right back. The kitchen's about to close."

"Right down the street?"

"The cabin at the end, facing the bay. It's got a loft and a gate at the walkway. You can't miss it. Right past that old brick brewery that's been redone."

It was all Cammie could do to keep making pleasantries with the woman after she'd learned what she'd come to find out. And though there was a chance this "Jerry" person wasn't Tyler, it sure sounded like the same person.

She left her car parked in front of the Goosedown Inn, tucked her woolen jacket closer to her body against a chilly wind and strolled in the general direction of "Jerry's" cabin. Her teeth chattered and her pulse raced along in anticipation.

It was crazy. She was crazy.

About four blocks later, she stood outside a shingled cabin with white paned windows whose back view consisted of the bay that stretched toward Washington State. She could actually see straight through a round, porthole-type window through a bank of rectangular panes and the dark water, glimmering beneath the lights of Bayrock, beyond.

Her view of the interior of the cabin itself was limited, however, and Cammie began to feel self-conscious as she craned her neck for a look inside. Was it really Ty's cabin? She felt ridiculous!

Pushing open the short white, wrought-iron gate which connected two ends of an equally short fence in matching natural cedar shingles, Cammie walked up a pebbled path to the front steps. There was a brass knocker, ravaged by the wind and weather to a beaten, greenish hue, in the center of the door. The round, porthole window just above eye level greeted her, and Cammie rose on tiptoes, trying vainly for just a glimpse of Tyler Stovall.

Holding her breath, she banged the brass knocker down, once, twice, three times. She waited what seemed an eternity, jumping up and down to keep warm, her hands thrust deep in the pockets of her red wool peacoat.

Nothing.

With a sigh, she tried again, feeling suddenly overcome with weariness from the emotional trauma of this odyssey. When there was no answer once more, she twisted the doorknob. To her surprise it opened beneath her touch, the door swinging slowly inward as if unseen hosts were beckoning her to enter.

Déjà vu . . .

Creeped out, Cammie stood on the threshold. "Hello?" she called, grimacing a bit at her boldness. "Anyone home?"

She wouldn't dare step inside without an invitation, would she? She wasn't completely without manners! What if it were someone else's place and the woman at the Goosedown Inn had misinformed her? What if she barged in on a total stranger?

But the place seemed deserted. Leaning inside, she gave it a quick glance around, impressed by the stone fireplace and fir beams and plank floors. Time passed and she feared the owner would feel the draft from the open door and come barreling down on her in a fury.

I'll look for him tomorrow, her cowardly conscience decided, and with that she stepped over the threshold to grab the knob and pull the door shut behind her—when she saw the legs sprawled across the floor.

Cammie gasped, frozen. Jean-clad legs and booted feet, hidden behind the sofa from the doorway, were suddenly thrust into her line of vision. Whoever they belonged to was lying on the floor, without benefit of carpet, it appeared, and after a moment of indecision, Cammie tiptoed within, wondering if she should help the occupant or if he was just asleep.

More *déjà vu,* she thought faintly as the whole body came into view. Ty Stovall lay spread-eagled on the plankwood boards, his arms flung wide, his lips parted while he breathed deeply in a comalike sleep that looked suspicious even without the uncapped bottle of scotch on the coffee table.

But this time he was fully clothed.

For a moment, Cammie's eyes just feasted on his male form. He was bearded, and there were the faintest traces of gray trying to form within that facial hair, but the thick shock of mane on his head was still a lush sable brown. Man oh man, he looked wonderful, she thought, feeling slightly faint, then as a blast of frigid air swirled through the room, she scurried back to the door and closed it firmly behind her.

Moments later, she whispered carefully, "Ty?"

He scarcely moved.

It was so strange and wonderful to see him. So incredible, after all this time! It was like he'd been a fantasy. Something she'd made up in her youth and now, with ten years of exile behind him, he was more legend than reality.

Except here he was—in the flesh! In much the same position she'd left him that fateful last night.

"Tyler?" she called again, louder, bending over his endearing face.

His lashes fluttered, gray eyes opening with a start. He stared at her uncomprehendingly for a moment while Cammie's heart jumped painfully.

"Cammie?" he muttered, echoing her own incredulity.

"Hi," she said with difficulty around a taut throat, her smile trembling.

"Cammie?" he repeated, louder, struggling up to his elbows.

"I—yes—I—"

"Get out!" he suddenly blasted her. "Get the hell out and leave me alone! I don't want to see you or anyone else. *Do you understand?*"

CHAPTER SIX

It was the stuff nightmares were made of. Cammie straightened abruptly, deeply hurt by his coldness. She stumbled backward and sat down hard on the sofa. Lord, she was mortified! What had she been thinking? Awash in rose-colored memories, she'd disregarded the fact that Tyler had run away from everything he knew because he'd wanted to. He hadn't changed his mind with time.

And she knew that! Hadn't she warned herself of the same, time and again?

Ty sank back to the floor, his vision centered on the fir beam that ran the length of the cabin and the open trusses that marched like soldiers from one end to the other. His brain swirled, and for just a moment, he almost forgot that he wasn't alone.

Good God, Cammie was here?

Or was it just a dream?

He staggered back to his elbows, fixing her in his line of sight, struck dumb by the vision of riotous auburn hair and wide, worried blue eyes, an upturned nose and full, sensuous mouth. She was more beautiful than she'd been as a teenager—at least in his rather murky opinion—and sadder, too.

"What the hell are you doing here?" he demanded, but his tongue felt sluggish and awkward. *Damn the scotch!*

"I came to see you . . ."

The words floated and shimmered. Tyler was certain he'd conjured this whole thing up. He couldn't cope. He just wanted to be left alone. *You called your father, you idiot!* his brain railed at him.

But it was Cammie who'd appeared, in a puff of smoke like a very enticing genie.

And suddenly the pieces fell together. "So it was you!" he snarled. "You!"

Cammie stared at him in confusion. Tyler, regarding her with a narrow-eyed glare that nearly froze the blood in her veins, looked ready to bodily toss her out—if he could have just managed it. "What do you mean?" she asked.

"And here I thought Sam was the one." His struggles to half rise appeared to be too much effort, and Ty flopped down on the floor again, clunking his head so hard that Cammie leaned forward to help in spite of herself.

"Don't you want to move to the couch?"

"No, I like pain," was his sardonic answer.

"Sorry to barge in on you. Really," she apologized. "I know you didn't expect me. I'm sort of surprised I'm here myself!"

His answer was a snort that could have meant anything. He'd closed his eyes again, and Cammie was glad. She wanted to look at him undisturbed, and with his lashes lying in a thick, dark sweep against his cheeks, she could examine him at leisure, protected from the censure she was sure to see in his own famous orbs.

He was a bit thinner than she remembered, but harder, too, as if physical exercise was an important part of his daily regimen. There were lines beside his mouth that hadn't been there before, and crease marks at the corners of his eyes a few shades lighter than his deeply tanned skin. He must spend a lot of time outdoors, she surmised, wondering anew what he'd been doing these past ten years. How had he supported himself? What were his plans?

Besides a pair of jeans, he wore a stereotypical lumberjack's shirt—flannel, in black-and-red plaid. The top buttons were left undone to reveal those same crisp chest hairs that had pulled at her senses so long ago. She was struck by a desire to run her hands inside that opening and caress his flesh. Shaking her head, Cammie tried to get hold of herself. Good grief! He'd just ordered her to leave in no uncertain terms. She was a fool not to listen, and she was certainly as silly and wanton as she'd ever been, when it came to Ty! Hadn't she learned anything over the years?

You still want him, a voice inside her head accused. *You've always wanted him. You're only going to hurt yourself if you don't leave now!*

"Why are you here?" Ty asked, his eyes still closed. One hand reached upward, fingers blindly rummaging across the tabletop for the near empty bottle of scotch.

"I told you. I wanted—to find you."

"But why now?" he insisted, on a path of his own that she couldn't understand.

"I don't know," she declared honestly. "I've just been thinking about you a lot lately."

"The hell you have. You found out my address. That's all."

Since this was, in effect, the truth, Cammie didn't know how to respond. After a moment of silence, Ty filled the gap.

"Should I expect the tabloids next?" he demanded, levering himself up so that his gaze could skim the tabletop in search of his bottle.

"Of course not. I came alone."

"Sure. The paparazzi with you? Just waiting outside?"

Cammie sighed. "You're not listening."

"Your timing . . . just a coincidence?" Shifting, he propped his head and shoulders against the couch, then squinted at her, as if she were out of focus. Most probably, she was.

"I don't know what you're talking about," Cammie said, feeling a bit of a fraud. Did he know about *Rock Bottom* somehow? Did he think she was here to solicit him for the starring role?

Ty's gaze connected with the bottle, and with a grunt of satisfaction, he collected the fifth of scotch by its neck and poured a wallop into his glass where half-melted ice cubes tinkled. "Wanna drink?"

"No, thanks."

"Women never drink scotch. It's white wine or nothing."

"You make it sound like a disease."

"It is." He nodded sagely. "It's all appearances."

"You're not making any sense."

"Really."

"Do you do this often?" she asked tightly, surveying the liquor and its effects.

"Every night," he agreed, regarding her so steadily that Cammie, who knew how priggish she'd sounded, dropped her gaze from his unnerving stare. "Twice on Tuesdays. I'm a no-good drunk. Get out while you can."

"You aren't as out of it as I originally thought," Cammie answered softly, "or you wouldn't be able to ridicule me."

Her words momentarily disconcerted him, and he glanced away. "You look good, Cammie."

"Thanks," she murmured. Now, *she* was disconcerted!

"Be a good girl and go back to Hell-ywood and tell whoever sent you that you didn't find me. Say the address was wrong. The burglars bungled it."

His patronizing tone got under her skin. Stung, she declared, "You lost me."

"Yeah?" With that, he swallowed another huge gulp, grimacing a little as the liquor burned down his throat. "So, how'd you get here?"

"By car."

"Oh, funny."

"If you mean, how did I find where you were, I did some searching until I got your address."

"Searching? Oh, searching," he muttered knowingly, nodding several times.

"I came on my own, okay? No one knows I'm here. No one."

"Yeah?"

"Yeah!" she challenged.

"How'd you find me then?"

"Well, from Sam . . ." she admitted, realizing she'd just caught herself in a lie.

Ty's reaction was galvanic. He leapt to his feet in a fury. "My *father?*" he roared, glaring down at her from his superior height.

Dimly, Cammie realized that he wasn't swaying or struggling that hard to maintain his balance. She'd been right. He wasn't as inebriated as she'd first suspected.

Not like the last time, anyway . . .

Shuddering at the memory, Cammie looked away from him. "He told me you were in Bayrock."

"It *was* Sam," Ty said reflectively, his features setting as he digested this information.

"He said he's had your address for some time. I tried to get Nanette to tell me, but she said she'd have to talk to you first."

"She never did."

"No, I didn't think she would. I—asked her not to. I didn't want to—"

"Tip your hand," Ty finished, as if he understood completely. He inhaled a long breath and rubbed absently at his beard. His initial antipathy seemed to be fading away, and Cammie dared to hope that meant he was changing his mind about throwing her out.

"I thought I would have a better chance of getting through if I surprised you," she admitted a bit humbly.

"You surprised me."

She flushed. He didn't sound all that thrilled about it.

"So dear old dad's had my address for some time?" Ty shook his head. "That's a lie. He stole my address."

"What do you mean?" Cammie questioned.

He shrugged impatiently and paced toward the fireplace. Kicking at a half-burned log, Ty forced ash-covered embers to suddenly glow scarlet and faint, darting sparks to scatter skyward like a rush of fireflies. "It doesn't matter," he stated flatly. "Why did he send you?"

"He said you wouldn't see him."

"Damn right!" Ty turned back from the stone fireplace in frustration, sinking down in one of the oversize chairs situated opposite the couch from where Cammie had gingerly perched. He set his glass back on the coffee table, his hands hanging between his knees. It was a peculiarly loose-jointed and therefore sensual position, at least to Cammie's overheated senses, and she struggled to maintain an outward composure when she was being hit at all levels by his attractive maleness.

Linking her hands together, she asked, "What—what have you been doing all this time?"

"Drinking," was his terse reply.

"Besides that."

"You don't have the right to ask any questions," he warned. "I ask the questions."

His arrogance was new. The old Ty hadn't been nearly so tense and sensitive. His attitude raised the hackles on the back of Cammie's neck, but she kept a rein on her own temper. After all, she was the interloper here, and for that she expected some touchiness on his part.

Ty's jaw was tight, his expression grim. After a moment, he said carefully, "My father gave you my address and said I wouldn't see him. But he gave the address to you." The look he sent her was full of unasked questions.

Here was the tricky part. Licking her lips, aware that she was treading a thin line between fact and fiction, Cammie said simply, "He knew I wanted to see you."

"How did he know that?"

"I—don't exactly know."

"Why did you want to see me? I mean, *why now?*"

Cammie gazed at him in desperation. She couldn't tell him about *Rock Bottom,* even though its existence had sparked everyone's sudden desire to find Ty. And when Paul and Susannah, and yes, Samuel, had asked Cammie to attempt the impossible and find Ty, she'd risen to the challenge, despite her own protests as to the improbability of its success.

"Because Samuel delivered your address," she stated.

"Out of the goodness of his big heart, he just said, 'Ty's in Bayrock. Go find him. Tell him hello!' "

"That's about the size of it," Cammie declared.

Ty barked out a humorless laugh. "Sure."

Cammie clamped her lips together, refusing to say more, especially when the full truth could get her into trouble. But his eyes drilled deeply into hers, and eventually Cammie couldn't keep up the facade. Flushing, she looked toward the fire where the embers had faded to the tiniest orange throb on the underside of the oak log.

"I'd believe he was with you, at a hotel somewhere nearby, if I hadn't just talked to him."

"You talk to him?" Cammie couldn't hide her surprise.

"*Talked.* Once. Earlier tonight. But hearing his voice slammed me back to reality in a big hurry. Then, fortuitously, you show up."

"I told you, I came on my own. Samuel may have given me your address, but that's as far as it goes. If you remember, he's not my favorite person," she added coolly.

"I remember."

As if he'd suddenly grown tired of the conversation, Ty closed his eyes and sighed heavily, one hand yanking on his beard in a restless movement she could picture him doing over and over again. "I haven't forgiven him, either."

"His egomania kills everything," Cammie murmured softly, drawing Ty's attention with a snap.

"Where did you hear that?" he demanded.

"Why—I don't remember," Cammie stumbled. Too

late, she realized those had been Ty's words that fateful night together, and there was no way she could have known them unless hearing them from his own lips. And apparently Ty did not remember anything of their night together, or it would have come up already. She didn't believe for one second that he would be able to keep from denigrating her with that information, too. He was too unhappy about being discovered to make allowances.

"You sure you don't want a drink?" he asked, after a long moment of consideration.

"Positive." Then, with a small smile, she added, "Unless you've got some white wine."

Her humor caused his brows to lift in surprise. Ty's gaze darted to hers, and when Cammie couldn't fight back a nervous chuckle, something inside him seemed to relax a little. He didn't actually smile back, but his expression softened. "There might be some here," he admitted grudgingly.

"I was kidding," she said when he got to his feet, grabbed the bottle of scotch and headed for the kitchen tucked beneath an overhanging loft.

"Yeah, well, I wasn't. I can't stand to drink alone, unless I am alone, which is most of the time," he admitted. "But when I have guests, it's social hour."

"Really, Ty—"

"Shh," he told her, and Cammie helplessly watched him rummage through his cupboards and finally locate an unlabeled bottle of some mysterious fluid that he declared was white wine.

"Home grown," he told her, "by some friend of a friend," as he handed her a healthy dosage in a goblet. Cammie sipped at it. "How is it?" he asked.

"Lighter fluid."

Ty grinned, a flash of white so overpoweringly male and sexy that Cammie slopped some of her wine onto the floor. In the years since he'd been gone, she'd made a point of watching all his old movies until the tapes were scratched and the audio skipping. His smile had been his trademark, and seeing it suddenly was a shock she'd been unprepared for.

"Let me refill that," he suggested.

"No thanks, really. I couldn't drink much more of this stuff if my life depended on it."

"Honesty," he said, pouring himself the remainder of the scotch. "I like that."

Cammie's smile trembled on her lips. She wasn't even close to being honest.

"You're funny," he said, as if rediscovering something he'd lost. "I remember that."

Do you remember anything else? Cammie wondered uncomfortably, but judging by Ty's attitude, she guessed not. Their night together was, as she'd expected, a forgotten dream for him. Which was all to the good, since she wouldn't know how to act if his memories ever became as crystal clear as hers were.

They stared at each other for long moments, and Cammie realized Ty, who had yet to touch his latest drink, was sobering up fast. Her nerves reacted accordingly. How would she feel when Ty, stone-cold sober, ordered her to leave? She didn't think she would be nearly so bold as she'd acted thus far.

Cammie took a breath. "I can't believe I'm here and we're talking. It seems so unreal."

"I've been gone a long time."

"A long, long time," she agreed.

Silence. Cammie counted her heartbeats, conscious of her elevated pulse as he gazed into her eyes, his own seeking answers.

"Cammie—"

"Ty—"

They spoke together, but before either of them could finish a thought, the telephone shrilled. Cammie jumped, and Ty glanced sharply at the offending machine, as if it were entirely at fault instead of the caller on the other end.

"Someone knows your number," Cammie stated, swallowing.

"Nanette," he said. "I used to be more paranoid. I wouldn't ever call her unless I was at a phone booth, but the public has a short attention span and they left her alone very quickly."

"Not all that quickly. The sheriff had to help," Cammie said, and Ty shot her a questioning look.

The phone rang on like a nagging shrew. Ty glared at it impatiently, undecided, then with a muffled oath, he snatched up the receiver.

"Yeah?" was his terse response.

Cammie could hear tinny squawking from the voice on the other end, but Ty didn't respond to its sharp tones for a long time. However, his expression subtly changed, and when he said, "Thanks," and softly hung up the receiver, Cammie sensed an electric change in the air, as if something monumental had happened.

"What?" she asked.

"My father had someone break into a friend's apartment and get this address."

She shook her head. "I don't believe that."

"Then you're a bigger fool than I am. My father directed you here for reasons I don't quite understand. But the fact is, you're here," he said, and Cammie felt the chill in his voice brush over her as if his breath were actually a stiff, frigid wind. "I wasn't thinking before. I almost forgot that he actually burglarized someone's home. I got all caught up in seeing someone I once considered a friend. Call me 'alcohol impaired.' But I'm back in my head now and I want you to leave."

"What?" She could scarcely believe the abrupt change in his demeanor.

But he was pretty clear when he stated tautly, "You're trespassing."

Still, Cammie hesitated. She hadn't come all this way just to turn tail and leave. "Who was that?" she asked, glancing toward the phone. Clearly, it hadn't been his mother.

If she'd hoped to divert him, it didn't work. Ty's stern countenance didn't alter an iota, and when he strode to the door, throwing it wide and silently gesturing for her to follow his order, she had no choice but to acquiesce.

Except she couldn't just go! "Ty, I'm not leaving Bayrock without talking to you."

"You just talked to me."

"You're not listening. I—"

"You're right, I'm not," he interrupted harshly. "If I wanted to be found, I'd have been found before. Now, get out of my house before I throw you out."

"I don't know what that person said to you, but I never hired anyone to do anything, especially breaking and entering! All I want to do is reconnect. That's all. I just want to—have some family again," she blurted honestly. "I just want to see you—again."

Her pathetic little speech appeared to have no effect, and Cammie could have kicked herself for sounding so lonely and needy. Of course he didn't want to see her! He'd made a pretty serious stand on this issue ten years earlier when he'd dumped his entire life and run away. What had she expected?

"Where are you staying?" he asked, as if the words had been dragged from some deep inner part of himself he would have liked to deny.

"Nowhere, yet. Maybe the Goosedown Inn? That's where I'm parked."

When she would have brushed past him, still doing his bidding, though reluctantly, her feet moving ultra-slowly, Ty's hand suddenly shot out and grasped her upper arm. For a moment he didn't speak, and she gazed at him uncertainly, afraid for what might come next.

She could smell the alcohol on his breath, but it was a sweet, warm scent that somehow stirred her blood. Memories flitted inside her mind, brushing like butterfly wings—memories of his lips and touch and hunger.

"You've turned into a beautiful woman," he ground out, as if the words were torn from him.

"Thank you." She didn't know what else to say. She was entrapped by the emotion in his eyes.

Did he know he was rubbing her arm with his thumb, a convulsive movement that belied his granite appearance of ultimate control. She couldn't breathe. The space was too tight, yet she wanted the moment to stretch out into infinity.

"If I let you stay—" he started, cutting himself off instantly, as if the words were blasphemy itself.

"I'm not going to tell anyone where you are. I have no interest in that."

"My father didn't send you? Hell, he had to have!"

"He told me where you lived. When I decided to find you, I left on my own. I didn't tell him. If anyone followed me, they were pretty cagey about it." A faint thought skittered across her brain, a sense of anxiety she couldn't quite put a finger on.

Ty shook his head. "It doesn't matter. I'm leaving this place anyway." But reluctance rang through his words. His feelings were plain.

"You're leaving Bayrock."

"I've got to! I feel the dogs panting at my heels. It's only a matter of time. And now you . . ."

"But you don't want to go." She voiced the realization.

"I don't know what I want!" he gritted out, clearly furious with his own indecision.

Why did you leave? she wanted to ask him. *Why for so long, so completely?*

"Go get your things," he said suddenly, the words fast as if he knew he was making a mistake and was in danger of changing his own mind before the words were even spoken. "You can park out front. You can have my room. I'll sleep in the loft."

"Ty, you don't have to—"

"Do it before I change my mind." Abruptly, he released

her arm. His mouth twisted into a sardonic smile. "I warn you though, I'm difficult as hell."

Without another word, Cammie strode across the threshold, knowing a gift when she received one. She moved with all due haste, half running through the frigid night because Ty's mercurial change of mood might last as long as his next thought, and she couldn't risk losing this windfall of an opportunity.

Ty slammed the door behind her, stared at it in total astonishment, then ran his fingers frustratedly through his hair. Damn, he was furious with himself! Hadn't Bruce just told him that he suspected Sam was behind the break-in? Hadn't someone called up and tried to access Tyler's records at work, posing as Samuel Tyler Stovall, Jr.? Sure, it could be some independent, but only Samuel cared; Ty was certain of that. And Bruce had to agree.

And so what if it were someone else? Sam knew enough about him to give the information to Cammie. Any way you looked at it, his cover was totally blown.

So, why was he waiting around for the axe to fall? Why had he invited the Trojan horse into his home?

Ty didn't even want to consider the answer. He suspected it was something more basic than he wanted to admit. One look at Cammie, and some dormant male hormone had jumped to life as if he were an adolescent.

It had been all he could do to try and behave normally.

Growling beneath his breath, Ty headed for his temporarily forgotten drink. But as he raised the glass to his lips, a lustful image of Cammie naked ripped through his brain. Ty blinked in shock. Was it memory? It couldn't be! But it was so incredibly sharp that his body reacted accordingly, and that ticked him off so badly he swallowed a burning gulp of liquor that caused him to choke and his eyes to tear.

Good Lord. She was practically a sister to him! Well, no. That wasn't true. She'd been a stepsister for one brief period of history in his life. He'd had other stepsisters as well, although he couldn't even recall their names and faces right now. Cammie was the one who'd mattered. The one who'd been a part of his life. But it was all so many years in the past that it seemed odd to have such familiar power.

"I've been gone too long," he said aloud to the empty room. "I'm delusional."

No, you're not, you ass, you're just horny!

That ticked him off anew because the truth of it was so darned obvious and so puerile. He'd had other women during his self-imposed exile. He'd had a number, as a matter of fact, Missy Grant being the one who lasted the longest, but the honest truth was, they were quick moments, transient encounters which were over even before the act of sex was completed, at least in Ty's mind. He couldn't connect. He couldn't love anyone, and when he actually warmed to a woman, invariably they began talking love, marriage, and children. It froze his blood.

At some level he wanted the first two, though he doubted he would ever find either. Love and marriage were the ideal. But he did not, and never would, want children; Gayle's death and his father's indiscriminate siring of children had cured him of any small interest he might have harbored for fatherhood.

Which didn't explain why he'd relented when it came to Cammie. Why had he invited her to stay? *Why?* Some infantile desire of his own in her professed need to "reconnect," he supposed. That was the worst of it. He was more of a sap than he'd ever believed, and it took a certain amount of serious, internal dissection of his feelings to make him recognize this aberrant new side to himself.

What was he going to do with her?

Setting down his drink, he walked down the short hall past the bathroom to his bedroom. Clutter reigned on the shelves. Books, mostly, and extra computer supplies that hadn't made it upstairs to the loft. There were no pictures, nothing to remind him of the past, except a ceramic cup that read "Jerry," a memento from his first film which was now used to store pencils.

Ty picked up a pair of jeans from the floor and carried them to the kitchen where, behind louvered doors, stood a tiny, stacked set of washer and dryer. He suddenly felt invaded, and he silently cursed the impulse that had caused him to invite a guest into his space.

But what a guest she was!

Picturing her wide-set blue eyes and lush auburn hair waving to her shoulders crowded out every other thought inside his head. He shook his head in disbelief, staggered a bit and realized he'd had way too much to drink. But was it really alcohol that was impairing his judgment and his reactions, or was it something far more treacherous?

With an effort, he headed back to the couch and collapsed into the cushions. Boxes lined the edge of the room, a reminder that he did have to leave. Putting off the inevitable was dangerous; if Cammie were already here, there was sure to be others, no matter what she said.

Still . . .

His head swam when he closed his eyes, so he snapped them open, staring up at the beamed ceiling. He was a master at holding his liquor, yet there was always that point of no return. Had he reached it yet? He hoped not. He so seldom drank hard alcohol anymore, for it reminded him of those terrible days just before he left Los Angeles for good.

He suddenly wanted to be stone-cold sober when Cammie reappeared.

What have I gotten myself into? he thought with an inward shudder, sensing in himself a susceptibility he'd hoped with all his heart had been killed when he'd learned of Gayle's duplicity and death.

Cammie dragged her overnight bag from the trunk of her rental. She was parked in Ty's driveway, directly behind the closed door to his two-car garage. The stiff breeze kept up a constant *whoosh* around the buildings which guarded this edge of the lake, and she could smell the dank scent of water and wet foliage.

Closing her eyes, she drew a deep breath, hiked up the overnight bag, then headed for the gate that led to the front door. She hoped he hadn't changed his mind. She hoped this was the beginning to something new and wonderful.

She hoped for a miracle.

Across the way and down the street, parked in the shelter of a couple of giant firs, Orren Wesson lowered his binoculars. She'd done it. She'd gained entry. And though he hadn't seen Mr. Tyler Stovall in person yet, the address was right and Cammie had found a way to gain his trust.

Twisting the ignition, Orren eased his car down the street and slipped into a space outside the brick brewery near the Goosedown Inn. The place wasn't exactly hopping, but there were enough people at the cluster of tables inside to toss him a few uninterested glances before returning to their ales and hefeweizens and microbrews.

Orren popped a quarter into the pay phone and dialed a credit card calling number, followed by the now memorized number of his current employer: Samuel Stovall.

"The fat lady's been singing for a while, just like I told you," he said.

"She found him?" The eagerness in the other man's tone caused Orren to smile faintly.

"Found him and talked him into letting her stay. She took her overnight bag inside and parked the rental in front."

A snort of amusement, or possibly admiration, followed. "Come on back and collect your money."

Orren grunted a happy agreement. This trip hadn't been

necessary in the first place, but if someone else was paying, why not? Still, he could use a little warmer weather. Hell, it was still *winter* up here!

Los Angeles was only a day away.

CHAPTER SEVEN

Samuel Stovall walked with the natural urgency of a man who can't bear to get behind, in time or in life. He strode forcefully, and though he was nearing sixty, he looked ten years younger and sometimes even managed to fool some into believing he was in his early forties. Of course, those were the people who remembered his son, Tyler, as he'd been when he left town: twenty-six years old and a spittin' image of the old man at the same age.

Only close friends and those who'd known Ty well realized the passing of the years; most of the public seemed to be content to expect time to have stopped, and Sam was in no hurry to argue with them, nosirree! If they wanted to believe the myth of everlasting youth, so be it. The value to him as a man was uncountable. His power at the box office had not diminished because of it, and if it weren't for a series of avaricious ex-wives, he'd be rolling in cold hard cash.

Still, he wasn't bitter. He could get things done. And when he wanted his way, he generally got it. It was just a matter of time.

With a grunt of satisfaction, Sam pushed open the door to William Renquist's office. As Sam's personal assistant, William had been asked to perform many a duty outside the "normal" expectations of a general dogsbody. And though Sam had seen some anxious expressions cross William's face from time to time, his man Friday seemed to manage—and quite nicely, too. William was worth the extra money Sam paid him and then some.

"So?" Sam barked by way of greeting.

"You were right. Wesson followed her, though she was a bit faster than he expected. Took a flight to Seattle the very next morning after you gave her the address. Rented a car from there."

Sam chuckled and rubbed his palms together. "She's staying with him!"

"Will she call, do you think?"

"Me?" Sam snorted. "Hell, no. The girl thinks I killed her mother. She's as distrustful as a wild colt."

William nodded. He was thin, and sharp as a steel point. He'd been with Sam through the last two wives, and he knew more about Samuel Stovall than any man, or woman, alive. His loyalty was based on more than money; Sam Stovall had paid off a debt William's sister had owed to some unsavory characters who'd threatened her with bodily harm. He'd done it to win William's unswerving devotion, and he'd succeeded.

But William thought Sam's use of Camilla Merrill was totally unnecessary, and he hadn't been exactly silent about his feelings. Samuel Stovall was thoroughly enjoying being right. "Are you going to Bayrock?"

"Good God, no!" Sam blasted. William was smart as a whip, but he knew next to nothing about Tyler. "Believe me, we need a woman's soft touch. That's Camilla's job."

"Your son isn't known for falling for women's charms unless it suits him," William pointed out.

"Not most women. But there have been a notable few."

"Who?"

Sam, however, wasn't willing to share a story that could

only make him look the villain. There were still a few details of life that even William Renquist wasn't privy to. "Never mind. Camilla's a great shot for this. It's brilliant. She's got a reason to want him back, and when he reads *Rock Bottom,* he'll be back in a heartbeat. He's not a fool. The role's perfect for him."

"And for you." William smiled.

"Well . . . it's more for Tyler." Sam pretended not to care, but his altruism was a sham and they both knew it. Though his box office appeal was still awesome, Samuel Stovall, and his audience, were aging. This meant less dollars spent by the average moviegoer, and therefore less total money earned by the film. But adding Ty to the roster was a guaranteed hit, no matter what the script! It was a stroke of genius on Sam's part, one he was certain he would have concocted without the help of Camilla's smarmy ex-husband, given the time.

"I hope you're right, and he jumps at the chance," William said, throwing in a little bit of negativism that Samuel did not need.

"Are you kidding? He'll lap it up. He's no idealist, no matter what the public thinks." Samuel shook his head and sighed with delight. How could it fail? The behind-the-scenes tale was a marketing man's dream: popular actor, rocketing to fame, disappears for ten years without an explanation and then suddenly reappears to take the lead in a small dramatic role. It was a sure win even without *Rock Bottom*'s fabulous script! And the public would flock to the box office in droves. Sam couldn't imagine a soul wanting to miss out on Tyler's comeback.

And Sam didn't want to miss the windfall that would pour down on the studio, production company and actors *et al.* when that happened! He planned to be first in line, standing at the front door, both hands outstretched and ready for every, and all, profit that would rain down in buckets.

"You're certain Ms. Merrill will be able to persuade him."

Sam winked at William. "I'm a gambler. She's a tough girl, our Camilla. I saw that when she was a kid. And I'm telling you, she made me feel like a criminal, when I wasn't doing a damn thing wrong." He smoothed his hair, an automatic gesture from years of unconsciously checking his appearance. "And I helped things along a bit by making certain she was Nora and Jim's first choice. Oh, I know that hustler ex-husband of hers thinks he got her the role, but believe me, he doesn't have the clout."

William nodded in agreement.

"When he first pitched the idea, I knew he was wasting his time. The Connellys didn't give a rat's ass about him. The only reason they even talked to him was because he threw my name around—Camilla being my stepdaughter and all."

William nodded.

Sam lifted his arms in guiltless glee. "I'm an opportunist. I admit it gladly! Paul Merrill was floundering around, boring everyone to tears, but he was close to the right idea. I remember thinking, 'Camilla can get to Ty.' That's when I put a little bug in Nora and Jim's ears. Simple."

"Brilliant," William concurred. But then he cleared his throat. "You're sure she wants this as much as you do?"

"Are you kidding? That young lady's hungry for a career. That nowhere soap opera of hers . . ." Now it was Samuel's time to snort in disdain. "Paul Merrill said the show was going in another direction, so I kind of suggested he get her axed a bit sooner than originally planned. Hah! I should get a medal. Gave the program a bang-up ending they wouldn't have had this season."

Privately, William believed Samuel Stovall was inclined to give himself too much credit, but he wisely kept that opinion to himself. "How long are you going to give her?" he asked.

"What?" Sam was lost in his own "feel-good" over his Machiavellian machinations.

"Summer Solstice won't wait forever. They're red hot

and ready to roll, so what kind of time frame are we talking about?''

Sam frowned in consideration, smoothing his hair once more. ''It's April. There's some time left.''

''They want production to start as soon as possible.''

''Well, of course they do! They always do,'' he growled, referring to production companies as a whole. ''We'll give her a few weeks. Maybe a month or so. They can hold off till August, if necessary. There's a bunch of preproduction still left that has nothing to do with the actors.''

''Will you still want to do the film if your son refuses?''

''Hell, yes. It's too good to give up. But Tyler will see the light, just you wait. The boy's got good business sense. The only one of my kids that does.'' A flash of bitterness swept through his voice.

They switched topics briefly, with William checking how things were going with Sam and his current wife, Felicia. This latest marriage was foundering, and though Sam showed some interest in keeping it together, he was more concerned in furthering his own selfish goals. In his later years, he'd turned his energies from philandering to the self-promotion of his career—much to Felicia's relief—but his ego was huge, his selfishness legendary. He was a difficult man at the best of times, and these, though not the worst, were definitely down the list a ways.

William was Sam's sole source of sanity and reason. Though Samuel Stovall heeded no one but himself, William at least had the power to pose possible avenues for Sam to reach his goals in the least destructive way.

But both men had one long-term goal that never wavered: to get Samuel Stovall everything he wanted.

''June on the outside,'' Samuel said now, as the conversation wound down and each man's thoughts returned to the issue on the top of both of their lists. ''If she hasn't succeeded by then, we'll just have to prod her along, won't we?''

William Renquist inhaled deeply through his nose, wondering exactly what that might entail. Orren Wesson had broken into that stockbroker fellow's house, which was felony by anyone's standards, and William was a bit faint-hearted when it came down to skullduggery of that nature. Still, his check was fat, his loyalty deep.

"June," he agreed, and both men smiled.

Cammie lay awake in the middle of Ty's king-size mattress, stretching her arms across the smooth sheets. The bed was enormous, made more so by the confines of the room, as it was tucked beneath the slanted wall where the stairs turned to the top of the loft. Everything was constructed of fir, warmed to a golden richness that seemed to envelop Cammie and make her want to snuggle further beneath the nautical blue comforter. Her gaze searched the nooks and crannies of the room, her senses soaking up more and more information about Ty Stovall.

He kept things. Whatever was purchased or given to him seemed to be set down and forgotten. There were books and magazines and a stack of blank computer paper. His office seemed to have spilled downstairs into his bedroom, and when she dared to open the drawer in his nightstand, she discovered Chapstick, several best-selling novels, a recent copy of *Popular Science,* and a stack of papers that looked suspiciously like a screenplay at first glance.

Footsteps sounded above her. Panicked that he would catch her snooping, Cammie shut the drawer so quickly she slammed her finger, hard. Pain shot through her hand and she involuntarily cried out, tears stinging her eyes.

Klutz! she railed at herself. Her index finger ached like a beast, and she'd done it to herself. Fighting back a moan, Cammie watched blood well around the base of her nail. Guilt wasn't enough, apparently. Throbbing pain beat like a pulse.

"Damn," she whispered.

Moments later, Ty tapped on the door. Curling her throbbing hand beneath the comforter, Cammie called, "Yes?"

"Are you all right?"

How odd, she thought. *I'm in his bed and he's asking me if I'm all right!* "I'm just getting up," she said.

"I thought I heard you—" His voice trailed off as if he couldn't quite figure out how to ask her about the noise she'd made. No wonder. *She'd* have a hard time asking him!

She struggled not to laugh, then bit back a groan of pain as the pressure in her finger increased. She'd really done it. She would undoubtedly lose a nail after the blasted thing turned every shade from red to puce to black!

"Cammie?" Ty was clearly puzzled.

"Just give me a few minutes. I'll be right there."

She heard him walk back down the hall, then she dared to look at her hand. It was already red and growing redder, and a dark purplish spot showed beneath the nail. The pressure was growing. She knew she'd have to do something to release it.

Why me? she thought with an inward sigh.

With difficulty she climbed out of bed, threw off the T-shirt she'd worn as makeshift pajamas, then struggled one-handed into a pair of jeans and white, long-sleeved cotton blouse. She made it through three buttons before she gave up and just held it closed with the good fingers of her injured hand. She wanted a shower anyway, before she was fully dressed, so grabbing up her makeup bag with her free hand, she stepped into the hall . . .

. . . and straight into Ty's warm, hard chest.

She gasped in shock. "Ty!" She hadn't counted on him being right outside the door.

"Sorry," he apologized, steadying her as he stepped back to arm's length. "I was just going to ask if you wanted your coffee black or with cream or sugar or . . ." His gaze dropped to her partially buttoned blouse.

Cammie knew an expanse of skin showed at the throat of her white shirt. With difficulty she managed a breezy smile and murmured something about a shower. Slipping past him, she sneaked into the bathroom and closed and latched the door.

Leaning against the panels, she squeezed her eyes shut tightly, exhaled slowly, then slowly lifted her lashes again. *Tyler Stovall! Good Lord, she was staying at his cabin!*

Shaking her head to dislodge the sense of disbelief, she examined her battered finger, turning her hand around to view it from all sides. Nothing life-threatening. Just swollen, sorely painful, and a reminder that she was absolutely no good at detective work!

She heard him in the kitchen, probably pouring the coffee. Unbuttoning her three buttons once more, she stripped off her shirt and jeans and slipped into the shower.

The spray hit her in a hot, steady shot, streaming over her head. She stood there for what felt like an eternity, until her nerves slowly calmed down and her breathing returned to normal. Good grief, she felt odd. Seeing Ty again had sent her emotions spinning, and though she'd expected to have some reaction, she couldn't get over the sense of displacement and all-out strangeness that had descended upon her.

What a weird night it had been! All the while she'd been gathering her things, she'd worried that as soon as she crossed his threshold again he would throw her out once and for all. She was certain he would change his mind, so she'd scrambled and rushed and scurried, parking the car with more speed than safety in a spot directly in front of the cabin. Once inside, she'd pretended with a bright smile that her being in Bayrock was all ho-hum and commonplace. What Ty thought of this performance, she couldn't say. He'd barely grunted at her when she returned.

He did insist she take the bedroom, however, and though she protested loud and long, she lost that particular battle before it had scarcely begun. Ty was deaf, dumb, and blind to anything she might say.

"I'm sleeping on the couch in my office," he told her flatly.

"But you don't have to. I feel guilty enough already,

barging in on you like this, so I refuse to throw you out of your bedroom."

"Give me a break," he said with a faint smile and trudged up the stairs while Cammie's protests floated after him.

Eventually, she did as she was bidden, checking the lock on the front door since Ty was particularly lax about privacy and protection. Then, tucked in the comfort of his huge bed, she'd lain awake for hours and hours, convinced she would never catch a wink of sleep.

She'd been overwhelmed by the idea that it was *his* bedroom, *his* belongings, *his* scent hanging in the air. He'd been gone so long from her life, and so long from the film industry and world as a whole, that he'd assumed mythical proportions in Cammie's mind. It was as if he weren't really *real,* and though she knew he was, Tyler Stovall had become to her, like most of the world, a person who existed only through the media. A celebrity, first, foremost, and only.

Cammie had entered his bedroom with a sense of treading on hallowed ground, and she simply couldn't shake the feeling. Tossing and turning, she prayed for the sweet oblivion of sleep and listened to her restless heartbeat, wishing deep inside herself for something she dared not name. In the wee hours of the morning she'd been unable to stand it any longer, so she'd tiptoed into the living room and sat down in front of the cold ashes of the fire. In the semidarkness, she reviewed the events that had brought her to this point, and, as ever, she felt uneasy inside herself.

Oh, she wasn't about to get down on her knees and beg him to accept the role in *Rock Bottom.* She wasn't a complete loon, and she'd purposely left the script at home. But she was afraid of what she, Cammie, might really want and hope from him, and knowing that made the hours tick by ever so slowly until daylight was a faint lightening of the deepest darkness outside the huge windows that faced the bay.

And that's when Ty showed up.

One moment she was lost in her own troubled thoughts, the next his footsteps sounded on the stairs.

And it didn't help that when she jumped to her feet, whipping around in surprise, it was to find him in a pair of dark boxer shorts and nothing else.

"Holy sh—" He stopped short. "What the hell are you doing, sitting here in the dark?"

His anger was from surprise. "I—I couldn't sleep."

"How long have you been there?"

"Not long. An hour, maybe."

"I'm thirsty," he admitted, after a long moment of assessment. With that, he ducked under the loft and flipped on an under-counter fluorescent light. Illumination bathed the tiny kitchen in an eerie bluish-white glow. Feeling awkward, Cammie couldn't think of anything to say or do, so she stood in utter silence, uncomfortably aware of everything about him. Of their own volition, her eyes focused on the narrow white strip of pale skin above his boxers. His tan was deep.

Ty poured himself a glass of water and drank lustily, wiping the back of his hand across his mouth. There was something so rugged and untamed about him that Cammie could hardly credit that this was the same urbane and controlled man who'd left Hollywood ten years earlier. He seemed like a mirror image, or a clone, or someone else. He certainly didn't seem like Ty.

"Do you want something?" he asked with forced politeness.

"Look, if you don't want me to stay here, I'm perfectly happy heading to the Goosedown Inn."

"Did I say I wanted you to leave?"

"No, but I—" She shrugged unhappily. "I just sense that you'd rather not have me here, that's all."

"I'm not exactly familiar with houseguests. No one's come to visit, for obvious reasons, and I'm probably doing a damn poor job of it."

"I wasn't criticizing you," Cammie put in hurriedly.

"I was criticizing myself."

His tenseness translated itself to her. Or maybe hers did to him. Either way, the moment stretched interminably, and Cammie found herself searching for a way to escape to the bedroom. But that would mean she would have to pass by Ty as he'd come to stand at the foot of the stairs, nearly blocking her route to the short hallway and bedroom. She didn't really want to get that close to him. She didn't know what she expected to happen, but she didn't want to find out, either!

Searching for something to say, she asked, "What do you do all day? I mean, what's a typical day for you like?"

"You mean, how do I survive without the confusion and insanity of stardom?" Ty's lips twisted.

"No, I just mean, what do you do? When you get up in the morning, what's the first thing you do? What's your routine?"

"What kind of a question is that?"

"I don't know!" Cammie declared in exasperation.

"I don't have a routine. I just get up and let the day happen."

"Do you work at all? I mean, at some job?"

She was struggling and she knew it, but what else was there to talk about? He was so closed off about the past, and if the truth were known, she didn't want to talk about it, either. She wanted the here and now.

"I'm in real estate," he stated blandly.

Cammie half laughed, then caught herself. "Really?"

"Is that funny?"

"No, I guess not. It just seems odd that—people around here—don't realize who you are."

"It's been a long time," he pointed out, scratching at his beard again. "Besides, I'm Jerry Mercer now."

"No one's ever asked you if you're Tyler Stovall?"

He shrugged. "People remark on the resemblance."

"I can't believe it. If you walked into any restaurant in Los Angeles, you'd be spotted immediately."

Ty shook his head, drank the rest of the water in his glass, then said, "Nobody thinks about me any longer, which is just fine with me. I'm yesterday's news. It takes a lot of energy to stay in the limelight, year in and year out, like Tom Cruise or Harrison Ford. You'd be surprised."

"You'd be surprised," Cammie muttered so softly that Ty cocked his head in her direction.

"What?"

"Nothing . . ." She couldn't go into all the hoopla surrounding *Rock Bottom* without giving away the impetus for her trip to see him. But she knew he was wrong about his fame. It was much bigger than he realized, immortalized by the very flight he'd chosen to try to make it disappear.

As if sensing what she'd elected not to tell, Ty set the glass down very carefully on the counter, then ran his hands through his long hair, his jaw tightening ever so slightly. "I hated it," he admitted through clenched teeth. "Every part of it."

Cammie didn't answer, unsure of what to say.

"All I wanted to do was act, but then things happened . . ."

"You must not have hated *acting,* then," she pointed out softly.

"No, you're right. But if I had it to do over again, I would choose another profession."

"Your father was awfully proud of you following in his footsteps." Cammie cautiously sat back down on the couch.

Ty snorted. "Are you kidding? He only liked it until he considered me a threat. He's competitive in ways you'll never know," he added with a taste of bitterness.

"Was that why you left? Because of your father?" Cammie asked, realizing she'd never considered that particular angle.

Ty's face shuttered, as if he'd realized he'd given too much away. "I wanted out of everything." Heaving a sigh, he joined her in the living room, flopping himself in the depths of the armchair across from where Cammie had uneasily settled on the couch. She couldn't look directly at him. There was too much skin, too many muscles, too much—*Ty!*

"So, what are you doing these days?" he asked. "What's your—routine?"

"Me? Nothing much." She shrugged.

"You were studying theater in college, weren't you?"

"Well . . . yes . . ."

"And?" He lifted one brow, waiting.

"I eventually got a job in television. It took awhile." She linked her fingers together.

"Acting?"

She nodded jerkily. Glancing around, she realized there was a television tucked on one of the shelves nestled against the rock fireplace.

"I don't really watch it," he admitted, following her gaze. "I don't even know why it's there." He gave her a searching look. "What television show?"

"Pardon?"

"What's the name of your show?"

"Oh . . . I was on a nighttime drama, *Cherry Blossom Lane,* but I've just recently been released from my contract."

"I've never seen it," he admitted. "Generally I check the stock market, sometimes the news." He shrugged. "It's not a priority." When Cammie didn't respond, he asked, "When does it air? Your show?"

"Oh, um, Wednesday nights. I don't know about here in Canada, though."

"That's tomorrow night," he pointed out.

The idea of Tyler watching her act suddenly filled her with pure fear. Why hadn't she considered that before? With all this talk of roles and films, she'd never thought about what it would be like to have him view her skill—or lack of it! "Well, it's probably not on at the same time here. I don't know. It's not something I'd change my routine for, that's for sure!"

"You're afraid of me seeing you," he realized.

"I'm—flat out terrified," she admitted in a rush.

His slow smile played havoc with her already overheated senses, spreading across his lips in a thoroughly sexy manner. Cammie felt mesmerized by that image, and the powerful masculine messages he was inadvertently sending her way.

Good heavens, if he didn't put some clothes on soon, she wasn't certain she could sit here much longer without wanting to touch that tanned skin. And wouldn't that just be great? Having "little sister" suddenly jump on him?

Like before . . .

"Something wrong?" Ty asked.

"No. Why?"

"You look like you're going to faint or something." With that, he suddenly moved to the couch, sinking down beside her. Cammie's heart leapt erratically in alarm at his proximity. She pulled back as far as possible without actually moving her hips from the depression his weight had created beside her.

Ty's gray eyes assessed her carefully, and she found herself holding her breath against her will. "What is it?" he asked softly, perceptively.

"What—what do you mean?" Cammie licked her lips, inadvertently drawing his attention to the pink tip of her tongue.

"What are you hiding?" he asked.

"Hiding?" Her attempt at laughter sounded as forced as it felt.

"You're trembling. Do I scare you?" he suddenly asked in surprise as the idea hit him.

"I'm just nervous," she admitted. Beside her leg, his hair-dusted, muscular thigh looked masculine and tough and thoroughly enticing.

"Why did you really come and find me?"

"I told you. I just wanted—"

"I know what you told me." He swept that away with an impatient gesture. "But now that I'm sober, I want the truth. Something's wrong, isn't it? There's some secret, or problem. What is it?"

Cammie swallowed. Beyond the window, the sky was turning dusty pink, harbinger to a vivid dawn that would fill the eastern skies very quickly. "It's morning," she said.

"Don't change the subject. It's not my father, is it? Is something wrong with him—apart from his being a bastard, that is," he added with only the faintest humor.

"No!"

"My mother," he choked out, his voice tightening.

"No, no. Nothing like that. Everything's fine."

His hand suddenly clasped her upper arm. Cammie squeaked out a protest, her eyes widening, but then she saw the flash of concern in his dark eyes. "Is it you? What is it? For God's sakes, Cammie, if something's serious, you'd better tell me quick."

"I'm fine! We're all fine! Why can't it just be that I wanted to see you?" she demanded desperately. "You've been gone so long, and it's just not—fair!"

Her outburst was childish and pathetic. She hated the words that came straight from her soul. And, as if Ty suddenly sensed their true meaning, the grip on her arm loosened but didn't quite relinquish. Instead, his thumb rubbed against her shoulder, sending a frisson of awareness down her arm to the pit of her stomach where tension formed into a knot. He had to stop doing that. If he was unaware of its effect—as she believed he was—then he had to be told. His touch was like a magic potion, overtaking her until her brain felt light and airy, her body hot and aching.

"I thought you'd be married by now, raising a family, living the whole lie," he said. "You seemed the type."

"What's that supposed to mean?" Would he ever let go of her arm? Her whole concentration was centered on his touch.

"Mom, Dad, apple pie, and a station wagon."

She shook her head, breathing sketchily. "You still think I'm your little sister."

"No, I don't. Not for years. So, no marriage, huh?" He flicked a glance at her left ring finger and found it bare. "No kids, either."

"I'm divorced."

"What's the bastard's name?" he asked humorously, responding to her tight tone.

"Paul Merrill."

"What happened?"

"I don't know . . ." She couldn't bring herself to go into it right now.

"Are there children involved?"

"No. None." Bitterness crept into her voice. He waited silently for further explanation, but none came. He could sense her sadness. "I'm sorry," he said softly, meaning it, and it was the worst thing that could have happened. His sympathy raked across Cammie's raw nerves. Feelings engulfed her. Misery. Despair.

"Don't be," she whispered, unable to meet his eyes. One moment he was an antagonist—a sexy, dangerous, and persuasive opponent—the next he was a reluctant ally, one who pitied and empathized with her. And Cammie, who'd been running on emotion for far too long, felt tears burn her eyelids and a huge ache swell inside her chest.

She tried to rise. To stand up and leave. But his grip never loosened, and when he pulled her into his arms she melted into a puddle of misery, crying silently on his shoulder, her salty tears dampening his warm flesh.

"Did that affect the divorce decision?" he asked quietly.

"What?" For a moment she'd forgotten her own words, awash in her own grief and shocked by the delight of being consoled in his strong arms. "Oh. No." She swallowed. "Paul didn't care. I mean, it wasn't an issue, really. We just couldn't get along."

"He couldn't get along with *you?*"

His faith in her character went a long way to restoring her equilibrium. She smiled. "We both thought we loved the same person. He just loved Paul Merrill a little more than I did."

"Ahhh . . ." Ty nodded. "He was an actor."

"A producer, of sorts. My mother thought it would be a good match. She wasn't—well."

He inclined his head in understanding.

"It's all right. The marriage is over, and we've both moved on. He actually worked with me on *Cherry Blossom*

Lane." She could have gone into how she'd helped him get his job and how he'd stabbed her in the back, but it was all water under the bridge and, besides, she was sick of talking about her own problems.

Tyler absorbed her information, then reluctantly—at least it seemed reluctantly—released his grip on her arm. "It's late. Almost dawn."

"We should get some sleep," Cammie agreed, feeling self-conscious at all the revelations of the night.

"You go ahead. I think I'll take a walk. Believe it or not, I'm not much of a serious drinker anymore, and I need to get these poisons out of my system."

"Sure . . ."

And so she'd scurried off to the safety of the bedroom and managed to drift in and out of sleep, but only after she heard his tread on the stairs up to the loft. She'd thought about his days and hours and minutes spent in Bayrock and marveled anew at his being in real estate. She'd fallen asleep thinking she'd like to know more, then this morning she'd seen the pages of that script tucked in the drawer, and her curiosity had gotten the better of her.

And I've got the throbbing finger to show for it! she thought with some remorse as she turned off the taps to the shower and flexed her fat digit.

Pressure had increased and now her attention seemed fixated on the pain. How was she going to hide it from him? She didn't want any more of his sympathy, and she certainly didn't want to explain what had happened! Their relationship was tenuous at best, and Ty would not appreciate her snooping through his things. He had moments of tolerance, to be sure, but she knew how she'd feel if someone were to go through her drawers.

You're such a silly fool! How do you get yourself into these predicaments?

A sudden rap on the bathroom door caused her to yank down a fluffy lemon-colored towel and wrap it close to her body. "Yes?"

"You okay? You've been in there for a hell of a long time."

"I'm fine."

"Good. Hurry up. Breakfast is waiting . . ."

Ty stalked away from the bathroom door, grimacing slightly at the pain in his head. His throbbing headache was definitely alcohol related, but the black mood dogging him had a name: Cammie Pendleton Merrill.

And why are you mad at her? he asked himself.

He sighed, knowing he was really mad at himself and his reaction to her. She flat out bothered him. Just thinking of last night's talk with her on the couch elicited a strange feeling inside his gut that he didn't like. Somehow, she'd dug beneath his tough skin and touched something vulnerable that he'd spent a lot of years denying existed.

He didn't like it at all. He didn't like thinking of her being married to some narcissus named Paul Merrill. He didn't like the infinite sadness that stole over her face when she'd revealed she couldn't bear children.

He, himself, thought the whole family thing was an overrated crock of bull perpetrated by insecure folks who needed everything neatly tied up in writing—usually for monetary gain. Cynical? He knew he was that and a whole lot more, but he honestly couldn't find proof to the opposite. His father had married and married and married and sired a passel of forgotten offspring. Sam's lack of parenting skills wasn't entirely his fault, but Ty didn't care anymore. He, Ty, had tried to follow in his father's footsteps and he'd been trodden on. Had Sam been proud of his son's ambitions? Hell, no! Okay, maybe in the beginning, but the man had quickly become threatened by his son's success, and then hell had really broken loose.

And Ty wasn't proud of the fact that it was Gayle's death that had brought him to his senses and sent him away from the insidious bonds of family and his own ambitions. Luckily, he'd left with his soul battered but intact.

That was the problem, then, with Cammie. He feared for her. She'd chosen a similar path to his own and though she seemed removed from Sam's web of deception, she was still a babe in the woods when it came to the machinations of the self-serving in Hollywood.

God, he hated it. And yet, he couldn't deny there was a fascination there that sent millions of fame-seekers to its golden Mecca. He was jaded and angry, and it wasn't really fair. Not to people like Cammie who still possessed a positive view of others.

Still . . . what was it about her that got to him so much? Had he been such a hermit that *any* reminder from his old life could awaken such powerful feelings? Why was he so touched that someone, even a pseudo-relative, cared enough to search him out?

And it had taken one long, long walk along the bay as the streaky hot pink light of dawn appeared against the horizon for him to get over that seductive feeling and remind himself that reuniting was no good for either of them.

Ten minutes later, Cammie appeared at the foot of the stairway. In jeans and a white cotton shirt, her feet bare, pink, painted nails peeking beneath the frayed hems of her pantlegs, her auburn hair damp and combed straight so that it waved gently beneath her chin, her blue eyes wide and a bit uncertain: she'd never looked so desirable. And that was the word, too. *Desirable.*

Ty swallowed and felt a bit like a masher. Wasn't he supposed to be her "older brother"? Maybe he didn't feel that way, but she probably did.

Her hands were tucked behind her, her stance one of a truant awaiting discipline. He said gruffly, "I've got toast, eggs over easy, and bacon. What would you like?"

"Just toast, please. Maybe one egg."

"Women don't eat bacon, either," he predicted with a faint smile.

"Actually, I like my bacon with white wine," she teased. "A few strips—no, a rasher—along with a carafe. Unless

I'm dieting, of course." She reached for the plate he handed her, wincing suddenly and nearly dropping the china dish in the bargain.

Ty steadied the plate in her hand and considered the frozen look on her freshly scrubbed face. "What?"

"Nothing."

Her wince had been of pain, he realized, and ignoring her protests, he pulled the dish away, spying her damaged finger before she thrust her right hand behind her back like a recalcitrant child.

"What happened?" he asked.

"I smashed it."

"Let me see it."

"Nope. Go on ahead with breakfast. Maybe you could just set mine down on the counter."

She was being awfully coy, Ty decided, but he did as she suggested—for now. What he really wanted was to yank her arm around and assess the injury.

He poured them both orange juice and sat next to her at the tiny bar that served as his eating table. She attempted to keep her right hand in her lap, eating with her left though it was an obvious and awkward effort. Eventually, Ty gave up waiting and clasped her wrist, bringing her injured finger within view.

"Ouch," he said, examining the swollen member. "Hurts like hell, doesn't it?"

"Mmmm."

"Looks like you just did it. What did you smash it in, the door?"

She swallowed some orange juice, gently extricating herself from his grasp. "A drawer."

An inkling of understanding slipped over him. "My drawer? In the bedroom?" When she didn't immediately respond, he asked, "What were you looking for?"

"Nothing! I just opened one."

Ty was beginning to grow amused. "Snooping. And you got caught at it."

She blushed prettily, the color covering the V of skin at

her neckline. Ty found himself so intrigued by this show of femininity that he forced himself to turn away.

And then he realized what she might have found . . .

"Which drawer?" he asked, his voice hardening.

She didn't answer.

"The nightstand?"

The bit of egg on her fork slipped back to the plate as her hand trembled ever so slightly.

"You were reading my script, weren't you?" Ty declared in a dangerously soft voice. To her continued silence, he demanded, "Weren't you? Answer me, Cammie. Is that what you were sent to do? Spy on me, find out what I'm up to? Report back to Sam and God knows who else! Who's paying you?" he demanded, his rage swelling furiously. "Tell me that. I think I have a right to know!"

CHAPTER EIGHT

To her intense embarrassment, Cammie was suddenly near tears. They burned hurtfully behind her lids and she blinked several times, her eyes unnaturally bright. Horror filled her; she was about to humiliate herself in the worst way.

"You're on someone's payroll, aren't you?" Tyler persisted angrily. "Damn it, Cammie! Answer me!"

"No!"

"I'm not going to believe you came here out of some misguided need for 'family.' I know how you felt after my father treated your mother so badly. I've got my own issues with him, too." He paused for breath. "But as you're talking to him again, somebody's got something to gain. So, what is it, hmmm? Why are you helping him?"

"I'm not helping him." Cammie was adamant. "I wouldn't help your father in any way! I'm sorry, but it's true. If you don't want to believe me, fine. I can leave right now."

"And go tell who?"

Fury finally took over, and she was glad. She was tired

of everyone telling her how *she* felt and what *she* wanted and what would be best for *her.* "All right, you caught me," Cammie declared hotly, throwing up her hands in defeat. "I've got a horde of reporters waiting right outside that door. Everyone wants a piece of you. We're all going to make a fortune off this! In fact, your father is in a nearby television studio right now, crying to a million viewers how he lost the love of his son. It's a reunion show and all I have to do is bring you there, and the audience will go mad with joy! Come on, let's go. It'll be a fabulous show and you'll be the star! Oh, and don't forget, *I'll* get a hefty finder's fee, so we'll all be just as thrilled as we can be!"

She nearly ruined it by breaking down and crying herself. Her lips trembled, threatening her hard-won composure. But she met his gaze with a cold one of her own, and in the end, Ty inclined his head and scratched his chin, fighting the stirrings of a smile.

"Okay," he said.

"Okay, what?" Cammie demanded.

"You've made your point. And, you might be a halfway decent actress, although the tears would have been over the top."

"You bastard," she said with feeling.

He grimaced and drew a breath. When he gazed at her, there was a touch of admiration in the depths of his eyes. "Since I don't think Geraldo or Leeza or Oprah are anywhere within a thousand miles, I guess I'm safe from the 'reunion show,' " he said. "I—apologize."

Cammie's pulse pounded in her head. His words effectively blocked the surge of rage that had fueled her tongue. She wanted to hold on to this fury. It was her protection against the attraction he couldn't help making her feel. Damn the man! It wasn't fair that she should be so ridiculously eager to please him, and make him happy, and want him to like her so much. Nor was it fair that he could hurt her so easily, distrust her on instinct, and drive her to rave at him like a crazy loon.

"You're amazing," he added, destroying her wall of anger still further.

"I'm not amazing. I've just been on television for three years, and I've seen enough tabloid TV to think like an idiot."

Holding out a hand to her, he shook his head. "I don't know how to behave anymore."

"You're doing just fine," she murmured tautly, too emotionally overwrought to place her fingers within his and expect to keep her wits about her.

"It's good to see you."

This heartfelt admission trampled her defenses yet again. She turned away, knocking her finger against the side of the counter. Yelping in pain, she yanked her hand close to her chest. Ty reached out and gently unfolded her fingers, examining her injury more closely. "It's throbbing like hell, isn't it? You need to drop the pressure."

"It'll be fine."

"I could drive you to a local clinic where they'd—"

"No," she cut in firmly.

"—take care of it, or I could relieve the pressure myself."

Her blue eyes looked into his bland gray ones. "You?" To his nod, she asked, "How?"

"A needle. I think I've got one in some travel kit around here."

"A needle?" she questioned, not liking the sound of that at all.

"A doctor would just drill a small hole in your nail to release the pressure. It'll feel better instantly, believe me. But I can sterilize a needle myself with alcohol and punch it through if you want me to."

"Good grief, no!"

He shrugged. "I've done it to myself before."

"Well, no thanks, mountain man. I think I'll just let nature take its course."

"If you change your mind, let me know," he said, turning back to his breakfast.

For her part, Cammie was having a tough time even

eating her toast and juice. It was easier to swallow coffee and hope for a little caffeine jolt. Even so, she felt bad that she hadn't done justice to the meal, and her mumbled, "I guess I'm just not hungry" was met with an indifferent nod on Ty's part. She noticed, however, that he hadn't had much of an appetite, either, and though she tried to help carry dishes to the sink, he gave her a long look that told her to stop being so helpful given that she only had one hand available.

But leaving Ty to those domestic duties only made her realize how superfluous she was. She stood in the middle of the living room, admiring the stone fireplace anew, though her mind was elsewhere. With a sigh, she turned her attention to the view from the massive windows, all the while fighting not to examine her injury.

Maybe she should just let him do his worst, she decided, wondering why she felt so compelled to thwart him. She wasn't quite as squeamish as she'd led him to believe, but for reasons that escaped her, she couldn't let him help her.

When he was finished cleaning up, he headed for the door next to the kitchen that led to the back deck. "Where are you going?" she demanded, afraid she was about to be abandoned.

"To split some wood. I thought we could use a fire."

"Oh."

His lips slanted. "Did you think I was leaving without saying good-bye?"

"Well, it wouldn't be the first time."

"Ahh . . . yeah . . ." he conceded, opening the door. A swirl of rain-drenched April wind blew into the room, as cold as any January bluster. Cammie shivered in her jeans and white cotton shirt. Ty, dressed warmer in a dark-green flannel shirt, blue jeans designed totally for durability rather than fashion, and a pair of thick brown boots, seemed impervious to the weather. Through the window she watched him head down a short flight of stairs to the back of the cabin where a thick round stump, axe buried deep inside its grayed wood, stood at the ready. Ty grabbed a hefty chunk of fir, set it on the stump, then swung the axe in a strong arc, splitting the fir cleanly into two manageable pieces. He sliced through these again, and when he returned to the cabin, it was with four solid blocks of firewood.

She held the door for him, and he entered in a swirl of damp breeze smelling slightly of the sea mixed with the dank, yet comforting, scent of wet wood. But when Ty dumped the chunks of fir into the fireplace and methodically stuffed the space beneath with newspaper, lighting the waiting pyre with a long match, the fir crackled and caught fire almost instantly, belying its wettened condition.

"The wood's dry," Cammie said, surprised, seeing its damp outer layer.

"It's been tucked beneath the deck. I just put some pieces by the stump last night because I thought I was going to make a fire. The wood's only damp from the wind driving spray water off the bay."

"The fire was out when I arrived last night," she observed, more for conversation than out of any real interest.

"I wasn't planning on hanging around here," was his slow reply. He glanced across the room to the row of boxes near the windows. "I decided to get drunk and pack instead."

"Pack?"

"I got a call that my hiding place had been discovered, then, lo and behold, you showed up."

"Who called? No one knew I was coming. Not for sure anyway."

"I got a call from a friend—the one whose house was broken into."

Cammie shook her head. "That had nothing to do with me," she stated positively.

"Maybe, maybe not . . . Dear old Dad seems the most likely culprit, however, and he sent you."

"He did not *send* me."

Ty pushed at the logs with his booted foot, causing sparks to scatter in a fury up the chimney. "I'm sorry, Cammie. It can't just be coincidence. Someone broke in and got to my files."

"What friend is this?" she asked, frowning.

"You don't know him. He takes care of my financial interests."

"And he lives in Los Angeles?"

Ty was beginning to believe she knew nothing about that particular break-in, which made him wonder if he wasn't jumping to conclusions after all. His father could have known his address for years, he supposed, although that was highly unlikely. Samuel Stovall wasn't a man of patience; far from it! Ty's instincts told him the break-in and Cammie's appearance were related in some way, even if she didn't know of the connection.

Which was all academic anyway, given that Ty's whereabouts were public knowledge no matter what the sequence of events. Now, he had to decide what to do about it.

"Forget it," he told her, since Cammie was regarding him with concern, her expressive face full of consternation that he might think she was somehow responsible for this state of affairs. "It doesn't matter."

"Are you seriously thinking of running away again?"

"I don't know why it has to be considered running away when all I want is some privacy," he said tersely.

"You'd never consider going back?"

"To Hollywood? To *acting*? Are you kidding?"

"Was it really that bad?" she asked, linking her hands together, then wincing at the pain in her finger. For a moment, she'd almost forgotten.

"Yes," he said shortly.

Cammie curled back on the couch, her knees tucked close together. "Why?"

Ty stomped on the chunks of fir again, although there was no need to fuss with the fire anymore. He just needed something to do, to get her slim, sweet image from imprinting on his brain. He was appalled at himself, yet he seemed incapable of looking at Cammie in any other way than as a male in search of a mate.

"Why was it so bad?" she persisted, either oblivious to his ostracizing stance or impenetrable to it. Either way, her probing bugged him, making him tense and irritable.

"Does there have to be a specific reason?"

"No . . . but you were having so much success, and then *poof.*" She snapped her fingers together. "You were gone. I always figured there had to be something more, and when I saw you—" She sucked in a sharp breath, shocked because she'd almost added, *"that last night we were together . . ."*

Ty jerked around. Cammie's eyes were wide and scared. "What happened?" he demanded. "Is it your hand?"

Her lashes swept downward. She moved her fingers as if they were stiff and unresponsive. "Ummm . . . yes . . ." she murmured.

"I'm getting that needle," Ty declared, stalking toward his bathroom and the overnight kit in the top drawer which contained a small sewing set.

Cammie stared after him in horror. It wasn't her hand. At least not at this particular moment. And it wasn't the fear of his intended minor surgery, either; she could handle that if she really had to.

No, she couldn't get over the fact that she'd nearly brought up *that evening!* That evening they'd spent making sweet and fiery love! That evening that he clearly remembered next to nothing about!

. . . *that last night we were together* . . .

Her own words, unspoken but so loud to her ears that it was like a roaring surf inside her head, had nearly annihilated her on the spot. If he didn't already remember—*and please, God, don't let him remember!*—she would just as soon he *never* remembered.

"Here." Ty reappeared, striding toward her with a small travel kit, a bottle of alcohol, and a bag of cotton balls filling his hands.

Cammie pulled back, a bit daunted. But it was his proximity that really got to her, not his intended role as healer of all wounds. He sank down on the couch beside her, his thigh hard against hers.

"Give me your hand."

Her heart was palpitating all over the place. She found it hard to remember to breathe. Her lungs had forgotten their involuntary movements, apparently, for she felt dizzy and starved for air.

He doused a cotton ball with alcohol, then liberally applied it to the needle. Next, he swabbed her fingernail, and she must have made some small protest, because his eyes searched hers. "You all right?" he asked.

"I'm such a wuss," she demurred.

"Don't look."

She tore her gaze from his and stared fixedly at the window. To her shock, Ty next placed her palm on his hard thigh. She glanced down, supremely conscious of the pressure of his muscles beneath her palm, but then he pressed the needlepoint onto her nail. A sudden sharp pressure. She moaned, inhaled a breath and squeezed her eyes closed.

Biting her lip at the tiny stab of pain, Cammie nearly drew blood from it. The needle pierced her nail. Instantly, the throbbing abated. Blinking against unwanted tears, she opened her eyes in time to see Ty regarding her with something approaching serious concern.

"Did I hurt you?" he asked tensely.

"No, no. It's fine."

"You're crying . . ."

"I am not!"

"There are tears in the corners of your eyes."

Tears of fear and reaction. "I told you I was a wuss," she disabused on a soft laugh. Her hand still lay on his thigh and she was loath to move it. Yet, the tensed muscles beneath his jeans were drawing all her inner attention even while she fought to keep her gaze anywhere but on Ty.

His fingers picked up her palm, examining his handiwork. As he'd predicted, the skin beneath the nail had filled with blood and a tiny droplet oozed from the minute vent hole.

Instantly, Cammie felt sick. She wasn't good with blood. She wasn't good with any of that stuff, though she sure as heck could pretend she had a stomach of iron.

"Cammie . . . ?"

Ty's voice sounded from far away. *Oh, for God's sake,* she thought in self-disgust, *I'm going to faint.*

And promptly did.

She awoke to a strange sense of coolness and realized a damp rag lay on her forehead. Her head pounded. She lifted a heavy hand to the washrag and heard a sudden rustling.

"Cammie . . ."

Ty's face swam into view above her. She was lying on his bed, she realized with a jolt. The thought of him carrying her limp body brought a new wave of humiliation crashing over her.

"I'm so embarrassed," she whispered.

"I should have taken you to the clinic," he berated himself. "What the hell was I thinking? You scared the living daylights out of me."

"No, no . . . I'm always like this. How long—how long was I out?"

"Five, ten minutes. Just long enough for me to bring you in here. I could call a local doctor and—"

"No! Don't make things worse. Please." Cammie struggled upward, and Ty gently pushed her arms back down. She felt weak. It was easy to give in and just collapse.

"I'll get you some water," he said, following a silent moment, and after he left, Cammie suddenly realized that her white shirt was unbuttoned to her waist. No wonder she'd felt a draft. With her good hand, she probed her bra and realized he'd left that alone. Its front clasp was still tightly closed and the lacy cups covered enough to make her feel her modesty was still intact.

Her thoughts were ridiculous! Ty had no interest in her that way. He'd loosened her blouse to increase air to her throat and lungs. He felt guilty about being the cause of her fainting spell, not lust! *She* was the one who noticed every little detail about the both of them in that man-woman way. *She* was the one making a fool out of herself over him.

With a groan of misery, she buried her face in the pillow. A moment of that, then she turned an eye to her finger and the result of Ty's minor surgery. Ugly blackness was taking over, but the pain was minimal. She could even flex her fingers a bit.

Ty appeared in the doorway and Cammie instantly tugged on her shirt to close the gaping front. Her movement caught his attention.

"Sorry. I just wanted to make sure nothing was constricting you." Flicking a look at her bra, he added, "I was just about to unhook it when you came to."

"I'm glad you didn't," she admitted, swallowing. He gave her a long look that did nothing to her already leaping stomach. "I'm usually not so squeamish. I mean, I'm squeamish, but not *so* squeamish! I feel like an idiot, and oh, thanks. My finger does feel better."

"Good." He set the glass of ice water on the nightstand, his gaze taking in the partially opened drawer—Cammie's nemesis. Crooking a finger beneath its beveled edge, Ty slid open the pine drawer and pulled out the sheaf of papers Cammie had so wanted to review.

Now she concentrated on the ceiling while still holding tightly to the two sides of her white shirt. Should she attempt to button it up? She didn't trust her fingers to be anything but clumsy, but it was ignominious, to say the least, to have Ty in the same room with her while she lay there, half dressed.

"You were looking at this," he said without rancor, as if he'd forgotten his earlier reaction to her snooping. But

Cammie wasn't likely to forget his irritation and anger, and she wanted him to know she wasn't a complete betrayer.

"I didn't get a chance."

"You got worried you'd get caught, shoved the script back inside the drawer, then slammed your fingers in the process."

"That's pretty much it," Cammie admitted with a grimace. "I guess I got what I deserved."

He shook his head slightly, as if negating her comment. Silence stretched until Cammie's nerves began to scream with the torture of being so close. "Are you writing a script?" she blurted out. "A screenplay?"

"I told you, I'm in real estate."

"Then whose is this?" She glanced at the pages in his hands. "I mean, it doesn't look like something you brought with you ten years ago, and unless someone's sending you their work for some reason, or you bought the script through an agency that sells them . . ." She glanced at the pages and added, "But those look fresh off a printer. I'm willing to bet that you wrote them yourself."

"And if I did, then what?"

"Then, nothing." She shrugged. "I mean, why not? You certainly have the acting background, and I remember you were good at writing as a teenager. And even Nanette was once a screenwriter, so it runs in the family."

"And besides, what else have I got to do with my time, right?"

Was he being sardonic? Cammie suspected so, though he made the comment cheerfully enough, as if he were trying to keep her off balance.

But there was no need for that! She was off balance enough. Good heavens, she'd hardly been herself since she stepped across his threshold. "Now that you mention it," she murmured, licking her lips a bit nervously.

"What?" He shifted his weight, setting the pages down, his hands on either side of her body, his face disturbingly close to hers.

"Selling real estate just doesn't seem like you."

"I don't sell it. Well, I sell my own," he amended. "I have different property around, but I'm not an agent, if that's what you mean. I'm a speculator."

"And you've been doing this for ten years?"

"Pretty much. I tried a bit of farming, but I'm better in theory than in practice. Got bit by an old ewe one day and she nearly crunched right through my hand!"

He was teasing her. She caught the light in his eyes, and she couldn't help responding to it. Remembering how much they'd enjoyed each other's company as teenagers, she spoke her mind without thinking. "I'm so glad to see you again."

Perhaps if they hadn't been in such a compromising position already. Perhaps if they'd had more time to reacquaint themselves as "brother and sister." Or perhaps if they'd both been just a little less lonely, the next few moments wouldn't have happened.

But Cammie's incautious words, coupled with a look of longing that suffused her face and deepened the aqua blue of her eyes, served to ignite a smoldering ember. She hadn't known that latent fire existed for Ty until that moment, thinking that her own emotions were the only ones involved. But when he shifted his weight to one arm and gently ran the back of his hand down the side of her cheek, she sucked in a sharp, excited breath.

"I didn't realize how much I've missed you," he admitted, the timbre of his voice deep and almost throbbing. It struck a chord inside Cammie, and she gazed at him with unknowing longing written all over her face. Any skills she possessed as an actress fled with the need to be with the man she loved—and had always loved, at some level. Ty's swift intake of breath said he didn't mistake the signs, but he still hesitated, his gaze dropping to her trembling lips as if he couldn't tear his eyes from their luscious pink contours.

"Cammie . . . ?" he asked uncertainly.

"Aren't you going to kiss me?" she heard herself ask from far, far away.

He smothered a sound of disbelief. "Yes," he admitted.

Putting action to words, he leaned forward. She could feel the heat of his skin through his shirt, and her hands released the edges of her blouse to ease their way up his chest. Through the flannel, his skin felt hard and warm, and she wanted to yank the offending garment from his body and crush his bare chest to her trembling breasts.

Her lashes fluttered closed. Her lips pushed upward, anxiously awaiting his kiss like a blossom opens to sunlight. She'd yearned for this since the night they'd made love, and even from before, when she'd been an adolescent awash in hormones and unrealized dreams, hungry for love and affection and the desire and touch of another human being.

She waited, suspended in helpless anticipation. She could hear his breath, strangled and uneven, could feel the strain and effort it took for him to hold himself above her by the weight of his arms. She wanted him to give in. To just drop down upon her and take what was offered . . . but after a few interminable moments when nothing happened, she opened her eyes to gaze at him doubtfully.

"I don't know what I'm doing," he said, and she realized remorse had struck even before the kiss!

And then, as if to put things right, he gave her a perfunctory kiss on the cheek and rolled to his feet. Bereft, Cammie couldn't shift gears as fast as he could, but his withdrawal dug away at her self-esteem. Oh, God! What did he think of her? He couldn't believe she was some besotted fan, could he?

Her cheeks grew warm. Then her whole body suffused with painful humiliation. She wanted to curl up into a ball and die.

For his part, Ty was trying to act like everything was as it had been before. He gathered up the sheaves of paper that had scattered across the bed and laid them on the adjoining nightstand. "I'm—sorry," he murmured.

Sorry? Now, he was sorry for turning down her invitation?

"You don't have to be sorry," Cammie declared shortly, trying desperately to hide the hurt of his rejection.

"I don't blame you for being mad," he said, misinterpreting her feelings completely. "I'm not normally—on the prowl," he said tensely, as if the words tasted foul. "That's my father's domain. I won't blame you for not believing me, however. For God's sake, I half undressed you when you were unconscious!" He let out a bark of embarrassed laughter, as Cammie struggled to a sitting position. "Put it down to the fact that I'm not used to an attractive woman lying on my bed."

"You weren't coming on to me," Cammie disabused, sliding onto her hip and tucking her knees to one side. Here she'd been denigrating herself for being so easy and eager, and all the time he was blaming himself. She couldn't have that. "If anybody was coming on to anybody, it was me to you."

Ty's brows jumped together. "What?"

"I thought you were rejecting me."

"*What?*" he repeated, but it was a whisper, a rhetorical question for the gods or the silent walls surrounding them. "What are you saying?"

I'm saying, I want to be with you. To sleep with you. I want your arms around me and your body to possess me. I want to forget about the world outside and make love like we're the last two people on earth.

"I'm saying—" she whispered, swallowing and licking her lips. "I'm saying—"

"You're saying," he urged softly, watching her mouth with pure fascination.

"Oh, Ty . . ."

That was all it took. Whatever misgivings he'd felt earlier were brushed aside in the wave of passion and heat that consumed them both. One moment he was staring at her, hard, waiting for her to voice her need for him, the next he was pushing her back against the soft coverlet, her blouse gaping open to reveal the scrap of lace that was her bra and the swell of her breasts.

"What are we doing? It's like a dream or something." His mouth pressed against her cheek, his hot breath and tongue dampening her skin.

"I don't know. I don't know." Her hands swept over his back, clutching his shirt spasmodically. *I want you,* she thought. *I want you. I want you. I want you!*

And then his mouth captured hers, his lips pushing down on hers as if to crush them to his, meld them together. A small sigh escaped her, half moan, half strangled cry of desire. His mouth was hard, and yet so, so soft. A paradox that fired her blood and made her want to hold his head in place so that the sweet fire of it would never, never stop!

His mouth traveled across the downy hill of her cheek to the lobe of her ear, biting gently, then a bit harder, striking fire to the inner core of her. Cammie clung to him, straining her body, wanting to be as close as possible.

When he kissed her again, his tongue thrust between her teeth, stabbing into the hot cavern of her mouth over and over again, mimicking the movements she wanted their bodies to perform. Cammie twisted beneath him, and Ty's hand slid over her rib cage and across her breast, pressing her flesh hard beneath the white wisp of lace. A second later, his thumb and finger unsnapped the front clasp and the lacy scraps fell away. But when he began kneading her breast, Cammie moaned, the hard button of her nipple pressing against his palm.

"My God . . ." he muttered, as if the small blasphemy was torn from him.

Don't stop, she thought incoherently. She linked one leg over his, a silly attempt to hold him to her. It was unnecessary, it appeared, as his body had begun that age-old rhythm against hers, their twin sets of jeans rubbing against each other, body parts that yearned to be together held in check and chafing. The hill of her femininity rose seemingly of its own volition to rub against the bulge at his zipper. Ty was no proof against it, pushing back against her with an urgency that caused Cammie's breath to expel in a gasp.

Then suddenly, the fingers at her breast were replaced by a hot, wet mouth. Ty's tongue circled the dark tip of her nipple. Cammie's hands tangled in his thick hair, guiding him, and her head flung backward against the pillow, her back arching. *My God! I'm going to climax just like this!*

Her hand slid convulsively down his back, reaching his hip and the firm hardness of his buttocks. She held him close, moving feverishly beneath him. Heat suffused her face and her thoughts splintered.

And then he pulled back. She whimpered in protest. But his head moved lower. She opened her eyes just long enough to see the dark crown of his head before she felt his breath heating the crotch of her jeans. Nuzzling the most secret part of her femininity through her clothes, Ty brought Cammie to a sudden, shattering climax. Her fingers clutched convulsively in his hair.

"Oh, God, oh, God!" she gasped, shocked, thrilled, and moving so fast, she reached the pinnacle with a sharp cry of ecstasy, her body straining and tense, reaching, reaching . . .

Weakness invaded her almost instantly. She lay limp, chest heaving. When Ty lifted his head, she caught a quick glimpse of the burning desire in his gray eyes before she squeezed her own closed, unwilling to let the embarrassment and humiliation she was sure to feel hit just yet.

She already wanted to apologize, but her head was a jumble of noise and impressions and sheer joy. *Later,* she thought dimly, knowing she'd never scaled the heights of passion like this before—*and they hadn't even made love!*

But Ty had other ideas, apparently, for he buried his face once again to the V of her jeans. She could hear the rubbing of his tongue against the heavy fabric but sensation was lost to her. It didn't matter. The thought, the idea, the mental image was enough.

Cammie climaxed again in sudden unexpected delight. She wanted to protest that this was all for her and nothing for him, but all she could do was form the words: *I love you, I love you, I love you . . .*

Whether she voiced them or not, she never knew. All she could think about was sensation, and Ty made certain of that fact, over and over again.

CHAPTER NINE

Ty inhaled deeply, raised the weights held in either hand above his head as he lay on the workout bench, then slowly dropped the weights to each side again before repeating the procedure. Sweat dripped off his forehead. His biceps bulged and ached in protest. He'd never worked out so long and so hard before. His normal routine was to do a light run down the main street of Bayrock, hit the small exercise club that was scarcely more than one mirrored room where a gung-ho entrepreneur had begun a small health club business some five years earlier, then finish off with some minor weight-lifting.

Today he'd been at it for more than three hours.

He glanced around the room. Most of the residents paid scant attention to this local exercise club, but visitors and new immigrants to the town seemed to like it. Ty was, however, a regular and accepted by one and all as Jerry Mercer. Sometimes he got stared at, but it was mostly with a quizzical expression. The general public seemed to have forgotten what the real Tyler Stovall looked like, and his face touched only some dusty corner of their memory.

Several people had asked if they knew him, and Ty's answer was always a terse, "No." His unapproachable and surly attitude kept most people at bay, though truthfully it was only the odd person who even approached him. Most folks came just for the workout, like he did, and they didn't bother with socializing of any kind. It was perfect for Ty, so he could use the facility at will as a place to physically expunge his frustrations.

And frustrations he possessed by the truckload—especially these days!

It had been almost two weeks since Cammie had appeared out of the blue. What had originally been a scare, then a pleasant novelty, was fast turning into an out-and-out problem. First, but not necessarily foremost, as it turned out, he hadn't left Bayrock yet. He was half packed and basically ready, but he was lollygagging around, tarrying like a lovesick schoolboy, mentally soft when it came to even looking at his lovely ex-stepsister.

What had happened? He didn't even know for sure. From those first hours of disbelief he'd progressed through a series of emotions that had culminated in a serious bout of foreplay that had sent her rocketing into ecstasy and him into self-recrimination and unrequited desire. His body clamored for some kind of release, had been clamoring like mad ever since he'd brought Cammie to the heights. It was all he could do to even *look* at her anymore without getting an erection!

But, if he'd harbored any false hope that there might be a second chance at physical closeness, Cammie had disabused him of that thought, right quick. She'd been pretty clear on that subject, all right. Crystal clear, as a matter of fact.

I should have kept right on, he thought now, straining against the weights. *At least I could be over this constant sense of sexual frustration. Or maybe still doing something about it . . .*

Moving the weights above his head, he held them suspended a moment at arm's length, staring at the barbells as if they held the answer to his dilemma.

That first morning together, in the throes of wild foreplay, Ty had had every intention of finishing what he'd started. What *they'd* started. But he'd taken too long. While Cammie still floated on the wings of sensation, Ty tenderly wiped back strands of moist hair from her face, kissed her softly, lost to his own desires, which were many at that particular moment. His hand slid downward, to the straining zip of his jeans, his body hard, ready and anxious.

"I love you," she whispered. "I love you, I love you . . ."

The words penetrated Ty's feverish brain. A tiny sting of something unpleasant followed. Memories danced around like fireflies, bright lights inside a dark space. Gayle's voice whispering those three terrible little words—words of betrayal.

"I love you," she'd purred. "Only you. You know that."

Ty had harrumphed some kind of response. He hadn't cared. They were in the heat and rhythm of lovemaking and he wasn't really paying a whole lot of attention, if the truth were known.

But Gayle was insistent about it, totally obsessive. "Say you love me. Say it, Ty. *Say it!*"

"I—my God, Gayle!"

"Say it," she demanded, picking up the rhythm and staring into his eyes. Ty wanted to turn away, to finish what they'd begun without all this silly drama. Well, all right, maybe it wasn't silly, not to her anyway. But making a man express his love in the heat of passion was tantamount to a shotgun marriage. It was meaningless. There was no heart, no spirit to the avowal.

And though Ty wanted to say what she longed to hear, he couldn't. He didn't believe in love, marriage and the whole fantasy. He'd seen too much evidence to the contrary, and though he loved his mother and he knew she loved him, that was the only form of love he'd ever known. That wild "you're all I need to live" kind of love was something he didn't believe truly existed. It was a fantasy, an excuse. An emotion created to salve consciences and make the sex act somehow legal and moral.

To him, it was all a bunch of bunk. Sex was sex, and desire was desire, and affection was affection, but there was no deep, abiding *something* out there for philosophers and poets and saps in general to talk about.

It didn't exist.

But Gayle was demanding. She nipped at his ear. "Say it, please, Tyler. I need to hear it."

He'd blocked his brain. Oh, he wasn't proud of it now; he hadn't been at the time, either. But he'd been too far along in the act of sex to just pull out, and he was simply unable to give her what she wanted. So, he ignored her demands and swept ahead on a wave of pure sensation, and when he came inside her and flopped down upon her body, it was just a release of tension, a fulfillment of need.

Of course, she'd been ticked off, royal. Squirming from beneath him, she actually struck at his head, slapping his ear in futile punishment as she rolled from the bed. "You bastard!" she screeched.

"Hey!" he demanded, grabbing her hands and pulling her back down on top of him. "Stop that. I'm sorry. You know how I feel."

"I'm pregnant, you louse," she cried, huge alligator tears spilling down her cheeks and falling all over them both.

Shock ripped through him, electric and devastating. "Pregnant?" he repeated dumbly.

"It's our baby, Tyler. Yours and mine. I want to love you and raise a family. But you can't even tell me you love me!"

She would have slapped him again, but he still held her wrists in a crushing manacle. All he could see was his father, indiscriminately siring children with woman after woman, never caring, hardly ever *counting* his offspring!

Revulsion kicked in. Revulsion at himself. How could he be so stupid? "But we were protected," he said, the first concrete thought that sank into his brain.

"That's all you can say?"

"Condoms," he said, his mind getting into gear at last. "We've been careful."

"Not careful enough!" She writhed and fought and bit at his fingers. He released her, suddenly as anxious to be free of her as she was of him. "Well, guess what, Tyler? One of those condoms must have been defective. How else do you explain it? And you know what? I don't care anyway. I want this baby *and I want you!*"

Tyler couldn't move. He'd already been the victim of one paternity suit—a false one, since he'd never slept with the starlet in question. But getting him into a drunken make-out session with her was, at least to her thinking, apparently enough. She hadn't expected him to even remember their evening together; she hadn't expected him to know the truth. And another time, she would have been right, because just before he left Los Angeles forever, there'd been a period when he'd had difficulty knowing when to stop. Hard liquor had accounted for more than a few blackouts . . .

But not with the girl in question, and when he'd demanded DNA tests, she finally backed off. Of course the whole damn thing got splashed across the papers first, and that's why he'd been so careful with Gayle. He couldn't *believe* this was happening!

"We can't have a baby together," he told her without thinking. "I'm not interested in marriage. We've talked about this."

"You've talked. I've listened," she said bitterly. "I want more, Ty. Much more."

"You set this up," he realized in dawning horror. "You did it."

"Bastard!" she cried again, striking at his face anew with flailing hands.

Anger swept away everything else. Oh, he'd been young and foolish and unable to see what was happening. The anger was more at himself, but he was furious with her, too, because so much of what he'd accused her of was true. He'd known Gayle's character flaws and wanted her just the same. She'd seemed like him, lonely and aloof and in need of companionship even while keeping her independence.

He'd been wrong, wrong, wrong.

"If the baby's mine, I'll pay for its support, you know that," he said through gritted teeth, clasping her arms again in a tight grip. "But I'll be damned if you rope me into something I'm not ready for."

"You'll be sorry," she whispered, and something in her face, some wild fury that swirled in her eyes, sent a shiver right down to the core of him. She meant it.

Later, he told himself he'd just been being melodramatic himself. Later, he believed that Gayle's outburst had been merely a result of dashed hopes, of having his disinterest in marriage and family thrown in her face, so to speak.

And though he continued to see her through a few more social engagements they'd already made, it had marked the end of their relationship. Meanwhile, he'd been finishing up *Escape From Eden,* and his disillusionment with his life—which seemed to echo the sentiments of the protagonist in that story—grew with each passing day. *What are you doing?* he continually asked himself. *Where is this going? What do you hope for? What, in God's name, is next?*

And then he was knocked down by a terrible truth, one that had the power to make him shudder to this day. He closed his eyes to the thought, nearly dropping the barbells at the memory, and with a sudden loss of strength he let them thunk to the floor on either side of him, his hands still gripped around the metal bar as if he couldn't bear to let go.

"Mr. Mercer?" the girl in the leotard who'd helped him get started asked tentatively.

"I'm okay," Ty muttered.

She giggled nervously. "Okay. We just want everyone to be safe and all."

He flicked her a look out of the corners of his eyes. She smiled and tucked a lock of blond hair behind her ear. Her eyes blinked rapidly, and he wondered idly if this was where the phrase "batting one's eyes" came from. Her whole demeanor was coy and interested.

And she was probably half his age.

It made him feel weary, as if life had passed him by long ago and at too fast a rate. It was his own fault, really, but that didn't help how he was feeling now.

Climbing up from the bench, he moved over to the treadmill, conscious of the girl's eyes following his every move. In the mirror straight ahead, he tried to assess what she saw in him, but he didn't see how the scowling countenance that met his gaze could hold the least bit of attraction for anyone. He wasn't fool enough not to understand his physical attributes; he'd been told about them so often that he'd have to be a complete idiot not to understand. He could, in fact, tick them off in a litany: strong, compact build; handsome, angular face; eyes as gray as the North Sea and possessed of a peculiar intensity that could range from anger to passion to anguish in the space of a heartbeat; and a slow smile that flashed with the kind of sexual brilliance that left his female fans swooning in the aisles.

Now, he snorted as he turned the treadmill to a faster clip that had him running hard on a slight incline. What a bunch of hype. Total crap, really. He hated it. Hated what he'd become, and he still hated it.

Yet . . .

Inside, an unfamiliar awakening was taking place, a desire. A damn near aching need. Since that morning he'd played sexually with Cammie, it had spiraled into some kind of weird obsession that left him half afraid of his own susceptibility. Why had he done it? Why had *she?* And though those three little words she'd spoken had momentarily stopped him, when he'd sought to regain the mood, she'd placed one soft palm against his thudding chest.

"I—I don't know what I'm saying!" she whispered in horror. "I'm sorry, Ty. I didn't mean it."

He hadn't cared. Not really. He was only intent on recapturing those luscious pink lips, but the mood was completely severed and nothing was going to put it back together at that point.

In fact, Cammie had suffered serious remorse, if he'd correctly interpreted her actions, which he was certain he had. She'd clasped her arms over her bare breasts in a thoroughly offended maiden pose, her eyes wide and round. And though he'd known her reaction was to her own confession, he'd found her sudden scruples both irritating and sweet. The innocence of it caught him unawares, and while he sorted through some conflicting emotions of his own, she yanked on the tangled mess of her shirt and rolled from beneath his weight to stand trembling at the edge of the bed.

It hadn't helped that her hair was a wild, unruly cascade of reddish curls flowing around her face. Or that her eyes glimmered a blue so deep he felt lost in them. Or that her limbs and mouth quivered from emotion. She was as beautiful as any woman he'd ever seen, and Ty stood by in numb amazement, wanting back those intense moments between them.

And that's when he made his mistake.

Reacting on impulse, he climbed off the bed and dragged her into an embrace. Unfortunately, he wasn't as cooled off as she was, and when she felt the hard evidence of his arousal, she whimpered in dismay and stumbled backward, away from him, until her back was up against the wall.

"Cammie . . . look . . ." he started to say, unable to clear his head enough to utter a thought. Everything about her distracted him, and though it hadn't been that long since he'd spent a night with Missy, it suddenly felt like a century. He wanted Cammie so badly it was embarrassing. And he couldn't think of one single thing to say except, "I want you," which was painfully clear already.

Her arms held him at bay. She shook her head. "I'll leave," she said, her voice still echoing the horror of her own sensuality. He knew what she was thinking, and he wanted desperately to let her know it was okay.

"It's okay to say 'I love you,' " he told her reasonably, but she uttered a moan of pure misery and ducked beneath his arms, putting the space of the room between them.

Her hands pressed against her cheeks, and she half doubled over, reacting in unmasked hysteria. "It is not! Oh, Lord, I'm such a sickening fool. I don't know what's wrong with me. No, no," she said, warding him off with one outstretched arm as he would have crossed to her again. "Please, please, leave me alone. Just go away—for a while—and let me be. Oh, I need some space," she groaned as if in pain.

"You're making a bigger deal of this than you need to."

"Shut up, Ty," she said without any real heat. "Just go—"

He'd had no choice but to leave the bedroom. He'd tried to reach her with a silent entreaty, but she'd turned her face away, unwilling to look at any part of him.

Now, looking back, he was torn between wishing he'd handled himself differently, that he hadn't fallen into the silken trap of his own emotions and nearly made love to her, and the certainty that he should have just forged ahead, ignoring her whispered pledge of love, and made love to her with all the pent-up physical desire and passion they'd ignited in each other.

"You've come a long way from worrying about her being your *sister,*" he growled beneath his breath.

"Did you say something?" the same teenage-girl employee yelled from halfway across the room.

Ty inwardly sighed. A heavyset woman on the treadmill next to him turned around in confusion and yelled back, "No!" to the girl, thereby saving Ty from another round of adoration by his would-be fan.

He'd had a hell of a time getting Cammie to put down her bag and stay with him. She'd been determined to move to the Goosedown Inn, or maybe just drive her rent-a-car back to Seattle. Only serious persuasion on his part had kept her at the cabin, and since that time, though they'd shared the same space, their conversations had been on general topics such as the education system, the state of the world as a whole, and the long term effects of global warming and El Niño. It was interesting, Ty had noted with a certain amount of self-deprecation, that the subtext body language denoted her anxiety, and though he'd tried to convince himself that she was overreacting, whenever Cammie spoke he could later only remember her tongue, teeth and feminine gestures, the look in her eyes, or the shine of her hair.

So, what did that mean?

He had no idea.

Snatching the towel from around his neck, he wiped down his face as he simultaneously lowered the speed of the treadmill to a walk. Finally, he turned it off, then stood there a moment, regaining his sea legs, so that when he stepped off he wouldn't stumble and fall, a phenomenon of riding the treadmill too long.

The girl, whose leotard swelled and tightened in all the right places, gave him a bright smile as he returned from the changing room wearing a lightweight black nylon jogging suit over his sweat-dampened clothes.

"Missy was here," she chirped in a voice as bright as her smile.

Ty drew a mental picture of Missy Grant, his sometime paramour: a pretty, thirtyish woman who longed to be twenty-two again, if one could base an assumption on her dress and manner. Ty had found her uncomplicated and easy to be with, but their worlds were as different as far-flung stars and he knew, as with everything else at Bayrock, that she was merely a nice diversion for him. At first she seemed to feel the same. She told him she was looking for fun, not a husband, nor a father-substitute for her only child. The relationship had run a fairly smooth course until he started forgetting to call. Complete apathy on his part. That's when he learned about the true Missy.

She'd rung him and rung him and rung him, and tried her darnedest to get him down to Rodeo Bob's, her place of employment and the restaurant and bar that he himself owned and that his friend Corky ran. Ty had danced around the whole thing. It was a shame about Rodeo Bob's, however, as he'd liked hanging out with Corky and some of his buds.

But he'd had no intention of leading Missy on any further. It was over. Although occasionally, when he was desperately lonely, he thought about calling her, just like the other night . . .

That was his problem, he realized with a rush of relief. Loneliness! That was why he'd wanted Cammie so badly. She didn't hold some strange spell over him. It was just lack of sex, pure and simple, that was making him feel so out of control, anxious and vulnerable, too.

Leotard-girl broke into his thoughts with, "I hope you don't think I'm being nosy. It's just that I know you and Missy were seeing each other, but I don't know . . ." She chewed on the edge of her finger, eyeing him hopefully. "Sometimes things don't work out, I guess."

"I guess," Ty agreed. Thinking of Missy still made him feel like a heel.

"So, what are you doing now?" the girl continued.

He read her pinned-on name tag: Karma. "I'm heading back to the cabin to work," he answered curtly. Good grief. Karma. Were *all* parents half crazed when they had children? He sometimes wondered if parenthood sucked all the brains out of people?

"Oh, that's right. Missy said you had a houseguest."

Ty jerked around in surprise, then covered the movement by digging into his gym bag. He hated being the speculation of anyone. Wasn't that why he'd left Los Angeles in the first place? And here he was, in this small tourist town, suddenly the center of attention. It was the same damn thing, except on a smaller scale.

"A friend," he admitted, heading for the door.

"Girlfriend?" she couldn't help calling after him, but Ty was through the door and onto the street, letting the afternoon sun touch his tense face.

Girlfriend . . .

No, she wasn't his girlfriend, but she wasn't any kind of sister to him, either. He didn't know what he expected her to be, but the idea that she would be leaving soon, a topic neither of them discussed but nevertheless lay between them like some huge, impenetrable wall, filled Ty with a sense of longing and dismay that couldn't be swept away by some platitude like "She's just come to reacquaint herself with family" or "She lives in Los Angeles and there's no way you can be with her."

There were issues they needed to discuss, he realized as he walked up the street to his cabin. A watery sun shone down and made an attempt to warm the ground, but the April breeze still blew chilly and strong, reminding him that winter was just a tiny step behind the nodding daffodils and rhododendrons.

It would be warm and sunny in L.A., maybe even hot. He rolled the idea around in his head, and though there was a prick of disgust, it wasn't the same kind of out-and-out revulsion he used to feel when he thought about his one-time home.

Maybe I'm healing, he thought with a certain amount of cynical amusement. That kind of quote was nineties psychobabble of the worst type. It sounded deep and important, when in reality it was just a bunch of words. It was a symptom of the bigger illness he'd run away from as fast as he could go.

Like you're so much better off now . . .

Ty sighed heavily. Though he could dismiss a lot of things out of hand, he couldn't dismiss his feelings for Cammie—complicated though they were—and when he pushed open the gate and walked to the front door, he grew annoyed at himself at the sense of expectation suddenly firing his blood. Just knowing she was inside thrust his body into teenage hormone mode.

But she wasn't inside, as it turned out. Ty strode through the cabin's few rooms and ascertained that disturbing conclusion very quickly. Had she left for L.A. without telling him?

Fear stabbed his heart and he threw open his bedroom closet door, relieved to see her overnight bag still in its place, her clothes neatly hung on their hangers. So, she was around somewhere. Possibly taking a walk along the waterfront. He hadn't seen her on his return, but that didn't mean she couldn't have stopped in somewhere for a bit of touristy-type shopping.

At least he hoped that's what it was.

Two hours later, he was starting to worry. Twilight had settled over the water, sending streaks of waving illumination across the moving surface from the many lights winking along the waterfront. Standing outside on his back deck, Ty cradled a beer between hands that were fast growing numb from the sharp wind feathering his face, neck, and any part not suitably covered. It was his first beer since Cammie's arrival, his first alcoholic drink of any kind. He'd been afraid he'd made a fool of himself that first night, and he'd steered clear of everything until now. He wasn't an alcoholic, but he definitely could abuse the stuff now and again. He'd paid the price in many whopping hangovers, and now, as he tipped back the bottle, he wished there was some other form of anesthetic for the torture that ailed him.

Do you really think she's left you? Do you?

A soft knock on the front door drew his head around. Spirits rising, he reentered the house, set his beer on the counter and moved quickly to admit Cammie.

"Where the heck have you been?" he demanded with more impatience than the situation warranted.

But it wasn't Cammie. It was Missy. In a dark-blue sweater and skirt, her blond hair twisted into a makeshift bun and clipped with a rhinestone barrette, her anxious face covered with mounds of makeup, she looked a bit like an over-the-hill starlet, desperately seeking her one big chance.

"Where have I been?" she echoed. "Where have *you* been? I don't hear from you for *months* and then you finally surface at the club today."

"Surface?" he asked blankly, his brain frantically searching for a way to ease her out of the way before Cammie returned.

"Well, Karma says you've been there before, but she said she actually talked to you today. She said you talked about me."

No way out of that one without creating a serious problem. Still, Ty hung by the door, reluctant to invite her inside. Nothing good would come of it, for him or for her.

"Karma's a friend," Missy added unnecessarily, stepping around him without an invitation, trailing a cloud of perfume in her wake. Its flowery scent wafted upward, thick and sweet and cloying. It seemed to mask everything else, and Ty realized belatedly, as his stomach jolted, that he hadn't eaten all day and his beer wasn't settling well.

Missy's hands reached for him, and it was all he could do to keep from backing up. She jerked playfully on his collar. "So, you have company, huh? I've never known you to entertain. I always thought you were kind of a hermit."

"Yeah . . . well . . ." Gently, he disengaged himself from her grasping fingers, softening the rejection by holding her hand and leading her to the couch.

"Did you sell that property yet? I don't see a real estate sign anymore."

"It's still on the market. The sign just fell over."

"Not very good business, would you say? I mean, who's your agent again? They should be johnny-on-the-spot. I'd fire them and get someone else."

Ty almost smiled. "Who would that be in Bayrock? Someone else from the same office?"

"Oh, I know it's small, but there's got to be someone else, doesn't there?" Missy shrugged out of her navy jacket. Her breasts were large and somewhat matronly, making her seem heavier than her true build. Ty couldn't help comparing them to Cammie's, and he found he preferred Cammie's smaller breasts and petite shape.

A moment later, he could have kicked himself for his musings. What was happening to him?

"Jerry, I've been thinking—" Missy began, when the front door opened once again and Cammie stood in the aperture.

She wore a soft green sweater, her ubiquitous denim jeans, and a pair of suede boots. Her hair was held back in a ponytail by a rubber band, and her cheeks were flushed pink from the weather. Aqua eyes glittered with lustrous good health, and the warm smile she greeted him with melted all Ty's concerns. There was something going on between them that neither could deny. Maybe they were both having a little trouble facing it, but its existence was unmistakable.

And then Cammie's gaze fell on Missy.

"Oh, hello," she murmured.

Missy's face was a frozen mask. "Hello," she answered shortly, turning accusing eyes on Ty.

"Missy Grant, this is Cammie Merrill," Ty introduced. "Cammie's a friend from a past life."

"Really?" Missy's lips tightened in reserved judgment.

"Missy and I are friends in the present," Ty went on, feeling a shift of mood in the room that surprised him. Being male and a confirmed bachelor, he wasn't as quick to pick up the underlying messages, but when he did, he wanted to laugh out loud. The two women were sizing each other up, deciding who had the most valid claim! He gazed at Cammie with affection. Didn't she know it was no contest? But it was gratifying nonetheless that her emotions were involved at a deeper level than he'd suspected.

It took an excruciatingly long time before Missy Grant decided to take her leave. Even then, she hesitated by the door, clearly resenting the fact that Cammie was invited to stay while she'd worn her welcome into the ground.

Jealousy ran through Cammie's veins like green poison. She was shocked by her reaction, even though it wasn't that unexpected if you looked at it right. But it made her feel small and insecure, as so much of the past two weeks had. She didn't trust herself with Ty. Good Lord! Their frantic petting was proof enough of that!

As soon as the door swung shut behind Missy, and Cammie had wiped her moist palms on her thighs, she turned to meet Ty's stripping gaze. That's what it was, too: *stripping.* Oh, not that she felt he undressed her with his eyes, though there was certainly an element of that in there, too, but because she felt he looked right through her into her soul. She was naked in front of him; all manner of deceptions lost to his knowing eyes. She'd felt that way the whole two weeks, and whenever she started to feel the least little bit safe, her mind cast back to those fervent, groping moments on his bed and her peace of mind shattered.

Still, she couldn't leave. She'd tried and tried. But apart from that first day, when she'd tossed together her belongings and bolted for the door, stopped by Ty's strong hands and even stronger persuasive manner, she hadn't physically attempted another departure. Any other leaving took place entirely in her head, a war she continually fought. In some ways this was absolute paradise, the fulfillment of her fondest, most impossible fantasy, but in another way, it was like Eve plucking the apple in the Garden of Eden: she knew it wasn't right, wasn't real, wasn't good. They had nothing to build on, no future to plan. The most she could expect from Ty was a long-term affair in a faraway town or village in some far-flung corner of the world. He wasn't going to come back to Los Angeles, for the "role of a lifetime" or anything else. She couldn't even ask him without appearing like she had her hand out. No, this was Ty's life now, and though he hadn't actually taken off and headed to a new place yet, it scarcely mattered, for that new place would be just as remote as this current one. That, she knew for certain.

So, where did that leave her?

Up the proverbial creek without a paddle . . .

"I don't think Missy approved of my being here," Cammie admitted after several tense moments. She clasped her hands in her lap.

"Want a drink?" Ty asked.

"Umm . . . no, thanks." Cammie was slightly surprised, since Ty had been a virtual teetotaler since she'd arrived, and he'd never offered her a drink past that first night.

"I need one," he stated flatly, as if expecting her disapproval.

"Go ahead."

"Thanks. I'm glad I have your permission."

Cammie slid him a look. "Ouch. Why are you mad at me?"

His answer was a long sigh, and when he returned to take the seat across from her, a newly uncapped beer in his hands, she realized he looked completely done in.

"Is something wrong?" she asked.

He shook his head, then ran a hand around the back of his neck in a peculiarly sensual movement that caused Cammie's eyes to follow his movements hungrily. She didn't know what to do with Ty. How long to stay. What to say. With each passing minute she felt more and more like the "uninvited" that she was, and yet she couldn't get up the gumption to leave. She wanted something *more.*

"I guess I just realized how little I wanted to be involved with Missy," he said heavily.

Since Missy had spent the last hour chattering away and offering innuendoes that she and Ty were seeing each other hot and heavy, and Ty had spent the same amount of time not refuting her, but gazing at her in a way that called her a liar, Cammie could have guessed that their relationship whatever it had been—was long over.

Missy had finally worn down and stopped talking, unable to sustain the fiction without some kind of help from Ty. Cammie had felt a bit sorry for her, but deep inside, a selfish piece of herself was just plain glad Missy wasn't her competition.

Which was insane, since she, Cammie, had no intention of throwing her career away to follow around a man who wasn't much more than a hermit these days!

Did she?

"I didn't get the impression that Missy wanted it to be over," Cammie murmured.

"No, I think she would have liked to continue."

"But you don't—want to continue?"

Ty slid her a look that sent a shiver through her veins. "No," he agreed. "Although I can't say I feel the same about you."

Cammie glanced away, afraid to read more into his words than he implied. As if regretting his own revelation, Ty immediately got to his feet, patrolling the confined space of the room and looking tense.

"Let's go to dinner," he suggested.

"Sure." She was relieved, having no wish to tread into areas she wasn't ready for.

But half an hour later, while they sat across from each other at a little bistro overlooking the bay, a candle on the table casting uncertain shadows on their faces as the sun dipped below the horizon, Cammie asked herself if she was proof against this sudden intimacy. For two weeks they'd led companionable but separate lives, Ty disappearing to his loft while Cammie spent the time strolling around the town of Bayrock, wiling away hour after hour. It was as if they were both in a dream, a holding pattern, a cocoon, and neither of them wanted the real world to intrude.

Cammie had called Susannah from the Goosedown Inn to report in, and though she'd been cagey about her whereabouts, Susannah hadn't pushed. She only cared whether Cammie was going ahead with the role in *Rock Bottom.*

"I don't know," Cammie admitted truthfully.

"But you're working on finding Tyler Stovall, right?" Susannah asked, her voice dropping to a near whisper.

"I—yes."

"Listen, my dear, everyone's talking about it. The inner circles have got him down for the part."

"What?" Cammie was incensed. "That's a little premature!"

"Well, you know . . . it was courtesy of his father. Samuel

Stovall's word is truth. But it's just buzz at this point," Susannah went on to assure her. "Nothing in the papers."

"Good! Because if Ty saw something, that would just finish it, once and for all."

There was a pregnant pause. "You've found him, haven't you?"

"Susannah, don't ask me anything. I'm trying, but I don't think he's ready to dip a toe in the cold waters of Hollywood just yet. I couldn't even ask him."

"My dear, it's the opportunity of a lifetime for you and *him!*"

"I'm so sick of that phrase," Cammie said with uncharacteristic bitterness. "There's more in life, you know. I just don't know what I want, and I can't talk any longer. Just know I'm okay, and I'll get back to you when I can . . ."

She'd hung up, then rushed back to the cabin, expecting her guilt to be written across her face. But Ty, who'd been wheeling and dealing with someone over one of his properties, had been absent when she returned, and by the time he showed up, a smile on his face over the signing of the property, Cammie had been fairly composed. Still, she felt like Mata Hari, spying on him and planning his downfall, so to speak. And yes, she wanted to work with him on the project, but as she'd learned over subsequent days, he was no closer to moving back to L.A. than he'd been ten years ago.

But even all of that just filled a small corner of her brain. Most of her mind contained images of Ty's lovemaking and the memory of her own response. She played it over and over again like a favored reel of film, remembering every touch, every sigh, every soft scent. She was ridiculous, letting her world spiral down to those few moments.

But she'd lived on them totally for the past two weeks, only waking from her self-imposed sleep when she encountered Missy and the realization that Ty had a life here in Bayrock before Cammie Merrill ever dropped on his doorstep.

A life she couldn't change for him.

"Tell me how you did it," she said now, running a nervous finger over the stem of her wineglass. Ty had ordered another beer, then changed his mind and asked for scotch, then refused to even touch the drink. Consequently, the ice cubes were melting, turning the mellow amber fluid a few shades lighter. Cammie focused on the drink because she couldn't face Ty's discerning eyes.

"How I did what?" he asked.

"Manage to disappear so completely. When I think what it would take to drop out of my whole life, I can't even imagine it."

He shrugged. "It wasn't all that difficult."

"Do you have fake identification?" She gave him a serious look.

"Yes," he said, as if she were incredibly dense.

"How?"

"It's easy enough if you know where to look. Los Angeles is full of hustlers. You can get a California driver's license for less than fifty dollars."

"Is that what you did?" Cammie drew her wineglass to her lips, meeting his gaze. His own eyes followed the rim of the glass as it reached her mouth, disconcerting her all the more.

He nodded. "Before I took off. The man helping me knew who I was. He thought it was a riot." To Cammie's look of confusion, he added, "The guy thought I wanted the ID so I could lead a secret life. You know, where no one knows who I am and I can do whatever I want."

"Well, yes, of course. In effect, that's what you did, isn't it?"

That stopped him a moment. "I guess you're right. Only that guy thought I was going to be Tyler Stovall by day and Jerry Mercer by night, if you get what I mean. I could slum it. Drugs, sex, whatever. Not something you can get away with as a celebrity."

"Oh." Cammie's own little bit of fame was enough to let her know how difficult being a celebrity could be. There was no privacy, no room for a "secret" life.

"Anyway, I have a friend who's helped me—my investment man."

"The one whose house was broken into?"

"Yep." Scowling at the memory, Ty finally picked up his drink, swallowing half of it down at once. Cammie watched this with a certain amount of disapproval, unaware that she'd revealed her true feelings until Ty demanded, "What's the matter?"

"Nothing."

"You don't want me drinking?"

"I didn't say that."

"You didn't have to."

"Whatever you choose to do, it's your life," Cammie said, hoping she didn't sound as priggish as her words sounded to her own ears. "I'm just a visitor here."

He set the glass down, eyeing her so intently that Cammie shifted uncomfortably in her chair. "That's right," he told her, and she could have sworn she heard a trace of bitterness in his voice

"So, then what?" she asked doggedly, seeking to keep their conversation on track. "You just opened an account at a bank. Isn't that illegal, or something?"

"Probably." He was completely unconcerned. "I don't know. Bruce sent me a cashier's check made out to Jerry Mercer. I *am* Jerry Mercer as much as I'm Tyler Stovall. In fact, I'm more Jerry than Ty."

"Bruce is your friend?"

Ty could have kicked himself. He was telling her far more than he'd ever said to anyone before. His recklessness appalled him. It was as if he *wanted* to be found out, for God's sake! But that was a lie.

"Yes," he answered shortly. "Any more questions?"

"What about a driver's license? I mean, how long is your ID good for? You can't use it to get a new one, can you?"

"You think too much."

"Well, I just know it would be hard."

"I've gotten new ID, okay?"

Cammie sipped her wine, wishing the waiter would come by and take their order. "How?"

Ty swore softly beneath his breath. "What, are you writing a book?"

"I'm just asking, that's all," she murmured.

His hand suddenly shot out and clasped her wrist. Cammie fought back a gasp of surprise. "What are you really doing here?" he asked. "It's not just to reconnect, is it? You're on some mission."

She shook her head, trying to deny even while she knew she was essentially lying. There was an element of betrayal in her visit, no matter how many ways she tried to cover it up.

"Cammie . . ." His voice lowered, and she suddenly remembered a scene from one of his films where he was trying to persuade the female lead to trust him. He was playing that scene right now—only this time it was for real.

"Look. Ty, I can see why you're so paranoid. You've got reason to worry. You're still an object of speculation for lots of people. But I would never turn you in," she declared emphatically, meeting his suspicious gaze. "That's up to you. I just want a little time with you, that's all."

"Why?"

She shrugged, feeling trapped. It was an effort not to squirm in her chair. "I don't know."

"You told me you loved me," he reminded her, and Cammie's cheeks flushed scarlet.

"I was under the influence of my own loneliness," she said stiffly.

"Do you say that to every man?"

He was baiting her because he needed to know the truth, and his intuitive nature told him she was holding something back. But it still hurt. Terribly.

"I haven't slept with anyone since my husband," she told him, lips taut. "Maybe I'm just needy."

"I'm sorry," he murmured, releasing his grip on her wrist. He felt like a heel. He *was* a heel!

"Forget it."

The waiter came at that moment. "You order," Cammie said, feeling drained. Ty grimaced, then asked for the special: baked salmon with dill sauce and lemon slices, a Northwest specialty.

"My last relationship with a woman in L.A. was with Gayle. She committed suicide," he said out of the blue, and Cammie's eyes widened in shock. "You probably didn't know about it. The whole thing was hushed up by my father." His mouth twisted. "She was merely a footnote in the *L.A. Times.*"

"Ty . . ." she whispered in distress.

"She threw herself out a window in New Orleans." He looked up at her with eyes so dark and gray, they looked bottomless with hurt and pain. "That's why I left."

IF YOU LOVE READING MORE OF TODAY'S BESTSELLING HISTORICAL ROMANCES.... WE HAVE AN OFFER FOR YOU!

LOOK INSIDE TO SEE HOW YOU CAN GET 4 FREE HISTORICAL ROMANCES BY TODAY'S LEADING ROMANCE AUTHORS!

4 BOOKS WORTH UP TO $24.96, ABSOLUTELY FREE!

CHAPTER TEN

"Oh, Ty . . ." Cammie breathed.

"I couldn't stay in L.A. anymore. I couldn't stand it. And there's more," he admitted after a long, silent moment. He picked up his drink and finished it.

"More?" Cammie asked with trepidation.

"She was pregnant."

Cammie's head reeled. Now she knew what had been bothering him that night she'd stopped by his house. Now she knew why he'd been out of his head with misery and alcohol. Ten years after the fact, he still hadn't completely recovered.

"And there's more . . ." he whispered again.

She couldn't even ask him. She was fairly certain she didn't want to know.

And as if he'd realized he couldn't bring himself to talk about it further, Tyler drew a harsh breath and sat back in his chair, his jaw tightening in resolve. With a slow shake of his head, he stopped whatever confession still hung, unresolved and unspoken. "That's why I left," he finished shortly.

Cammie slipped her hands across the table. Reaching for his, she clasped them tightly, silently offering all the love and support she possessed. Tyler looked down at their entwined hands. To her intense surprise he leaned down and kissed her fingers. When he lifted his head, her heart was beating like a drum, her pulse hammering inside her veins, her chest heaving as if she'd run a marathon.

"Make love to me," he said.

Cammie hesitated, thrilled and a little stunned. Before she could answer, the waiter came with their food and Cammie was obliged to drop his hands.

They ate in tense silence. Cammie wasn't certain what she was going to do. She felt light-headed, giddy and free. She wanted him and he wanted her. What more could she ask for?

Love, the tiny portion of her rational mind that still functioned reminded her. *Love.*

Tyler loves me, she answered back silently. *He's always loved me.*

Not the way you want . . .

Her meal was fabulous, but she barely remembered it: melt-in-one's-mouth flakes of salmon with creamy dill sauce dripping over each bite; soft, dry wine; slices of carrots and tiny bits of broccoli drizzled in butter. Outside the window, the bay was gorgeous: black water and shimmering lights waving streams of illumination extending across the bay. A sense of wildness and freedom and being at the most beautiful edges of the world.

But Cammie only saw Ty. She remembered his touch, the sweet insistence of his tongue, the glaze of passion in his eyes.

I'm done for, she thought as Ty paid for their meal and she walked up the street beside him like an automaton. He could ask anything of her, anything at all, and she couldn't deny him. Was that love or infatuation? She almost wished it were the latter, because then she could recover. But she knew how she felt and it was deep and impossible to ignore.

At the cabin, the atmosphere grew even more stifling, if that were possible, with Cammie fighting for each breath. Ty was remarkably quiet and had been since his revelations about his ex-lover. She understood his disillusionment and pain now, though his rejection of everything to do with Los Angeles and Hollywood still seemed a bit over the top. It was almost as if he'd needed an excuse to throw it all away, and Gayle's suicide while she'd been carrying his child had been more than enough.

"Could I have a cup of coffee?" she asked, stalling. As much as she wanted Ty—and there was no denying her feelings just based on the way her body felt drawn taut as a guitar string—she couldn't quite bring herself to just jump into a sexual relationship with him. Apart from all the obvious drawbacks—the biggest being the fact that they lived in two different parts of the world and neither was willing to give up their life for the other—Cammie hadn't made love to any man before or after Paul, save Ty himself. And that time with Ty, well . . . she'd responded to some aching need within him and thrown caution to the winds. At that moment she hadn't really cared about her own future; she'd given in simply to assuage the terrible pain of the man she loved.

Now, however, it was a whole new proposition. Ty was ready, willing, and able, and if she embarked on a sexual exploration with him, there was no one to blame but herself and her own carnal needs.

Still, as Ty set the coffee maker to dripping, she recognized that the dialogue going through her head was all academic. If he asked again, she would say yes.

He handed her a cup and Cammie cradled it within shaking palms. Her injured finger was black beneath its nail and she gazed down at it ruefully. "It still looks terrible."

"It will for a while," Ty conceded.

"But your magic did work. I haven't felt any pain since."

One eyebrow lifted. "My magic?"

For some reason, that reminded her of those moments

on his bed, their bodies writhing together, and Ty's intimate perusal of her body . . .

"Your surgical magic, if you can call it that," Cammie stated jerkily. "Aren't you—having any coffee?" she asked when he didn't pour another cup for himself.

"No, and I'm having a hell of a time staying away from another drink."

"If it's because of me, I'm sorry. I don't mean to come off as a nag! Do what you want."

"Oh, it's because of you," he agreed.

"It's your—your life, Ty!" she stammered. "I can't change it! Goodness, I'm surprised you even listen to me."

"I don't." He was terse.

"But you just said—"

"I said you're the reason I want another drink," he clarified, sighing deeply and running his hands through his thick hair. The movement separated his shirt from his jeans and she caught a glimpse of a flat, muscular abdomen with dark hair arrowing down to below his belt.

A curious melting feeling followed. *Oh, Lord,* Cammie thought. *I'm as bad as Donna Jenkins, my love-starved* Cherry Blossom Lane *alter ego!*

Something in her face must have registered, because with a sound of frustration, Ty took the cup from her unresisting hands and pulled her toward him, his arms surrounding her, his chin resting on the crown of her head. She counted her heartbeats, aware that there was no turning back. With a sigh of surrender, she pressed her cheek against his flannel shirt. Fleetingly, she warned herself not to tell him she loved him, but then he stirred, his mouth pressing kisses against her temple and the lobe of her ear, and all conscious thought fled.

Her fingers dug into the soft fabric of his shirt, bunching it spasmodically as his teeth bit the lobe of her ear, tugging gently and causing curious sensations to swirl inside her. She'd been married, but was still inexperienced when it came to sensual pleasure. Paul had been fairly quick in his lovemaking, almost clinical sometimes, his mind unable to disengage from the next plot or plan to spend a lot of time pleasuring his wife. Cammie had felt that was the way it was supposed to be, except for that encounter with Ty. Even in his numbed alcoholic state, his hands and mouth and body and overall need had worked their magic to turn her into a quivering mass of desire. She'd cried out with every plunging thrust, begging for more even while a distant part of herself marveled at her own wantonness. She'd wrapped her legs around him and urged him onward, her only regret that the experience was over much too quickly.

Of course, other regrets had come later. But right now, with her flesh shuddering and her lips reaching up to meet his, those thoughts were distant little pinpoints of light, fading away into a black vortex that seemed to be pulling her under. She met his kiss urgently, and when he groaned softly, pressing her weight against the counter, his own weight hard against her yielding contours, her knees turned to jelly.

"Cammie," he murmured, his hands sliding into the curtain of her hair, holding her head hostage to his plundering mouth and tongue. That tongue stabbed between her parted lips. The tip of Cammie's tentatively reached forward and Ty sucked it between his own lips. A swirling sea of emotion overtook her, weakened her already puny resistance. Resistance? What a laugh! She wanted him as much as he wanted her. More, probably. And though there was no future in this, no positive ending, she couldn't stop herself, because she wanted it too badly.

"Don't stop," she whispered when he drew back to look at her.

"I can't," he admitted simply.

And then his fingers began unbuttoning her blouse. She watched it fall away and one of his tanned hands reach forward and twist the front clasp with an expertise that left her feeling even weaker. She gazed up at him.

He sucked in a sharp breath. "Don't look at me like that!"

"Like what?"

"Like a trapped animal."

Cammie half-laughed. "You're reading me wrong. My God. Ty. . . I want you . . ."

That did it. Whatever eleventh-hour nobility had possessed him was shattered. With renewed vigor, he kissed and caressed and pressed his body against hers. His hand cupped her breast, kneading it, his finger and thumb rubbing the hard button of her nipple between them. His hips pinned her to the counter, and there was no mistaking his urgent arousal. With a feeling of stepping outside herself, Cammie's fingers reached down and slid over his sex, cupping it. A moment later his hand came to help, rubbing her fingers over his manhood in a smooth motion that quickened Cammie's blood.

He groaned deeply, releasing her a moment later to grab the snap of her jeans. With fingers grown clumsy from desire, he yanked on her zipper, snagging it, then muttered a suppressed oath.

Cammie swept his hands aside and performed the deed herself, her jeans sliding helplessly down her hips. His hand instantly insinuated itself in her most feminine area, sliding beneath the band of her silky panties to touch the hub of her pleasure.

Cammie gasped, shocked by the stab of pure sensation. She'd never been quick to arouse with Paul. In fact, she was damn near impossible to excite. But this, *this!*

Her hands were now at his shoulders, pulling him closer even though their bodies were practically fused. This time, when his head bent to her breast, her hands curled in his hair, pulling and releasing rhythmically. Sensations ran from her breasts to the core of her femininity as if pulled by strings. She wanted to lie down on the floor and let him have his way. She wanted to moan and writhe and cry out like a primal animal.

"Ty . . . Ty . . ." she breathed.

And when his head bent lower, his tongue licking a trail over the soft hill of her abdomen, his fingers parting the way for his intimate penetration, she simply lost all strength. She slid down the counter to the floor, and as Ty's hot tongue teased and tormented, she let out a sound between a scream and a whimper, reaching a climax so fast her body convulsed in wild ecstasy.

It felt as if she surfaced from some distant netherworld, her brain slowly engaged to realize that Ty was frozen against her, his body poised but immobile, his own motions in tandem with hers, subsiding with the spent relaxation of her own spasms.

Embarrassment wanted to cloud her judgment, but she pushed those thoughts aside, her fingers burrowing between them to release the zip over his straining manhood. He pressed his face to the downy curve of her cheek, letting her undress him until they were both naked, their jeans and underclothes kicked away.

And Ty, balancing himself above her on his locked arms, looked into her sultry eyes and said, "The kitchen floor?", to which she broke into paroxysms of laughter.

He grinned as well, then hauled her to her feet, sweeping her into his arms before that same old embarrassment could do more than pinken her cheeks. Carrying her to the bedroom, he laid her on the bed, then slid down beside her, one hand running from her neck to her thigh in a soft, sweet motion that incited her sleeping desire once more. She couldn't get enough of him!

"I'm a shameless hussy," she said on a gurgle of laughter.

"Good," he admitted.

"I'm going to hate myself in the morning."

"No, you're not," he said, and the amused look on his face slowly dissolved into an urgent hunger that made Cammie catch her breath.

"No, I'm not," she agreed, but the words were stolen from her as his hard mouth pressed down on hers. His hands cupped her rounded bottom, fusing their bodies, even as his knee nudged her legs apart. Then he lay atop her, and Cammie, whose memory of their one night together superimposed upon this time, wound her arms around him, her ankle entwining with his leg, holding him close, as if she feared he would leave her before she was satisfied.

But this time Ty had no intention of going partway. He simply couldn't restrain himself. His hard member rubbed against her warmth and she could feel the flooding of herself she would have found impossible to stop if she dared try. Meanwhile, his mouth kissed her with urgency, all over, and her own tongue tasted the taut skin at his shoulder and neck, reveling in the masculine saltiness. When she felt the tip of him nudge entry into her womanly flesh, her hands slid down his thigh to grab his hips, urgently yanking him closer until Ty gave up every hope of resistance and thrust himself inside her.

Cammie gasped. It had been a long time since she'd made love to Paul. Longer yet with Ty, and she'd forgotten the sweet feeling of possession, of desirability, it engendered. But then Ty began a rhythmic movement, and she was lost in helpless desire and memories. Paul had never taken such time with her; she hadn't even realized that fact until now when she could recall every breath and touch from when they'd made love before.

Her sensitized skin responded with a shudder. She sighed, then caught her breath.

"Cammie . . ." Ty whispered longingly.

"Please . . ."

She wanted him to do something more. To stop this slow, delicious torment, to hurry. Her hands begged with fervent demands, pulling his hips close while she strained against him. But Ty refused to change his rhythm and soon Cammie's head tossed about on the pillow. It was sweet torture! She couldn't stand it. She cried out, begging something unintelligible.

His mouth pressed hot against her neck, his tongue licking in tandem to his thrusting body. When she came, it was a skyrocketing climax, her whole body convulsing, her words sweet pleas and declarations of love.

She collapsed, drugged with sensual pleasure, chest

heaving, lost in lovely numbness. And then she heard his tense voice.

"Do you use birth control?"

"What?" she asked, dazed.

"Cammie, please, I can't hold off much longer."

Reality truly was a cold dash of water, she thought dimly, her brain clicking into reluctant action as his words penetrated. She felt cold, doused with icy fluid, all joy and warmth and love eradicated under a cascade of frigid reality.

Ty was struggling, his body telling him one thing, his brain another. He didn't want children, she remembered. Maybe because of Gayle's deliberate murdering of his unborn child, maybe because of his father's absentee parenting, or maybe because of less dramatic reasons, such as simply not being interested in fatherhood. The one thing she held most dear, and he was fighting it!

"It's taken care of," she stated bitterly, that old familiar pain seeping into her soul.

"Cammie . . . ."

"Shhhh . . ." He didn't believe her completely. Why should he? He didn't know her situation, and this was certainly not the right time to tell him. But still, her heart spilled over with love, and she wanted this lovemaking, this union, more than anything. "Don't worry," she whispered, and when her hands slid between them to lightly feather the skin of his abdomen and tentatively touch the place of their joining, Ty's defenses crumbled.

With a groan he ground himself against her, his body hard and thrusting, surprising Cammie by bringing her to sudden, unexpected climax once again. She panted and whimpered and Ty bucked in a last drive that sent his seed spilling hot inside her at the same moment she cried out again in a rush of pleasure. He collapsed against her seconds later, and her arms crushed him close, cradling his head as she brushed her lips across his angular cheekbone.

And Ty slowly raised himself above her, the look on his

face impossible to read. Cammie's lips quivered. What was he thinking? Was he regretting their coupling already?

But his next words, though they explained his reaction, shocked her to her very core.

"Have we done this before?" he asked incredulously.

CHAPTER ELEVEN

The walk to the Goosedown Inn seemed way too short today. Cammie hurried along, half walking, half jogging, glancing over her shoulder from time to time in guilty worry that Ty might somehow be following her. She needed no coat all of a sudden, as the rain-laden breeze had disappeared and a soft, yellow sun parted the clouds in the afternoon sky.

Spring was well on its way, and soon it would be summer. Summer . . . Summer solstice . . . She uttered a sound of worry as she hurried up the steps to the picturesque hotel. With a nod to the girl at the desk, she tucked herself in the alcove beneath the stairs where two public phones stood. Neither was occupied, and with nervous fingers, Cammie dialed Susannah's number collect.

"Coburn and Associates," Teri's cheery voice answered the phone.

"Hi, Teri, it's Cammie," she said. The skin at the back of her neck feathered and she glanced around sharply. No one was there.

"Oh, hi! Susannah's in a meeting with a client," Teri said. "Can she call you back?"

"Um . . . no, not really. I hate to bother her, but is there any chance I could catch a few minutes of her time."

"Sure," Teri answered, her doubtful voice revealing her true feelings.

Cammie drummed her fingers on the receiver, waiting impatiently for Teri to convey the message. The girl at the desk walked by Cammie, bestowing a smile of recognition on her as she passed. Cammie had become a fixture at the Goosedown Inn, having made this trek several times. The girl, who was not the same one who'd answered all Cammie's questions that first night in Bayrock, had come to know her. Cammie wasn't sure how to feel about that, but there it was. She had yet to engage her in conversation, figuring it was better to keep her identity as secret as possible. She would hate for Ty to learn of her ulterior motive before she was ready to tell him about it, if, indeed, that day ever came.

"There you are!" Susannah declared, sounding breathless as she clicked on the line. "I had to run down to the phone in my office because I was in the client room with an actor."

"Who?" Cammie automatically asked, using nosiness as a means to delay her own reason for calling. Susannah was not going to like what she had to say.

"Oh, you don't know him," she brushed off. "He's too good-looking for words, but he's got this way of coming on to every woman he meets, as if we're all dying to be seduced. He doesn't know any other way to relate, and believe me, he'll never get a role with that sleazy, chauvinistic attitude."

"But you're his agent."

"Not yet," Susannah stated emphatically. "Maybe I can change his ways. Too early to tell yet. He's such a jerk!" With scarcely a pause, she added, "But enough about him. Where *are* you? And, more importantly, when are you coming back?"

"I don't know," Cammie murmured, heaving a sigh. "I don't know."

"Is that what you called to tell me?"

"I told you I'd call."

"That's the only reason? You mean to tell me, you don't care what's going on here?" Susannah sounded appalled.

"What do you mean?"

"Everybody's going crazy over *Rock Bottom.* It's scheduled to start production in July!"

Cammie's heart lurched. "Oh, I see."

"You see what?" she demanded. "Cammie, you've got to get back here, with or without you-know-who!"

Cammie slowly inhaled through clenched teeth, wishing she could feel some kind of inner peace. As it was, every time she called Susannah, she just tensed up. So many people seemed to be counting on her, and she was failing them at every turn. "They're going to have to recast, aren't they?" she asked, resigned to her fate. She couldn't accept the role. Not now.

"They're going to have to cast somebody," Susannah averred. "And if it's not you, then someone else. But, Cammie! You could have this! Just get your tail back here ASAP."

"They'd hire me without that contingency? The reason I left?" She hated being so oblique, but there were ears everywhere. She didn't want to be the one who finally blew Ty's cover. Let it be from some other source.

"They want *him.* Samuel's practically apoplectic!"

Cammie gasped involuntarily. "You saw Samuel?"

"The man's been a fixture around here," she stated dryly. "He's not particularly good at waiting, and I have to admit, I'm getting pretty sick and tired of it."

"He's hanging around *your* office? Why?"

"Why do you think? Because of *you!*"

"Me?"

"Oh, Cammie, for pete's sake. The man's obsessed with this idea of all of you working on this film. It's amazing it hasn't hit *Variety* yet, or any of the other trades. But Nora and James are getting itchy, you know what I mean? They want this thing signed, sealed, and delivered. Everyone's waiting for you," she added on a sigh.

"Well, they can't!" Cammie declared, distressed. "It's not up to me."

"Oh? Then what are you doing in God-knows-where? Taking up residence? You've been gone over three weeks, my dear. If you haven't found what you're looking for, then you're on some other quest you haven't come clean about." There was a pregnant pause during which Cammie gathered her uneasy thoughts. Susannah waited for an answer, then finally, when she realized Cammie couldn't give her one, she cajoled, "Come on, girl. Level with me. Have you found what you're looking for?"

"I—think so," Cammie admitted uncomfortably.

"You think so?" Susannah was cautious in reading too much into her words.

"Susannah, I'm not sure I want to come back," Cammie admitted in a rush.

"Oh, come on!"

"No, I'm serious. Ever since I had that first meeting with Dr. Crawley, I've tried to figure out what I want. I don't know if acting—a career—is the most important thing to me."

Susannah was clearly poleaxed. "Well, what else do you have?" she asked, puzzled, unwittingly hitting the bull's-eye of Cammie's insecurities dead center.

"Not a heck of a lot," Cammie admitted with false lightheartedness. Inside, something crumbled and fell apart, some last hope for marriage and family and love. Though Susannah didn't mean to, she struck to the heart of the problem, reminding Cammie of how little she possessed in the way of happiness, and how farfetched any chance for achieving it truly was.

"Look, hon, I don't mean to be a downer. Good God. I *love* you!"

"I know." Cammie could scarcely squeak the words past her lips.

"But please, think about what you need. Think about what *I* need," she added in a humorous aside. "You've got a career on the rise that most people would kill their best friend for."

"A career on the rise," Cammie repeated a bit sardonically.

"I'm not kidding. Even without this opportunity, you've got solid standing in this community. Don't throw it all away just because you're at a low point. Come back. With or without the man of the hour."

"The Connellys won't use me without him," Cammie reminded her.

"Oh, pooh. Who cares? I'm still working on them. Just come back, so I can show them that one of their stars really exists."

"Do they know what I'm doing?" she asked suddenly, alarmed.

"How could they? I haven't told them."

But maybe Samuel Stovall has.

The thought churned across Cammie's brain, sending a cold frisson up her spine. She mumbled some platitudes and good-byes to Susannah, then walked to a chair in the lobby and sat down hard.

What are you afraid of? she asked herself. *Tyler's father? He can't hurt you now. He knows you have no interest in bringing Tyler back so that he can be exploited.*

She was still sitting there when Missy strolled into the foyer, her eyes searching the room as if she were looking for someone before her gaze fell on Cammie. To Cammie's intense dismay, she strolled over to her. "So, what are you doing here?" she asked. "I thought you were staying with Jerry."

"I am," Cammie admitted, wondering how long she needed to make polite conversation before she could lam out of the hotel. She did not want to discuss Ty, or Jerry, as the case might be, with his ex-girlfriend.

"Ahhh . . ." She touched a finger to the corners of her mouth, examining her lipstick. "Are you having lunch?"

"No, I was just—looking around."

"Then have lunch with me," she pressed. "I've really got some things I want to talk about with you."

"With me?" Cammie stalled. She didn't want this. No, no, no!

"Please . . ." she begged. "Jerry's a great guy, but there's some things, you know?" she added ambiguously.

Cammie was intrigued in spite of herself. This woman knew the Ty of the last ten years better than most. Hating herself a little for her prurient interest, Cammie accepted the invitation. Besides, it was better than going back and facing Ty again, right now. She still hadn't gotten over that comment from yesterday, after their frantic and wondrous lovemaking. She'd just begun to think she was safe when he'd uttered those bone-chilling words: *Have we done this before?*

Of course she'd denied it. She'd pretended to be at a total loss, calling on acting skills she'd thankfully kept honed. She'd even gone on to ask him what he'd meant by that, and Ty, either because he was less guarded because of what they'd just shared, or because he was reeling with memories as she was, memories he hadn't known he possessed, chose to be completely candid.

"I feel like we've made love before. The way you pulled me close and kissed me just now, at the end . . ." His voice trailed off as his gray eyes studied her flushed face closely. Luckily, her color could be put down to exertion rather than emotion, and Cammie acted as if she were amused and flattered rather than scared spitless, which was her true reaction.

"When we were kids?" she teased, letting him see how ridiculous the idea was.

"No." He rolled away from her, staring at the ceiling in hard thought for a few seconds before shaking his head dismissively.

And as soon as that disaster was avoided, Cammie suffered a wash of humiliation as she considered the little love words and moans that had issued past her lips. Had she told him she loved him again? She'd struggled so hard not to, even while the phrase sang from her heart and filled her head. But she'd made other sounds, small mewls of pleasure that had climbed to near howls, that made her want to cover her head and hide in embarrassment.

Still, pledging her love at the height of ecstasy was the worst, and she seemed to have avoided it, at least that time.

And they'd made love again. This morning. And several more times during the night before. She'd been in a little better control after their first endeavor, and although the experience had been no less enjoyable, she'd at least managed to keep a cooler head. Ty, too, for that matter. The first time, they'd reached for each other like they were drowning for each other's love; the second, third, and fourth times, they'd been less desperate and therefore Cammie felt a bit safer about the whole thing.

Safer? That was a laugh. She was out of her league and she knew it. There was no feeling safe with Ty; her emotions were too intrinsically wrapped up in everything about him.

And now she was treading into another treacherous place by allowing herself to share a meal with Missy. She was completely, utterly nuts.

They were seated at a table near the window, just a few down from where she and Ty had eaten dinner the night before. Cammie's eyes kept straying to the currently vacant table, and her thoughts were distracted by bits of remembered conversation and mental images of her body wrapped up with Ty's . . .

"I saw you come in here," Missy confessed, disconcerting Cammie to the extreme. "I thought maybe you were already getting something to eat. What were you doing?"

"As I said, just looking around."

"There's not much to see," Missy pointed out. "It's just a kind of boring hotel."

"Hardly boring," Cammie protested in spite of herself. "It's really beautiful here."

"Well, maybe when you've lived somewhere all your life, you don't see it that way." She shrugged. Today she wore a red dress that looked out of place in the casual atmosphere of the place. It was almost as if she wanted to be noticed. Cammie had always erred on the side of understatement, in her dress and her manner, and she always felt slightly embarrassed for those who didn't, even though they clearly wanted to create the very impression she found so uncomfortably obvious. Cammie herself wore black slacks and a blue collarless cotton blouse. She'd tossed her hair in a quick knot at the base of her neck; now loose strands were escaping from it. Compared to Missy's primped and sprayed blond curls, Cammie knew she looked underdressed. Still, Missy's choice of dress was almost out of place and contrived in the comfortable surroundings of the Goosedown Inn, while Cammie could have stepped out of the pages of Martha Stewart's *Living*.

Which didn't mean Missy wasn't attractive, Cammie conceded, looking at her from a purely adversarial position. They were just two very different people with very different backgrounds, and, in the long run, when it came to Ty's affections, there was no real certainty that she, Cammie, would win. After all, Missy lived here in Bayrock, while she was a vagabond, at least at the moment, a displaced Hellywood actress, which counted for less than nothing in Ty's eyes.

Which was depressing, to say the least.

"So, how long are you staying for?" she asked.

"I'm not really sure."

"Don't you have a job, or something?"

"Not currently," Cammie admitted. She was glad this girl didn't appear to recognize who she was. Having to explain how a television actress would be such close friends with Jerry Mercer might be a little difficult. "What do you do?"

The waiter came and Missy ordered a wine spritzer. Cammie settled for a diet cola, which made Missy's lips delicately curl in disgust. "I work at Rodeo Bob's, just outside of town when you're coming in to Bayrock? It's a steakhouse. Country western, you know. I'm the manager when Corky's not there."

"Corky's the owner?"

"Oh, no. Jerry's the owner." She smiled at Cammie as if she were dense. "My goodness, you don't know that much about him, do ya?"

"Well, I know he's into real estate," Cammie said, forced into defending her association with Ty. She was surprised, though. Ty's roots were deeper here than even she'd guessed.

"Oh, Jerry owns lots of stuff. Property all over the place." She waved an arm to encompass the surrounding area. "Corky's just the manager. I'm the assistant manager," she explained.

"What other property does—Jerry—own?"

"Well, not the Goosedown. At least, I don't think he does." She giggled. "He's got a ton of money, but you probably know that."

Cammie smiled noncommittally.

"So, how do you know him? His past is such a mystery."

"We were friends."

"He said you were sister and brother."

Cammie nearly choked on her drink. She hadn't guessed that Ty might have talked to Missy in the past few days. "We were once stepbrother and stepsister, but it didn't last all that long."

"And that was—where?"

Her probing bugged Cammie, but she'd let herself in for this, hadn't she? Hoping to learn something about Ty, she'd forgotten that she knew more than anyone here, and what she knew could damage her relationship with him forever.

"You and Jerry were lovers?" Cammie counterattacked, needing the space.

"Well . . ." She smiled, running a hand through her hair and drawing a stiff blond curl across her lips. "Yes. Didn't he tell you?"

"Yes, he did, as a matter of fact." Cammie relied on her

acting skills yet again, pretending not to care other than simple interest. "But he didn't say how you first met."

"Oh, that was when he was buying Rodeo Bob's. I was hostessing then. Jerry walked in, and *bam!* It just hit me, y'know? I thought, my God, he's so handsome. And he looks a little like that actor who was real popular once, Tyler Stovall. So I told him that, y'know," she went on, oblivious to Cammie's stiffening at the mention of Ty's real name, "and he said he heard that a lot. I just bet. But he's older looking and he's got that beard, and everybody knows that actor was gay anyway."

Cammie couldn't prevent a muffled exclamation.

Missy picked up her wineglass, sipped from its contents, and eyed Cammie knowingly. "Well, it's true. Jerry says so, too."

"Does he?" Cammie gulped down the rest of her cola and wished she'd ordered something stronger after all.

"Sure. So, anyway, Jerry and I hit it off and started seeing each other. At first I sorta thought he wasn't going to stay in Bayrock. I thought he might move on. But he'd been here awhile before we met apparently. Then he built the cabin, and wow. . . he owns tons of land. The old Richards place, and some timber land, I think. I don't know. He doesn't talk about it all that much."

"What does he talk about?" Cammie asked curiously.

"Oh, anything, except his past." She laughed. "He never mentioned you, for instance, until you showed up."

"I don't think he was very happy," Cammie said softly. "He'd like to forget it all."

Missy eyed her shrewdly. "I've got a theory. Maybe you can tell me whether I'm right."

"Don't look to me for answers!"

"There's an ex-wife somewhere, and she's nasty as a hive of hornets. She'd like nothing better than to sink her claws into him. At first, I was afraid she was you!"

As Missy waited with avid interest, Cammie sought for some kind of answer. Clearing her throat, she inclined her head, hoping Missy would think she was betraying a dear secret. "I wasn't that close to—Jerry—for a lot of years. You could be right. It's only recently that it was possible to even get near him again. He likes his privacy."

"Don't I know it!" she sniffed. "Sometimes he's just a bear about it."

"I've seen that side of him, too," Cammie admitted sardonically.

The waiter came to take their order, but before Missy could choose, Cammie said, "You know, I really don't have that much of an appetite. You go ahead. I'll just have a—glass of Chardonnay," she said to the waiter.

"You sure?" Missy asked, frowning.

"I'm sure."

That was the one thing Cammie was sure of: she could use a drink. Her nerves were shot. Except she couldn't afford to loosen her tongue too much. Missy had a way of burrowing to the truth that put Cammie on edge, and if she could possibly have figured out a way to end this lunch date early, she wouldn't have ordered the wine. But as there seemed no easy way to extricate herself without raising the other woman's suspicions, she figured she'd just sip away at her drink, soothe her jangled nerves, and outwait Ty's sometime-girlfriend.

A change of air pressure, or some sixth sense that feathered across Cammie's skin, caused her to shiver and glance around. Her heart nearly stopped. Ty himself stood a few paces away, his expression unreadable, his mouth drawn into a sharp line.

Had he overheard her?

"Jerry!" Missy called, waving furiously at him, as if there was any chance he could miss seeing them.

Cammie swallowed and pasted on a welcoming smile. Ty shot her a glance, then strode toward them somewhat reluctantly. Cammie got the impression he was sorry he'd stumbled upon them together. For her part, Cammie could have sunk down beneath the table. She felt like a traitor, somehow, but Missy welcomed his unexpected appearance with obvious delight.

"We were just talking about you!" Missy declared, patting the chair next to her. "Sit down. Cammie's not having lunch, but I am. You want something? I'll buy."

"No, thanks." He accepted the seat a bit reluctantly, Cammie thought, since it put him in close contact with Missy. Cammie was almost glad he was on the other side of the table; she didn't think she'd be able to keep her wits about her if he was seated next to her, his thigh millimeters from hers, the heat of his body close and warm. Their relationship had definitely changed and Cammie was still getting used to the shock.

Missy chattered away, delighted beyond bearing that Ty had come within her circle again. She seemed to have forgotten her animosity over learning Cammie was his "friend," at least for the time being, and instead used the opportunity to ply Ty with questions about what he'd been doing lately.

"You know, I've been asking Corky what happened to you. You've been like a ghost around Rodeo Bob's lately. I thought maybe you'd sold it, or something."

"I didn't realize you'd diversified into the restaurant business," Cammie put in.

"I only own the property. Rodeo Bob's is Corky's brainchild. I'm basically a landlord."

"With part interest!" Missy declared. "Corky said you loaned him money!"

Ty was clearly irked by all this discussion of his finances. Cammie didn't blame him, but Missy was oblivious to his darkening mood. "That doesn't make me a partner."

"Whatever." Missy waved her hand, dismissing the finer points of financial ownership as undeserving of further discussion. Cammie knew Ty was just glad to have the subject change, whereas Cammie wondered how extensive his financial dealings were in this Canadian border town. It looked as if it wouldn't be as easy for him to pull up roots as he'd first let on. Maybe her appearance was just an excuse for him to stay, which was fine by her.

"What if I wanted to open my own place?" Missy asked teasingly. "I could use a partner."

Ty's gaze swept over Cammie's face before she averted her eyes. This was getting sticky, and she was fast becoming embarrassed for all of them. "I'm more of a solo operation," he said not unkindly. "You know that."

"It doesn't have to be that way—forever," Missy suggested on a murmur.

Ty didn't answer, which left Cammie with food for thought.

Thirty minutes later, when Missy had finished most of her sandwich and Ty and Cammie could make a polite escape, Cammie stepped ahead of Ty through the Goosedown Inn's front double doors, the oval, beveled glass mirroring their images in the soft afternoon light. Missy was right on their heels, still carrying the bulk of the conversation, but when Cammie and Ty began to walk in the direction of his cabin, she asked pathetically, "Mind if I join you? I've got nothing to do tonight?"

Ty hesitated, and Cammie was afraid he was going to turn her down. "Sure, come on," she invited, drawing a frown across Ty's face. "We'll make popcorn and watch TV."

"I'll be right there! I've just got to pick something up!" Missy called, half-running across the street to her car.

"Now, why did you do that?" Ty wanted to know as soon as Missy was out of earshot.

"Do what?"

"Invite her over. If I didn't know better, I'd think you were trying to avoid being alone with me."

"You do know better," Cammie reminded him softly. "I just didn't want her feeling bad. She's got a serious thing for you."

"And you think this is going to help?"

"No." She grimaced. "I just couldn't leave her hanging

like that. I know, I should have asked if it was all right with you, but she was so . . ."

"Needy?" Ty suggested.

"Yes."

He sighed and raked a hand over his beard. "Believe me, you'll be sorry for acting like a saint," was his strange reply as he linked her arm through his, much to Cammie's delight, and they strolled back to the cabin, arm in arm.

"So, after that, I wouldn't let him come near me anymore," Missy stated, her hand hovering over the popcorn bowl as if she'd just been hit by another thought. "I mean, he just wanted to make Jerry jealous, after all."

"Jerry" couldn't help a small sigh from escaping his lips. His eyes were on the television, glued to it as if it held all life's mysteries. In reality, he couldn't remember what the name of the program was that they were watching. The whole evening had been interminable, and unless he could find a way to dislodge Missy, it was only going to get worse.

For the better part of two hours, Missy had hinted about all the men who found her attractive, making certain that although she was sought after by a host of eligible bachelors, her heart belonged to "Jerry." It made Ty want to crawl under a rock. He'd ended his abortive relationship with her several times, and only let himself be sucked back in by pure loneliness. But this last time, he'd ended the relationship once and for all, and he thought she'd gotten the message. From the onset, he'd been plain about his feelings on love and marriage, and though she'd acted as though she understood, he was now beginning to wonder.

Cammie's appearance in Bayrock had effectively restarted Missy's campaign, apparently. And since she believed Cammie was somehow related to him, and therefore not a threat, she'd become all sticky sweet and proprietorial, and Ty was about to jump out of his skin.

He'd warned Cammie, but she hadn't realized what would happen. Did she realize now? he wondered, as he slid her a surreptitious look. She was curled up on the couch, her feet tucked beneath her in that thoroughly enticing way, her auburn hair pulled back in a loose ponytail while errant strands curved beneath her jawline. She was gorgeous. A drop-dead beauty. The kind of woman he'd made a practice of staying away from because, in his experience, the prettier the face, the bigger the insecurities. Any actress he'd ever dated was an out-and-out basket case. And Gayle, though she'd worked in production instead of in front of the camera, had turned out to be as messed up as any of them.

Gayle . . .

Sadness and a renewed spurt of anger rushed through him. His sorrow over her death, and guilt, had ended up being replaced by a whole new set of emotions, ranging from disbelief to fury, when the truth had finally come to light after her swan dive.

A truth he still couldn't bring himself to talk about. Her pregnancy . . .

"We need a DNA sample," his lawyer had said, "to be sure the child's yours."

Ty had been too numb to understand. He'd been living in a fog, aided by the evils of drink, and the man's words seemed nonsensical. "What does it matter now?"

"Your father wants to know." To Ty's incredulous look, the lawyer added with a look of sympathy, "He thinks it might be his."

Ty had come unglued. He'd rushed over to his father's house and blasted him with the news in front of his latest wife, while she held his latest son screaming in her arms. What a scene. Scripted right out of a melodrama. Samuel hadn't denied the accusations; he'd just wanted to know if Ty had agreed to the tests. The answer to that was an unqualified, "No!", then he'd slammed out of the place and driven back home, drinking himself into an alcoholic stupor that had lasted the better part of a week. When he'd finally recovered, he'd left L.A. No regrets. No second thoughts. Just a desperate need to shake the dust of that miserable place behind him.

He didn't know to this day whether Gayle's unborn child had been his or his father's. Samuel had wanted to know for reasons of his own. Ty figured his father could give the DNA sample, and to hell with it. He'd mourned the loss as if the child were his anyway, no matter how much he'd tried to tell himself it had nothing to do with him.

When he'd first arrived in Bayrock he'd kept to himself with almost fanatic perverseness. But time is a great healer of ills, and finally he broke through the shell of his own paranoia and started to rediscover a life. He'd met a few of the locals, and had even dated a bit, but always at arm's length. He had no interest in encouraging anyone, but as the years passed, he slowly began to feel a bit of safety, and then, finally, a recognition that it just didn't matter as much anymore.

So, when Missy crossed his path after he helped out Corky, he let himself start seeing her. She was uncomplicated. More rural than urban, and though she played her little games, they were easily dismissed. Only when he realized how involved and insistent she'd become did he start to ease away, and when that began to happen, she doubled her efforts to hold on to him, which was the death knell itself to their relationship.

He'd just about given up on women entirely until Cammie walked through his door. She'd knocked him sideways, and even though he knew it had more to do with his lack of female companionship than her feminine wiles, it hardly mattered. He was won before she dropped her coat on the couch.

And that was why he'd been so damned testy these past few weeks. He was in a quandary, a vortex, a terrible place, where lust and love swirled together into a potent mix in which he felt he was drowning. At first he'd tried to call her his "sister," thinking that would help. But they both knew that was a crock, and when she'd looked so vulnerable, yet slapped him with that sassy tongue, he'd been undone.

Finally, finally, they'd made love, and though it had been a fabulous, soul-defining event, he could sense her wariness and ambivalence. She was a fabulous sexual partner, so giving and luscious and deliciously demanding, a mixture of virgin and wanton that could turn a man's brains to mush, his body into a hormone-raging group of jerking muscles, his soul into slavery.

When she'd disappeared this afternoon, he'd pretended it didn't matter. What the hell. She was free to go where she pleased. But it had dug into his skull like a screw, and he'd been unable to work on anything, not his business papers or his screenplay, and though he'd called himself every kind of fool, he'd gone in search of her—and discovered her with Missy, of all people.

And now all he could think about was burying himself inside her warm sheath. It boggled the mind. How could it be that he, Tyler Stovall, was so obsessed with sex? There'd been a time in his life when it was so readily available that he could scarcely work up the enthusiasm. He couldn't count the times he'd gone through the act by rote, even with Gayle. In those days, Cammie Pendleton was a little girl, at least in his mind, and not interesting to him in that way. She was his little buddy, if he thought about her at all, and mostly he didn't, because he was a young jerk who thought only about himself.

So, how did this happen? And how was he going to get rid of Missy? He had to do it soon or his body, which was receiving lusty messages from his brain about Cammie, was on the verge of reacting in a way he wasn't going to be able to conceal.

Absently, he pushed the buttons on the remote, waded through a few commercials as Missy prattled on, and finally settled on a drama with young, fresh actors and actresses who Ty didn't recognize. Apart from a few names that were perennially on the Hollywood top-end list, there was seldom a celebrity who could keep his or her fame going full tilt, as so many of them were wont to do. For Ty, fame had been like carrying the weight of a dead elephant around. As the lead singer for the Rock group INXS had once been quoted, "Fame is like the ocean. It's pretty from afar, but if you jump in, you'd better know how to swim." He, like Gayle, had suffered a premature death.

"So, what is it you do again?" Missy asked Cammie. "I don't remember what you said."

Since Cammie, as far as Ty could tell, had never mentioned her profession, it stood to reason she didn't want Missy to know. Whether that was to protect his identity, or because she was as uncomfortable with that "celebrity" thing as he was, Cammie had been very quiet about being an actress.

He glanced her way and caught a sideways look from jewel-bright aqua eyes. Cammie knew Ty found humor in the situation, but she didn't want Missy to know anything about her. "I'm out of work at the moment," she said.

"Oh, yeah?" A thought struck Missy. "Are you looking for work *here?*" she asked, seeking to keep the horror from invading her voice and failing utterly.

"Not really. I'm not sure—" Cammie cut herself off as her gaze riveted momentarily on the television set.

Oh, God, no! she thought.

There she was, on the small screen in all her glory as Donna Jenkins, straight-jacketed and wild-eyed as gas hissed through the vent of the room in the sanitarium.

"Carbon monoxide," Donna Jenkins mouthed in the faintest whisper, her fate sealed as someone watched her struggle for air outside the room, through the tiny window.

And so ended the final cliffhanger from this season's finale of *Cherry Blossom Lane* . . .

Both Tyler Stovall and Missy Grant stared at Cammie in varying degrees of amusement and wonder.

CHAPTER TWELVE

Ty could have laughed out loud at the consternation and suppressed horror written across Cammie's face as she viewed herself on television.

This, then, must be Cammie's nighttime drama, the one she'd been fired from by her Judas of an ex-husband.

Missy gazed blankly from the screen to Cammie, then to Ty. "Was that you?" she asked Cammie, completely lost.

Cammie was half inclined to lie, but she'd put her fingerprints all over the thing by reacting so violently. "I'm afraid it was," she admitted.

"You're—you're—on television!" Missy fairly shrieked.

Cammie winced, wondering just how far a leap it was for Missy's brain to sizzle through the connection to Ty. She would know who he was. It would be too obvious.

"The truth comes out," Ty said lazily, not nearly as worried as Cammie felt he ought to be.

"You're on television," Missy said again, staring at Cammie in total disbelief.

"I was. My role on *Cherry Blossom Lane* is over."

"Her ex-husband took care of that," Ty put in, earning

him a killing look from Cammie, who felt everything was unraveling at much too fast a pace.

"Ex-husband? Who's he?"

"One of the producers." Now it was Cammie who wished she could find a quick way to get rid of Missy, but this latest revelation had left Missy with even less desire to leave.

"I don't believe it!" she sputtered, blinking rapidly. "You're an actress. On *television.* I've never met anyone who's an honest to God actress. How did you get the part? Did you know someone? Do you have an agent?"

"Yes," Cammie admitted, helpless in the face of this onslaught of questions.

"Do you live in New York?"

"Los Angeles," Cammie said.

"Oh, yeah. Of course. Hollywood." She shook her head. "Wow." Slowly, as the neurons began to fire and deductions were invariably made, she turned to look hard at Ty.

"I was a stunt double," he said, lying with such practiced ease that Cammie's lips parted in surprise. "You said yourself I bear a resemblance to Tyler Stovall."

"You do!" Missy's head bobbed excitedly.

Ty grimaced. "Yeah, well, it was great at first. They used me once or twice on his films, but then the fool took off and that ended my career." Ty sighed and shrugged. "I hung around for a while, but the work dried up. Decided to pack it in, and I sort of fell into real estate development and property management."

Acting. He was acting, Cammie realized with a certain amount of admiration. He was so good. So natural. She almost believed him herself.

"You never told me!" Missy declared now, playfully slapping at him.

Ty slid Cammie a conspiratorial glance that Missy couldn't see even while he lifted his shoulders in an uncaring gesture. "I like my privacy."

Someone had once told Cammie that the truly gifted liars always kept close to the truth. And she'd also heard that the best way to deal with a potential problem is to point an arrow at it and explain it away before the first question even arose. Ty had successfully done both, but then, he'd had years to manufacture this story.

How strange that her climactic scene on *Cherry Blossom Lane* had aired tonight. She'd almost forgotten that other life, she was so embroiled in this one. But it was a reminder that time was passing and decisions were going to have to be made.

"What an idiot!" Missy declared vehemently. "He just takes off and doesn't even think about it. He ruins your career in the process, too." She sniffed. "Selfish bastard. Probably ran off with his gay lover."

Ty rubbed furiously at his nose, fighting back a storm of mirth that threatened to crack his facade. Cammie's eyes twinkled in shared merriment as they met his, and he had to restrain himself from rushing over and swooping her into his arms, kissing her all over.

It took another thirty minutes to roust Missy out, and even then, it was only because Cammie feigned tiredness, managing to fake a few yawns. Ty jumped on that excuse and expertly maneuvered his ex-girlfriend to the door. Cammie sped up the process by waving good night to Missy as she strolled down the hall to Ty's bedroom. Closing the door behind her, Cammie then pressed an ear to the panels to hear what Ty said next.

"She sleeps in your room?" Missy questioned.

"Yes," was Ty's answer. His voice warned her not to travel that road further, but Missy, as Cammie had learned, wasn't good at picking up the subtext of any conversation.

"And where do you sleep?" she demanded.

"Wherever I damn well please."

"Jerry, you know what I mean!"

"Yes, I know exactly what you mean," he agreed almost gently. Cammie winced, aware that Ty was trying to leave Missy a chance to back out gracefully. But it wouldn't work. Missy wasn't made that way.

"You act like she's your sister and all, but she's not,"

Missy barreled through, proving Cammie right in her next breath. "So, what's really going on? I have a right to know."

"Missy, go home. Go to bed. Don't think about it."

He was still trying to be kind, but it was too much for Missy.

"You haven't seen her in years! She didn't even care enough about you to come visit until now!"

"You don't know what you're talking about," he said flatly, a further warning she refused to heed.

"Just because her husband left her doesn't mean you have to play the knight in shining armor! Come on, Jerry, wake up! She's just lonely."

"Missy . . ."

Cammie felt bad, wondering if she should do something to stop this escalating fight. But maybe it had to happen. Ty certainly needed to clear the air with her; maybe today's events were the precursor to the inevitable.

"Jerry . . ." she pleaded.

That was all the eavesdropping Cammie could stand. She moved quickly away from the door, rubbing her hands over her elbows. She didn't know what she was doing here herself, and Missy's pain and disappointment made her feel all the worse.

Eventually, Ty tapped on her door. Cammie opened it, glancing past him.

"She's gone," he told her on a sigh.

"I feel—terrible," she said.

"Don't . . ." He shoved his hands in the pockets of his jeans, clearly at a loss to what to say next.

"It makes me feel weird to hear her call you Jerry," Cammie admitted, grimacing. "Doesn't it bother you?"

"I've gotten used to it. Sort of. It's been a lot of years," he reminded her on a short, humorless laugh.

"I hardly knew what to do when *Cherry Blossom Lane* came on. I thought she'd realize who *you* are. I'm amazed she didn't."

"Nobody believes I'm Tyler Stovall," he said without rancor. "Give them half an explanation and they'll take it. You saw how she reacted when she realized you were on television. It's just too hard to believe. Actors aren't real people," he added ironically.

"Still . . ." Cammie wasn't completely convinced, even though she'd gotten a little of that herself. The public believed she was Donna Jenkins—period. There was no Camilla Merrill there at all.

"No one recognizes me because they don't believe there's any possible way I could be Tyler Stovall. It's easier to think I'm a stunt double."

"That was inspired," Cammie said with a smile.

"I've had a long time to come up with every excuse in the book," he admitted. He eyed her with a certain amount of detachment. "Do you plan to stay in it? Acting, I mean."

Cammie didn't quite know how to respond. And she didn't think saying "It all depends on you!" would be the right choice. "I guess."

"You're not dying for the fame and fortune?"

"A couple of years on a television show cures you of that. But I'd like to keep my hand in it somehow. I love doing it."

Her honesty reached him. Everything she said, everything she did, just fascinated him all the more, and he wanted to wrap her up and keep her close. A ridiculous idea, since they were at polar opposites in their choice of lifestyle and career.

Except there was that script . . .

Ty lowered his lashes, thinking hard and unwilling to let her read anything in his eyes. He'd taken that copy of his script from its nightstand drawer and squirreled it away upstairs with his other, newer copies. He'd been working on the damn thing for over a year and it was nearly finished, and although he had no plans to ever turn it over to Hollywood, it had been a therapeutic experience for him, a balm to his unhappy soul.

"I want to show you something," he heard himself say, then gestured for her to precede him out of the room. Cammie hesitated a moment; he didn't blame her. Ever since she'd arrived, they'd embarked on this wild, furious, roller coaster of emotion that neither had expected. It was glorious and frightening and downright pleasurable, and Ty didn't want the ride to end.

But it had to . . . someday.

Just don't make that day today!

He led her upstairs to his loft office. Cammie followed with both anticipation and trepidation. He hadn't allowed her into the loft since the first day he'd shown it to her. Oh, it wasn't that he'd written some huge "Keep Out" placard; he'd just made it very clear that his office was his private work area. He also had taken up sleeping on the sofa tucked beneath bookshelves at one end, and so Cammie had respected his privacy completely. And after his annoyance when she'd discovered his script, well, it was a slam dunk that she wasn't going to be stepping over that particular line again.

Thinking of the script she'd barely caught a glimpse of reminded her of her injured finger. The nail was cracked and split and the underlying skin blackened, but there was a tiny moon of new pink where the nail had begun to grow out.

"Does it still bother you?" Ty asked, following her gaze.

"Oh, no. It's just so ugly."

"Nothing about you is ugly."

The compliment made her blush. Cammie felt as ridiculous and callow as a schoolgirl. Her voice was light as she murmured, "You could make a girl's head turn, you silver-tongued devil."

"Oh, by the way, my mother called," he said. "She still didn't say anything about you."

Nanette had placed several calls to her son since Cammie had been staying with him, but as yet she hadn't mentioned Cammie had been by to see her. She was keeping that secret safe for the time being, though she now had a tendency to sing Cammie's praises at each and every opportunity, according to Ty.

"You should tell her I'm here," Cammie said.

"I thought about it."

"Why didn't you?"

"I don't know," he admitted honestly. "I guess I just don't want anything to—spoil this."

Cammie knew exactly what he meant. She didn't want to spoil this time-out-of-time together, either. But it would have to end soon, no matter what either she or Ty wanted. The clock was ticking and eventually the bomb would explode. Samuel Stovall had to know she was here, and he wouldn't wait forever.

"So, what did you want to show me?" she asked, pushing her worries aside.

"Well, I was thinking about how you got that injury," he said. Reaching for her hand, he gazed down at her fingers. "You were looking at my script."

"I really didn't see any of it," she told him again. "A few words and then I panicked and slammed the drawer on my hand."

"I remember," he said sardonically.

"It's your private property. I understand. Really."

"No. I shouldn't have gotten so protective about it. It's just that I never intended anyone to see it."

Her attention was riveted to the warm touch of his hand holding hers. He could distract her so easily, and right now, she did not want to be distracted. "No one?" Ty nodded, and Cammie asked, "So, why write it at all?"

"Call it a catharsis. I don't know. Some things happened that I didn't handle very well, and oh, I don't know . . ." He sighed. "Therapists say if you write it all down, it doesn't seem so terrible."

"Therapists?"

He smiled. "I've never been to one personally, but hell, everyone else in the business has! I don't know how many times some 'date' I was with started in on what her therapist had said. With the hours I've put in, listening, I've probably got a degree!"

He sounded so disgruntled that Cammie laughed. The music of her laughter caught his attention, and suddenly he pulled her into his arms, kissing her ravenously on her face and neck. Cammie giggled louder, scrunching up her shoulders. "You're tickling me!"

"Good," he growled against the skin of her neck.

"Stop it!" She squirmed and gasped, her aqua eyes full of mirth. "I mean it."

"No, you don't."

"I'll scream!"

"Go right ahead," Ty invited, his own eyes full of a lazy humor that made Cammie catch her breath, the tenor of the moment changing from playful to desirous. He picked up the change in mood immediately, his gaze dropping to the pink crescent of her mouth. "Go right ahead," he invited again, his voice deepening to a husky drawl.

"You were going to show me your screenplay," she reminded him.

"Was I?"

"You know you were."

"It can wait." His gaze dropped lower, to where her heart beat at the base of her throat. Gently, he touched a finger to that pulse point. "I thought you were going to scream," he reminded her softly.

"I don't think I can. I don't think I want to anymore." Her voice was a thready whisper.

"What do you want, then?"

Her lips twitched. "If you don't know by now, you're not paying close enough attention."

Their eyes met, his, narrowed between thick lashes, a bright beam of silver with hunger flashing in their depths, hers, a soft, slumbrous aqua, full of deep emotion. With a groan, Ty captured her lips with his, the force of his body pushing her toward the office couch. When the backs of her knees encountered the cushions, she slipped down with a thunk and a gasp.

"Not fair," she declared, pretending outrage.

Ty's grin was devilish. "Yeah, well, tough." He sank down beside her, one hand clasping her outer thigh and twisting her until she faced him, their knees touching. That same hand started a bold foray across and up her leg. Automatically, she stopped his hand with hers.

"You're heading toward dangerous territory," she warned softly.

"Really. How dangerous?"

"Things have changed since you left L.A."

"How do you mean?" But he wasn't really listening. His teeth had clamped gently on her earlobe and he was biting and nibbling. It nearly blew Cammie's concentration, but she enjoyed their playful bantering, something she'd never experienced with Paul or any other man. Everyone was just so *serious* all the time. It was as if people in general had forgotten how to have fun.

"There's such a thing as asking before you touch," she told him haughtily. "Sexual harassment is a serious offense."

"Sexual harassment?" His voice was laced with humor. "I haven't been gone that long!"

"How do you know this is what I want?" Cammie argued. "You could be misreading the signals."

He pulled back to look at her. "Y'think?"

"For all you know, you could really be invading my space!" Cammie's laughing eyes spoiled her argument.

"Maybe I should do a test," Ty suggested.

"What kind of test?"

"I'll make some little move, and we'll see from your response whether it's good, bad, or indifferent."

"What kind of little move?" Cammie asked suspiciously. She was sure this wasn't going to last very long at all, since every touch, every whisper, and every slanted glance of desire sent her fluttering pulse into overdrive.

"Let me show you."

Ty situated himself next to her until only their knees were still touching. His arms lay across the top of the couch, his body as lazy as a jungle cat in repose. She shot him a sideways look, then averted her eyes. He was flat out irresistible, and a part of her, while enjoying the game, felt a quiver of fear that this could matter so much to her.

What would happen when it ended? Would she be able to cope with the loss? Was she that strong?

"What is it?" he asked suddenly, reading her swiftly changing expression.

"Nothing. Why?"

"You looked so—sad, for a moment."

"I have this bad habit of reading the future and not liking what I see."

His gaze searched her face. "Our future?"

"Something like that."

He reached out and cupped her chin, his thumb rubbing sensuously against her lower lip. "I don't want this to change," he whispered urgently.

"Neither do I. But it can't stay like this forever, can it?" Her voice broke, revealing her feelings.

For an answer, or maybe because there was no satisfactory answer to her question, Ty leaned forward and kissed her, his mouth fusing with hers, his arms squeezing her tightly as if he were afraid to ever let her go.

I love you, she thought, aching inside, but this time she kept her tongue silent and instead wound her own arms around him.

They kissed over and over again, then Ty's fingers found the buttons of her shirt, pulling it apart so that cool air swept across the skin of her abdomen and shoulders. Unsnapping the clasp of her bra, Ty's hands freed her breasts, which slid into his welcoming palms. His thumb rubbed the bud of her nipple and she moaned her desire involuntarily.

"I'll take that as a 'yes,' " he murmured achingly, and Cammie's silent laughter was captured by his marauding mouth.

By the time they uncoiled their tangled limbs, it was well past midnight. Moonlight streamed through the circular window above Ty's desk, bathing them both in a soft, bluish glow.

"It's getting warmer," Cammie murmured. "Time's going by. It's May, and soon it'll be June."

"You're going somewhere with this, I can tell." His voice still sounded husky with the aftereffects of their lovemaking.

"I don't want to leave," she admitted.

"Then don't."

"You know what I mean."

"I only know that it feels like you've been a part of my life forever, and I can't imagine giving you up now."

She gazed at him through the darkness, lifted her hand to his cheek and rubbed adoringly down his bearded contours. "The first time we made love here, you said it felt like we'd made love before."

"Mmmhmmm." He collected her fingers and delicately sucked on their tips.

"Stop that, or I won't be able to continue," she murmured gently, pulling back her hand and touching her curving lips lightly to his. "I've got to tell you something."

"I need to shave off this beard," he said suddenly. "I'm sick of it, and I don't think I need it to hide anymore. If they find me, they find me. I'm not leaving Bayrock."

"Listen!" Cammie commanded, refusing to be deterred when she was ready to confess.

Her tone amused him. His teeth flashed white in the semidarkness and he sketched a salute.

"Ty . . . ?"

"Yes?"

"That first time? It wasn't the first time we made love," she admitted in a rush.

"What do you mean?"

"There was another time. Back in Los Angeles. I was glad you didn't remember. But now I can't stand keeping the truth from you. It feels wrong! Like I'm a liar, or something, so I just want to let you know and damn the consequences."

Her rush of words left him speechless for a moment.

"What in the world are you talking about?" he finally said on a half-laugh.

"There was a night—at your house—before you left?"

"I'm not getting this. Are you joking?"

"No." Cammie drew a breath, then launched further in her tale. "I came to see you one night, to talk about our parents. I wanted your dad to go see my mother because she was so unhappy. But you were drunk. Out of it. You were . . ."

"I was?" he prompted. She'd gotten his attention now, and he was stock-still, frozen, waiting for some kind of explanation. She was almost sorry she'd begun this confession.

"You were—in your bedroom. On your bed. You were, well, you were naked."

"When was this?"

"I don't know. Right before you left, I think. You kissed me and you were so—I don't know!—*vulnerable,* and I had a terrible crush on you since we were kids, and I just let it happen!"

"Let what happen?" he asked slowly, though she'd already told him. He just needed to hear it again, as if that would make it more real.

"We made love. I made love to you, and it just happened, and then you called me Gayle. I deserved it. I know I did, but I just ran out of there. When I thought about talking to you about it, it was too late. You'd gone, and I hoped you didn't remember, which you didn't."

Silence met this last pathetic confession, and Cammie waited in tense anticipation for God knew what. At length he asked incredulously, "It was you?"

She nodded, figuring he'd found some glimmer of remembrance somewhere deep in his memory.

"At my house."

"Yes."

"When I was drunk and you came over to—" He sucked in a sharp breath, jerking a bit.

"What?"

"That must have been the night I learned of Gayle's suicide," he said wonderingly. "I thought I dreamed it. I knew she was dead, but it felt like she was there and that we were making love." A second later, he demanded, "You're serious. This is for real."

"I wouldn't make it up."

He stared at her, and Cammie had no way of knowing what he was thinking. "Good God," he muttered after a moment, as if his brain couldn't put it together.

"I came to see you to reconnect, like I said, but a part of me wanted something more," she forced herself to add, though it was likely to kill her. "I've never quite forgotten that night," she added lightly. "It's haunted me, and when the opportunity arose to search you out, I guess I had some selfish motives of my own."

"The opportunity?"

For a heartbeat Cammie considered blurting out everything: Samuel, the script, her chance to co-star with him, the Connellys and Summer Solstice . . . But those reasons weren't truly important to her; they never had been, and they never would be. She'd wanted to see Ty again for herself, and it felt wonderful to get that off her chest, no matter what he thought of her now.

"The opportunity that your father gave me when he told me where you lived."

"So, you really didn't come at my father's request."

"No, I didn't."

Her voice rang with truth, and Ty apparently heard it, for he shook his head and said, "You amaze me. I was so certain there was an ulterior motive."

Licking her lips, Cammie murmured, "I told you. I just wanted to be with you again."

"Well, yes. But you never told me this!"

"Somehow, I didn't think I could just blurt it out. You weren't all that excited to have me here in the first place, and then to suddenly say, 'Hey, Ty. Remember the last time we saw each other? Was it good for you?' "

He broke up on that one, laughing out loud and easing

Cammie's tension. "I wouldn't have believed you anyway. But after making love . . ." He trailed off. "It just feels *right!*"

"Do you mean it?"

He nodded. "Why? What did you think I'd do?"

"I don't know!"

"Accuse you of sexual harassment, or worse?" He shook his head. "It sounds like I was a willing participant."

"Well, you were. Obviously." Cammie blushed.

"Obviously," he agreed, grinning.

"You just didn't have all the facts until now."

"Wow . . ."

"Yes, wow. I feel strange telling you this."

"No, I remember vaguely. So, that was you, huh?" he murmured, as if he couldn't get over it. A moment later, he shifted gears. "And then I just left. My God. And you've held this in all these years."

"I didn't know where you were," she said, "and even if I had, I'm not certain I would have told you. It's difficult telling you now."

"Cammie . . ."

Crushing her close, he dispelled any lingering doubts she possessed about telling him the truth about that night and her feelings. Because she couldn't help herself, Cammie whispered, "I love you. I know you don't want to hear it, but it's how I feel."

"Shhh . . ." He was overcome by emotion; she could sense it from his trembling body. "Let's just take one day at a time," he said, pulling her close, burying his face against the skin at her throat, his breath hot. "I've been marking time for ten years, and now things are happening so fast."

"I don't mean to scare you," she said.

"I'm not scared. I'm just not sure where to go from here."

"Neither am I," she admitted.

Moments passed. Long moments where both of them

were lost to their own thoughts. Finally, Ty said gruffly, "Come on, let's go to bed. We'll figure this out tomorrow."

"I'm with you."

Guiding her to her feet, Ty half led, half carried her downstairs and to the bedroom. At the bottom rung, Cammie stopped short.

"You were going to show me your screenplay," she remembered belatedly.

"Tomorrow," he assured her. "And we'll take care of this beard then, too. For tonight, though, we've got a lot of things to think about."

"All right."

Exhausted, Cammie tumbled into the bed beside him, curling up to his warmth and his incredible acceptance of her story. She'd expected far worse, just based on the fact that she hadn't been honest right from the start, but it appeared Ty had overlooked that transgression, even understood it. She thanked her lucky stars for such an unexpected gift.

His arm lay heavy and possessive around her shoulder; her cheek rested on his hair-dusted chest. For the first time since she'd embarked on this journey, she had hope for the future. If they could jump this hurdle, couldn't they find someway to make the separate paths they were traveling converge?

I love you, she thought again with pure joy, squeezing closer against his hard contours. He squeezed back, and, for now, that was enough.

CHAPTER THIRTEEN

Setting down the last page of the script, Cammie mouthed a silent "Wow" to the empty room. She straightened the papers and set them on the kitchen counter, full of awe and a certain amount of trepidation at the tale she'd just read.

Ty was a gifted writer. Perhaps he'd inherited his talent from his mother, Nanette. Maybe he'd even taken a class or two, although she suspected there hadn't been time in his pre-Bayrock life, and there was certainly no one around here whose forte was screenwriting.

The most likely answer was that he'd read enough screenplays to know the mechanics and was gifted and diligent enough to actually create the work. But even beyond the writing itself was the story—a tale that was definitely autobiographical in nature. If it wasn't Ty's own story—the tale of a man's stormy relationship with his famous father—then it was so close to the truth as to brush the bone.

And there's more . . .

Ty's words came back to her with a vengeance. If she

could believe everything in this screenplay, then Ty's relationship with Gayle was a lot more complicated than he'd let on. In the script, the protagonist's girlfriend was pregnant and committed suicide, but there was a question of paternity.

The hero's father was accused.

That can't be true. Samuel can't have been sexually involved with Ty's lover? That can't *be true!* Cammie thought desperately, afraid deep in the core of herself that it was. It explained so much.

But it was impossible! Ty must have taken some literary license here. She couldn't believe that Samuel had been sleeping with Gayle.

Yet . . . yet . . .

Cammie inhaled a long, slow breath, exhaling slowly until her lungs ached from the starvation of oxygen. Her next breath was a sharp gasp. Something, *something,* had sent Tyler tearing away from Hollywood. And it had to be something so terrible and vital that it would engender complete and total exile—something as awful as the scenario in this script.

Should she ask him about it? It was so highly personal that she didn't dare, yet he'd let her see his work even though he'd never intended it to be read by any eyes other than his own. That must mean something. Some kind of trust gained. After all, he'd been flat out furious when she'd glimpsed part of it that first time, so for him to hand over the whole manuscript now and let her read it must mean something monumental. In any event, it certainly was a huge step on the road to trust.

Which only made her feel worse about her own deception. Maybe she should tell him what his father had asked of her, what the Connellys had asked of her, what Paul and Susannah had asked of her . . . Maybe if she explained that *Rock Bottom* was merely a tool she'd never intended to use.

"Who am I kidding?" she asked aloud, her voice echoing off the rafters in the empty hollows of the cabin. Ty had gone to work out at his health club, but Cammie, though invited along, had chosen to stay at the cabin and read his screenplay. She suspected he was secretly glad she'd remained; he hadn't wanted to be in the room while she read his work. In fact, physically working out had probably just been a ploy to give her some privacy, which was fine with her because she wouldn't have been able to lose herself in the story if Ty had been sitting across from her with bated breath, waiting for her review.

But it was a marvelous story, and more than once she'd felt tears burn the backs of her eyelids. She could just imagine the power this story would have on film, yet Ty had sworn it would never see the light of day in Hollywood; it was far too personal.

Far too personal . . .

Cammie closed her eyes, switching her thoughts from the manuscript to her own recent memories, specifically the stretch of lovemaking she and Ty were enjoying. Her cheeks reddened at the memories and her lips curved into an embarrassed smile. For it *was* embarrassing! They devoured each other. It was like two lost souls, clutching at each other for salvation, finding deliverance in the glory of touching and discovering each other's bodies.

Sensations swamped her just at the memory. While his lips had trailed a hot line of fire from her mouth to the crest of her nipple, her hands kneaded the muscles of his back and her own mouth sought the curves of his ear, her tongue darting in and out until a low moan issued from his lips.

Somewhere, deep in the night, he'd groaned, "Cammie, what are you doing to me?"

"No more than you're doing to me."

Then this morning, while she lay sleeping and dreaming beside him, he'd awakened her in the most delicious way. Pulling back the covers, he'd exposed her smooth, honey-gold skin to his questing tongue. Warmth suffused her, spreading like molten lava through the most intimate parts of herself. Cammie's head lolled back and she opened herself totally to his skilled seduction.

He'd tried to hold off, to drag out the moment, but she'd slid her hands over his hips and straining manhood. Lightly, she brushed her nails across his most intimate parts, earning hard, burning kisses against her mouth, his tongue thrusting deep inside that moist cavern, foreshadowing the ultimate possession yet to come.

"Hurry!" she'd begged against his persuasive lips.

His answer was a half laugh, half groan of torment. Before falling asleep, she'd managed to slip on a pair of panties. Belatedly discovering them, Ty had growled in protest, yanking at the tiny scrap of fabric with urgent hands. Out of the corner of her eye, she saw the wisp of her panties tossed blithely through the air; her amusement at this vision quickly vanquished by a host of wild sensations as his hands explored every vital area. When his fingers parted her most secret femininity, she simply relaxed and gave herself up to his lovemaking. She gazed into his passionate eyes and drew his face to hers, kissing the slightly salty skin, rubbing her cheek against the beard that she'd grown so used to.

When he slipped inside her, she was wet and ready in a way that a distant part of her mind marveled at. How could it be this way? Loving him, wanting him, was all that was needed to turn her into a wild wanton. Her behavior both shocked and awed her; she hadn't known she would feel this way. She'd made herself believe that their one night together in Los Angeles was an aberration, a beautiful fantasy that could never be repeated.

But she was fast learning that loving Ty was an experience she could enjoy over and again without fear of losing her desire. She craved him again already, and it had been mere hours since their last fervent encounter.

The front door suddenly blew open. May sunshine flooded the cabin, brightening the honey-toned fir beams and planks, sending a soft enveloping breeze to warm the morning air. Outside, birds twittered and the smell of summer was just around the corner. Cammie, whose back was to the door, gathered the screenplay in her hands, climbed off the stool, then turned slowly in Ty's direction, her gaze still fastened on the pages of his work.

He stopped short upon entering.

"Ty, this is amazing work," she said. "It's very, very good. In fact it's . . ." She glanced up, then gasped in shock, the manuscript fluttering from her hands to the floor.

"What do you think?" Ty asked her.

The beard was gone. Shorn. Completely eradicated.

Cammie gulped. "Whoa."

"Whoa?"

Years had been lifted in the process. Ty looked younger, more vital, full of strength. He was, in fact, the image of himself at twenty-three. A decade had been shorn along with the beard, and just looking at him stirred strange feelings and memories inside Cammie. His gray eyes seemed bigger, deeper; his brows sterner. Dimples played beside his mouth, dimples lost in the thick fur of his facial hair. That simple beard had, in many ways, covered up the real Tyler Stovall.

He smiled, throwing her a flash of white teeth that melted her feminine soul. "I shaved at the club."

"No kidding. You look—amazing."

"I look too much like I did, don't I? The girl working reception stared at me as if I were a ghost."

Cammie could believe it. "Do you think she knew who you really are?"

"Maybe. No." He frowned. "I hope not. I should have told her some story she'd believe, but I just wanted to get back here and see you. I'll deal with her later."

"You'll have to come up with a whole new repertoire of lies. You look like Tyler Stovall now. Just like you were."

He eyed her soberly. "I'm glad."

Cammie's heart thumped. "Are you saying—you're ready to go back?"

"I'm just not as ready to hide," he answered, picking

his words as if he were just understanding the truth himself. Gazing at the untidy papers spread at Cammie's feet, her earlier words finally penetrated his brain. "You liked it," he said, and she knew he was pleased.

"I loved it."

Cammie bent to pick up the scattered pages. Ty came to help and, when the manuscript was gathered together, she handed it to him. Her fingers trembled a bit, which bugged her to no end. So he had a "new look." So he was more like the old Tyler. So what?

Crossing to the couch, she plopped down on it. Her own susceptibility was an embarrassing nuisance. She wished she could be more nonchalant where Ty was concerned; if she couldn't, she was destined for heartbreak.

Ty glanced down at the pages of the screenplay he'd dubbed with the working title, *Father Knows Worst*. He was glad he'd let Cammie read it. He'd needed a fresh eye, just for confirmation that his instincts were right about the story. Though he never intended to turn it into film, he felt vindicated somehow, just knowing that someone recognized its worth.

And that someone was Cammie.

Sliding a sideways glance in her direction, Ty was overwhelmed anew at what she did to him. She'd changed into the usual jeans and a greenish-blue corduroy shirt, a shade that matched her eyes. No proof against the fetching picture she made, Ty reached her in two strides, then stood gazing down at her, suddenly humbled by the tender feelings she engendered in his heart. Her hair tumbled in red-streaked waves across her shoulders, and her eyes were still heavy from lack of sleep, a condition he was totally to blame for. As he looked down at her, her lips parted, moist and full and so enticing that Ty groaned and flung himself on the couch beside her.

"What's the matter?" she asked, alarmed.

"Nothing."

There was something so pure about her that he couldn't get over it. It wasn't real; he knew that. It was some silly picture he placed over the truth to wipe away all the tawdriness he'd known in the area of love.

Love . . . He shuddered at the idea, because he wasn't sure he believed in it beyond the love of a mother for her child. Okay, fathers loved their children, too. Some fathers. But romantic love had no place in his beliefs. Most cultures, as it turned out, agreed with this philosophy. Arranged marriages were the norm, where parents were supposed to know best in these matters. Only in western society was the idea of an arranged marriage abhorrent.

Well, I would never trust my father to pick out a wife for me! he had to admit to himself. *That would be a one way ticket to divorce-ville!*

Still, it didn't mean that there existed, between a man and a woman, a true romantic spirit that could last and endure beyond the physical. And he was too old to hope for its existence now . . . . wasn't he?

Just because you're attracted to her beyond all sense doesn't mean you are in love with her. You know better.

With that thought squarely in mind, Ty bounded to his feet again, still hanging on to the pages of his screenplay while Cammie looked at him as if he'd lost his mind.

"I'm glad you like it," he told her gruffly.

"I don't expect you to sell it to Hollywood," she said. "It was too—telling."

"Was it?" he asked rhetorically, for he knew fully what she meant.

"Yes," she answered, and he glanced over at her again. His senses stirred again in spite of himself. She had the most outstanding effect on him!

"It got to me," she added. "I wanted to break down and bawl like a baby a time or two." She hesitated, grimacing before pointing out the obvious. "It would be amazing on film."

"No." He was adamant.

"Is it true? I mean, *all* of it?"

Her eyes were filled with uncertainty; she didn't want to pry. Ty gnashed his teeth together, almost afraid to admit to such terrible truths. With an effort, he nodded curtly, and cringed when Cammie swept in a sharp breath of disbelief.

"Disgusting, isn't it?" he declared bitterly.

"Sad," she answered gently. "Your father doesn't know how to act like one, that's all."

"Is that some kind of excuse?"

"Not at all. It's just that—there's something unformed about a person who's in such desperate competition with his own son."

He stared at her. She was uttering thoughts he'd believed to be only his own. Glancing at the sheaves of papers that made up *Father Knows Worst,* he asked, "You picked that up from this?"

"I never thought about it before, but now I believe, well, that your father went out of his way to thwart you. He professed to be so proud of you, but it was really just envy."

Ty felt slightly dazed. She'd echoed vague thoughts he'd never quite put into words. Thoughts that had found their way into his screenplay through the action he described between himself and Samuel. Oh, he'd changed the names, unable to write his and his father's names on the printed page. It had seemed safer, somehow, to keep it in the abstract even while he was laying it down, step by step, just as it had occurred in life.

"You know what I'm going to say next, don't you?" Cammie asked, her gaze soft and tender.

"Don't . . ."

"You should send this to a producer, or a production company."

"No."

"It's a beautiful story with a poignant ending."

"Beautiful!" he rasped, shocked.

"Ty, it's a story of triumph," Cammie said. "Look at it objectively. The hero's a man who ends up in the most unlikely of places—a small, cowboy town in the Northwest where the seamy tawdriness and trite ugliness of an unhappy childhood in the spotlight is replaced by a love for simplicity. And that's where he finds his true self."

He shook his head and argued, "It's a story of a powerful father who despises his own offspring while he continues to populate the earth with them as a means to prove his own immortality!"

"That, too," she agreed. "But it's so much more, and you know it."

Did he? Tyler, for all his self-confidence, had little faith in his ability to express himself through screenwriting. Yes, he'd picked up a few subliminal tips from his mother when he was a child, and yes, she'd answered some knotty problems from him when he'd queried her on the phone while he'd written the thing. But he hadn't believed it was any good. Not really. Because it was too personal and because just reading it over still had the power to inflame his sense of injustice and helplessness where his father was concerned.

There was no way he could allow it to be filmed.

"You don't have to make that decision today," Cammie said. "I just want you to know that it's really a worthwhile effort. It's loaded with the kind of truth that hits you in the gut. And let's face it, that's what everybody's looking for."

"I could never put my life out there like that—exposed for everyone to see." He snorted derisively. "These people who write those tell-all books are gluttons for punishment! The whole world thinks they know you. Everybody's an expert. I did this for a sense of closure, that's all."

Cammie nodded. "I couldn't bare my soul for public viewing, either. But that doesn't make this any less powerful. That's all I'm saying." The corners of her mouth lifted humorously. "And if this ever saw the light of day, your father would have a coronary!"

"That's the first argument you've made that I'm willing to listen to!" Ty declared with a snort.

"I know you left because of Gayle's faithlessness," Cammie said. "Her suicide was terrible and shocking, and destroying her own child . . ." Cammie shook her head. "It's unconscionable. But finding out she'd slept with your father was soul-destroying," she added softly. "I know that's what sent you here, to Bayrock."

"I never loved her." His voice sounded strange to his own ears.

"I know. It's all in there." She inclined her head toward the screenplay.

"She said she wanted me. She said a lot of things that I believed, and when she told me she was pregnant, I told her I'd pay for the baby."

"Pay?" Cammie questioned.

"For its upkeep. Its cost. I didn't want to marry her, and she didn't want to marry me, either." He smiled without humor. "At least, I wasn't her first choice. I wasn't as established as my father."

"You don't know what she was thinking," Cammie murmured, hurting for him.

"I know she was pregnant, and I know she was having an affair with Samuel. Or, at least I learned that the hard way. I should have guessed, though. She was so . . . difficult, toward the end." He ran his hands through his hair and closed his eyes, thinking back. "Any woman my father was associated with was a whore, according to Gayle. I didn't understand it at the time, but I think now she saw herself more with him than with me."

Cammie nodded. The screenplay hinted at everything Ty now corroborated.

"But she didn't want my money. She was upset. Who knows what would have happened if things had been different. But, according to dear old Dad, the baby was his."

"Was it?"

"I don't know. It was such a mess, and I was so angry and sick and fed up. My father was, of course, married and, unlucky for her, currently not interested in another divorce. She should have just stuck around," he muttered bitterly. "He would have got there in time, I'm sure."

"Maybe she loved you. Maybe Sam was just a tool, a way to make you want her more."

"Oh, no." Ty's mouth curved bitterly. "She had me first. I told her I'd stick by her. But I was merely the stepping-stone, although I didn't know that for a fact until after her death. She wanted my father."

"Maybe."

"She wanted the prestige of being Samuel Stovall's wife—like so many others before her."

Cammie glanced down at her nails. "Like my mother, you mean?"

Ty sighed. "No. You were right, and I was wrong. Your mother really loved him. At the time I just didn't want to face how selfish and awful my father was. It was easier to blame your mother."

Cammie gazed up at him with love. "Thank you for that. I know it doesn't seem like much, but I needed to hear it."

"I was such a bastard," he said, grimacing.

"You weren't. You were just protecting Samuel, and in a way, that's admirable."

"Completely back-assward and stupid. But admirable."

Cammie smiled. "That's not what I meant."

"Yes, it is. And I deserve it. It's okay."

They smiled at each other with renewed tenderness, crossing a huge gulf that had once seemed unpassable.

"Whew!" Cammie declared. "Look how far we've come in so short a time. I feel like all these terrible little issues that were digging at me are being put to rest, one at a time. I'm so glad."

"Me, too," Ty agreed, and it was as if those same nagging issues had been resolved for him, too. He felt stronger. Tougher. Less influenced by his previous life which had haunted him for so long.

"You know," he said thoughtfully, "I'm tired of all this wallowing in the past. Let's get out of here. Do something different."

Her brows lifted delicately. "Like what?"

"A boat ride. I know a guy who'll rent me one anytime I like. Let me take you for a tour around the bay. What do you say?"

"Now?"

"Sure. Why not?"

Cammie glanced outside. Sunshine slanted from the sky in visible rays, cutting through grayish clouds that were rapidly scurrying away. It was warm, but the weather was iffy, as if it couldn't quite decide whether to rage on toward summer or hang on to the last vestiges of a cold spring. The ubiquitous breeze flitted through the green leaves of a stand of nearby birches, reminding her that it could be raw as December up here, even in late May.

But Ty was already heading downstairs. He grabbed a red-and-black-checked, lumberman's-type flannel shirt from a peg in the hall.

Cammie slipped past him into the bedroom and dug through her small bag. She needed something warmer. Ty appeared behind her, and as she pulled out a pair of black leggings, she said doubtfully, "Maybe I could wear these under my jeans."

"I've got a pair of sweats you could put over those," he suggested.

Cammie twisted to look at him and caught him stuffing the tails of his shirt into his jeans.

"What?" he asked to her look.

"There's something sexy about a man in jeans and a flannel shirt." Her eyes teased him. She was loving this new freedom to say how she felt.

"Yeah?"

"Yeah," she agreed, then squealed in surprise when his arms suddenly surrounded her and he dragged her to the bed. "Excuse me, sir," she said, her hair tumbling richly around her face, a crown of reddish-brown silk. "What thoughts cross your mind?"

"I think you know."

"Are they of an indecent nature?"

"You'd better believe it," he growled against her neck,

and Cammie shrieked and giggled and pretended to fight, finally giving in with a satisfied sigh as her arms enfolded him.

"Boat ride, schmoat ride," she murmured.

"It can wait . . ." was Ty's muffled response, his mouth covering her uplifted lips.

An hour and a half later, they stood on the pier near the Goosedown Inn and listened to instructions from Earl, a garrulous old fellow who was extremely leery about lending out his boat. Ty may have rented from him previously, but either he'd had a lapse of memory, or this was a regular routine with him. Either way, he eyed Cammie as if it were somehow her fault that he was in this position.

"*Libby Lou's* kinda temperamental sometimes," Earl said, patting the hull and squinching up his face to gaze at the horizon. "You get caught out there, you gotta baby her along."

"The engine?" Ty questioned.

"Nah. Just the connection, y'know? Don't get overanxious and flood her. Treat her like a lady." He gave a sideways glance to Cammie. "You know how to do that, right? Or, do I gotta help you there, too?" He chuckled as if he'd told the funniest joke on record.

Ty smiled and shook Earl's gnarled hand. The glance he sent Cammie said he'd been through this scenario several times before. For her part, Cammie had serious doubts about the seaworthiness of the *Libby Lou,* but Ty had assured her, the small motor boat had performed perfectly every time he'd taken it out. Earl never could quite remember who Ty was, and only when Ty reminded him that Corky from Rodeo Bob's had introduced them did Earl seem to gather an inkling. Of course, Ty certainly looked different without the beard, but Cammie was convinced this exchange would have taken place no matter what his appearance was.

But it didn't matter anyway, for as soon as Ty started

talking dollars and cents, Earl babbled on about what the *Libby Lou* could, and couldn't, do.

"I've thought about buying a boat of my own," Ty told Cammie as he helped her step across the gunwale. "But I don't know if I want a motor boat or a sailboat." He inhaled deeply, sighing as Cammie clasped his hand and jumped into the boat beside him. "Of course, that's if I intended to stick around here, and that looks like it's in jeopardy as it is."

"How do people manage to be fugitives?" Cammie asked as Ty took the wheel and she cuddled her red peacoat around her in the passenger seat. Ty's sweat pants were practically falling off her, but she didn't care. They were warm and they were his, and that was good enough for her.

"It's a hell of a job," Ty muttered. Gently, he twisted the ignition key and the *Libby Lou* fired up as if she'd been just waiting for the right man.

Earl waved them away and headed back up the pier to his small marina and boat shop. He was one of the colorful locals, and Cammie realized Ty was more tied into this community than she'd first guessed. Maybe he didn't realize how much himself, although it was obvious he dreaded the idea of pulling up stakes and finding a new place to hide.

But maybe that wasn't really necessary anymore. Ty had made some peace with himself. He'd written his screenplay as a catharsis, and she believed it had worked. Maybe he wasn't ready for all the hoopla of Hollywood, but his existence might not have to be such a secret any longer. Maybe he could live happily somewhere, even if the world knew where he was and what he was doing.

She knew his reappearance on the planet would create a minor sensation; his sudden flight ten years earlier had set up that scenario. But after the initial fuss, wouldn't he be left alone? Or was that just wishful thinking on her part?

"Wouldn't you like the 'fugitive' part of your life to be

over with?" she asked, revealing her thoughts, as Ty eased the *Libby Lou* from her berth.

He gave her a look and shrugged. They'd been over it and over it. Something would have to change before any serious decisions were made about the future, and when that happened, their idyllic time together would be over.

With expert hands, Ty guided the small boat into deeper waters, and soon they were speeding away from Bayrock and toward the Washington State shore. The stiff breeze ruffled the water into small, frothy whitecaps, but overhead the sky had turned a lovely dusky blue instead of the gray that had dogged the area since her arrival.

"Do you know why the sky is blue?" she asked, huddling inside her jacket.

Ty glanced her way. The wind created from their speed tossed his hair away from his forehead and made him seem even more wild and free. "Okay, I'll bite. Why?"

"This isn't a joke. It's just a little fact I learned. Light travels at different speeds through different atmospheres. Sunlight heads to earth through space which is a vacuum and therefore light travels faster through space than our atmosphere. When it hits our atmosphere—our air—it has to slow down."

"Okay." Ty was enjoying this. "I'm with you so far."

"When it slows down, it bends. The angle it bends is relative to the speed that it slows down."

"Go on."

"Now, think of a prism. The bend of light, or refraction, through a prism creates a whole spectrum of color. But the speed of sunlight is such that when it hits our atmosphere it bends at short, or blue, wavelengths. And that's why the sky is blue.

"However," Cammie continued, "when the sun is setting, the angle of refraction is different. The wavelengths grow longer and on a clear night—"

"We see reds, oranges, and pinks!" Ty finished, catching on.

"Very good, sir."

"Has anyone told you that you're a smart girl, Cammie Pendleton?"

"Woman," she corrected. "I'm a smart woman. And, it's Cammie Merrill these days, Mr. Jerry Mercer."

"So I read in the credits."

"You may just turn into a huge fan of *Cherry Blossom Lane,*" she said blithely. "It has quite an audience you know."

"Except that my favorite character just suffered an early demise."

"Dead, in the world of soap opera, isn't really dead."

"I'll keep that in mind."

Cammie's eyes crinkled at the corners. She enjoyed being with him so much, it was totally insane. She refused to think about the future and the departure that had to come. These moments were too precious to squander by worrying about the future.

And it felt great to skim across the bay as if to outrace a pack of wolves at their heels. It just felt great to be with Ty.

As they closed in on the Washington shore, Ty pulled back on the accelerator. They glanced across at the picturesque town in their sights. "We could dock and take a look around," he suggested.

"I like it right where I am."

He reached a hand out and caressed her knee in a familiar fashion that nevertheless sent a thrill down Cammie's spine. "Me, too," he admitted.

As the afternoon wore on, they cruised around the bay, gazing at the scenery from one vantage point to another. The sky slowly darkened. Later, Cammie couldn't remember what they'd discussed. It didn't matter. It was all just mundane conversation meant to break the silence. The real communication was in the looks they sent each other, the cool, silky feel of the breeze, the beat of their hearts, and the musky scent of bay water. Finally, when they both felt they'd exhausted their tour, Ty guided the *Libby Lou* back to shore.

As they were tying up, Ty said, "There's something I want to talk about with you."

"Oh?"

"It's been kind of bothering me."

"Shoot," Cammie said, grabbing on to his hand for support as she stepped across the gunwale to the pier.

But Earl appeared at that moment and wanted to hear all about how his lady fair, the *Libby Lou,* had handled. Ty gave him a running account of the boat's engine and how she dipped and yawed and turned and responded to the point that Cammie lost interest. While they talked at length, she turned her face in the direction of the Goosedown Inn and the soft yellow light glowing from its windows. Her teeth began chattering as if on command, and she shot a look at Ty, seeking to catch his attention.

His gaze shifted briefly her way. Signaling that she was going inside the inn, Cammie caught his slight nod before she hurried to warmth and security. Surprisingly, the place was hopping, and she learned from the hostess of the restaurant that a tour group had chosen to make a side trip to Bayrock on their way from Vancouver, British Columbia, to Seattle. The Goosedown Inn was full to the gills.

"What's the story?" Ty asked, coming in to stand beside her. He smelled of fresh air and the sea, and she impulsively slipped her arm through his and burrowed close to his side.

Her move surprised him, but he seemed pleased enough. "Tourists," Cammie explained.

"Aaahh . . ."

"What did you want to talk to me about?"

"Mmmm. It can wait till later." He looked thoughtful. "How would you like to go to Rodeo Bob's?"

"And meet Corky?" Cammie grinned, then her smile practically fell off her face. "And Missy . . ."

Ty chuckled, then threw back his head and laughed, drawing collective looks from the curious tourists who were still being seated. Realizing he was dragging undue attention to them both, Ty hustled Cammie out of the inn and down the street toward his house.

"I'm not interested in Missy. You know that, don't you?"

"Yes."

"Then, come on. We'll talk later. Right now we're going for some western cuisine at its most—western."

"What does that mean?"

"Not to expect a gourmet meal," he said humorously as he led the way to his Jeep.

CHAPTER FOURTEEN

Rodeo Bob's wasn't much to look at: a long, rectangular, red-shingled building with a thick, shake roof and only a tiny grouping of windows along one short end. Ty led the way into an anteroom, then held open saloon doors which gave way to the main restaurant and bar. A dance floor took up the whole of one end, and a *Cheers*-type bar divided the barnlike space in half. The floors were plank board and covered in a thin coating of something like sawdust. Upon closer inspection, Cammie realized it was peanut shells, pulverized beneath thousands of boots.

"Wednesday night is peanut night," Ty explained. "Free peanuts, as much as you'd like, with an order of beer or soft drinks."

Cammie smiled. "Interesting."

"Hey, this is slumming at its finest."

'I'm not being a snob. I like peanuts."

'Good. Peanut night was my idea . . ."

She would have liked to retort that she'd understood he was the landlord, not part owner of the business, but Ty had spied a man with curly gray hair in the "older men's" horseshoe, who was currently involved in a rather heated discussion with someone sitting at the bar.

"Hey!" Ty yelled, oblivious to the mood of the discussion, which was on the verge of openly hostile.

The man behind the bar looked up. His frown cleared upon spying Ty. "Hey, buddy!" he boomed out.

"Corky, this is Cammie," Ty introduced. "Cammie . . . Corky."

She shook hands with Rodeo Bob's owner/manager, receiving a strong, enthusiastic clasp and a bright grin. "Maybe you can knock some sense into Joey, there. The bastard thinks I owe him a free drink."

"What for?" Ty asked, glancing at Joey.

Joey was fifty if he was a day, and his expression was surly. "He shortchanged me last time," was his bitten-off reply.

Ty glanced to Corky for confirmation.

"Yeah?" Corky demanded of Joey. "And before that, you slipped on my front mat and wrenched your knee. Tried to sue me for all I'm worth. And before that, you complained that one of my glasses was chipped and you cut your lip. I've been giving you free drinks for years, pal. And you know what? I'm through!"

Joey glared at him.

"You must be really unlucky, pal," Ty pointed out reasonably.

"You can both go to hell!" Joey growled, sliding his glass down the bar with enough force to send it over the bar's rim and into the lap of another patron.

"Hey!" the customer yelled, jumping up from his stool, fists at the ready.

Joey pretended to be unaware as he strode quickly through the saloon doors, slamming them as hard as he could so they flew wildly in the wake of his departure, as if in a state of agitation themselves.

"Never a dull moment," Corky muttered, turning to the hapless customer who was staring down at his beer-soaked jeans. "Hey, pal, how about a pitcher on the house? Give the man a pitcher of whatever he's drinking, Carl. He's the one who deserves a free drink!"

Carl, helping at the bar, set down a pitcher of a wheat beer in front of him. Gratefully, the beer-soaked patron sat back down on his bar stool and poured himself a frothy mugful.

Appeasement all around.

Ty surveyed the melee with amusement. "So, what do you think?" he whispered in Cammie's ear. "A far cry from some of those chichi Hollywood hot spots."

"I wouldn't be all that excited about getting a beer tossed in my lap," she admitted. "But, hey, when in Rome . . ."

"It's normally not quite so 'Wild West' here, but there are sometimes guys like Joey, who're more interested in chiseling than getting along, everywhere."

They sat down at a small table to one side of the bar. Corky came over and wisecracked with Ty awhile. They enjoyed a rapport that Cammie would have described as a "guy thing." It pleased her for reasons she couldn't quite analyze, though she suspected it had something to do with the fact that her ex had alienated most people, men and women alike, with hardly any effort at all. Paul's selfishness just couldn't be hidden for long, and only Cammie, for all the wrong reasons, had fallen for it.

"You've gone all quiet on me," Ty observed as Corky brought them a pitcher of the same burnished-gold wheat beer that the unfortunate man at the bar had ordered.

"I was just thinking."

"About what?"

"Paul," she sighed, not really all that eager to discuss her ex.

"Mmmmm." Ty didn't sound all that eager, either.

"He didn't really make friends. He wouldn't know how to joke around like you and Corky do."

"Corky's a good guy," Ty said, a smile touching the corners of his mouth. "He never asks too many questions. Face value is all he needs."

"How did you meet?"

Ty poured them each a mug, then took a long draught of the amber fluid. Setting his glass down, he said reflectively, "Corky had a little beer spot tucked back near the waterfront. It was kind of raucous and loud. Everybody wanted it moved. Part of the problem was, it was just too small. I spent a lot of hours there when I first arrived in Bayrock. Too many." He gave her a swift look, and she could well imagine Ty drowning himself in brewskies on a stool at the end of the bar. "I told Corky he needed to move, but there wasn't really anywhere to go unless he built something new. That wasn't in the cards money-wise, so I contracted this building and Corky moved in."

"That's the kind of real estate you're in? New construction?"

"New construction, renovation, raw land . . ." He shrugged. I've gotten involved in all phases. It's something to do."

"What are you going to do now?" she couldn't help asking.

"You mean since you found me?"

"Well, yes . . . I guess so."

Ty's lashes swept downward, and when he looked up again, his gaze was sober and intent. "I don't want you to leave."

Gratified, Cammie admitted, "I don't want to leave."

"Then don't," he said urgently. "Stay here with me."

The offer was darned near irresistible. "How? What would I do?"

"You don't have to do anything."

"Ty—"

"Just share my life. Be a part of it. If that's selfish, I don't care. It's what I want. The question is: is it what you want?"

Cammie had no answer for him. Her head felt muddled and thick, and some strange, exuberant part of herself was joyously awakening and saying, "Yes, yes, yes!" Still, she wasn't a complete romantic. She knew better than to wrap up all her hopes and desires in someone else's dreams. "You wanted to talk to me about something earlier," she reminded him, needing to change the subject. "Was it something else?"

Ty looked as if he would like to keep on pushing the issue most important to him. But he nodded and took a breath. "Well, yeah . . . I've got a few questions about us. About you, actually," he amended.

"Me?"

"Cammie, we haven't used birth control that I'm aware of. You said it doesn't matter, that it's taken care of. But I'd like to know . . ."

She couldn't blame him. He needed an answer. She sure as heck would want one if the situation were reversed. But she couldn't do it. The idea of blurting out her most dire problem drove a cold spike through her heart. "It doesn't matter," she sidestepped hurriedly.

"Why doesn't it matter?" he asked, watching her carefully, almost suspiciously to Cammie's way of thinking.

For all her ability to talk honestly on most issues, she just couldn't discuss her barrenness. It was too awful, too raw. She was too fragile. "I can't . . ." she mumbled, suddenly feeling as if the room were too tight, the air thick and choking.

"Cammie." Ty reached across the table to clasp her cold hands between his comforting palms. "You've got to tell me. I don't want any children. As far as I can see, we've been playing with fire, and since I have no intention of going celibate with you around, I'd like to be assured that we're safe."

"We're safe," she repeated flatly.

"Not good enough."

"I can't have children," she whispered.

"Can't?" He leaned closer, trying to meet her gaze, but Cammie's eyes had shifted and she gazed blankly across the room. It was the glassy stare of the grief-stricken. The hopeless. For Cammie, the noise in the surrounding room seemed to meld into one, long distant roar, and to her horror, misery welled up inside her, filling her chest, prickling her eyes until tiny tears collected on her lashes.

"Cammie?"

Jerking her hands free of his, she suddenly stumbled to her feet, then stood shaking a moment, fighting for control. But it was a losing battle. Suffocating, she ran blindly through the saloon doors, pushing herself through to the outside and the brilliance of a moon-bright May night.

Sounds escaped her lips. Choking mews of pain. She hesitated, turning blindly from side to side. There was nowhere to go. Her lungs ached for air. She couldn't breathe. The noises issuing from her throat were pathetic gasps of misery.

She could hear Ty calling after her. Stumbling, Cammie ran headlong for the road, blinded to everything but her own inner torment. For a normally levelheaded individual, she reacted with pure, primal intensity, and only when she was out of breath, chest heaving, head spinning, stomach churning dangerously, did she stop running and lean over to balance her hands on her knees. Her hair curtained her face, which was just as well, for silent tears streamed over her cheekbones to collect on her chin and drip to the ground.

Ty was beside her in an instant. His palms gently grasped her trembling shoulders and he rotated her to face him. "I'm sorry," he said in a tone both concerned and baffled.

"It's—not—you," she gasped out.

"I didn't mean to bring up something so painful to you."

"No, no, it's all right."

"No, it's not." Lifting up her chin with one finger, he gazed into her tear-drenched eyes. "Come on. Let's go home . . ."

Home, Cammie thought with a wrench. "I—can't."

"Yes, you can." He collected her in his strong arms and led her to the Jeep, tucking her inside. She stayed in the exact position he left her, a limp rag doll with no will of its own.

* * *

Fifteen minutes later, she crossed the threshold into Ty's now familiar cabin on unsteady legs. *Home,* she thought again. A few weeks earlier, she hadn't known this place existed, now he'd called it *home* and it made Cammie's heart ache with a pain so intense she wanted to cry out.

It wasn't her home. It could never be her home. She had a life waiting for her somewhere else, and she couldn't just give it all up for Ty. She couldn't. But her love for him made her crazy. She was acting like a madwoman—all irrational emotion and no sense. Her reason had deserted her, and she felt so vulnerable that it scared her to absolute silence.

Ty led her unresistingly to the couch, and when she was settled, he touched a flame to the newspaper and firewood he'd stacked earlier in the grate. While he returned to the kitchen, she waited in a kind of frozen stupor, paralyzed by the decisions she had to make. Ty set a kettle on the stove, and when it was whistling like a tiny toy train, he poured her a cup of tea, then pressed her numb hands around the hot mug.

"I'm sorry," he apologized again, watching her take a first, tentative sip.

"It's not your fault." Her voice was a near whisper.

"I touched a sensitive nerve." When she didn't respond, he added softly, "A secret sorrow."

Cammie glanced away. If he kept this up, she'd be bawling again for sure!

"You can't have children. It hurts, and I'm an insensitive jerk because, since I don't want any, it's hard for me to see."

"Don't you really want any?" She gazed at him, her eyes naked with pain and incomprehension.

Ty had to suck in a swift breath against her appeal. He wanted to gather her in his arms and soothe her fears. But he knew it was wrong for him to lie. "No," he admitted a bit regretfully.

"Never?"

"After my father . . . after Gayle . . ." Ty searched for the right words but they eluded him. "It's not something I want, that's all."

"It's everything I want!" she admitted. "Someday." Her voice broke despite her efforts to be brave. "But I can't have it, and I know that. It's okay, most of the time. It really is."

"Cammie . . ."

"Don't feel too sorry for me. You'll only make it worse."

Ty touched her trembling chin with his thumb. "If I could, I'd fix things for you, but since I can't . . ." He hesitated a moment before gently pointing out, "Maybe we're perfect for each other. I don't want any, and you can't have any."

Cammie blinked and lifted a hand to her brow, feeling as if she were in a fog. The next moment, she dropped her arm, the effort too much.

"My father sired about a dozen kids, give or take a few, legitimate and otherwise," Ty went on with a trace of bitterness. "His twisted need to form a dynasty."

"You would have helped Gayle raise your child," she reminded him.

"Monetarily speaking." He inclined his head. "I do have some responsible tendencies, you know."

"No, it's more than that. You would have helped even if you'd learned later about Sam," she said on a note of discovery. "Even if the child were his."

"I wouldn't have had to. Dear old Dad would have stepped up to the plate." Rotating his shoulders to relieve tension, he added, "But Gayle realized she wouldn't get what she wanted, so she decided on a permanent way out."

"Or maybe she was just so terribly miserable," Cammie suggested, "that it seemed like the only solution."

Ty's mouth turned down at the corners. "At the time, it just was too much. I was shocked and then I was angry, and then when I found out about her and *Dad* . . ."

"It seems like a shame to me that you're letting *that*

decide whether you have children of your own," Cammie said softly, after a long, tense moment. "It's like some kind of punishment, and I don't think you deserve it."

"It's not just Gayle. Samuel played his part."

"But you're not anything like Samuel."

He didn't answer that. Instead, he shook his head, as if sweeping the cobwebs out of his brain. "I almost called my father the other night," he reflected moodily. "I *did* call him, actually, but when I heard his voice . . ." He drew a breath, his lips twisting. "Maybe I'll need another ten years before I don't care anymore."

"You might be too hard on him," she surprised herself by saying.

"Are you kidding? After what you know he's like?"

"People change," she murmured, feeling too weak to fight, but unwilling to let Ty's anger toward Sam control all his feelings, even down to fathering his own child.

"Sam's always the same," Ty assured her.

"How do you know? You haven't talked to him in ten years."

"Are you defending him?"

She almost laughed. "Are you kidding? He's not my favorite person by a long shot. But he's your father, say what you will. Someday, you'll have to face that."

Ty didn't argue with her further. Instead, he asked, "How are you feeling now?"

"Better," she admitted, sipping the tea gratefully.

He nodded, then said, picking his words carefully, "I don't mean to sound callous. Just because having a child's not right for me, doesn't mean everyone should feel that way. Because you want it so much, I wish you could have a baby."

His tender tone scraped raw nerves and new tears threatened. Cammie cleared her throat and tried to fight them back. "I'm okay."

"It doesn't matter to me that you can't conceive. Maybe it's fate. Like I said before, maybe we're meant for each other." He heard how that sounded, and he shook his head, raking hands through his hair in a gesture she recognized as a sign of supreme emotion. "Cammie, I want you in my life."

Cammie's lips parted to refute his erroneous belief that she couldn't conceive; that wasn't the problem. But then the rest of his words sank into her brain. *I want you in my life.* This was a huge admission for Ty, as close to a declaration of love as he'd ever come. Hope soared inside her, only to be shoved back down by reality: she couldn't stay here in Bayrock.

"What is it?" he asked to her swiftly changing expressions.

"I have to go back."

"Why?"

"I'm not cut out to be a hermit."

"It's not all that hermitlike here," he pointed out. "And we would have each other."

"You know it's not right, Ty," she said achingly. "You're asking me to give up everything that's important to me, except for you."

"It wouldn't be forever." The words sounded wrenched from somewhere deep inside him.

"How long?" she queried, but he couldn't answer her. "Ty, I'm not asking you to return with me. I know you're not ready, and that you might never be ready. But I've got a life I can't just drop out of."

His gray eyes bore deeply into her blue ones. "How soon?"

"What?"

"How soon before you leave?"

She swallowed. "Soon." She had to get back. If nothing else, she had to shut off the "let's get Tyler Stovall to star in our film" machine. She had to protect him from the clamoring producers and opportunists and fans who would kill his soul in their need to have a piece of him.

He sighed in reluctant acceptance, joining her on the sofa. Cammie drew him near, kissing his face with a hundred soft touches of her lips, caressing his back and arms and hips, and holding him close. Ty's fingers unbuttoned her blouse. Lovingly, he reached inside her bra and softly kneaded her breasts until the nipples were straining hard against his palms.

After that, there was an urgency neither could deny. They ripped off their remaining clothes, kissing and straining and desiring a union that was both tender and shattering. In the aftermath of their fiery passion, Cammie held his cheek to her breast and considered telling him about *Rock Bottom.* He needed to be warned. He needed to know that others would follow after her. She could try to divert and delay them, but she suspected it would all be futile in the end. He hated the Hollywood life. He shouldn't be dragged back there for the selfish purposes of others, herself included. He should be left to make his own decisions.

"Ty . . . ?"

"Mmmm," he murmured, his tongue licking a lazy circle on her breast.

Cammie shivered and smiled. "Stop that. I need to be serious a minute."

"Go right ahead."

"Oh, sure. Like I can concentrate with you tasting me!"

"I'm sure you could. You're just not trying hard enough. Besides, you taste good."

"Ty!"

"All right, all right," he grumbled good-naturedly.

"Let's get dressed and then I'll tell you all about it."

"It?" he questioned, picking up the serious vibes.

"It," she agreed, struggling upward as Ty finally reached for his discarded jeans and shirt.

Ten minutes later, Cammie was finger-combing her hair and standing in front of the fire. She wore jeans and a cream-colored sweatshirt. Her feet were bare, her nails a pale peach color, and Ty had all he could do just to keep his mind on her voice because the overall picture was so sexy and alluring.

"I haven't been completely honest with you," she said, linking her fingers together in a thoroughly fetching way. She reminded him of a schoolgirl again, and yet her curvaceous body and independent soul were those of a total woman.

He realized, with a sudden shock, that he loved her. Or, at least he felt something he'd never felt before. Love? He hadn't believed he could feel that emotion, but this new sensation, this pulse-pounding, light-headed, silly, rapturous joy that made him want to alternately sing at the top of his lungs and whisper softly in her ear was entirely new.

It was a revelation that sent his brain spinning, and he realized after a couple of moments that he hadn't heard a word she'd said.

"What?" he asked dumbly.

"Ty!" she declared in exasperation.

"Sorry. I lost track for a minute. What did you say?"

Her lips pressed together, as if she were struggling to contain some overwhelming emotion. "I'm making a confession here," she said doggedly.

"Sweetheart, didn't you hear me?" he asked tenderly. "I don't care that you can't have children. I'm not going to change my mind. I think a bigger problem is where we're going to live, don't you?"

That caught her attention. "What?"

"All right, you can't stay here, I don't blame you. It's not exactly a bustling metropolis. We can move. And I know you want a career in television or film. That's—not impossible, I guess. I don't really want to go back to L.A., but maybe we could try New York. An apartment in the city, and then a place upstate. Maybe a farm. I don't know."

He was surprised at the words passing his own lips. A few days, even a few hours earlier, thoughts of leaving Bayrock were misty half-formed ideas floating in the far corners of his brain. But for Cammie, for a chance at love, he would do it. He would do damn near anything.

"Are you kidding?" She was stunned, disbelieving.

"No."

It was the God's honest truth. And it was a small sacrifice, he realized, recognizing how selfish he'd been to expect her to join him in his self-imposed exile. And foolish, too. Pointless. It was time to face the music, at least at some level, and he knew he could do it with Cammie.

"Ty," she whispered, completely undone by his aboutface.

"Don't make it so hard," he urged gently. He crossed the small space that separated them, waiting until her hopeful eyes turned up to meet his. "I can compromise, if I have to. I don't want to lose you."

"Ty!"

She flung herself into his arms. Ty grinned, kissing her warm neck, feeling freer and younger than he had in years. He was an idiot. A romantic, lovesick fool.

"Oh, Ty, are you sure?" she asked tentatively.

"Completely."

"You won't—you won't change your mind?"

"No," he answered gently.

Bzzzzzzz!

The buzzer at the door made them both start. They stared at the door in unison, as if it were the intruder itself. Cammie was lost in ecstasy. She didn't care who was trying to break into this heavenly moment; nothing could change how she felt.

"Go away!" Ty yelled.

"Yeah! Go away!" she called after him.

Bzzzz! Bzzzz!

It sounded like angry bees, and with a groan, Ty disentangled himself from Cammie's warm embrace and headed for the door. His shirt was untucked and wrinkled and his hair was mussed. Add to that, the sense of fulfillment that fairly reeked from him, and it wouldn't take the newcomer too long to figure out what had been going on between them.

Cammie couldn't have cared less. She grinned at him,

her own hair wild and free, her eyes flashing with merriment. Wiggling her fingers at him, she winked and lifted her brows up and down several times, silently inviting him to join her as soon as he'd dispensed with the intruder.

Ty flashed her a grin and twisted open the knob.

The look that crossed his face was indescribable. Instantly, fear clutched Cammie's heart and she shot to her feet and scurried to his side, her gaze locking onto the newcomer.

Pure shock bolted through her.

"Hello, Son," Samuel Stovall's unmistakable drawl greeted Ty. "Long time no see . . ."

CHAPTER FIFTEEN

"I should have guessed," Ty said into the tense aftermath that followed. He hadn't exactly offered Samuel any kind of welcome, but he hadn't slammed the door in his father's face, either.

Samuel Stovall stood near the fireplace, surveying Ty's hideaway with a look that hovered somewhere between appreciation and disbelief. Cammie stood near Ty, wondering why she, too, hadn't believed Samuel would follow her. After all, she'd been here too long, and the movie machine in Hollywood cranked along regardless of the fact that Cammie Merrill no longer wanted to be one of its cogs.

"You've been here for ten years?" Sam repeated, as if he couldn't fathom how anyone could transplant themselves to a place as remote as this.

Ty responded with a terse, "How did you find me?"

"I have a man who—does things for me," Samuel admitted, his craggy, handsome face carefully neutral. "You remember William Renquist?"

"*Renquist* found me?" Ty was incredulous.

"With the help of a private investigator."

"Ahhh . . ." Ty's jaw was a rock. "So Renquist didn't burglarize my stockbroker's home. That was the work of someone more qualified."

Samuel eyed his son carefully, weighing his words. Clearly, he wondered how much Ty actually knew, and how much he was guessing at. Cammie remained silent. Her own judgment by Ty was bound to come soon—as soon as Samuel brought up *Rock Bottom.* The truth would kill her. All her dreams would be smashed to smithereens. Still, her mind raced like lightning, searching for an answer, an excuse, a way to keep the axe from falling on her own vulnerable neck.

As if on cue, Samuel said, "We were expecting Camilla back long before this," jumping right to the heart of the matter.

Ty frowned, clearly at a loss, while Cammie held her breath in expectation. "We?" he demanded.

Samuel sent a look Cammie's way, silently asking her what she'd already told his son.

Her heart thundering, Cammie declared tautly, "I don't report to you or anyone else." She hated herself, her own cowardice. "You gave me Ty's address. I didn't ask you for it."

"I know that, dear. And you seem to have convinced Ty of the same. So, I'm the enemy, and Cammie's the ally?" He glanced at his son for verification, but Ty's face was granite. An answer wasn't necessary anyway. Cammie knew her relationship with Ty was too evident to miss. And Samuel Stovall, for all his faults, was an astute man. She glanced down at her blouse, rumpled from their earlier romantic fumblings. Glaring signs. Telltale evidence.

"Why did you come now?" Ty gazed straight into his father's eyes.

"When Camilla didn't immediately return, I felt I should—"

"No, I mean, why after ten years? Ten years . . . and then here you are. All of a sudden."

"Time passes . . ." He spread his hands.

"No." Ty slowly wagged his head from side to side, refusing to give Samuel an inch. "There's a reason. Bruce was burgled for my address. Tell me why now."

Cammie's heart thundered so hard it almost deafened her. Sweat broke out on her back and under her arms. Ty was tough, angry, and implacable. He would never accept that Sam wanted to "reconnect": her own weak excuse. The web of lies she'd spun couldn't save her now from the plain truth.

Sam flicked her a look and Cammie stiffened. He had to know she hadn't delivered *Rock Bottom* as promised, otherwise Ty would have mentioned it by now. The guillotine was poised, the firing squad at the ready.

She waited in agony.

"Do you mind if I have a brandy?" Samuel asked.

"I've got scotch."

"That'll do." Samuel cleared his throat and seated himself on the couch. Cammie's nerves screamed for him to get on with it. She couldn't bear the hope that somehow this would turn out all right. It was unfair.

Ty fixed his drink, and, after a brief hesitation, one for himself as well. Without asking, he made a third and pressed it into Cammie's cold hands. They all looked at each other, and Samuel was by far the most relaxed.

"Oh, stop looking like the apocalypse has arrived," he growled in exasperation to both of them.

"What prompted this invasion?" Ty reminded him. He gazed without liking at his father.

Cammie swallowed, forgetting to breathe. Her head was airy, her knees jelly. She couldn't move for fear of falling down. Clutching the scotch, she dimly wondered if it truly contained restorative powers. Deciding there was no harm in finding out, she lifted the glass to her lips. Gulping, choking, and ultimately gasping for air, she swallowed a healthy dose. While Ty and Samuel's eyes silently dueled, Cammie staggered on unsteady legs to the armchair across from Samuel, collapsing into its depths.

I deserve this . . . I deserve this . . . I deserve this . . . but oh, my God, I can't bear it!

Ty moved to her side, touching her arm. "You okay?"

"Fine," she squeaked out.

"It's the scotch," Ty told her, not understanding.

"The stuff's pure poison," Samuel observed with a smile, sipping his own drink and making a mockery of his words. Ty shot him another look and Sam took a deep breath.

Cammie waited in a dull haze.

"I've got a story to tell," Samuel began. "One you only know parts of, but it's really what provided the impetus."

"What story?" Ty propped himself on the arm of Cammie's chair.

"It's about you and—Gayle." He let his words sink in and Cammie gazed at him incomprehensibly. *Gayle? What was this? Why wasn't he bringing up the screenplay?*

Samuel lifted his palms, his lips parting. He hesitated a moment, as if searching for the right words, then suggested to Ty, "Maybe this should just be between you and me."

Cammie's heart jerked in fear. Bad enough to hear by her own ears; worse to have Samuel explain all the whys and wherefores to Ty without her present.

There's no hope anyway. None. What does it matter?

"Cammie can hear whatever you have to say," Ty told him coldly, and Sam inclined his head, as if to say, "It's your funeral."

He cleared his throat. "All right. It started ten years ago. Not long after Gayle's death and just about the time you left."

"What started?" asked Ty.

"I received a demand for money that I couldn't ignore," he stated flatly.

Baffled, Cammie lifted dazed blue eyes. Samuel didn't even flick her a glance. He looked thoughtful and serious and was embroiled in a story that seemed to come out of left field.

What's he doing? Why isn't he telling the truth about the film? Why is he lying? Who's he protecting?

"A demand for money? Blackmail?" Ty's brows lifted. This was clearly coming as a surprise to him, too.

"Gayle's maid. Or maybe she was a personal assistant, I don't know. A rather fierce and tenacious woman named Phoebe came to see me straight after Gayle's death. She had a note with her, in Gayle's own hand."

Ty blinked. "A suicide note? I don't remember a suicide note."

"It was a letter actually, addressed to me. Phoebe brought a photostat to me. In it, Gayle said good-bye to me, and good-bye to you. She said she was killing herself and her baby because I didn't love her. She wanted me to know it was all because she'd caught me in our bed with another woman." Samuel shook his head. *"Our* bed? Where did she come up with that? I was married to Felicia, and Gayle burst in on us in bed one time! It scared Felicia out of her mind and me, too, for that matter. The lady was plain bonkers!"

Ty's face was stone. Judgment reserved.

"Come on, Son. You can't deny that she was a kook! She was always doing something weird. You'd had your fill of her, too, don't say you hadn't."

"You were having an affair with Gayle. She obviously thought it meant something more."

"I was married to Felicia," Samuel reported stubbornly, as if that had any bearing on his actions, then or now.

"The woman was a manic-depressive, my shrink said," Samuel went on. "She had delusions about me, and about you, too. She was always doing something nutty."

"She wanted you to marry her," Ty reminded him.

"What?" Samuel laughed. "She jumped on me because you didn't want her, though I didn't know it at the time! Later, she transferred her sick desires to me. It was a mess."

"You didn't have to sleep with her," Ty reminded him.

"I shouldn't have," he agreed.

"Why did you?"

"I don't know really. I guess, because she was yours . . ."

This admission was more than Cammie would have

believed possible for the arrogant, egomaniac who'd sired Ty. Her expression must have said as much, for Samuel shrugged. "I've faced a few things over the years. I had a few—problems with your success. After years of therapy, I can admit it now. Gayle was a huge mistake." He grimaced and swallowed half his drink, scarcely reacting to the burn at all. "A huge mistake."

"She was pregnant," Cammie murmured.

Samuel narrowed his eyes, obviously not liking to be reminded of that fact.

"Whose baby was it?" Cammie dared to ask the question Ty had been torturing himself with for ten years.

Both men looked at her, but it was Samuel who murmured, "So he told you. I'm surprised. Ty can be awfully touchy about his personal problems."

"I never did the DNA tests," Ty said.

"Yeah, well, I did . . ." Both Cammie and Ty gazed at him in reluctant anticipation. "It was yours," he told Ty.

"What?" Ty was staggered. "Is this some sick joke?"

"Of course not!" Samuel was affronted. "She tried to say it was mine. Maybe she wanted it to be. But the tests proved differently, and it was all academic anyway since she killed herself and the baby before anyone knew the truth."

"So, what were you blackmailed over?"

"The whole sordid mess. Me, you, Gayle, paternity tests, suicide . . ." He grimaced. "What an unholy mess."

"So, this Phoebe came to you with a good-bye note. And she wanted money," Ty took up where Samuel left off.

"She wanted some cash. A solid amount, but not tons. Just enough to send her son, Warren, through law school. I debated. Good God, it was a disaster. Felicia didn't want the whole sordid story to hit the press, and it sure as hell wouldn't have helped my career—or yours, for that matter—so I debated fiercely about giving her the money. But it rankled, you know? Like Gayle reaching out from the grave."

Cammie turned away. She didn't approve of blackmail,

but Samuel's casual insensitivity curdled her stomach. To him, Gayle and her unborn child were a nuisance, nothing more.

"So, I'd just about decided to kick her butt out of my office when you hightailed it to God knew where!" Samuel glared at Tyler as if the whole thing were his fault.

For his part, Ty was still coping with the thought that the child had been his, *his!* He'd never believed it. Never. He'd proved phony paternity claims before. This was just another one. Until now . . .

"You looked guilty as hell!" Samuel went on.

That broke Ty's reverie. "Guilty? Guilty of what?"

"Pushing her to suicide!"

"Oh, come on!" Ty slammed his half-finished drink on the table. The amber fluid jumped out of the glass and puddled on the coffee table's cherry top.

"I wasn't going to have the scandal," Samuel declared, "so I paid for her precious son's law school, not that the slimy little creep deserved it."

"You're nuts," Ty said. "You should have just weathered the storm."

"You shouldn't have run!" Samuel's jaw jutted forward pugnaciously. "I had to pay Phoebe to kill the scandal before it even started, so all's well that ends well."

Ty shook his head in disbelief. "You're the one with a guilty conscience."

Cammie had to agree with Ty. Only a guilty conscience would bend to such ridiculous, outrageous demands.

With a sigh, Ty said, "That still doesn't explain why it was suddenly so imperative for you to find me now."

"Phoebe died last December. Her son, Warren the *lawyer,*" he bit out, as if the word tasted bad, "discovered Gayle's note. Apparently, Phoebe kept it in a safe-deposit box with a list of all the payments I'd made to her. He brought it up to me again."

"You did it to yourself," Tyler said, torn between horror and disgust. "You paid the blackmail and left a trail right back to yourself!"

Samuel didn't like his son's implications, but he was bound and determined to carry on with his tale. Cammie, though rapt, kept wondering when *Rock Bottom* was going to be brought into the conversation. Or, had the screenplay just been a convenient excuse? A way to approach Ty that, in the end, hadn't needed to be used?

It didn't make a whole lot of sense, but Cammie was at a complete loss when it came to Samuel Stovall anyway. He was a man pursuing his own goals, and those goals were a mystery, it appeared.

"I thought the little scoundrel wanted to take up where his mother left off, but no, Warren went to the police."

Cammie's brows lifted. "The police? Why?"

"Apparently, he felt there was something more to the story. Something I was trying to hide." Samuel's mouth tightened with remembered fury. "The bastard didn't even bat an eye when he learned how his education was paid for. But, by golly, he wasn't going to be tainted by it! Lily-white, he is, now that he's got that damned degree in his tight little fist."

Samuel's outrage was almost comical. Cammie swallowed and threw a look at Ty. He seemed as poleaxed as she was. His father couldn't see that he'd made his own bed—and was now forced to lie in it.

"Warren went to the police," Ty prompted his father.

"They wanted to know why I'd paid the money. I was furious. Then the flatfoots started asking about *you*. The DNA tests were brought up. They showed the child wasn't mine, but it was close enough to be an almost-match. They wanted to know how that was possible. The obvious answer was that the child was yours. You'd been dating Gayle, et cetera."

"And?" Ty's eyes were dark, his mouth tight.

Here, Samuel hesitated, coughing into his hand. "They wondered if your sudden flight might have been motivated somehow by these events. Gayle was pregnant, after all. And you'd already fought one paternity suit . . ."

"And won," Ty reminded him tautly.

"But they figured that maybe you didn't want to go through it all again, the legal way, especially since the child could be proven to be yours."

Samuel's craggy cheeks seemed to slacken at this admission, making him appear, suddenly, every one of his sixty-odd years.

"You made them think Ty was responsible for Gayle's death?" she declared, aghast.

"No, no, no!" Samuel was adamant. "They tried to twist it all around, and I wanted to kill that weasel, Warren. It was just speculation and assumption that all got blown out of proportion, but it's all been put to rest now. Don't worry, I took care of everything. You're not wanted by the police."

"Oh, thanks," Ty said harshly.

"I'll accept a certain amount of blame," Samuel said stiffly, "but I'm not the one who ran away and made myself look guilty! You did that all on your own. And, whether you like it or not, that's what it looks like."

"You're the one who paid blackmail. You made it look that way," Ty pointed out.

"I did what I felt was best. Anyway, it's all over and done with now. Gayle's death was a suicide. There was no evidence of foul play. She threw herself out of a window because she was mentally unstable. She wanted a Stovall, any Stovall. She had us mixed up together. You should read the note."

"No, thanks."

"So, this is why you wanted to find Ty?" Cammie asked him, a flick of anger burning inside her at the way everyone had been used, even herself.

"I have a lot of reasons to see my son again," he reminded her tautly, his taut gaze loaded with extra meaning. "But after that go-around with the police, I decided it was high time to get over this nonsense," Samuel admitted. "What good does it do to hide out here anyway? It's ridiculous and melodramatic. It's time you grew up and came home."

Ty just stared in disbelief at his father.

Samuel clasped his hands together. "If you came back now, it would have great impact, fabulous resonance. All would be forgotten as soon as you reappeared and started making films again."

Cammie couldn't believe it. "Gayle committed suicide. She killed herself and her baby. Ty's baby," she told him intensely. "And just when that all came crashing down on him, he learned his father had been having an affair with *his* woman, and that, furthermore, the baby might be his father's. And all you can say is that his return would have *fabulous resonance?*"

"I don't need your sarcasm," Samuel declared.

"Get out," Ty growled.

Cammie, once started, couldn't be stopped. "It's an ugly, tawdry tale! And you don't seem to grasp its significance. You contributed so much to Ty's reasons for leaving, and now you just think everything's 'all better'! You want him to come back, so he should come back. End of story!"

"Stay out of this, Camilla," Samuel warned.

"Your son has a battered soul, Mr. Stovall, and he's spent a lot of years trying to mend it," Cammie stated tautly. "Whatever your reasons for coming here, they're clearly not in Ty's best interest."

"Get out," Ty ordered again, staring his father down. "You remind me of every reason why I left."

"Tyler, there's more."

There's more . . .

The words were prophetic. She'd heard them from Ty's own mouth, and they, too, had involved Gayle. The tragedy of her death haunted like the notes of a half-remembered song.

"I don't care what it is." Ty moved toward the door, his stern, steady gaze silently inviting his father to accompany him.

Sam, however, took no notice of his son's warning. He remained where he sat, albeit tensely, as if he knew he was pushing too hard. "Even though the police have put the case to rest, I'm afraid there's been some interest by the press."

"Oh, God . . ." Ty shook his head in disbelief. "Why would you think I would ever want to come back?"

Cammie's heart sank. Any good she'd done, any bit of encouragement to get Ty to rethink his reasons for leaving, were being slammed down by Samuel's story. If Ty's father had really wanted him to take the role in *Rock Bottom,* he was burying the chance before it even saw the light of day.

"Do you know what you've left behind?" Samuel asked him rhetorically.

"Oh, yes."

"I don't think you do. People struggle all their lives for one smidgen of the fame you hold in your hands—and you're not even trying!"

"Fame—or her perception of its worth—destroyed Gayle," Ty stated flatly. "If either you or I had been a—small-time real estate speculator in a Canadian coastal town, say"—his eyes glinted with ironic humor—"then she would not have hitched her wagon to our stars. Simple."

Samuel gestured impatiently with one hand. "Gayle was Gayle. It's over, and that's it."

"You just said the press wants to make something of it."

"Well, of course they do! They're always scrounging for something. My point is . . ." He hesitated, as if realizing his next words wouldn't be taken in the vein he wanted them to be. "My point is that this is an opportune time for you to return."

"You mean, *use* this! This *publicity!*"

Ty's horror couldn't be disguised. Cammie, too, felt completely affronted.

"How horrible!" she declared.

"It's going to be there anyway—the whole publicity," Sam said with a dismissive shrug. "Don't you see? This story's been percolating for ten years. It's going and going and going, and no matter when you come back, it'll bite you. I'm just saying that you might as well use it. That's all."

"You're incredible." Tyler gazed at him in a mixture of disgust and reluctant admiration. "You'll use anyone at anytime for any purpose. You're a complete opportunist. What do you really want me for? Tell me. Nothing you can say can shock me now."

Cammie dug her fingernails into the arms of the chair. Samuel regarded Ty assessingly, as if wondering just how close he could come to the truth. It appeared as if Ty were warming to him a bit, despite all Samuel's selfish explanations. But appearances were deceiving, and Cammie knew the extent of Ty's acting prowess. She knew, even if Samuel, who was blinded by his own desires, didn't, that Ty would never come back to Hollywood on a wave of free press, a wave thundering to shore with the wind of scandal at its back.

"I want you for me," Samuel said bluntly.

"For you."

"Yes, for me. I want my son back. I want him to resurrect his career. Whether you believe me or not, I want what's best for you. Father to son."

Ty's jaw tightened and relaxed. "You have never been any kind of father to me," he said in a low voice. "Not when I was young, not when you slept with Gayle, and not now."

"I helped get your career going, and don't say I didn't. If you'd been a nobody, it would have been harder."

"So, I owe you something for that."

"Damn it, Tyler!" Samuel jumped to his feet, thunking his empty glass on the table. "You're as stubborn as a mule and only half as smart. Look what you've done!" He swept an arm around the cozy room. "You've collected dust for ten years! Get out and live, boy, before you're old!"

Like me . . .

The words weren't uttered, but they hovered in the air anyway, betraying Sam's feelings in unexpected eloquence. He wanted Ty back because it felt like his own youth was slipping away like sand through his fingers. Cammie could almost feel sorry for him.

Almost.

"I'm not interested in returning right now," Ty told him, his voice gentler. "Whether you think so or not, I have a life here. Maybe it's not perfect, but it's close." A frown marred his brow. Was he remembering her? Cammie wondered. And the knowledge that this life would be one without her? That location was their enemy?

Or, was that putting too much emphasis on what she meant to him?

As if hearing her thoughts, Samuel swung his tyrannical gaze on her. "And what about you, Camilla?"

"What do you mean?" she answered automatically.

"What do *you* want?"

"This isn't about me." She shook her head. "I thought you were here to change Ty's mind."

"I thought you were, too," he reminded her, shooting an icicle of fear through her heart.

"No," she denied quickly. "What I want and what Ty wants aren't necessarily the same. I wouldn't expect him to change his life so drastically, just because I can't live here."

Samuel's brows lifted, and the glint in his eyes could only be described as diabolical. Cammie began to sweat even before his first syllable was uttered. "So, you've thought about staying on, then? In this one-horse town?"

"What do you want to hear?" Ty interrupted. "That we've been seeing each other since she arrived? That we're—*involved?* Okay, we're involved. It's been—great."

If he'd thought that might derail Samuel, he'd only inadvertently greased the wheels. "You've gotten pretty cozy with each other," he observed. "Romance. It's a beautiful thing."

"Cut the sarcasm." Ty sounded tired.

"You're all trusting and close and loving."

"Samuel . . ." A livid warning rested in Ty's tone.

"Am I wrong?" He gazed innocently at Cammie whose

mouth had turned to cotton. He had the power to ruin her, and that moment was close—very close.

"I don't know what you're driving at, but you know what? It's none of your business." Ty, who had moved away from the door, now returned to it, silently asking his father to leave once again.

"What about the screenplay?"

Samuel's bomb landed with a thud, or at least it sounded that way to Cammie, whose ears suddenly thundered with a swoosh of air, as if a hurricane were rushing throughout the room, rendering her deaf.

"The screenplay?" Ty repeated in a deadly voice.

"Camilla . . ." Samuel clucked his tongue. "You didn't show him?"

"Show me what?" Ty asked, but he was looking at Samuel.

Cammie turned to Ty, to the man she loved, feeling as if she were in a vortex. His image seemed fuzzy and unformed. She couldn't see. She couldn't speak. "I—didn't—" she stuttered.

"Your loving little friend has something to say," Samuel prompted.

"Get out!" Ty yelled at him again. "Get out now!"

"Tyler!"

"If I have to, I'll bodily throw you out! Get the hell out, *now!*"

Samuel opened his mouth, then snapped it shut again. Ty's tense, murderous gaze said it all. No more explanations. No more waiting. No more secrets revealed.

"Go," Ty urged, his voice so soft, Cammie wondered if she'd read his lips instead of hearing the sound.

Frustration tightened Samuel's lips. He hated being thwarted. But he'd done it to himself! In his desire to get Ty to do his bidding, he'd thrown Cammie to the wolves, thereby sabotaging any hope of achieving his goal. Now, he strode stiffly to his son, but Ty's eyes clashed furiously with his own. Still, he couldn't quite admit defeat. "Ty . . ."

A pungent curse escaped Ty's lips, punched with power, made more so by the fact that it was spoken so softly.

Samuel hesitated one last time. His lips parted, but Ty's expression was stone. Expelling a furious snort, Samuel departed with ill grace, striding stiffly outside. Tyler gently shut the door behind him.

He turned to face Cammie, his back against the door. "What screenplay?" he asked.

The moment had come. Cammie felt suspended, floating. She'd set this up all on her own. It was no good blaming Samuel; she'd taken the bait and run with it. And her innocence, if it could be called that, wouldn't be acknowledged. She'd tricked Ty, though not in the way he would assume; she was only guilty of withholding the truth, but that, in its own way, would be damning enough.

And she'd known it all along. Why, oh, why hadn't she come clean in the very beginning? Now, it would appear she'd been Samuel's cohort from the onset—which was not that far from the truth.

"What screenplay?" Ty asked again, his voice flat, wiped clean of emotion.

Cammie licked her lips.

"My God. You told him about *Father Knows Worst!*"

"No!" That brought her to her feet. Ty's stunned expression was more than she could stand. "He doesn't know about your screenplay. He couldn't!"

"Couldn't he?"

"No." Cammie was emphatic. "I don't see how. I haven't talked to him since I left L.A."

"Then what did he mean?"

"Ty, take a seat," Cammie begged, gesturing to the couch Samuel had so recently vacated. She couldn't have him standing there, legs spread apart, expression tense and accusing, while she dissolved into the armchair, weak and guilty.

"Do I need to sit down?" he questioned in a voice that was hard to read.

Cammie nodded jerkily, and Ty, after a short hesitation

where his jaw perceptibly tightened, strode stiffly to the couch and eased himself down onto it, his gray eyes searching Cammie's face, reading God knew what. Her own features felt tight and frozen.

"Go," Ty clipped out.

Cammie swept in a breath and let it out slowly. "I haven't been completely honest with you—I'm sure you've guessed that by now. Your father gave me your address, that much is true, but he did it for other reasons than the ones he gave you."

"What other reasons?"

"He wanted you back. He wanted you back as an actor. And a son, of course," Cammie stumbled on, knowing she was digging her own grave.

"Of course."

"Ty . . ."

"Just tell me." His gaze was cold as the North Sea.

"There is an opportunity for you," she admitted in a low voice, unable to put any power behind her words. "A lead role in a Summer Solstice production."

Cammie cringed, waiting, but Ty looked more perplexed than angry. "Summer Solstice?" he repeated blankly.

"A husband-and-wife production team. They're the ones producing *Rock Bottom,* the screenplay Samuel's talking about."

"You mean, this is about a part?" Ty asked slowly. "That's all?"

"Well, y-e-ss." She drew out the word, waiting for the volcanic reaction that was sure to follow.

But she was wrong, it appeared, for Ty looked merely relieved, and then almost amused. "The answer's no. I'm not interested. End of story."

Cammie had no response, mostly because she didn't know which tack to take. He didn't understand all the complexities yet, and when he did, he wouldn't be so blasé.

"Was there something else?"

Cammie sighed heavily. She sensed she was at the end of her relationship with Ty no matter what she said, what she did. She felt outside of herself, watching the pathetic soul lost in the depths of the chair, knowing that poor fool was about to have her rising hope and burgeoning love quashed forever.

"There's more, obviously," Ty answered his own question. "Go on."

"When Samuel learned I wanted to see you, he gave me a copy of *Rock Bottom* in exchange for your address. He wanted me to convince you to come back and take the role."

"Okay." He waited, but Cammie, unable to continue and bring about her own demise, merely shook her head. "Where's the copy of the screenplay?" Ty asked.

"I—I didn't bring it with me."

"Why not? Wasn't that your bargain with the devil?"

"I couldn't do it. I just—let him think I could," she admitted wearily.

"You thwarted him." Ty's lips twitched with amusement.

Cammie could have cried out at the unfairness of it. She could have been forgiven. He would have forgiven her! Bringing him the script would not have been a crime in itself; she was the messenger, not the message. But when he learned of her own personal stake, of the part she herself had been offered, there would be no convincing him that the role had no bearing on her feelings and reasons for searching him out.

"You heard him. Samuel had me followed, so I guess I didn't really thwart him much."

"Don't worry so much, my love," Ty told her. He knelt beside her chair and pulled her cold hands in the comfort of his own, gently urging her forward into his arms. She felt shaky and lost, and a protest issued involuntarily from her lips. "Don't let him ruin this for us," Ty urged into the glory of her hair, his strong arms enfolding her, his heartbeat strong beneath the cheek she rested against his chest. "We have each other. We'll figure this out. We couldn't stay on in Bayrock anyway; I guess I always knew that. You want to go back to L.A. Maybe it's not impossible.

Maybe I could find a ranch out there somewhere, like my mother. I don't know."

"Oh, Ty!" She could have cried over the unfairness of it.

"Take it easy. Samuel wants the past swept under the rug, and he wants me back in Hollywood. It has nothing to do with you."

"Yes, it does," she argued. "I want you back, too. You know that."

"Then I'll give it a try," he said soberly.

Disbelieving, she pulled back to gaze into his beloved face. "Do you mean it?"

"Yes. Dear old Dad's right about one thing," he said, his lips twisting ironically. "It's time to put the past behind me, and that's never going to happen unless I face my own ghosts."

"Are you serious?"

"Completely. I'm almost sorry you didn't bring the damn thing with you."

"You mean the screenplay? Are you *interested?*"

"Oh, there's a twinge," he admitted. "I liked acting. But when I relived all the sordid details surrounding Gayle's death"—Ty pretended to shudder from head to toe—"all those terrible feelings came right back. Over the years I've sometimes wondered whether running away was the best choice, but when Samuel brought up the past, it convinced me leaving was my only choice. I knew it then; he reminded me now."

Cammie clung to him, to his warmth and support. He kissed the top of her head, pulled her to her feet, then slowly set her at arm's length from him so that he could stare into her eyes.

"Why do you look so frightened?" he asked, perplexed. "I don't blame you."

Cammie choked out a hysterical laugh. "Not yet."

"How could I blame you for Samuel's treachery? He hasn't changed a bit! He's selfish and egocentric, through and through. He has his moments, but they're not enough."

"Ty . . ."

"Cammie, you said yourself you didn't bring the screenplay. That oughtta tell me something." When she still couldn't relax, he asked, as a means to lighten the mood, "So, what is this screenplay about?"

"*Rock Bottom?* Do you really want to hear?"

He stroked her hair, willing her to get over the harsh interruption of Samuel's arrival. Once over the initial shock, he himself was almost relieved to be found out. It made his next course of action inevitable. And he felt more tethered, though he was loath to admit it. Seeing his father again had made him recognize that family thing that Cammie had first touched again. It was important, no matter how much he tried to run from it. "Start with Summer Solstice Productions. Who's this husband-and-wife team?"

"Nora and James Connelly. They've become very successful in the last few years. Everyone's clamoring to be in one of their films. A Summer Solstice film is as close to a sure bet as it comes in this industry."

"So, why do they want to resurrect me?" Ty gently steered Cammie away from the living room and toward the short hall that led to the bedroom. He was done fighting his father and the ghosts of the past for one night. All he wanted was to fall asleep in the shelter of the arms of the woman he loved. *Loved.* It was getting easier by the minute to say, to accept.

"They want you because you're perfect for the role," Cammie murmured, letting herself be led. "It's a great part."

"You've read the screenplay."

"Mmmhmmm. I read it the night your father gave it to me."

Ty stopped for a moment. His hands cupped her chin, lifting her reluctant gaze to the scrutiny of his. "Did you think I would actually come back to Hollywood for a role?"

"I said you wouldn't," she admitted honestly.

He regarded her thoughtfully. "It's that good?"

"Yes."

"Do you think I should go back for it?" he asked curiously, without any real intent behind the words.

"I think you should do whatever you want to do. Based on what your father said tonight, and what I now know about Gayle and everything, I wouldn't blame you if you never returned!" She kissed his now smooth cheek, loving the smell of him. "But I also know that if you did go back, it would be because you'd come to peace with the past. Nothing, certainly nothing as superficial as a film part, could lure you to Hollywood unless you were completely ready."

"You sound sad, like you expect it to never happen. Didn't I just say I might go back?"

"But you won't."

She was so positive, all of a sudden, and Ty couldn't understand her attitude. It was as if she didn't want him to answer "yes." Something else was going on, but for the life of him he couldn't figure out what it was.

Bang! Bang! Bang!

They both jumped at the harsh knocking on the front door. Muttering to himself, Ty reluctantly released Cammie and strode to the entryway. A glance through the triangular windows revealed his father had returned.

"Dear old Dad," he groaned. Cammie's already ashen face grew still whiter, bewildering Ty anew. "What's wrong?" he asked, his hand on the knob.

She shook her head.

"Cammie!"

"Answer the door. Find out what he wants. He won't go away unless you do."

"I should just let him rot out there," Ty muttered.

"Your father's bullish." Cammie's smile was wan. "Runs in the family."

"I'll take that as an insult," he said, loving her all the more. She seemed so fragile to him tonight, totally unlike the independent, smart-tongued woman he knew her to be.

Bang! Bang!

With an oath of repressed fury, Ty threw open the door, meeting his father with an icy glare. "There was something else?"

"You bet there was," Samuel answered, having clearly recovered his full composure. The minutes since his departure had convinced him he didn't have to listen to his son. Samuel Stovall's recognition of self-worth was ever-present. He'd just forgotten for a moment that *he,* not Tyler, was the boss, forever and ever.

"Ahhh . . ." Tyler said as his father thrust a sheaf of papers at his chest. The title *Rock Bottom* jumped out at him.

"Read it, damn it," Samuel bit out. "You can do that much, can't you?"

"It won't do any good."

"*She* should have given it to you," Samuel declared, throwing a vitriolic glance Cammie's way. "What were you thinking? You can't just stay here indefinitely. Nora and James don't want you that badly," he told her, and Cammie's breath caught in her throat.

Here it comes!

Ty glanced from Cammie to his father. "If they don't want me that badly, why are you insisting I read it?" he asked Samuel, missing the messages entirely.

"Not you. *Her!*" Samuel's furious brow suddenly cleared, as he realized the truth of the moment. "Didn't she tell you?"

Ty, sensing he was out of his depth, stood in silence, waiting.

"I was offered a role, too," Cammie broke in with a rush.

"*What?*"

"Offered a role?" Samuel barked out an ugly laugh. "That's the reason she came to find you, Son. They don't want her, unless she gets you! It all hinges on you." He shot Cammie a pitying glance. "Camilla, my dear, you really ought to learn to throw your cards on the table. Did you think he wouldn't find out? Tyler, if you take the part, Camilla is your co-star!"

CHAPTER SIXTEEN

Needles of hot spray beat into Ty's face. He turned toward the nozzle in blazing defiance to the scorching temperature and blasting water pressure, uncaring, unfeeling, and desperate for something to wake him from his nightmare.

Because it was a nightmare. A trough. A black hole of betrayal.

He couldn't think about it; he could think of nothing else.

When his father had bitten out those damning words, Ty's brain had sluggishly refused to hear the intent. Cammie, his co-star? A project for the two of them? For the barest of moments he'd surged with joy. The idea, still not fully coalesced, brushed some hidden desire within him, and he saw the possibilities.

He'd half turned toward Cammie. To what? Embrace her? Tell her he'd changed his mind, that this chance was all he wanted? This chance with *her*?

One look at her face and hope withered and died. Shock, misery, and guilt—first and foremost, guilt—were plainly stamped on her beloved face. She was all Samuel accused her of. All that, and more.

And then he saw with pure, painful vision the scope of her betrayal, and the depth of his own gullibility. Every touch. Every gesture. Every whispered word of love was a lie.

Lies. Bitter, bitter lies. All of it.

She said something then. Something about loving him, of rejecting the offer. But Samuel pooh-poohed her. "Rejected the offer?" he bellowed from the doorway. "Hardly. We've all just been *waiting* for her to get you to sign. If she couldn't pull it off, she was out of the role. Period."

Ty couldn't think. Could scarcely breathe. Vaguely, he remembered closing the door in his father's face, then staring down at the unfamiliar stack of pages in his hands. The script. *Rock Bottom.* A pretty good description of how he felt at that particular moment.

He'd ordered Cammie out of the house. Not in the loud, belligerent voice of his father. In a quiet, deadly tone that sounded menacing even to his own ears.

"I need to explain . . ." she'd stammered.

"You had weeks. Get out of my sight. I never, ever want to see you again."

He'd turned and walked through the cabin and out the back door into a warmish night filled with flickering stars and a yellow moon, the air full of familiar and welcoming brackish scents off the bay. Stumbling down the steps to the ground, he'd picked up the axe, swinging it in an arc toward the chunk of fir already sitting on the stump. Shards of wood flew like shrapnel all around him. Setting a second piece of wood in its place, he shattered it just as quickly. He couldn't recall now how much wood he had split, nor how long he'd chopped and flailed away in the moonlight before exhaustion took over.

He'd sensed once that she was standing at the back windows, but he hadn't looked. When he finally finished, gasping and spent, sweat pouring in rivulets down his face, neck, and back, he'd glanced up to see the windows blank. Stumbling, swiping at the welling perspiration, he'd climbed the back steps, thrown open the door and staggered inside. He was alone.

Now, he stood in the shower, a punishment and a cleansing all in one. He wanted to die. He wanted to bellow like a wild boar. He wanted to cry.

He ran the tank out of hot water. One moment, he was facing a warm, but cooling, stream; the next, icy spray stung him full in the face. Slamming off the taps, he leaned an arm against the tiles, head bent, water dripping off his wet hair and down his limbs. Those limbs were quivering. He felt ancient and used up and so very lost.

Ten minutes later, he flopped facedown, naked, atop the bed. He smelled Cammie's scent all around him. Lifting his head, he blindly looked for her, realizing even as he did so that the aroma emanated from the bedding where she'd lain.

He couldn't sleep here. He didn't want to anyway, with so many recent memories crowding his brain, making him ache in a way he hadn't believed was possible since those terrible days after Gayle's betrayal and death.

Feeling as old as Methuselah, he stumbled up the stairs to the couch in his office, throwing a blanket over his shivering body. His last conscious thought was that for once oblivion was reached without the help of alcohol.

A strata of intense pink clouds layered the eastern horizon outside Cammie's window at the Goosedown Inn. She stared blankly at the beautiful sight, watching silently as dawn burned through the clouds, changing them to faded peach and finally white with faint gilded edges. Bayrock was glorious this morning. Water glittered. Seagulls swooped and cried plaintively. Sailboat spars were white arrows pointing skyward against a sky growing bluer by the moment.

She'd grown used to this small town the last few weeks.

She'd known she would have to leave soon, had thought and talked about it ceaselessly. But now that the day was here, she felt miserable, depressed and frozen into immobility. She couldn't go. She couldn't go without Ty. She just—couldn't.

But now he would never leave with her. She'd made sure of that. And even though she should have known this would be the only ending possible, some silly, hopelessly eager part of herself had simply charged ahead and made plans without doing the requisite "reality check." She'd made herself believe there was a chance for them. Now she knew there wasn't.

So, here she was. Time to check out. Time to return to the life she'd put on hold.

With a heavy heart, she turned away from the spectacular morning splendor and concentrated on the task at hand. Last night, she'd packed her things like an automaton, aware only that Ty's wrath would not abate, his forgiveness would not come.

Now she examined her meager amount of clothes, refolding them one last time into the overnight bag that had been her companion all these weeks. Staring down at the bag, she was overcome with misery. It sapped her remaining strength, and she sank onto the bed. Last night, she'd stood at Ty's cabin door, one hand on the knob, fighting the urge to rush to the back deck and desperately beg him to forgive her. She'd silently wished for help—some kind of divine intervention!—but it was no use. The fates were against her.

If fate were a woman, I wouldn't be in this situation.

"Hah," Cammie said on a gulp. She'd made all the choices herself.

Twisting on her heel, she surveyed the cozy room through dull eyes. The Goosedown Inn boasted rooms wrapped in tiny rose-printed wallpaper and fluffy beds designed to prove the inn was as good as its name. Antique furniture, restored to its original luster, was tucked beneath angled ceilings. It was gorgeous and warm and wonderful, and Cammie had slept as badly as she ever had. Tossing and turning, she'd reviewed the events that had led her to this fate and had come up with the same conclusion time and again: It was her own fault.

And it was time to leave.

With limbs that felt held down by weights, she moved through the motions of getting herself ready: a shower, a brisk brushing of teeth, a touch of makeup. Dragging on her jeans, she ran fingers through her wet hair, tousling it dry. Still on its hanger, her white shirt waited for another wearing. Cammie adjusted the collar of her white shirt, supremely conscious of the soft, yet sharp scent of detergent from its most recent washing at Ty's cabin . . .

Sucking in a tortured breath, she ordered herself not to think anymore. Thinking was bad. Thinking brought on fresh pain.

With difficulty, she thrust her arms through the sleeves of her shirt. More difficult yet was the task of examining her own taut reflection in the oval mirror above the dresser. Unhappiness covered her face. With an effort she pulled her lips into a smile, but it looked forced, which it was.

What am I going to do? she thought in despair. *What am I going to do?*

A knock on the door caused her to whirl around. Joy surged through her.

Ty!

Yanking on the handle, she flung the door wide, then stood in shocked dismay to see her nemesis, Samuel Stovall, standing on the threshold.

"You were expecting someone else," he observed without rancor.

"Well, yes, I was hoping," she admitted.

"Aren't you going to invite me in? We're neighbors." He inclined his head. "I'm right down the hall from you."

"How nice."

"Don't be nasty, Camilla. Clearly, Tyler's as disappointed in you as he is in me, otherwise you wouldn't be enjoying the hospitality of this fine establishment."

"Disappointed? That's a little tame for what Ty thinks of us, I'd say."

Ignoring her, he swept on. "If we put our heads together, we can come up with a mutually beneficial solution."

"No! No, no, no! Don't tell me anything more about Ty! I was a fool to listen to you in the first place. I shouldn't have come here. It's just made everything a thousand times worse!"

"Oh, don't be hysterical." Samuel frowned at her pessimism. "This isn't the end."

"It is for me. And it should be for you, too. Ty doesn't want either of us in his life. We took care of that once and for all."

Samuel's brow lifted. "I'm surprised you're shouldering some blame."

"I know what's my fault," she said bitterly. "Believe me."

"Camilla, it's going to be okay." His tone was surprisingly tender. "Ty just needs some time to cool off and think things through. He's got the screenplay now. He'll read it."

Cammie's lips parted. "You leave me speechless."

"He will," Samuel insisted. "Tyler's curiosity will get the better of him, if nothing else. He'll stop being angry at you." Samuel waved her fears away as if they were so much nuisance.

"You don't understand how hurt he is. How betrayed." It was an effort to force the words past her lips. Every breath she took felt like a knife in her heart. "He'll never believe I didn't care about the role in *Rock Bottom.* If I were him, I wouldn't believe it, either."

"It won't matter what he thinks," Samuel dismissed. "He'll get there in the end, all the same."

"Get there?"

"Where he's meant to be. To the job. To his home. He can't stay here forever. You know that, and he knows it, too. He needed this incentive. He won't blame you."

"You don't understand anything!"

He shook his head emphatically. "I might have agreed with you before, but not now."

"What do you mean?"

She was scarcely listening. This was just the last scene to a very bad film, and she wanted it to be finished and done with. She wanted to close the door in Sam's face and roll the credits. It was time to vacate the premises.

"Ty loves you," he said matter-of-factly. "That was plain. He'll get over this infantile rage because he'll have to. Let him have his fit. Get it out of his system. Then he'll come looking for you."

"My God. You are so deluded!"

"Realistic."

"Well, he'll have to find me in Los Angeles, because that's where I'm going. I blew it, Samuel, no matter what you think. If you want to hang around and try to change his mind, be my guest. But it hasn't happened in ten years, so I wouldn't hold my breath."

"Camilla, you can't leave!"

His arrogance never ceased to amaze her. "Watch me."

"I need your help!"

Cammie attempted to close the door in his face, but when he stuck a foot in the crack, she uttered a muffled curse, tossed up her hands in exasperation, then turned to the remnants of her belongings which were scattered across the rumpled bed.

Following her inside, Samuel said, "He may have had time to read *Rock Bottom* by now. All we need to do is go see him. He won't want to admit how good it is, but he'll know. He's too much of a professional not to. Camilla . . ." Samuel grabbed her arm, attempting to prevent her from packing.

Cammie stiffened and sent him a freezing glare.

"Do you love my son or not?" he demanded, switching tactics.

"I love him enough to respect his choices."

"Oh. Ouch." His lip curled. "Then, let me ask you this:

Do you think he's completely happy being a hermit up here in the Canadian wilderness?"

"It's hardly the wilderness," Cammie muttered, stuffing her bag and straining the zipper as she yanked on the tab.

"Is he completely happy?" Sam pressed.

"You'd have to ask him."

"I'm asking you."

Cammie gave Samuel Stovall her coldest glance. He was the most aggravating human being she'd ever had the bad luck to run across. Yet, it was hard to stay completely furious with him at all times. He was too *juvenile* to allow it! Too self-serving, in a sophomoric way that made her want to scream and pull her hair out.

Still, he was ruthless, too, and, she knew by experience, heartless at times. "Stay away from me," she warned. "I don't like the way you treat Ty, and I don't like the way you treated my mother."

"If you won't go see him for me, or for Tyler, go see him for yourself." Samuel was perfectly serious. "You don't have to like me, Camilla, but you can't deny that some of what I've said is the truth. He loves you, and you love him. Tyler's type of love is—er—more substantial than my own." This admission was made with an inclination of his head, to which Cammie lifted her brows in surprise. Concessions were not Samuel Stovall's way. "You can't turn your back on that kind of love. It's up to you, because Ty's pride won't let him come to you now that you've left. Do it, Camilla. Do it today, before it's too late . . ."

"I can't."

"You have to," he said in his most matter-of-fact tone. "Or you'll kick yourself the rest of your life."

She didn't want to listen to him; she didn't want him to be right. But there was resonance in his words that couldn't be denied, and now, two hours and a dozen cups of coffee later, Cammie stood outside her rental car, which was parked, once again, in front of Ty's cabin. Her heart beat strong and heavy, and sweat formed on her upper lip and between her breasts. The weather was downright warm, and she felt hot and feverish, full of fear.

She was surprised she'd listened to Samuel Stovall, of all people, but sometimes the truth slipped from the lips of those you least expected. Still, there was something strange about Samuel's attitude. Something that bothered her. And it wasn't just the fact that he had a huge stake in her success with Ty. It was something else.

But she couldn't think about that now. She couldn't think period. Her mouth was dry and her brain whirled with fear. She had to get through the next few minutes, one way or another.

Boldly, screwing up what little courage she still possessed, Cammie strode through the gate and up Ty's walkway, rapping loudly on the door. He might not be home. He might refuse to answer her summons. Good Lord. He might do a lot of things she couldn't face, and her bravado was so fragile she was afraid she would break into a million pieces if he so much as frowned at her. But she *had* to take this chance. In that, Samuel Stovall was one hundred percent correct.

The door suddenly swung open. Cammie stepped back, her breath sweeping in on a gasp.

Tyler stood there, his expressions as cold and hard as granite, his gray eyes meeting hers in a narrow stare that spoke clearly of his disgust in finding her on his doorstep.

"I—couldn't go—without talking to you," Cammie stuttered. "I know there's no explanation, no excuse. But I love you. *I love you.* I really do, and I don't care about anything but you and I never have. Don't—please, don't—turn me away. Oh, Ty, I love you so much!"

Cringing inside, Cammie gazed at the man who held her happiness within his hands. Her aquamarine eyes misted with the eloquence of her feelings. Ty's hands hung loosely at his sides, and she belatedly realized that he held *Rock Bottom* in one. His gaze traveled the path of her own, to where the source of their contention lay. Slowly he lifted the manuscript, holding it as if he were about to read it.

"Have you—" Cammie began.

"Yes," he cut her off.

Cammie held her breath. There was nothing more to say anyway. He'd read the screenplay. She waited for his assessment.

"My father was right. It's good."

He sounded so thoroughly disgusted at that particular turn of events, it was almost comical. Cammie exhaled in a rush of hope. Indicating the screenplay with a jerk of her chin, she said, "It's not why I came to Bayrock."

"So you've said."

"May I—come in?" she asked tentatively.

He hesitated for a tense moment, then stepped away from the door. Cammie crossed the threshold into the now familiar cabin. *Home,* she thought with a lump in her throat. Only it wasn't her home and was never likely to be.

Linking her hands together, Cammie stood stiffly in front of the fireplace. The beauty of the late-spring day slanted through the windows facing the bay. Eyeing the sailboats dotting the rippling water, Cammie said, "I couldn't just leave. I know you ordered me out, but I had to try to—explain."

"There's nothing to explain."

"Yes, there is."

"I understand."

"No, you don't," she insisted.

"Cammie . . ." Ty's voice was husky with repressed emotion.

Surprised, she gazed at him with dawning hope. "You've forgiven me?"

"No."

"No?" she choked.

"I mean, there's nothing to forgive. I don't care what motivated you to come to Bayrock and find me anyway. I'm just glad we 'reconnected,' as you say. And I've been worrying all morning that you'd already left. I wouldn't blame you," he rushed on, while Cammie tried to interject. "I was a bastard last night."

"No, you weren't!"

"I wanted to believe the worst. I *did* believe the worst. And it was a hellish night, I'll tell you. But this morning, it just didn't make sense. You haven't been faking the feelings of these past few weeks together; nobody's that good of an actor! Oh, Cammie . . ." Ty crossed the room in three swift strides, cradling her close. "My love," he murmured brokenly.

"Oh, Ty!" She clung to him in joy and disbelief. "I almost left. It was only your father," she bubbled, "who convinced me to give one last try. I thought you hated me!"

"My *father?*"

"He came to see me this morning. He wanted me to convince you to go back, but I told him you would never listen to me. But I had to see you. *I had to!* And he told me not to give up on love."

"My father told you that?"

"In so many words. He convinced me, or maybe I just wanted to be convinced."

"He was acting, then. Those lines are straight out of one of his roles."

Cammie's mouth dropped open. Of course! Now that Ty reminded her, she could visualize the entire scene of one of his earlier films. "Now I know why it sounded so familiar! That—that—rascal!" she bit out, for lack of a better adjective.

They pulled back to stare at each other, neither knowing quite what to think. Then Ty threw back his head and laughed, and Cammie, relieved and delighted, shook her head and chuckled. "I was totally fooled!" she declared. "Totally!"

"He's always been a good actor," Ty admitted grudgingly. "Fair to poor as a father and human being, but he's earned his success in films."

"Oh, Ty."

"Come here," he said gruffly, kissing her hard until Cammie's limbs felt as if they were weightless. "I don't want to think about anything but us right now."

"I agree," she sighed happily, and that was enough.

An hour later, they sat curled together on the couch, watching the sun-dappled water turn to a sheet of molten gold. Summer was on its way.

"I had a terrible night," Ty murmured into the warmth and sweetness of her nape. "All those feelings came back: betrayal and anger and helplessness. I wanted to kill my father, and I wanted to hurt you like you'd hurt me."

"I love you," she said by way of answer.

"God, Cammie . . . I love you, too."

His utterance to the words he'd so long denied shocked them both. But once said, Ty refused to take them back. He squeezed her tight, afraid to let go. "I guess I can't help myself. And somewhere in the middle of the night I realized that fact. Then it didn't matter anymore. I didn't care. I'd already determined I was going to catch the first flight to Los Angeles and find you."

"You're serious?" Cammie twisted to stare into his eyes.

He nodded.

"I don't believe this," she murmured wonderingly. "I didn't think you would ever trust me again."

"Why not? In the first place there was the indisputable fact that you didn't bring the screenplay with you. And even if you had, well, things changed between us pretty fast, if you know what I mean."

She fought a smile. "You mean, sisterly and brotherly affection changed?"

"Uh huh. In a big way."

He kissed her ravenously all over her face and neck until Cammie was squealing with delight, scrambling to get away. "You're tickling me!"

"Good."

"Stop it, Ty! Oh . . . good grief . . . damn . . . *oh!* You

. . . stop!'' she squealed, just as a banging sounded on the front door again.

''Samuel,'' Cammie murmured.

Ty groaned in frustration, collapsing against her at this latest interruption. ''Go away!'' he yelled.

They both gazed expectantly at the door, and sure enough it opened beneath the intruder's hand. Samuel stuck his head inside, spied them together on the couch, and his handsome, craggy face relaxed in a grin.

''Well, finally,'' he declared. ''Now, we can get down to business . . .''

If Cammie had been asked to script what a showdown between Ty, his father, and herself would entail, she could not have imagined any kind of happy ending. But now, hours into the discussion among the three of them, as she replaced the filter on the coffee maker, filled the carafe, then set the whole contraption in motion one more time, she almost believed it could be.

Watching the brown fluid drip into the carafe, she listened to the quiet drone of Samuel's instructions to his son. Oh, not that Ty was carefully listening; she suspected he'd checked out hours ago. And she'd performed this coffee-making task too many times over the course of the afternoon and evening to count. But she and Ty were both content to let Mr. Stovall, Sr., have his say, mainly because it was the only way they could think of to get him out of their hair.

Samuel had plunked himself down in the armchair, acting as if nothing untoward had ever taken place between him and Ty. He'd then set about making plans for all three of them, and it was a testament to Ty's newfound patience that he let his father ramble and plot and cajole. What he thought about the proceedings, Cammie could only guess.

In logical order, Samuel laid out the facts of how *Rock Bottom* was to be produced, when, and by whom. He was a far better advocate for the project than Cammie could ever have been. He cared, whereas Cammie had simply let it all happen around her. She was glad she'd never had to truly be *Rock Bottom*'s guiding emissary.

Now, slipping a steaming mug between Ty's hands, Cammie raised her brows in a silent question to Sam, asking him if he'd like the same.

"No, thanks," he answered. "Unless you've got some brandy?"

"Scotch," Ty reminded him.

"Never mind."

Cammie sat down by Ty on the couch. Lovingly, he placed one hand on her knee. Samuel barely flicked it a glance; he was on a track and nothing could derail him. "So, what do you think of it?" he asked into the pause that followed. He gestured to the copy of *Rock Bottom* which lay on the coffee table between them. "No more beating around the bush. What do you honestly think of it?"

"I told Cammie already. It's good."

"I mean as a project for you," Samuel pushed impatiently. "Are you interested?"

"I live in Bayrock."

Samuel muttered a few unintelligible words that sounded like half-formed curses to Cammie's ears. Ty merely looked amused. "Will you come back and take the role?" Samuel rephrased, his mouth a hard line, his own patience razor thin.

"You spent hours yesterday telling me how the press is ready to pounce on my bones. There's no going back without setting off a media circus."

"There isn't anyway," Samuel interrupted. "Your return will headline every channel."

"And that's supposed to make me want to come back?"

"*Rock Bottom* is the reason to come back. And Camilla," he put in as an afterthought. "You've obviously got deep feelings going here, and she's not crazy enough to give up her career and live like a mountain man's dimwit bride."

Ty rolled his eyes. Cammie was too happy to take offense one way or another, but she did manage to say, "This is hardly a 'mountain man' abode."

"My point is, the media storm will follow you regardless. Come back and do the film. It's perfect for you, and I know you want it. I want it for you."

"No offense, but I don't trust your 'fatherly' feelings."

"It's all I want, Tyler," Samuel insisted, looking for all the world like he really meant it. But then, he was a consummate actor, as Cammie appreciated more with each passing minute.

Ty gave his father a long look, then turned to regard Cammie thoughtfully. "What do you think I should do?"

Cammie's lips parted. "Ty, this is entirely up to you. Are you—seriously considering returning?"

"Do it!" Samuel jumped in. "This is the opportunity of a lifetime, don't you see? It's time to take control. You are Norm Franklin," he insisted, referring to *Rock Bottom*'s central character.

"And redemption's the theme," Ty finished with a faint smile.

"Ridicule all you want, Son. In this, I'm right. I'm always right when it comes to picking a film."

Ty gazed at the man he'd hated for so many years. His emotions warred with his intellect. A great many of the things Samuel said were true; a great many were selfish fiction. He had half a mind to tell his father where to stick it, but juvenile "feel goods" were always hollow and unimportant.

With a sigh and a sense of coming home, Ty said simply, "All right, I'll do it, on one condition."

"What's that?" Samuel asked a bit fearfully.

"That Cammie is definitely my co-star. No ifs, ands, or buts, and no changing at the last minute."

"Done!" Samuel declared, rising and thrusting out his hand to his son to seal the deal. "I'll call the producers at once. Welcome back, Tyler. It's about time!"

CHAPTER SEVENTEEN

Tyler wiped the sweat from his brow as he climbed from the workout bench and got to his feet. The smiling girl at the desk looked eager to help, but he just signaled her with a shake of his head and a mouthed, "Thanks" to let her know he was in no need of assistance. Heading outside, he walked back to his cabin and the boxes that awaited him.

Two nights earlier Cammie had left for the bright lights of Los Angeles. She followed in Samuel's wake, but he, Tyler, had stayed on to complete the final touches of his departure from this town which had been his home for so long.

He'd already said his good-byes. He'd stopped by Rodeo Bob's and explained to Corky that he was leaving. Corky, who'd been poleaxed by Ty's appearance *sans* beard, protested long and loud about his friend's decision to leave. Ty had nearly told his friend the truth about his identity, but he just couldn't bring himself to do it. It would spoil their relationship; he'd had it happen to him too many times in the past. And he wanted to remember Corky as the friend who thought he was Jerry Mercer, not Tyler Stovall. Eventually, of course, the truth would come out and Ty would have to come back to Bayrock and face Corky, but he wanted to get through the baptism by fire in Hollywood first.

Ty had then made a point of running into Missy. After exclaiming over his shaven chin, she'd boldly stepped forward and hugged him close. "You really look like that actor now!" she laughed.

The truth grated along his nerves; the pain was almost physical. He hated this. Hated having to be "that screen idol" again, and yet, he wanted to go back to filmmaking. He hadn't been able to confess the truth to Missy, either. He'd even stalled telling her he was leaving because he really didn't want to face her histrionics. And he had a mental picture of her stunned by the realization she'd been a paramour of the infamous Tyler Stovall himself—then selling the rights to her "tell-all" book to the highest bidder. The thought curdled his stomach. He managed to mumble to her that he was leaving Bayrock, but whether she understood that it was forever, he couldn't tell. She stared at him with huge, uncomprehending eyes.

Maybe he was a coward, but he wanted the people of Bayrock planted in his memory just the way they were. Besides, he had enough problems with the uncertain future ahead of him.

You're nuts. Completely crazy. You have no idea what's in store. It's a nightmare. The words reverberated silently.

But there was Cammie. He loved her desperately. Loved her in a way that amazed and humbled him. And the timing was right to go back. For Cammie, and for his own sense of self, he knew he was making the correct choice.

Still, it was hard, and when he'd given Missy a last, platonic kiss good-bye on the cheek, he'd felt like a charlatan. Tears welled in her eyes and she choked out, "You really love her, don't you?" Ty, after a brief hesitation, had nodded. Yes, he really loved her.

Now, stepping inside his cabin, Ty glanced around the

familiar environs, his heartstrings tugging. So, here he was, ready to go. He just needed to put the finishing touches on his packing, and he was set to leave. He'd shipped a ton of stuff already to his pal Bruce's place. And he'd called Nanette, who'd been rapturous over his confession of love for Cammie, but less enthusiastic about his return to Los Angeles.

"Don't let them eat you up," she warned.

Ty had been amused. "I can handle myself. And I can handle my father."

"I'm going to brace myself for the hue and cry. Keep Cammie close. You'll need her."

"I'll be okay."

Now, as he took one long, last look out the windows to the bay, Ty closed his eyes and imagined Cammie's soft smile, jewel-like eyes, and tender touch. She was his bright light, and he'd almost thrown her away over silly fears that nevertheless hung in the corners of his mind like cobwebs.

"The past is dead," he said aloud, his voice sounding unnaturally harsh and loud in the empty room.

The future was waiting.

Los Angeles lay brown and dusty beneath an unusually hot sun as the jet screeched and lurched to a stop on the landing strip. Cammie waited until the pilot pulled up to the gate before unclipping her seatbelt. A flurry of passengers yanked luggage from the overhead bins. With barely concealed impatience, she waited until the aisle was clear and she could make her way up the jetway.

Susannah paced about at the gate, much to Cammie's amazement.

"You came to meet me?" Cammie's lips curved into a surprised smile.

"Are you kidding? You call and tell me Tyler Stovall's coming back, and you expect me to just sit on my hands! Of course I came!" she nearly screeched.

"Shhh . . . I told you he's not on this flight. He's got some things to take care of first."

"I know. I know! But I couldn't wait to hear the details. And besides, you could use a lift."

Cammie's amusement continued. Susannah, who was as harried and busy as any successful agent could be, did not make a habit of picking up her clients and/or friends at the airport. In fact, this was the first time on record, Cammie was certain.

And though Cammie had told Susannah about Ty's decision to step into the shark-infested waters of Hollywood again, she had neglected to bring up the information of her own relationship with him. That secret was too new, too raw, to reveal right off the bat. Let Susannah, and the rest of the world, get used to having Tyler Stovall and all the resulting media frenzy that would surround him for a while before adding to the melee.

"So, spill!" Susannah insisted as she and Cammie climbed into her white convertible. The top was up though the sun was shining. Susannah wasn't fool enough to completely lose her coif.

"I told you almost everything already," Cammie insisted. "I couldn't bring up the screenplay. I just couldn't do it."

"But Stovall Sr. took care of that, right?" Susannah stated grimly.

"Among other things," Cammie muttered.

"So, then what?"

"Ty was—I don't know—sure he'd been used and tricked by his father again. And by me. But then he thought about it, and well, *Rock Bottom* speaks for itself. Everything kind of came together. End of story." She sighed. "I still can't believe it!"

"When's he getting here? When's he talking to the Connellys?"

"Samuel's been after him, but Ty made it clear that if anyone said anything before he was ready, he would back out. I don't know if he really would, but Samuel's not taking any chances." Cammie shook her head. "What's his stake in this anyway? I mean, you'd think he was the one up for the role, not Ty."

Susannah gave Cammie a searching look. "Oh, my God. Of course you don't know. I just found out myself."

"Don't know what?" Cammie asked, alarm feathering along her nerves.

"I was in a meeting with the Connellys and your lovely ex."

"Paul. Yes, yes." Cammie was impatient.

"Apparently, there have been some extra negotiations taking place."

"With Samuel?" Cammie asked, her heart sinking.

"Jim and Nora wouldn't really say. Not to me, anyway, so I'm just guessing here, but you know the part of Norm Franklin's father?"

"Oh, no . . . !"

"I'm thinking the Connellys have agreed to give Samuel the role. It makes sense, doesn't it? I mean, after all, he's perfect. And the publicity over father and son in the same film. . . . Well, it's a gold mine."

"Oh, I hope you're wrong. I really hope you're wrong."

Susannah grimaced. "Unfortunately, I have instincts over these things."

"Susannah, Ty will never do it." Cammie's brain spun wildly. "He'll think we set him up. *Again!*"

"It might not even be true."

"But what if it is. I can't even imagine what he'll think!"

"It's not your fault."

Cammie gazed at her friend in despair. Susannah didn't know the tricky ins and outs of her relationship with Ty, so she had no way of understanding how Ty would react to—what he would view—as this newest betrayal. "Somehow, it will reflect on me." She sighed.

"Stop being such a pessimist. You don't have to bring it up. Wait until he gets here."

"Oh, no." Cammie shook her head emphatically. "That'll be worse. He needs to be warned."

"I shouldn't have told you." Susannah gripped the

wheel with extra force, pushing her toe on the accelerator with sudden emotion. "We don't know anything for sure."

"You don't understand. I can't even think straight about this!" Cammie collapsed against the leather upholstery, as spent as if she'd run a marathon. "And to think that I almost felt sorry for Samuel a time or two, when he was acting all miserable about how his relationship with Ty had turned out."

"Whose fault is that!"

"Exactly. But I wanted them to reconcile, I guess. I wanted them to put the past where it belongs: in the past. It makes me feel used that he had this other agenda all along. I should have known! There's not an altruistic bone in Samuel Stovall's body. It was all about what Ty's return would do for *him!*"

"He's a bastard," Susannah agreed without heat.

"I have to tell Ty," Cammie said, feeling tired all over. "I have to."

"Do you really?" Susannah silently beseeched her, but Cammie slowly nodded, knowing that another betrayal would push Ty away from her forever. "Then we've got to buy some wine to drown our sorrows," Susannah capitulated on a sigh, taking the exit that led to Cammie's apartment. "And a lot of it!"

Half an hour later, while Susannah fussed with the cork on a *primo* bottle of Chardonnay, Cammie slowly replaced the receiver for what felt like the fiftieth time. She exhaled a pent-up breath. A glance at the clock convinced her she'd been too late: Ty was already on his way to join her in Los Angeles. He'd turned off his answering machine—had probably already packed it—and obviously was no longer at the cabin.

So, her news would have to wait.

"No luck?" Susannah inquired, handing Cammie her goblet of the shimmering, clear fluid.

"No luck."

With a sense of foreboding, Cammie swallowed a gulp huge enough to make her choke. She tried to make small talk with Susannah but failed utterly. In the end, her agent and friend gave her a hug good night and the platitude, "Don't worry. It'll all work out," before leaving the apartment. Cammie cleaned up the wineglasses, methodically wiping the rims and inner bowls, her mind tiptoeing through the minefield of the future.

She spent a hellish evening and sleepless night. The burden of Samuel's latest deception lay heavy on her conscience, and it felt as if a band were ever tightening around her chest.

When will he arrive? she fretted. *Should I check with the Connellys first? Or Samuel?*

Ty had told her he planned to check in at a hotel as soon as he arrived in town, for the home that he still owned—where Cammie had stumbled upon him naked and they had enjoyed their first night of lovemaking—was currently rented by a producer out of New York who used it whenever he was in town. Ty's first order of business would be to stop at his friend Bruce's place and check the lay of the "financial" land. Cammie's shy suggestion that he could move into her apartment for the time being had been met with a leer and a last trip to the cabin's loft for some "afternoon delight." But then Ty had told her he thought it would be best to keep their personal relationship low profile for at least a little while. Seeing it from that angle, Cammie had nodded in fervent agreement.

Now, as she looked around the appointments of her small but cozy kitchen and dining area, she wondered how long she and Ty would have to remain apart. As soon as the media caught the buzz, they would be harassed to the full extent of the ravenous press. Until the pending hoopla died down, there was nothing to do but wait.

Shuddering, she dreaded what was to come. Poor Ty, she thought with a grimace, recognizing that if she were already shying away, his feelings of aversion would be so much stronger. The whole thing would be as bad, or worse, than even he had envisioned.

Digging through her purse, she pulled out the business card Ty had given her for Bruce Cramer. Fingering the corner thoughtfully, she wondered if she should call Ty's stockbroker friend and see if Ty had contacted him in the last couple of hours. Bruce knew about their relationship; Ty had made that clear. But would he want her to call and question him about Ty's movements? Maybe she should wait for Ty to call himself.

As if on command, the telephone shrilled. Cammie snatched up the receiver on the first ring. "Hello?"

"Hey, there, beautiful!" Ty's voice greeted her. In the background she could hear the roar of traffic.

"Where are you?"

"Just off the freeway in Oregon. I think I'll stop somewhere later tonight. See how it goes. Probably cruise into L.A. sometime tomorrow."

"You shipped all your stuff?"

"Most of it. The Jeep's stuffed. The furniture's in storage—I might give it to Corky—and the rest's on its way to Bruce's. I might even beat it there."

"I can't wait to see you!"

"I can hardly hear you," Ty shouted over the noise. "I'm at this truck stop."

"I said, I LOVE YOU!" Cammie shouted, enjoying the freedom of admitting her feelings.

"WHAT? Oh! Did you say I love you? If you did, I LOVE YOU, TOO!"

"TY!" Cammie called, sensing he was about to hang up. "THERE'S SOMETHING I'VE GOT TO TELL YOU."

"I CAN'T HEAR YOU. SAVE IT TILL I GET THERE. BYE, MY LOVE."

Cammie stood with a dead receiver in hand. She replaced it and swallowed, then rubbed her tired eyes.

Get over it, girl. This is just the beginning.

Drawing a breath of courage, she murmured aloud, "It's the end I'm worried about."

* * *

With a feeling of being "over the rainbow," Ty drove his Jeep down familiar Los Angeles streets. He debated on staying at the Wyndham Bel Age, just off Sunset, but decided if he were going to reappear, he might as well do it in true Hollywood style. So thinking, he turned the steering wheel in the direction of the famous, pink-stuccoed Beverly Hills Hotel.

As soon as he yanked on the brake, valets raced to his dusty Jeep. Ty levered himself from the seat, easing tension from his back. Last night, he'd stopped at a motel just outside the California border, slept about three hours, then climbed back in his vehicle and driven the rest of the way straight—about twelve hours. He looked like he felt: weary and rumpled. Still, there was a strange sense of homecoming that threatened to reveal his world-famous smile for all and sundry to see.

"Here you are, sir," the obsequious young man said, handing Ty his parking validation. "Don't worry, it'll be safe with us," he added, referring to Ty's belongings which were crammed to the roof inside the Jeep.

"Thanks."

Ty strode into the foyer. He'd never stayed at the Beverly Hills Hotel, having no need since he'd lived in L.A. all his life until his escape to Bayrock. But he'd had drinks in the bar where the famous and infamous comingled. It was in his mind to head straight for a frothy beer when a prickling along his nerves, a premonition, caught his attention, and as he walked toward reception, he realized his days of obscurity were over: a row of eyes and smiling lips greeted him like a long-lost friend, the reception staff recognized his famous face.

"Mr. Stovall," one said, an attractive brunette with a drop-dead smile of her own. "We've been expecting you."

Before Tyler could react to that stunning announcement, the bellman was at his elbow. "Could I take that for you?" he asked, referring to the overnight bag Ty had stuffed with the items he needed most at hand.

"Uh . . ."

It was a dream. A washed-out transparency from which he viewed real life. A key was pressed in his hands. Directions to the room. The bellman took the bag Ty relinquished from slack fingers. An elevator dinged softly somewhere outside the misty tunnel of his vision.

Then he was at the door of his room. He entered in that same dreamy state to the lush appointments of a suite, complete with wet bar.

We've been expecting you.

Reality crashed. Heading straight for the phone, he punched out his father's number, clicking the receiver before it even had time to connect. No, he didn't want to talk to Samuel. Instead, he called his buddy Bruce who was already at home, awaiting Tyler's appearance.

"Bruce," Ty rasped, when his friend answered the phone, "I was *expected* at the Beverly Hills Hotel!"

"I know," Bruce sighed.

"How? I didn't tell anyone I was going there except you!"

"Word got out at my office," Bruce confessed. "An eager-beaver office gofer heard 'Stovall' and thought I was talking to your father. At the same time, I'd pulled up your account which, of course, reads Mr. Samuel Stovall, Jr.," he reminded Ty with a wince in his voice. "The gofer still thought it was your father. He told the financial advisor to Samuel's account who apparently took offense that I was poaching on his client, so he called Samuel, who then learned of your intentions and well . . . I'm sorry."

"My father," Ty murmured, exhaling a breath. A moment later, he said, "It doesn't matter. It was bound to happen sooner or later, but I'll tell you, it was eerie to walk in like I'd never left."

"I'll bet," Bruce said with feeling. "I didn't know how to reach you. Your cell was off."

"Yeah, I packed it by mistake. Figured it wouldn't matter. Anyway, never mind. The fact is, I'm here."

"How does it feel?" Bruce asked curiously.

"Strange as hell."

"Are you coming over to the house?"

"I'm going to call Cammie, then take a shower and get things together a bit," Ty said. "I'll be over right after."

So saying, he pressed a finger to the receiver and released it, all the while pulling a scrap of paper from his pocket with two fingers. Cammie's number wasn't committed to memory yet. But as he began punching the buttons, he thought better of it, replacing the receiver. Shower first. Phone call later.

Ten minutes later, while he toweled his hair dry, he began to dial Cammie's number again, cradling the receiver to his ear and absentmindedly picking up the TV remote with his free hand. Waiting for her to answer, he checked on the five o'clock news. Traffic problems in the city. Big surprise.

"Hello, there," he said with a smile in his voice as Cammie's voice came on the line. "I've got a picture in my mind of you right now. And you know what? You're not wearing anything."

"Untrue." Her own voice was full of mirth. "I am wearing one thing: Passion Flower Red polish on my toes."

"Woman," he growled as her laughter broke free, "you're going to drive me crazy!"

"Where are you?"

He told her, then said, "Meet me at Bruce's in about an hour. You know where he lives?"

"I've got the directions. But Ty, there's something I've got to tell you about your father."

Ty groaned. "Save it till I see you at Bruce's. I want to get moving."

"Really, Ty, it can't wait. And—you're not going to like it."

"I wouldn't expect to, if it concerns dear old Dad. Cammie, I—" Ty broke off on a sharp inhalation of breath at the image suddenly filling the TV screen. His face. From ten years earlier. Swearing pungently, he snapped up the volume. "Turn on your TV!" he ordered. "The you-know-what has definitely hit the fan!"

The drive to Bruce's house, situated on the edge of Beverly Hills, was a nightmare. The burden of telling Ty about Samuel's hidden agenda constricted her chest. If only she'd been able to come clean, but Ty's discovery of his own mini-biography being played on the news had superceded all else. Which was understandable, as Cammie herself had been knocked sideways by the story.

The press wasn't only ferocious—it was *fast!*

Cammie's hands tensed and relaxed on the steering wheel. Ty's return to Hollywood was treated with joy, disbelief, and speculation. The worst of that broadcast was the innuendo. Somehow, the bright, all-knowing woman reporter had unearthed a bit of the scandal surrounding Gayle's death. Conjecture was that her suicide prompted Ty's flight.

There was enough truth in her words to make Cammie wince; she could just imagine how Ty felt.

We needed more time, she thought futilely. *More time together. More time to plan. More time to think things through before facing the lion.*

Too late now.

Cammie gasped as she turned up the street to Bruce's home. The road was nearly blocked by TV news vans and crews. A policeman impatiently waved her on by. She had to park blocks away and then she sat in cold fear inside her BMW, heart pounding erratically as she recognized that the second volley in the match between Tyler Stovall and the fourth estate had been shot.

Samuel Stovall, she thought, sending the blame to its most likely source. *He's the one who's blabbed to the media.*

Infuriated beyond all reason, she slammed her car door and stalked in the direction of Bruce's house. The home was small compared to some of the massive Beverly Hills structures nearby, and somewhat unimposing, but a beautiful rolling lawn curved down to the street, bisected by a manicured drive that led to the front door. But that drive was currently stuffed with vehicles of all descriptions, and to Cammie's annoyance she was halted from stepping a foot onto its concrete surface by one of Beverly Hills' finest.

"I'm sorry, ma'am, but this is not a tourist attraction. Everyone is being asked to keep moving," he told her, his eyes already shifting past her to survey the sea of cars, trucks and camera people positioned about the area.

"I'm expected," she said flatly.

His gaze swiveled to her face. "Ma'am?"

"Mr. Cramer and his guest are expecting me."

"Your name, please?"

Cammie told him, then followed slowly behind as he headed up the driveway to check her story. Newsmen and women, tucked into tight bunches, swiveled their heads in Cammie's direction, then descended upon her in a horde. A battery of microphones were thrust in her face.

"Is Tyler Stovall inside?" one thin-faced woman demanded.

"Are you a friend of Mr. Cramer's? Has he been hiding Tyler Stovall all these years?" someone else yelled above the din.

"Are you in on the plot?" still another asked.

"What's your name . . ."

"Would you care to make a statement . . ."

"Is this another publicity stunt . . ."

"Quick, get her picture before she turns away!" someone screeched as Cammie ducked behind her blue-suited guide.

At the front door, the policeman turned to the crowd, one hand motioning Cammie to ring the bell. "Stand back!" he boomed out. The hungry news people ignored him completely.

Cammie pressed the buzzer, hearing chimes ring inside the two-story stucco house. She wasn't certain exactly what to do, but then the door cracked open and she was practically yanked inside. The crowd surged forward, but she was hustled to the back of the house where curtains were drawn across a wall of floor-to-ceiling windows, making the place seem like night had already fallen.

She didn't recognize her savior. Blinking at the dark-haired stranger, she said shakily, "Bruce Cramer?"

"Cammie Merrill?"

They shook hands on faint laughs. At that moment, a pair of double doors slid open to reveal a study, and Ty hesitantly stuck his head through. He motioned Cammie forward and she hurried to collapse inside the warmth of his welcoming arms.

"God, I missed you," he murmured into the softness of her neck.

She breathed deeply of his uniquely male scent. "I'm so glad to see you. What happened here? How did they know?"

"I barely got through the door when they descended like a pack of hounds!"

"Scum," Bruce muttered, his expression dark. "Word leaked out at work. They staked out my house."

"I was sure it was Samuel's doing," Cammie muttered.

"I wouldn't count him out." Ty tightened his grip, as if she were his sole support. "My Jeep's outside with all my stuff. I can't get to it. Bruce called the police and they're just starting to push people off the property."

He sounded angry and discouraged. "Well, we knew it was going to be bad," Cammie murmured. "I just thought we'd have a little bit more time."

Bruce stepped toward a smaller window which flanked a stone fireplace and opened onto a side yard. He peeked through vertical blinds, and said, "They're everywhere."

"Ty, about your dad . . ."

"Oh, yeah. What?" He was distracted.

"I think there was more to his wanting you to come back now. It may be that he's been angling for a part in *Rock Bottom*—Norm Franklin's father."

Ty swore pungently. Cammie held her breath, but she felt better just having unburdened herself.

"Figures," Bruce said, eyeing Ty carefully. Like Cammie, he knew how much each extra betrayal hurt.

But Ty, after raking hands through his hair and closing his eyes in momentary meditation, shook his head and stated firmly, "I don't care. I'm back now. It doesn't matter."

She knew it did matter, but she was glad Ty was willing to set the matter aside, at least for the moment. And it didn't appear that he blamed her. Her own confession helped keep his trust.

"I could call Susannah, my agent," Cammie suggested. "She could help contain this." She swept an arm to indicate the mob outside.

Since there didn't seem to be anything better in mind, Ty and Bruce agreed. Cammie put through the call, and when Teri, Susannah's assistant, heard what the trouble was, she eagerly took down Bruce's number and promised that Susannah would call back ASAP.

It took twenty minutes, however, for that miracle to happen as Susannah was in a meeting at that very moment with the Connellys and Samuel Stovall.

"It was a command performance," Susannah declared breathlessly, from the hallway outside the Connellys' private production offices. "I tried to call you, but you weren't home."

"I came to see Ty," she said simply, "but his friend Bruce Cramer's house is surrounded by—"

"Jackals," Bruce interrupted.

"—news people. And did you catch the news earlier? We're in the hurricane."

"And we'll all weather it," Susannah assured her.

"What's going on with Samuel and the Connellys?" Cammie asked, to which question Ty's lips tightened but he didn't make further comment.

"They're discussing *Rock Bottom,* of course. Everyone's on pins and needles waiting to meet with the infamous

Tyler Stovall. Does he, um, have an agent?" she asked diffidently.

Cammie grinned. "An agent? I don't think so."

"Tell her she's hired if she can get this riffraff off Bruce's yard," Ty drawled. Cammie relayed the comment and Susannah promised to send a barrage of publicity people to contain the impromptu press conference.

"Your lovely ex has been hovering around like a bad smell," Susannah went on, after she'd taken down all the pertinent information. "I'm sure he's afraid he'll be cut out somehow, and I think the Connellys would love to get rid of him. He might have put the deal together with you and therefore Tyler, but man, oh, man, he's a pain in the butt!"

"Tell me about it."

"Yeah, well, he's bound and determined to hang in there. It's his nature."

"The less I see of him the better."

"Ain't that the truth! Look, I gotta go. Meet me at my office tonight. I'll be there at eight o'clock with Karen Walthers. She's a publicity expert, and, honey, you need one! Bring the man of the hour, too. I'll take care of the mess in Mr. Cramer's yard. 'Bye."

Cammie hung up the phone, wondering when she and Ty could safely leave.

"The police are backing them off the driveway," Bruce reported from his view at the edge of the windows.

"Let's face the music," Tyler said.

Both Cammie and Bruce gazed at him blankly. "What do you mean?" Cammie asked. "Now?"

"It's time to go out, make a statement and be done with it. Hiding in here makes me feel like a criminal."

"Shouldn't you—check with a publicity specialist or something?" Bruce suggested.

"Susannah wants us to meet with someone tonight," Cammie informed him.

Ty shook his head. "I can speak for myself. Let's put

this to bed." Bestowing a faint smile on the woman he loved, he asked, "Care to be my right-hand woman?"

Cammie shrugged her shoulders. "I'm there," she agreed, loving him for his courage.

With that, Ty crooked his elbow and Cammie slipped her hand through his arm. Bruce led the way to the door, holding it open for them, and they strode onto the wide brick porch as one. A wave of noise and exclamations emanated from the retreating crowd. Instantly, they surged forward again, to be halted by several stern, immobile officers who guarded the drive. The insistent crowd clamored to move closer, but Ty, with Cammie firmly at his side, strode toward them.

"Are you Tyler Stovall?" someone yelled, and into the sudden, expectant quiet that followed, Ty said simply, "Yes, I am."

Pandemonium ensued. Microphones waved and people pushed. The police could only hold the crowd back so far. It was Ty who lifted his arms and called for order, and eventually questions came thick and fast—a barrage worse than what had assaulted Cammie on her way in.

"I have a statement," Ty yelled above the commotion. "And it's all I'm going to say." He waited for the din to lessen a bit before speaking. "I chose to leave ten years ago for personal reasons. There's no great mystery about it. Now, I'm ready to come back. Yes, I am talking to producers about a possible role, but nothing's been decided yet."

Questions pounded from all sides.

"Which producers?"

"Where were you all this time?"

"What have you been doing for a living?"

"Are you romantically involved with Ms. Merrill?" someone shouted, louder than the rest.

Though she knew how quickly information passed through the system, Cammie was still surprised they already knew her name. Ty tried to ignore the question, but the clamor broke out again. Throwing a glance at Cammie which could only be interpreted one way, he answered curtly, "Yes," to which several microphones were quickly packed up and a section of the crowd sped away. First to get the news, Cammie thought with a twinge of disgust.

"I would appreciate some privacy for my friend," Ty glanced toward Bruce. "This is his home. If you want further information, contact my father, Samuel Stovall," Ty added with a flash of inspiration. "He's the man with the answers."

After that, Ty hustled Cammie back inside, and he, Cammie, and Bruce waited for the hubbub to die down. Hours later, when only a few scattered paparazzi hung at the end of the drive, Cammie and Ty left in her BMW, allowing the hungry, independent photographers to trail them to Susannah's.

Karen Walthers was a tall woman, topping six feet by Cammie's estimations, and she held out a strong, welcoming hand as the two of them appeared in Susannah's office. She was also very, very pregnant, and the sight of her beautiful, full body brought Cammie up short, reminding her of an emptiness she'd pushed aside in the midst of her happiness with Ty. With an effort, she pulled her thoughts away from the woman's burgeoning girth and the life growing inside, instead concentrating hard on Susannah, whose wild curls looked even wilder, as if she were bristling with electricity.

Sensitive to her swift change of moods, Ty asked, "What is it?" But Cammie shook her head. She couldn't trust herself to talk about Karen's pregnancy with any degree of control.

A TV flickered at one end of the room, but the sound had been muted. Susannah glanced at the screen and said, "Karen's been on the ball, getting rid of the mob, but you're bound to be on the tube again later."

"Ty made a statement," Cammie said.

Karen and Susannah turned in surprise to Ty, who paraphrased what he'd said for the cameras. "Well, you'll be all over the eleven o'clock news," Karen said with a slight frown. Clearly, she wouldn't have advised Ty to make a statement.

"You two are an item?" Susannah questioned. To Cammie's shy nod, she said, sounding a bit hurt, "You didn't tell me!"

"It's rather—new," Cammie defended herself lamely.

"They put you on the spot," Karen said to Ty, referring to the press. "Don't let it happen again, if you can help it. You're the main entree now, Mr. Stovall, as I'm sure you know, and they'll twist and turn every syllable you utter."

"I know. I've been there before." He exhaled heavily. "I knew it would be like this, but reality's always a shock, isn't it?" His mouth twisted into a smile. "Can you make it all go away?"

Karen smiled back. "All I can do is ease the path."

"Good enough."

"The Connellys would like to talk with you as soon as possible," Susannah informed Ty.

"And I'd like to talk to them." He gave her a sideways look, assessed her with lightning speed, and said, "As my agent, would you set it up?"

Susannah grinned, a hand over her heart in delight. "Done." She headed to the phone.

"How serious are you two?" Karen wanted to know.

Cammie and Ty looked at each other. Things were happening so fast, it took their collective breaths away. "Serious," Ty admitted lightly, settling into a chair and tugging at Cammie's hand so that she tumbled onto his lap.

Susannah made a strangled sound that could have meant anything, but then Cammie saw her blinking back sudden tears. She sent Cammie a wobbly smile of happiness and gave her a thumb's-up sign, then her attention snapped to whoever had answered at the other end of the line.

Cammie's brief moment of melancholy lifted. What was the matter with her? She had the world by the tail, for pete's sake!

Karen took out a pen and pad from her briefcase. "Okay,

I'm going to set up a couple of interviews for you: Morning shows, late night, the works. We'll work out a script, based on whatever you want the public to know. Be specific, but make your life sound tame. Don't invite more speculation."

"Okay."

"Susannah tells me you were living in Bayrock, British Columbia. Do people there know you? Do they know who you are?"

"They think I'm someone named Jerry Mercer. A Tyler Stovall look-alike."

"Then you'd better start telling them the truth. They're going to be bombarded. Is there anything about your time away that might come back to kick you in the teeth?"

"I lived a pretty simple life."

"Ex-girlfriends? Lovers?"

Ty hesitated. "I wasn't celibate," he admitted tensely.

"It'll all come out, you know. Bayrock inhabitants are about to have their fifteen minutes of fame . . ."

Karen's warnings went on and on, and Cammie and Ty both began to feel more and more depressed. The tip of the iceberg had been his return; a whole lotta ice would be revealed before the entire thing was uncovered.

Susannah made a strangled sound, "Look!" she cried, covering the receiver with one hand and pointing to the television set with the other.

Samuel's familiar face swam onto the screen during a news update. Karen flicked off the mute button in time to hear Samuel say, "No comment," to five questions in succession.

"Well, he finally decided to keep his mouth shut," Ty drawled with amusement. "Better late than never."

Cammie smiled, then froze in disbelief as Samuel's image was replaced by Paul Merrill's.

"Ugh," Cammie declared, as Paul explained that he was not currently at liberty to explain the details of the arrangement that had "lured Tyler Stovall home," but that he was indeed responsible for the prodigal's return, ınd that yes, Camilla Merrill was his ex-wife. He preened 'atuously for the camera.

Tyler observed him with interest. "So, that's the ex."

"He got me fired from *Cherry Blossom Lane,*" Cammie ;aid aloud. "I'm sure he's clapping himself on the back 'or his 'brainstorm' of sending me after Ty."

"I thought that was dear old Dad's point of honor," Ty ;aid with a grin.

"I'm glad you're taking this so well," Cammie mur-nured.

"Keep up the lighthearted spirits," Karen said with ıpproval. "It's the only way to get through this." She rose from her seat, her cumbersome shape making it a bit of ı struggle.

Cammie tried not to eye her pregnancy with envy. "When will it be over?"

"It can't be that big of a story," said Ty.

"It's the biggest thing since Monica Lewinsky," was Karen's spirit-dampening observation. "Expect it to go on awhile. Just hold on to your sense of humor for all its worth—you're going to need it."

CHAPTER EIGHTEEN

". . . Warren Galloway's accusations of blackmail and cover-up have shed a new light on Tyler Stovall's reasons for leaving Hollywood. Mr. Galloway insists there's more to the death of producer Gayle Muldoon than has yet been reported. The police are reluctant to continue investigations, however, and insiders speculate that icon Samuel Stovall has used his enormous clout to stall further inquiries . . ."

Ty flipped off the TV in disgust, tired of the same tripe that had played over and over again the past few weeks. That particular clip was from *The Final Truth*, an investigative television program which had interviewed both him and Warren Galloway. Though it had eventually shown Ty in a favorable light, he was sick of hearing about himself, sick of being bombarded with questions, sick of everything except his work on *Rock Bottom* and his relationship with Cammie.

The worst of the media frenzy had ended in the first four days, but Gayle's story had been resurrected several times by Warren Galloway's desire to be kept in the limelight. Samuel, it appeared, had assessed Galloway's character correctly: the man wanted his pound of flesh and twinkle of celebrity sparkle as well. The truth didn't matter

For about the billionth time, Ty wished he could just do his job without all the resulting hoopla, but wishes neve seemed to be fulfilled.

Karen had instructed Ty to remain at his hotel, awa from Cammie, in order to douse further flames of contro versy over his current romance. It was good advice for both him and Cammie, though it was difficult sleeping apar from her. Still, they'd managed to get together here and there. For now, it had to be enough.

Ty had struck a deal with the Connellys that was generou and fair. Cammie had not been privy to that inner sanctum meeting; it was between Ty, the Connellys, and their agents Susannah had given Cammie the thumbs-up sign when she'd rushed through her office where Cammie was anx iously waiting, but apart from a "Ty'll tell you all about it," Susannah had been very professional about not blabbing about other actors' contracts.

Which had ticked Cammie off to no end and amused Ty, who'd given her all the particulars later when they'd reaffirmed their feelings for each other in bed.

"Karen's having her baby soon," Cammie had said tha particular afternoon, alerting Ty to her state of mind.

"Don't torture yourself," he whispered in her ear, let ting his tongue explore its soft pink shell.

"I don't," she said, but the wistful lilt of her voice came through loud and clear. For the time being, Ty left the subject alone, knowing there was nothing to do about i anyway.

For a while everything had gone smoothly until the day on the set when Ty had grown so annoyed with his father for wanting things *his* way, no matter what, that he had blurted to Cammie, "That man is the most self-serving individual on this earth! He treats everyone else like a slave. It's a blessing we won't have children, Cammie. I'm not kidding. I never want the chance of a relationship like the one I have with my father!"

Reckless, reckless words. Especially given Cammie's fragile state on this issue. He'd felt bad when she'd gone completely quiet, but he'd meant what he'd said, and he hoped, in the end, she would come to understand his feelings.

Now, glancing out his window, Ty examined the hot, palish-blue Los Angeles sky. Paparazzi still hung around the Beverly Hills Hotel, but the boiling fever of Ty's reemergence had dissipated to a small simmer. For that he was supremely grateful, even if these infernal broadcasts kept cropping up.

And true to Karen's prediction, the residents of Bayrock were duly interviewed. They expressed wonder and awe that "Jerry Mercer" was truly Tyler Stovall, not some mere look-alike. The whole town was amazed. When Missy was interviewed, Tyler braced himself for a storm that never came. Missy's report could have been embarrassing to the extreme, given the truth of their relationship, but she'd been so poleaxed by the fact that she'd had a relationship with the famous actor himself, she could do little besides whisper, wide-eyed, "Wow, I don't believe it!" Reporters quickly tired of her star-struck behavior and went in search of juicier tidbits of information. Count that one as lucky. Missy's physical relationship with Tyler would never be believed even if she were to suddenly start telling all and sundry about it; it smacked too much of pure fantasy.

Thank God for small favors.

During the resulting interview with Corky and acquaintances who were seated at the counter inside Rodeo Bob's, Ty fared a little better than with Missy. Though self-conscious of the cameras, the group had only nice things to say about the "star" who'd dwelled in their midst. "He's a good man," Corky stated with a shrug. "No matter what his name is. Hey, Jer," he added for benefit of the camera, lifting a mug to the lens. "This one's for you, pal. Keep cool."

Nostalgia cut a hole in Tyler's heart, but he vowed to keep plowing ahead with *Rock Bottom.*

But then Warren Galloway got cooking and Karen calle a quick meeting to assess what was what. Ty reluctantl explained the circumstances of Gayle's death, so Kare suggested a defense of “no comments” by all. It was trick especially when Warren took his tale of suicide, decei and blackmail to a particularly obnoxious morning sho host—and bared the extent of Samuel's misguided cove up. Warren described Samuel and Tyler Stovall as ev partners in a plot to drive poor, pregnant Gayle to suicid in order to kill the “love child” who had been fathere by one of them. The melodramatic and ludicrous tale hel just enough truth to be seriously considered; even th LAPD were named as part of the conspiracy to cover u the dastardly deed.

And it had gone on from there, losing fire, but neve fully extinguished. Samuel's prediction had come true The past haunted from beyond the grave.

Annoyed himself, Samuel had rung up Tyler one evening and boomed out, “I'm calling a press conference You've got to be there and help field questions.”

Ty had simply slammed down the phone.

“Enough,” he'd growled to Cammie who sat on th edge of one of the chairs in Ty's private suite. “I'm sorr about Gayle and the baby, and I'm sorry my father buckle under to blackmail. But I'll be damned if I'll go and digni slander. Samuel got himself into this, he can get himse out.”

Gayle's suicide and the death of her unborn child go a lot of play in the papers. Pictures of the deceased woma were splayed across papers and magazines. Warren Galloway was reportedly signing a book deal.

It all made Tyler sick.

And Cammie, oddly teary-eyed over the whole ordeal said miserably, “They just harp on this tragedy over an over again. I hate it.”

“Forget about it, sweetheart. I hate it, too.” Ty pulle her into his arms and Cammie clutched him tightly.

"I don't know how she could—" She gulped, cutting herself off.

"Kill her child?" Ty suggested softly, brushing back her hair, saying the words she couldn't form.

"I'd do anything to have my own baby. Anything! And the way they muckrake Gayle's story. It's flat-out criminal!"

The flap over Warren's allegations grew to fever pitch and Karen had to reverse her earlier proclamation. She suggested that Ty address the issue of Gayle and her unborn child. The swirling innuendo over the baby's paternity had grown with Ty and Samuel's silence over the issue. Ty balked at airing the dirty laundry, but Karen splayed her hands and pointed out, "Your sensibilities can be affronted all you want, but it won't cool the public's ardor. Tell them the truth. Tell them it was yours. Tell them you didn't know until it was too late, and tell them it was why you left."

It went against everything Ty believed in. The idea of baring his soul to a hungry, avid public was anathema. He couldn't do it. He couldn't betray himself so thoroughly. He was furious with Samuel for putting him in this position. And yes, he was angry at Gayle, too, for destroying herself and another life just for the sake of revenge. For that's what it had turned out to be. Written in her own hand, Gayle's suicide letter to Samuel had been all accusations and blame, and it had been used as a tool of blackmail all these years.

Ty thought to ride it out, but instead of abating, the buzz continued right up to the first day of shooting for *Rock Bottom.* Feeling like he was somehow buckling under and being untrue to himself, he nevertheless agreed to an interview with a reporter from *The Final Truth,* an hour-long, in-depth investigative news program along the lines of NBC's *Dateline* and CBS's *60 Minutes.*

Cammie chose to stay home while the episode was taped, and when Ty came back from the ordeal it was to her apartment. "Screw the media," he muttered as he drew her into his arms, having successfully shaken a paparazzi from his tail. "I'm sick of being today's flavor, and I'm even sicker of being polite." He managed a short bark of laughter. "Every time somebody thrusts a mike in front of me, I want to resort to rude noises and gestures."

"That ought to win over your public," Cammie responded with suppressed mirth.

"They'll all wish I'd stayed missing."

"Not all of them," she murmured, her aqua eyes filled with a come-hither look Ty felt he could drown in.

"Come here, woman," he muttered.

Cammie draped herself across his arms. "I love that He-Man stuff, Mr. Stovall."

"Yeah?"

"Take me to bed."

He lifted a knowing brow. "Well, put it to me that way . . ."

He kissed her hard, and she grinned against the curve of his mouth. Following her commands dutifully, he carried her into her bedroom and they made love with passion and love and a need deeper than Cammie had experienced before. When it was over, she lay across his chest, her hair splayed in a soft, reddish wave. Ty contemplatively drew an auburn tress through his fingers. "I tried not to talk about it," he confessed. "I did everything I knew how to avoid the questions."

Cammie opened her eyes, staring across the half-darkened room. "How do you think it went?"

"Okay," he admitted, sounding a bit surprised. "They got a few answers out of me, but there's no altering the fact that Gayle took her own life. My leaving was a reaction to all the ugliness. That's all there is to the story."

"Good." Cammie's voice was light. "It sounds like our troubles are behind us and we can look to the future."

"I hope you're right," he said, and Cammie wrapped her arms even more tightly around his hair-roughened chest, supremely happy.

That particular program aired a week later. Though Ty had told her it would come off okay, Cammie had been unable to watch without biting her nails. She was at Susannah's office, and Susannah, spying her nail-chewing, slapped at Cammie's hands. "He was great!" she declared, and a relieved Cammie had to agree.

Ty wasn't with them. He and the Connellys and the *Rock Bottom* crew were still filming that night. Cammie wasn't due on the set until later the following week, so she'd spent the time pacing the confines of her apartment, driving Susannah crazy and reading over her lines. "Co-star," as it turned out, was an inflated term for the small role. The story was Ty's and Ty's character, Norm Franklin's. She was a catalyst for the change in Norm's sordid life; she kick-started his salvation. But that didn't mean she had a huge part, though it was meaty. So, Cammie was forced to wait around while Ty worked on what he termed his rusty acting skills.

Samuel, for his part, had been careful to stay in the background. Ty had confronted him about his hidden agenda when it came to bargaining for a role for himself. Samuel, unrepentant, said simply, "Stop looking for a worm under every rock. It's not like you haven't benefited yourself!"

Ty had shaken his head all over again. "He never ceases to amaze me," he told Cammie.

"How are you dealing with it?"

"I just don't think of him as my father, then it doesn't matter," was Ty's solution.

Now, as Ty prepared for another day of shooting, he tried to push his annoyance with his father and the continuing media storm aside. He loved acting and he loved Cammie. Nothing else mattered.

Cammie parked her BMW outside Susannah's office, walked inside the lobby and punched the button for the elevator. Stepping inside the car, she hit the lighted number two. The elevator lurched upward. A wave of intense nausea washed over her, and when the doors slid open on

Susannah's floor, Cammie stayed put for a moment, one hand leaning against the wall, the other clutching her stomach. Gingerly, she stepped into the hallway and walked with careful, mincing steps to Susannah's office door.

"Hey, there." Teri called, upon seeing Cammie. Then quickly, "Are you okay?"

"Water . . ." Cammie croaked out.

She was herded into Susannah's inner office by solicitous hands. Susannah, as ever, was on the phone, but spying Cammie's unnatural color, she hung up with unaccustomed speed.

"Whoa, what's wrong, hon?" she demanded.

"I feel—sick."

"Come on, let's get you to the bathroom!"

Susannah practically yanked Cammie from her chair and helped her to the bathroom. Cammie waved her away. It was too, too embarrassing! Reluctantly, Susannah obeyed. Light-headed and seeing tiny spots, Cammie then beelined for the toilet, wretching violently.

Long minutes later, she flushed and then rinsed her mouth and face at the sink, staring at her ghastly green-tinged reflection in the mirror as the bell to Susannah's office buzzed from down the hall, announcing a new visitor.

"Ohhh . . ." Cammie groaned, not interested in seeing anyone in her current condition.

Current condition . . .

Shockwaves of heat ripped through Cammie's veins. Her face flushed pink in front of her eyes. *Pregnancy?* She'd just assumed she'd caught the flu, but since she'd experienced no other symptoms, the obvious answer was something else. Clapping a hand to her mouth, Cammie thought back to her other, brief pregnancies and recognized joyfully that this was exactly how she'd felt before!

A baby. A family. The man she loved!

Thoughts jumbled through her mind. Dangerous heady dreams. Fear followed in rapid succession: a return to reality. It wasn't that she couldn't conceive. That had never been the problem. It was that she couldn't carry a healthy baby to term.

Despair followed rapidly on the heels of ultimate joy. With an effort Cammie pulled herself back under control. She had to think, *think!*

She hadn't seen Dr. Crawley since she'd returned from Bayrock. She'd been too swept up in the megaevent of Ty's return. She would make an appointment tomorrow.

For tonight, she would keep her secret safe.

"You okay?" Susannah asked when Cammie reappeared.

Cammie opened her mouth to assure her when, behind Susannah, she recognized the newest arrival. Lounging in one of the chairs, looking as if he owned the place, was her unmourned-for ex-husband. While Cammie sought to keep the annoyance out of her face, he gave her a searching once-over. "You look like death," he observed. "Susannah said you were sick." His gaze sharpened instantly, and to Cammie's horror, he jumped straight to the right conclusion: "Don't tell me you're pregnant again."

"You know that's impossible," she managed faintly. "What are you doing here?"

"I came to see you, actually. It appears I've been usurped on *Rock Bottom.*" Anger turned his attention back to himself and away from Cammie, much to her relief. "I'm superfluous, or so I've been told! Very politely, I was asked to leave."

"Well, of course you were," Susannah declared, as if he were the densest individual on earth. "This is the Connellys' show. You helped them, but it's their baby. You knew that going in, Paul."

He couldn't argue with her, so he just flattened his lips in stubborn resentment. Cammie was too absorbed with her own discovery to pay much attention. Finally, when it appeared he would receive no help or sympathy from his ex-wife, Paul left in a sulky huff.

Then, Susannah turned to Cammie and said, "Better get to that gynecologist of yours ASAP, don't ya think?"

"You can't believe everything Paul says," Cammie demurred.

"My instincts—remember? Honey, I'm so hardly ever wrong—it's scary."

"It can't be, though." Hope whispered through her words.

In response, Susannah came over and hugged her fiercely. Tears starred Cammie's lashes, and Susannah said on a mock groan, "Just don't let it mess up *Rock Bottom*, please, please, please! That's all I care about."

"Oh, sure."

Susannah understood Cammie's medical problems only too well. Giving Cammie one last squeeze of affection, she said, "All right, I'm a big softy." A pause. "So, when it's all confirmed, when—and how—are you going to tell the proud papa?"

"I have no idea," Cammie admitted, swallowing. "No idea at all . . ."

In the safety of Ty's arms three hours later, back at her apartment for a few stolen moments before he had to leave for his hotel, Cammie still couldn't stop her internal shaking. Paul had effectively shattered her nerves with his blasted intuition where she was concerned; Susannah's voicing of her own worries had practically pulverized her.

"Hey, relax," Ty whispered. She could hear the smile in his voice as he nuzzled her ear. "It was bound to happen sooner or later."

"What?" she asked faintly, believing half hysterically that he somehow *knew!*

"That Paul would get the message. He's pretty persistent, however. He never let anyone forget that he put the deal together. On the bright side, he nearly drove dear old Dad crazy."

It's not about Paul.

Cammie closed her eyes and swallowed. They were cuddled together on her love seat. She hadn't been able to let go of him since he'd sneaked off to join her at her apartment.

"Paul's lucky that television drama still employs him," Ty added.

"*Cherry Blossom Lane,*" Cammie whispered by rote.

"Stop worrying about him. He's just part of your past, and that's what this time is all about—burying the past."

Cammie nodded silently. She fervently wished it were true, and she hoped against hope that she truly was pregnant. They were entering a whole new realm. Wouldn't it be wonderful if all the beautiful pieces fell into place?

Except Ty doesn't want children. Not that you could go to term anyway. If you are, indeed, pregnant . . .

"You're awfully quiet," he observed.

"I'm—tired."

"Then let me put you to bed. I've got an early call tomorrow, so I should be on my way, too." He rose from the love seat and gently pulled her to her feet.

"I love you," she declared suddenly, kissing him with extra need and ardor.

He grinned, pulling back to read her expression. "I love you, too," he said, the words growing easier by the day to admit. But her eyes were anxious, her mouth tense. "What is it?"

"I just want everything to be perfect. I don't want anything to spoil this."

"Like what? We've walked through the fire together."

Cammie nodded. "You're right."

"You don't sound convinced."

"No, I am. Really."

"Then what's wrong?"

"Nothing. Ty . . .?"

As they strolled toward her bedroom, arms surrounding each other, Ty gazed down at her, loving her sweetness and beauty and support. "Yes?"

"Everything's just so *right.* Sometimes it scares me a little. I've always dreamed about someday, you know?"

"Someday?"

"About the day when everything is perfect. When I find everything I want."

Her tension bled into him, and Ty peered in the half-light of her tiny hallway to examine her face. "Are you getting closer to 'someday'?"

"I'm almost there, Ty. *We're* almost there." She was fervent. "I've got—a family—again. I feel connected."

"Well, good," he said, a little at a loss.

"Maybe it's already here."

When she hesitated, Ty waited, feeling slightly uneasy. He could tell she was trying to express herself, but something wasn't quite coming through. He was about to push for more information when she shook her head and bestowed a brilliant smile on him that took his breath away.

"I'm being silly," she said. "Don't listen to me."

"Then everything's okay?"

"Perfect."

She ended the conversation by lifting her lips to meet his. No proof against such an attractive invitation, Ty pulled her close and buried his face in the silken wonder of her hair.

"Don't worry, my love," he said, offering encouragement for something he didn't really understand. "Nothing can come between us now."

For an answer, she shuddered silently in his arms.

Dr. Crawley regarded Cammie thoughtfully over the top of her half-moon glasses. "Everything looks fine."

"I'm pregnant," Cammie breathed, repeating the words she'd heard just moments before. "I'm pregnant."

Dr. Crawley refrained from offering either advice or predictions about the outcome of this pregnancy. Cammie understood, but she wanted assurances anyway.

"I want this baby," Cammie whispered. "I really want it."

"I understand."

"Isn't there anything I can do? Anything . . .?"

"Take good care of yourself and don't overtax."

"I've got this film role I'm starting next week. It's not hard, but if you think I should quit, I would in a heartbeat."

The doctor smiled and shook her head. "No. Not now anyway. You're a healthy young woman who understands the risks involved with endometriosis. Keep your fingers crossed and your faith strong. Medically speaking, it's just a matter of wait and see."

Impulsively, Cammie hugged Dr. Crawley around the neck, surprising her. "I'm sorry," Cammie whispered breathlessly. "I just want this so much!"

"I know."

They hugged for several moments, until Cammie could let go of her fear long enough to release the doctor.

"Have you told the baby's father?" Dr. Crawley asked as Cammie stepped back.

Cammie shook her head. "Not yet."

"Will he be as happy as you are?"

Cammie thought about explaining that the baby's father was none other than Tyler Stovall. Whether Dr. Crawley knew about Ty's disappearance and reemergence, and his reported relationship with Cammie, was anyone's guess. It was all over the news, but Dr. Crawley didn't bring it up and Cammie couldn't find the energy to explain.

"I think he will," she said after a moment of reflection, mentally crossing her fingers. "He's coping with all kinds of changes in his life right now. I think he'll cope with this."

The doctor's brows rose slightly. "That doesn't sound like a ringing endorsement."

Cammie laughed nervously. "Well, I guess it's not. Do you know—about what's happening with me? I mean, have you been watching the news?" Cammie managed to ask.

"It would be hard to miss," was the doctor's dry response.

Cammie was relieved she didn't have to explain too much. "Then you probably guessed the baby's father is Tyler Stovall."

She nodded.

"Ty's been dancing around with the press since the moment he returned. It hasn't been easy."

"You're saying this baby will be an extra pressure he doesn't need right now."

"No." She winced. "Well, yes, maybe. I don't know."

"Have you talked about having children together?"

Cammie's hands were cold as ice. All the things Ty had said about never wanting children flooded through her brain. But that was different! That was before he'd managed to find a way to deal with his own father. Wasn't it? "We haven't even set a wedding date yet," Cammie admitted a bit shakily.

"Does he know about your medical condition?"

"Yes, in a way. I haven't explained the details about endometriosis, but he knows—there's a problem." She bit her lip. *He thinks I can't have children at all.*

Dr. Crawley didn't offer any further advice, but Cammie picked up the message loud and clear: *Perhaps you'd better talk about this situation right away.*

Back at her apartment, she paced around, wringing her hands like some damsel in distress from an old B-movie! How could she tell him? How could she not? What if he turned away from her? What if he thought she was a liar? What if he seriously didn't ever want a child after all the misery Gayle had caused in that regard?

What if he's as happy as I am!

"I don't know, I don't know," she whispered aloud to the empty room.

It was late before Ty himself showed up at the apartment, and by then Cammie had moved to the back deck, her foot pushing the wrought-iron swing chair into a gentle, rhythmic sway.

"Hey, beautiful," he greeted her tiredly. He flopped into the companion chair. "What a day!"

"Tough, huh?"

"Only because dear old Dad makes it so." He groaned and closed his eyes. "My mother stopped by. I asked her to. Apart from a few minutes here and there when we're not running from the paparazzi, I haven't really had a chance to see her."

"She's a breath of fresh air, isn't she?" Cammie murmured, her thoughts elsewhere.

"Mmmm. Not like my father. Samuel has got to be the center of attention—always. And you know, he'll never change, never grow. I've gotten over hating him, but I'll never like him or trust him."

Cammie looked down at her hands. They were shaking. "I'm sorry to hear that."

Ty slid her a sideways glance full of questions. "Well, I don't think that's any surprise. I know you're happy to be part of a family, but Samuel's a poor excuse for a father in anyone's book."

"Fatherhood's important, though." Cammie was earnest. "I hope you're not dismissing it because of how poor Samuel is in the role."

"I'm not dismissing it. It's great for some people."

"But not you."

"Cammie, this isn't exactly a news bulletin. We've been over this before."

"I know. I just don't quite understand it, that's all."

"Well, I'm glad I don't have to make that choice," Ty said. "I never want to let someone down like Samuel does."

"But you wouldn't, Ty," she said softly. "You're not made that way."

"What is this?" Ty asked, reaching across for her cold hand and stroking the delicate skin at her wrist with his thumb. "If you're thinking about adoption, I'm not sure I'm cut out for that, either."

"I'm not thinking about adoption."

He gazed at her hard, trying to read her mind. Eventually, he shrugged. "Things happen for a reason. You can't have children and I don't want any. It's the best solution for us, given the circumstances and how we feel." Running his hands through his hair, he sighed and closed his eyes, looking for all the world as if he would fall asleep on the spot. "If you could have children, we'd have a bigger problem."

"What do you mean?" Cammie asked, a catch in her throat.

"Well, then choices would have to be made. And I would end up disappointing you."

She gazed at him in silent, quiet fear. "Why?"

"You know why. I wouldn't want to give you what you most desire, and it would break us up. You wouldn't choose me over the baby."

Cammie yanked her gaze away from his beloved face with an effort, staring out at the jagged, building-studded horizon, her view nearly eclipsed by the multi-storied offices and surrounding apartments. "I guess I would hope you would change your mind," she whispered.

"Luckily, it's not an issue," he murmured on a yawn, giving her hand a squeeze.

"Ty . . .?"

"What?" he asked drowsily.

"What if it were an issue?"

"Then I guess we'd have to face it."

His eyes were shut, his posture relaxed. He wasn't even really listening. Cammie couldn't come up with any other way to broach the subject. She sat staring at him for long minutes, heart pounding, palms sweating. As if picking up the intensity of her emotions, Ty's eyes slowly opened. His gaze searched her face.

"What are you trying to say?" he asked, his voice tense.

"I—I went to see my gynecologist today. Dr. Crawley."

"And?"

Cammie's face glowed with hope. Lips quivering, she declared happily, "Ty—I'm pregnant! I'm *pregnant!*"

CHAPTER NINETEEN

Pregnant!

Tyler gazed down at his script for *Rock Bottom,* struggling to make sense of the words while his mind still whirled with the shock of Cammie's announcement the night before. The scene was one he had down pat, but this afternoon, during take after take, he'd flubbed his lines time and again. James Connelly, *Rock Bottom*'s producer and director, had prudently called for a break, and now Ty sat in a chair in his dressing room, a makeup artist fussing over him while he tried to collect his thoughts.

Pregnant!

He couldn't shake that shocking truth from his head no matter how hard he tried. Cammie's words had echoed and echoed, and for a split second after their issuance Ty was certain he was dreaming. His first response was a harsh, automatic accusation: "You said you couldn't get pregnant!"

Cammie's joy dissolved in front of his eyes. "I said I couldn't have children," she softly corrected.

"What's the difference?"

"I'm able to conceive, but the chance of carrying to term is very slight."

Ty shook his head. His brain effectively shut down at that point and apparently wasn't coming back to life anytime in the near future.

Pregnant. Cammie was pregnant! He'd felt a brief spurt of betrayal which had quickly washed away. She hadn't lied; he'd misunderstood. The news apparently left her stunned and thrilled and tragically hopeful, but Ty's less than enthusiastic reaction brought her to earth with a crash.

"Don't worry," she declared bitterly. "This baby won't be born. My body won't let it."

Of course he'd felt like a heel. Too late, he'd tried to convince her that he was at least excited at the possibility, but Cammie was too sharp to buy it—and too hurt to hide her pain. Tears seeped from the corners of her eyes, tears she angrily swiped away. When Ty tried to help, she politely asked him to leave.

"I would like to be alone," she gulped.

"Cammie . . ." Ty ached for her.

"Please."

She'd been deaf to any excuses he could make. He couldn't blame her. Her hope was as fragile as a butterfly's wings, and he'd crushed it without even trying.

So now, here he was, lost in his own self-recriminations and unable to do the job that normally came so easily to him. He'd tried to call Cammie several times but had only reached her answering machine. Either she was screening her calls or she wasn't taking any at all. He hoped it was the latter. He hoped she didn't hate him for being the unfeeling bastard he'd shown himself as last night.

In a state of unhappiness that was self-inflicted, Ty had phoned his mother and blurted out the news. Nanette, typically, was as elated as Cammie. Instantly, she started making breathless plans, ending with a crisp, "You'd better get to the altar soon, my boy. She won't want to wait any longer for you to get off your duff. Oh, my God, we've got a wedding *and* a birth all at once!"

It was only then that Ty's continued silence penetrated Nanette's excitement, and she got her first inkling that something wasn't right. "What is it?" she demanded, and, perversely, when Ty opened his mouth to explain, he suddenly couldn't talk. His throat closed, and all he could choke out was a mumbled, "I'll call you later," to which Nanette quickly inserted, "I'll come by the set this afternoon."

She had yet to show, and Ty wondered if she'd gone to see Cammie instead.

If only he could make things right, but every move, every word would now sound false to Cammie's ears.

"That's the best I can do," the makeup girl declared, meeting Ty's gaze in the mirror in front of his chair.

"Thanks." Ty was unusually curt. She left him then, no stranger to stars' mercurial mood shifts, apparently. When he was alone, Ty stared at his grim reflection for several moments, struggling within himself to put his personal thoughts aside. Failing, he jumped to his feet and strode to the closet where his cell phone waited inside his jacket pocket. Phoning Cammie again, he wasn't surprised to get her answering machine but this time, instead of merely hanging up like a beaten pup, he said urgently and tensely, "I love you. I LOVE YOU. And I want a baby with you. And I'll do anything in my power to make that happen! Please, believe me. Cammie, my love, don't turn away from me. I want us to get married and—"

A knock on his door. "Mr. Stovall, you're wanted on the set."

Biting back a sharp retort, he said into the receiver, "Just remember I love you. Please."

Samuel Stovall stood on the edge of the ongoing scene where several "day" players were working on their blocking. Arms folded across his chest, Sam wondered why he felt so dissatisfied. He'd gotten everything he'd wanted, hadn't he? Orren Wesson and his right-hand man, William Renquist, had aided and abetted, and now Ty was back and they—he and his son—were finally working together on *Rock Bottom.*

So, why wasn't it enough?

Sighing in frustration, Samuel gazed across the set where Ty was just finishing up a conversation with Nanette. That bugged him, too—this closeness between mother and son—and he wished there was some way he could undo that bond. He felt itchy and unhappy. He wanted something more, something he couldn't quite name, an unusual situation for the man who demanded, and therefore achieved, everything he wanted.

With systematic precision, Samuel ticked off the positives in his life: a resurrected career; a faithful wife whom he felt comfortable with, even if it wasn't a grand passion any longer, a raft of children who spent a good portion of their time fawning over him, hoping for a handout or two; a prodigal son who had finally returned; the chance for another grandchild.

That thought brought him up short. A grandchild? He'd never put much stock in future generations before. It had never seemed like any great benefit to him. But the thought of Tyler having a child gave Samuel serious food for thought. Maybe Tyler would marry Camilla and give him a grandchild. Rolling the idea around in his head, he considered the benefits. More publicity. More notoriety. Now would be a perfect time.

Enormously pleased with the idea, Samuel didn't stop to ask himself why Tyler's child would mean more to him than a son or daughter by any of his other children. Tyler was the one he loved best, period, and he made no excuses for it. Samuel was a man who acted on emotion more than common sense, a fact that neither disturbed nor interested him.

Of course, Nanette would tell him he only loved himself, but he'd stopped listening to that skinny, cranky woman years earlier. Glaring across the room at her made Samuel feel better. *She* didn't know the first thing about how to behave in this town.

With a sniff, Samuel dismissed her, then straightened when the woman in question suddenly hugged Ty, then headed Samuel's way. Her gray hair was in that confounded braid again, he thought with disgust, and she'd wrapped a still trim body in faded, dusty jeans. No common sense, that woman! Growling beneath his breath, Samuel demanded in an icy whisper as she approached, "What are you doing here?"

"I had a meeting with our son. I'd heard you'd wangled a role out of this deal."

Her gentle amusement rankled. Silently, Samuel listed off all the reasons he and Nanette had divorced so long ago. He was incredulous that they'd ever been married. She wasn't his type at all.

Still, she was a character.

"Tyler and I are working together," Samuel clipped out.

"Is Cammie on the set yet?" Nanette asked, glancing at the cameras and thick wires which crisscrossed the floor like fat gray snakes.

"Not till next week."

"How do you feel about Ty's relationship with her?" Nanette wondered. Her eyes searched his face, and Samuel carefully kept his expression neutral.

How did he feel? "It's their business, isn't it?"

She grinned like a Cheshire cat, which unnerved Samuel to no end. "Not if you decide to make it yours. My advice to you, Samuel: leave them alone. For some reason God saw fit to give you a second chance with Tyler. Try not to blow it this time."

"You're really an old hag, you know that."

For an answer Nanette patted him affectionately on the arm, then turned to meet James Connelly, who'd chosen not only to produce, but to direct *Rock Bottom* as well. Samuel was infuriated. Gritting his teeth, he tried to ignore his ex-wife as she schmoozed with Connelly. Why did everyone act like she was so scintillating, so extraordinary? She was just an old broad with an attitude, he reminded himself, but a part of him couldn't help admiring her a little.

If things had been different . . .

A moment later, Samuel caught himself up. Growing maudlin over past mistakes wasn't his style, and he wasn't about to start now. Still, the thought of Tyler and Camilla having a child—a son—for him to dote on filled him with a sense of longing and need he'd heretofore never known.

Good Lord, I'm getting old! he thought with horror.

Swallowing, Samuel hurried back to his dressing room and spent the rest of the afternoon on the phone to Felicia, his wife, who heard the panic in his voice and soothed his worries with compliments and reminders of his continued manliness.

With a sigh of relief, Samuel Stovall's tilted world righted itself. Gazing at his own reflection, he quirked a brow, trying on a sophisticated, man-about-town persona. Okay, so the role he was relegated to was nothing more than that of an old grouch, but he still was Samuel Stovall, actor and icon.

Of that much he was certain.

Cammie replayed Tyler's message for the twentieth time. Warmth invaded every pore from head to toe. He'd come around. Completely! Though she'd prayed for just that scenario, fear had wrapped itself around her heart and she'd spent a really terrible stretch of hours while he sorted through his feelings.

Thank you, God, she prayed in silent gratitude.

Snatching up her purse, she headed straight to the Beverly Hills Hotel to wait for Tyler to get off work. When he stepped inside his room, she was already waiting, naked on his bed, courtesy of the room key he'd given her earlier. Spying her, Tyler smiled, then called over his shoulder, "Yeah, come on in, Jim. You, too, Nora. We'll go over that scene—"

Cammie shrieked and dived under the covers, burying her head beneath a pillow. Ty's deep laughter penetrated and she slowly peeked out and glared at him. "You big liar!"

"I couldn't help myself." He grinned from ear to ear like a little boy.

"I'll never be able to do that again."

"Oh, come on." He slid the chain across the door, slowly stripped off his own clothes, then slid in bed beside her, his body warm and familiar. Cammie rubbed her cheek against his hair-roughened chest. "I'm sorry about last night," he murmured.

"Don't be. I know what a shock it was. I'm still numb. Happy, but numb!"

"We're going to have a baby," he said, as if tasting the flavor of his words.

"Maybe," Cammie cautioned. "If all goes well and the stars align and the gods bequeath it."

"I love you."

"I love you, too," she sighed.

"We've got to make wedding plans."

Her lips curved at the welcome words. "Tomorrow," she murmured, capturing his mouth with her own. "Tonight, you're mine . . ."

Cammie started shooting the following week. She spent her first afternoon sauntering down a hot, cordoned-off city street, conscious of someone—Ty's character, Norm—following her. But instead of falling into place, the simple scene was plagued by one problem after another: cameras failed, people crowded the shot, the heel broke off Cammie's shoe, until the light failed and they had to quit and begin again the next day.

After that, the shoot went relatively trouble free until unexpected rain clouds burst in a heavy deluge over the city, sending everyone scrambling for cover and creating enough confusion and colorful language that the produc-

tion crew decided to move indoors until the summer storm
traveled eastward and out of their way.

Cammie learned her lines religiously, pushing aside he
secret joy until a more convenient time. Wedding plan
were discussed, but everything was put on hold until *Roc*
Bottom wrapped. Ty had told Nanette about the baby, bu
afraid of jinxing the whole thing, Cammie kept the infor
mation to herself, although Samuel Stovall made enoug
remarks about grandchildren to make her accuse Ty o
telling. He shook his head and spread his hands. Ther
was no understanding Samuel Stovall. He was one of
kind.

Throughout the rest of the shoot, Ty was loving an
supportive, and when a bold reporter pushed his wa
through the crowd to reach Ty and Cammie as they strug
gled to get into a waiting limo, he refused to rise to th
bait though the questions came sharp and fast.

"Is there a marriage in the future when *Rock Botto*
wraps? Are the 'brother' and 'sister' about to become ma
and wife? Have you plans for a family?"

Ty merely answered, "No comment," a touch of humo
lacing his tone.

"Come on, Tyler," the man said, as if they were ol
friends. "Give us something."

"After that brother and sister remark? You've got to b
kidding." His smile flashed. He wasn't a fool when it cam
to the press, no matter how irritating they could be.

"Tell us your plans. Let us in on them."

"When a man disappears for ten years, it's a good be
he prefers his privacy," Ty drawled.

"There's talk of a wedding? When?" The man turne
to Cammie and thrust a microphone in front of her lips
Behind him, cameras rolled. "After the film?"

"Well, it's not going to happen during the film." Cam
mie smiled and edged to the car.

"There must be something you want to say," th
reporter pestered Tyler. "We've got word that elopement'
possible."

"Isn't there some other news somewhere?"

"No. This is it." The reporter laughed, conceding Ty some space as he stepped back.

The reporter's capitulation won him far more than his plaguing questions had, for Ty gazed thoughtfully at Cammie for a moment, then drawled for all the world to hear, "I hope to have a wife to come home to very soon." That said, he helped Cammie inside the plush interior of the limo before sliding in beside her.

"Tyler Stovall? Tossing the press crumbs?" Cammie asked, pretending shock.

He grinned, threading the fingers of one of her hands through his. "Did I say something wrong?"

"Not a thing," she assured him.

"*Rock Bottom* wraps in a couple of weeks. Then we need to start planning."

"I'm with you, sir," Cammie murmured happily.

Several days later, as Cammie was preparing for the last of her scenes, she received an unwelcome visitor to the set: Paul. With an inner groan, she tried to pretend some enthusiasm.

"Don't look so excited to see me," he declared with a sniff of derision. "I've come with good news."

"Paul, I don't think we have anything to talk about."

"You don't?"

"No." She was emphatic, in no mood for word games with him or anyone else.

"Well, since I've been away from this project," he said, looking around a bit angrily, clearly resenting the fact that the Connellys hadn't wanted him as part of the package, "I've been back at negotiations with the folks at *Cherry Blossom Lane.*"

"Negotiations?" Cammie lifted a brow.

"They want you back, Cammie. Or, more accurately, they want the character of Donna Jenkins back."

"What? Donna's been asphyxiated!"

He waved that aside. "In the world of soap opera—"

"Nighttime drama," Cammie corrected, fighting a smile.

Paul conceded with a nod of his head. "Nighttime drama. Nothing is forever. The letters poured in after Donna's demise, so I did a little string pulling and *voilà*, my girl's back on the job."

"Paul, I'm not your girl."

"Yes, so I hear." His lips tightened. "There's a meeting next week. I left a message with Susannah's secretary, but I thought I'd come see you personally."

Cammie's head whirled with the news. It was more likely that Paul had nothing to do with this extraordinary turn of events; he was just good at taking the credit. But the idea of returning to *Cherry Blossom Lane* was one she hadn't considered in the least, given the way she'd been summarily dismissed.

She couldn't do it. Not with a baby on the way. Not with the delicacy of this pregnancy. She'd already determined that as soon as *Rock Bottom* wrapped she was taking time off—to plan a wedding and prepare for a baby.

Still, it was nice to be wanted back.

Her thoughts tripped like lightning, and seeing Paul watching the rapid series of expressions across her mobile face, Cammie cleared her throat. "I'll—I'll talk to Susannah," was her unsatisfactory answer.

"First shows start shooting next week."

"Paul!" she laughed in exasperation.

"Donna doesn't have to resurrect until later. You might not be needed on the set until the end of September. We'll work it out!"

"PAUL!"

"What?" he demanded.

"You're not my husband, nor are you my boss. Go away and I'll let you know," she said a bit more gently.

He pinched his lip between his thumb and forefinger. "Cammie—"

"Good-bye, Paul." She grabbed his elbow and turned him toward the exit door. "We'll do lunch . . ."

* * *

On Cammie's last day of work on *Rock Bottom* Karen Walthers delivered a healthy baby girl. With tremulous joy, Cammie headed to Karen's home the day after wrapping her first feature film. Karen had just gotten home that morning and looked radiant, tired, and a bit bewildered all at once. Cammie carefully and gently cradled the little bundle swaddled in a pink blanket in her own quivering arms.

"You are so lucky," she told Karen on a half whisper.

"I know." The proud mother beamed.

"I hope one day that I'll be able to have a child."

"You will," Karen assured her, a bit perplexed by Cammie's uncertain emotional state.

"Yes," Cammie agreed, nodding. Then, "Yes," more firmly, as if saying the words would make them come true.

She'd had some spotting. Not much, but enough to alarm the heck out of her. Dr. Crawley had been cautiously concerned, but an examination proved everything was still all right as far as they could tell at this early date.

Ty was currently out of town. He'd returned to the cabin in Bayrock to liberate some belongings he'd put in storage and tie up some loose ends. He'd asked Cammie to accompany him, but she'd been too nervous. She was half inclined to take to her bed indefinitely, but since the bleeding had stopped and everything looked okay, she'd chosen instead to keep everything status quo. No need to panic yet, though she had no plans for work in the immediate future.

Though Cammie had assured her agent she couldn't take on the role of Donna Jenkins right now, Susannah insisted she meet with the producers and staff of *Cherry Blossom Lane* anyway. Susannah was naturally distressed and confused by Cammie's reluctance, unaware of Cammie's condition.

"For pete's sake, hon," she pointed out on the phone the night before. "This is your bread and butter. Sign on for a year, that's all. Then *Rock Bottom* will come out, and who knows! Instant stardom—after years and years of obscurity, of course," she added dryly, referring to the fact that every "instant" star had a history somewhere.

"I don't think it'll work out," Cammie vacillated.

"One meeting! Good heavens! They're apt to recast. Do you want that?"

"No-o-o—"

"Then, what?"

There was nothing to do but tell her the truth. "Susannah," Cammie confided, chewing on her lower lip. "I'm pregnant."

"I knew it," she breathed. "Oh, my God. Oh. What about—?"

"It's a long shot," Cammie agreed. "I may not make it full term."

"Oh, wow. Oh, wow." A pause, while she reassessed. "Ty knows, I hope."

"Yes, he does."

"Good. Good . . ." Cammie could practically hear the gears turning in Susannah's head. "Okay, then. What'll we tell *Cherry Blossom Lane?* You don't want to work, I take it. Or, can't you at all?"

"I'm afraid to," Cammie admitted.

"Right. I understand. Well . . . that puts a new wrinkle on things! Oh, man. The publicity. We've gotta get that wedding going! Don't tell Karen about this yet. She'll try to put some plan together and she's got her own little baby to take up her time at the moment. I'll think of something," Susannah went on, more to herself than Cammie. "Don't you worry about a thing—Mom."

As she hung up the phone, a lump in Cammie's throat swelled until it nearly choked her. She'd had to sit down for a few minutes and struggle to pull herself together. Now, cuddling Karen's pink-faced angel, she thought briefly of confiding her news to the publicist, but in the end, she took Susannah's advice and refrained. Anyway, her news was too fragile, too easily spread, and if she should miscarry again, she knew she wouldn't be able to handle the public knowing as well. It would be bad enough handling the disappointment on her own.

Ty returned the following Tuesday, catching a taxi at the airport and heading straight for Cammie's apartment. No photographers lay in wait, as enough time had passed to take Ty and Cammie off the front page, at least for the moment. Slinging his overnight bag over one shoulder, Ty wrestled with the bouquet of roses he'd picked up on the run. He mounted the stairs two at a time, then leaned against the buzzer with his elbow.

Cammie opened the door, and Ty swept in on a startled breath. She wore a red velveteen bathrobe that skimmed her feet and left a narrow V from the hollow at her throat to the center of her breasts. Her hair lay in soft, touchable auburn waves, brushing her shoulders, and her cheeks were flushed a pretty pink. Turquoise eyes sparkling with merriment greeted him and she leaned up to kiss his jaw.

"I've been waiting ever since you called from the airport," Cammie whispered. "Oh!" she cried, as he slid the roses from behind his back and placed them in her hands.

"For you, my love."

It shocked Ty sometimes how far he'd come in accepting Cammie as the woman he loved. As she clasped his now free hand and led him inside, he marveled at how comfortable, how *right* it felt to be with her. There was such a thing as romantic love after all. He just hadn't experienced it until now.

Cammie put the roses in a narrow vase, fussing until the heavy, fragrant red blossoms tilted to her satisfaction. "Thank you," she said, admiring their nodding heads.

"I figured it was time to celebrate the beginning of our life together," Ty said, dropping his bag on one of the kitchen chairs. At Cammie's bewildered look, he added, "If it's all right with you, I'm finished with hotel living."

"Good!" She was glad he would be with her.

"I've started looking for a place; the real estate agent's got a couple of houses in mind already. Later this week, we can check them out and see if they're up to your satisfaction."

"You're buying a house?"

"*We're* buying a house," he corrected. "I've still got my other one, but I'd like to have something new for us. A place with no memories except the ones we make together."

Cammie was thrilled. "I'd love to look at houses."

"Good. Now, c'mere and sit on my lap and tell me how much you've missed me," he growled. "You can't wear that robe without letting me find out what's underneath it."

"A whole lotta nothin'," she admitted, sliding onto his lap and slowly untying the loose belt. Ty slipped his hands around her narrow rib cage, his thumbs just beneath her breasts.

"Mmmm," he murmured, kissing the downy curve of her jawline while the pads of his thumbs brushed her nipples.

Cammie could feel the thrill right to the center of her womanhood. Unable to stop herself, she squirmed atop him, causing a deep chuckle somewhere in Ty's chest.

"You like that," he said with pure masculine superiority.

"So do you," she countered, feeling the hard evidence of his reaction to her provocation.

"Maybe we ought to move to the couch."

Ty picked her up and carried her to the love seat, pulling her down atop him. Her hands reached for his belt buckle. A soft jingle as it slipped apart, then she set about on an exploration of her own that had him straining his hips to meet her tender touch.

"Cammie," he muttered, sliding the robe from her ivory shoulders and tossing it on the floor. She wore nothing underneath, and with swift movements he removed his shirt, pants, and underwear, then he twisted onto his back, pulling her full length upon him.

She realized, dimly, that he was holding back, and she lifted her head from a deep, delicious kiss. "What?"

"Is it—all right? I mean, tell me if you think we should be more careful."

Realizing he meant the baby, she whispered, "I think we're okay. Just no whips and chains this time."

His lips curved beneath hers. "I'll try to restrain myself."

Then there was no more teasing. His hands on her hips guided her over his straining erection. Cammie took him fully inside her, in the way they'd grown so used to feeling. It was as if they'd been made for each other, and now, with some history between them, she easily matched his movements in a familiar rhythm, adding soft sighs and touches in the way that pleased him, and therefore herself, the most.

The pace quickened. Desire licked through her and she moved faster and faster. Another time it would have been embarrassing, the way she rode him, but she knew Ty enjoyed it as much as she did, and with the confidence of his love, she let her emotions run wild. Her hips moved rapidly. Ty's breathing shortened with the tempo. She heard him moan and instantly slowed down, but he would have none of it. His hands grasped her buttocks and he physically moved her until suddenly she was on the brink.

"Ty . . ." she moaned.

"God, Cammie," he ground out through clenched teeth, then groaned as she felt the hot spill of his seed inside her. The next moment her own climax took hold and she cried out, clinging to him as his hips thrust hard against hers.

In the quiet aftermath, she smiled to hear their rapid heartbeats slowly return to normal levels. "I love you," he murmured, tucking sweat-dampened tendrils of her hair behind her ears.

"I love you, too," she whispered.

The future was theirs for the taking. They had each other, a love that bound them, plans for a home to share and a baby to adore on the way. A family, Cammie realized, hugging Ty close. Finally. A family of her own!

Lazily, Ty drew his tongue along the edge of her ear. Cammie shook her head.

"You're tickling me."

"That's the idea."

"No, no . . ." She climbed to her feet and, ignoring Ty's groan of protest, slipped the red robe back on, grabbed his hand, and pulled him to his feet. "Time for other sustenance besides the fulfillment of the flesh!"

"Do we have to?"

She grinned at his "little boy" pout. "Yes."

While Ty reluctantly redressed, Cammie searched in her small refrigerator for some kind of makeshift meal. She was hungry. Pregnancy had created a ravenous monster inside her.

"How about an omelet? I've got cheese, scallions, and mushrooms."

"Sounds great." Ty opened his bag and pulled out a thick sheaf of papers that looked vaguely familiar. Cammie glanced at the manuscript and realized he'd brought his own screenplay, *Father Knows Worst,* to Los Angeles.

"Are you thinking of selling it?" she asked in surprise.

"Good God, no. I just saw it when I was in Bayrock, and I remembered how I felt when I wrote it. It was so hard, and there was so much anger, I just . . ." He broke off, frowning, struggling for the words. Lifting eyes to meet hers, he said simply, "I don't feel that way anymore. I don't *need* it, the catharsis, I mean."

"So, what are you going to do with it?"

"I don't know. I think I'll change the ending and then put it away somewhere. I might get a good laugh out of it someday."

"Why would you change the ending?" She cracked eggs into a bowl and stirred them up with a wire whisk.

"Because it's not right anymore."

Cammie thought of Ty's protagonist's continued anger

nd hurt over his father's callousness, even to the bitter nd, and she looked over at him for explanation.

"The father character is flawed and selfish, but he's not n object of hate. He's not wicked, he's just misguided nd riddled with self-doubt, and he uses people. Spencer inally realizes it," Ty added, referring to his protagonist. 'He comes full circle and all the old animosity vanishes."

"That's a nice ending," Cammie said softly as she poured the eggs into the frypan and added grated cheddar nd chopped green scallions. The mixture sizzled gently, breakfast aromas filling the air.

"I just wanted to finish it," he explained, shrugging.

"Of course."

"But it's not for sale."

"Your life is not for sale," she said, showing she understood as she slid the fluffy, folded omelet onto a plate and et it on the table in front of him. "Eat up, my love."

"What about you?"

"I'm making mine right now. Have I told you how much love you?" she asked happily.

"Never," he lied, digging into the omelet with gusto.

She sang out, "I love you like the sea loves the shore, ike the wind loves the trees, like the day loves the dawn."

"You've got to get a little more original or I'm outta here," he teased around a mouthful of food.

"Hey, I made dinner. My poetry is the price you pay."

With that, Ty couldn't stand it anymore. Shoving back his plate, he came up behind her as she whipped up more eggs, grabbing her around the waist and kissing the back of her neck. Cammie squealed in surprise and tried to elbow him away.

"I'll spill it!"

"Go right ahead."

"Mr. Stovall, go sit down and finish your meal. The kiddo and I are hungry, and you're getting in the way."

He dropped her at once, looking stricken. "Why didn't you say so? I didn't have to eat."

"Oh, for pete's sake. Sit down. Finish your meal. I'll

have mine in a minute and then we'll—pick up where we left off. You don't need to coddle me," she added when he still didn't move. Pushing at him gently, she said, "But don't get between a pregnant woman and her food!" she warned with mock seriousness.

Lifting his hand in the traditional, Boy Scouts two-fingered pledge of honor, Ty vowed solemnly, "I pledge to be good from now on."

"Have I told you how much I love you?"

"Later," he suggested, wiggling his brows at her, and they laughed together.

Thursday dawned gray and smoggy, depressing after several clearish days of pale-blue sky and high hopes. Cammie ignored the pall and concentrated on her own plans. She'd reluctantly agreed to go with Susannah to the production offices of *Cherry Blossom Lane*. Susannah had promised not to spill the secret of Cammie's pending birth, but she refused to completely give up the idea that Cammie could be reinstated on the show.

"Maybe there's a way to make it all work out," she insisted. "Never say never."

They drove to the television studio together in Susannah's car, though Cammie felt some tiny, sharp pains in her abdomen. Was this normal? she fretted. Was it a normal part of pregnancy, or her endometriosis? Or was it the harbinger of something worse?

She didn't want to think about it. With damp palms, she followed Susannah down the familiar hallways that led to the offices, sound stage, and dressing rooms of *Cherry Blossom Lane*.

Paul was waiting for them, arms outstretched as if he were welcoming a long-lost relative. "Come in, come in. You look a little tired, Cammie. Here, let me take that."

He reached for her handbag, a huge faux alligator monster that Cammie habitually slung over her shoulder. Dumping the thing was a relief, and Cammie realized belatedly that she'd stuffed *Father Knows Worst* inside its depths when Ty forgot to replace the manuscript in his bag. She intended to return it to him tonight when she met him at one of the houses from the realtor's list, the one he liked best. The plan was, he would call on her cell phone and give her the address later today.

"Thanks," Cammie said gratefully.

Paul shrugged and placed the bag next to his desk. "Let's get down to business." He indicated where he wanted Cammie and Susannah to sit. Moments later, several other members of the decision-making force for *Cherry Blossom Lane* showed up, and everyone shook hands and started negotiations. Cammie's mind wandered; she couldn't help herself. As much as she'd loved working on the program, her life was moving in new directions and she had no great desire to go backward.

But when money was brought up, she stared at Glen Edwards, the man who'd offered the deal, in utter surprise. "Why am I worth so much more now?" she asked, the answer pounding into her brain even before the final syllable was formed: She was Tyler Stovall's girlfriend.

Her cheeks pinkened while Glen stuttered around for a viable explanation. Words like "recognition of worth" and "ratings bonanza for the season finale" and "association of your face with the character of Donna Jenkins" were filled with elements of truth. However, the true reason was a slap in the face, and Cammie grew angry at the inequities of a system she already *knew* wasn't fair.

Keeping her lips tightly closed, she let Susannah do all the talking, though her agent glanced at her from time to time, sensing her simmering fury.

Suddenly Cammie could take it no longer. She felt ill and uncomfortable. Jumping to her feet, she muttered hasty excuses, then raced to the nearest bathroom where she splashed cold water on her face.

She would tell Susannah there was no chance. She couldn't accept the part.

How noble you've become! she silently mocked the strained

image appearing in the mirror above the sink. *Sudden you're above the wiles and ways of Hollywood. It wasn't that lon ago that you charged after one missing Tyler Stovall, the offer a part being wagged beneath your nose as a carrot. Where wa your nobility then?*

"I don't care," she said aloud, her voice booming out startling her.

The door squeaked open and Susannah stuck her hea around the jamb. "You okay, hon?"

"I'm ready to go home," Cammie said on a sigh. "Tal to me about *Cherry Blossom Lane* tomorrow. I'm too tire today to make a rational decision. All I want to do is fin Ty and fall into his arms."

"Gotcha," Susannah said with an understanding smile

"I'm not saying no; I'm not saying yes. I just want to le this pregnancy get past the 'crossed fingers' stage. Yo think they can wait that long?" she asked, jerking her hea in the direction of the offices they'd just vacated.

"They'll wait," Susannah promised, then, with a twitc of her lips, added, "You're Tyler Stovall's fiancée!"

"Thanks a whole lot!"

And the two friends embraced and laughed at the fates

CHAPTER TWENTY

Ty strolled around the spacious rooms of the three-story house, quietly excited about the possibilities. The bedrooms were on the top floor and the master suite swept up all the square footage of the west end. Stately palms swayed outside the window and, beyond them, a view across the pink-tiled roof of the nearest neighboring home and then the horizon where somewhere below lay the Pacific Ocean. The place was elaborate and expensive by most standards; relatively modest by those of Beverly Hills.

Ty dragged his attention from the view to walk through a small anteroom off the master. It was on the opposite side of the room from the master bath and walk-in closet and held a vanity and mirror on one side, an extra closet on the other. Through a connecting door lay a room that could be considered a small bedroom or den.

A nursery.

Ty swallowed, thinking of his impending fatherhood. For Cammie, he was excited. He wanted the world for her, and if this was it, then full steam ahead. For himself, he was filled with trepidation. There were so many pitfalls to parenting, so many traps. The Ron Howard film, *Paren-hood,* had expressed the joys and traumas of being a parer so well that Ty had never been able to watch that particula movie without feeling somewhat anxious.

His mother had pooh-poohed his fears. "You're lettin Samuel's selfishness stand as your prototype. You kno you're better than that, Tyler."

She was right. Logically, he knew she was right. But i his illogical, scarred heart, he feared that somehow h would make worse mistakes than his father and ruin hi unborn child's life.

Ridiculous fears. Unable to eradicate.

Part of his problem was that he didn't trust happines In the midst of all this "growing" and "accepting," th old Tyler Stovall still expected some godawful cataclysn to smash his beautiful new world to smithereens. Betraya was so common. Selflessness and love and pure giving wa the rarity.

But he had that in Cammie, didn't he? Yes, there ha been some hurdles, some truths he'd had to face an examine and understand before there was trust. She' come for him in Bayrock because she loved him, period It wasn't for the co-starring role, though that had bee her initial introduction to the plan. But that hadn't bee Cammie's true motivation; that had been Samuel's.

To add insult to injury, Samuel had jumped onto *Roc Bottom* himself, wangling a role for himself in the film a well. Luckily, Cammie had warned him before he'd learne some other way. She understood his paranoia about thes things.

Then there'd been all the hoopla over his return t Hollywood. Enough to drive a sane man crazy. Sometime when he thought back, he was amazed at his own tolerance especially since that particular trait wasn't exactly his lon suit.

Now, Ty rubbed his hands together, feeling oddly cold Lastly, there'd been Cammie's unexpected pregnancy He'd thought she couldn't conceive; he'd thought that' what she'd told him. But instead, the root cause was some other malady . . . .supposedly.

Hearing his own thoughts, Ty brought himself up short. What was he thinking? What kind of traitorous ideas were humming inside his own head! Of course she'd told the truth about that! Just because he didn't know the full extent of her feminine problems didn't mean she'd lied to him. It was just this damn fear over being a father. He was letting it infect his reason.

Anyway, all that was in the past now. The future was set, and it was a bright future. He and Cammie were ready to face the world as a team. This anxiety he currently felt was probably due to a lot of reasons, chief among them the fact that he'd finished *Rock Bottom* and was experiencing a strange kind of letdown. He'd been here before; it was normal, after so much energy had been placed in a project, to mourn the ending a bit. That's all he was feeling. Nothing more sinister.

Don't get all weird and fanciful. Let the rest of the populace of this town look for signs and answers and meaning. Get back to reality.

"Damn good advice," he growled to himself, hearing a car turn into the circular drive outside. Cammie.

He bounded down the curved stairway that wound to an octagonal entry hall, the floor of which was composed of rectangular, gray slate. The front door itself was arched and painted to look distressed, with huge iron bands running horizontally near the top and bottom. It resembled the door of an old church or monastery, something out of a postcard from the ruins of Europe. Ty loved it.

But it wasn't Cammie standing on the other side of the threshold. To his amazement, her ex-husband, the ubiquitous Paul Merrill, stood on the stoop.

"I know you're meeting Cammie here," Paul apologized. "She left her purse in my office and I'm returning it."

Paul held out Cammie's familiar faux alligator bag, which was about the size of a small suitcase, a point they'd often laughed about. Ty accepted the bag but did not invite Paul inside. It wasn't his house yet, and he'd promised the real estate agent he would take care of the place as long as he and Cammie could have it to themselves, just for tonight. Because he was *the* Tyler Stovall, the friendly agent had gone against policy and handed him the key. One of the few perks of "celebrity-ism," in Ty's mind.

But Paul didn't take the hint. Clearing his voice, he glanced down at the other bag in his hand, his own black leather briefcase. "There's something I'd like to discuss with you, and I'll be honest, I'm not quite sure how to go about it."

"Why don't you save it till later?" Ty suggested, as with relief he saw Cammie's blue BMW suddenly squeal in behind Paul's black sedan.

"I'd rather get this out right now," Paul said hurriedly, balancing the briefcase on his knee and snapping the locks. He glanced back at Cammie as if afraid.

"What's the rush?" Ty teased her as she jumped from the car before it barely had time to come to a full stop. "We have first option on the place, I swear!"

She strode toward him and Paul, her mouth set, her gaze fixed, but there was a strange light of fear in those fabulous turquoise depths. Her attention was on Paul.

Ty glanced in confusion from Cammie's beloved face to Paul's sheepish one. And sheepish was the right word as Paul, handing Ty a sheaf of papers, suffered a wave of dark, unattractive color invading his cheeks. "I took the liberty of reading it," Paul confided. "It's the best thing I've seen in years."

Confused, Ty dropped his gaze to the manuscript. A familiar coffee stain marred the front page of *Father Knows Worst* even before he read the title. His heart beat fast.

"I left my purse in his office by mistake . . ." Cammie's voice came from a long way away, rippling like water.

"She gave it to me," Paul denied, charging her with a glare to deny him.

"I didn't!"

"I want to produce it," Paul jumped in. "It's fantastic. nd your father will play the part in the film, naturally. t's a perfect fit."

"Ty, he took it and read it without my consent." Cam- nie's voice shook. "You should be strung up, Paul."

"Oh, come on. You stuck a corner out of that monster andbag and set the whole thing on my desk. What? You idn't think I'd catch the invitation. Don't worry. There's part in it for you, too, but I guess you knew that, didn't ou?"

"You're despicable!" Cammie was appalled. "You took ny handbag from me!"

Paul shrugged, as if it were of no consequence. "I'm nerely practical."

Ty stepped away, unable to listen to more. *Betrayal. Lies. Deceptions.* The words flitted across his brain. He couldn't ear very well for the surf in his ears and the thick, pound- ng heartbeat that threatened to pulse right out of his hest.

"Go away," he said thickly.

Cammie's beautiful eyes begged forgiveness. "Ty . . ."

"GO AWAY!"

"Ty!" she cried in agony.

He slammed the door in their faces. It shook in its frame. The flesh of Ty's palm turned red and throbbed from pain. He stared at it uncomprehendingly. Staggering, he urned in the direction of the kitchen.

Three steps, and the front door swung open behind him. Cammie slipped inside. Belatedly, Ty realized he hadn't lipped the dead bolt in place.

"I won't let you do this," she said in a quavering voice hat revealed her feelings.

"Where's your cohort?" he demanded.

She shook her head. "Paul's not my cohort. He's noth- ng to me."

"You told him where I was."

She shook her head vehemently. "He must have over- heard me repeat the address when you called on the cell phone while I was at the studio. I didn't tell him. wouldn't!"

An engine fired up outside. Paul was leaving. Ty stro to the front window to watch Paul's black vehicle tear on the road, leaving him alone with Cammie.

"For God's sake, Ty. You know Paul means nothing me. I would never work with him on anything. You *kn* it!"

"I only know what you've told me."

Ty's harshness cut Cammie like a knife. She could believe it. Not now. Not after all they'd conquer together. "He's my ex-husband. A mistake from my past She swept an arm toward the screenplay Ty still held his hands. "It's just these kinds of manipulations that ma me realize what a snake he is! Tyler, please. He stole th from my purse!"

"He just *happened* to find it there."

"Yes!" Cammie was emphatic, but her body still quiver from head to toe with fear. She had to make him see, ma him understand. "I had it in my purse, and, . . . and wasn't feeling well, so he took my purse when I enter his office this morning. I was glad, at the time. You calle and told me about the house. Then, later, I just couldr sit there any longer in that meeting. I felt—bad. I prac cally ran out of the room. Susannah took me home and didn't think about my purse until I was getting ready meet you here. Then it was too late to go back to th studio. I called Paul, but he was gone."

"On his way here," Ty clipped out.

"I suppose. Anyway, I figured I'd get my purse later, b I never thought about your screenplay! Even if I had, wouldn't have believed Paul would be so bold, even kno ing what I know about him! He's just so desperate f success."

"That sounds like an excuse."

His stony countenance played havoc with Cammie emotions, which were unstable anyway in her conditio Her eyes searched his beloved face for some sign of unde standing, or, failing that, forgiveness, but she dimly realized she'd reached the end of his patience and belief in her. It hurt to know there was still some distrust yawning between them; she'd thought they'd breached the gap entirely.

But what could she do but plead her case? "I know it's impossible for you to believe I wasn't part of this."

"You're a part of everything," he pointed out.

They were standing in the hallway between the entry and kitchen, a narrow alley with a built-in glass-fronted cupboard on one wall, a sideboard on the opposite one. Feeling weak, Cammie leaned on the sideboard. "Please, Ty," she begged.

"You came to Bayrock to find me and you were given a part in *Rock Bottom.* You pleaded innocence, but you got my address from my father. You convinced me it was all on the up and up, but then Samuel was suddenly in the film as well. You told me you couldn't get pregnant, but you did."

"I told you I couldn't have a baby!"

But Ty ignored her. "And you told me you understood how private my screenplay was, how it was just a catharsis." His gray eyes bored into hers, heavy with accusations. "What are you going to tell me now that I could possibly believe?"

Tears filled her eyes, drenching her lashes. Her fight for Tyler had been an uphill battle from the onset, one she'd valiantly fought out of love. But she was tired, and this lack of belief in her motives hurt so much she could scarcely breathe. And it made her angry, too. How could he think this of her? How *could* he?

"You haven't given me a lot of faith in your words, either," she declared bitterly, to which Ty's brows snapped together.

"*I* haven't?"

"All your philosophy of love only being for others . . . all your talk about not wanting to be a father . . . all your sarcasm and snobbery about returning to Hollywood . . . It was all lies!"

For a moment, Ty was too dumbfounded to react to he
outrageous statements. And Cammie was too angry to sto
the floodtide once it had begun. "Acting! That's what
is. A convenient dogma to be thrown out like a shiel
You've been hiding behind it for years, and whenever yo
feel threatened, you just start blaming everybody els
before they can get close."

"What are you talking about?" he demanded, mo
amazed than angry.

"You. Tyler Stovall." Cammie pressed a hand to th
small of her back where a spreading ache was developin
"It's so easy for you to disdain everything. Everybody el
has got to have a hidden agenda, some secret, nefario
purpose that will somehow serve them and work again
you. You're paranoid, that's what it is. So certain that-
that—" She swept in a sharp breath.

"Certain that what?" Ty demanded, too distracted b
her words to pay much attention to her body language.

"—that there isn't any *good* in anybody. You try an
convict people just like that." She snapped her finger
Pinpoints of light flickered in front of her eyes and
distant humming seemed to swell loudly. She turned i
bewilderment to what she thought was the direction of th
sound, but the humming built to a deafening crescend
all around her. Distantly, she realized the sound was insid
her head.

"I think I have just cause," Ty bit out, but his voice wa
wavy and far, far away.

"Oh, my God," Cammie said suddenly. "I'm going out.

"Out?"

Ty's attention snapped back just as Cammie crumple
into his arms. Her face was white as alabaster, smooth an
innocent. Concern flooded through him. He carried he
carefully to the living room which was at least carpete
but in the process he felt a sticky warmth. He looked dow
at his hands.

Blood.

The baby. She was miscarrying the baby.

Panic ran through his veins like ice. For a moment, he tood in utter silence. Guilt slammed like a hammer inside is head, but he shoved it aside. No time for recriminations. ammie needed action.

As if the scene had been rehearsed, he carried her irectly to his car, struggling for tense, precious moments vith the lock on the front door, then the keys in his pocket, hen the car doors, seatbelts, and finally ignition.

He dialed 911 on his cell as he pulled from the drive, emanding the address of the nearest hospital. He gave is name and Cammie's, then reported his current posiion. They asked him what he believed was wrong with Ms. endleton, and Ty choked on words of explanation.

She's losing my baby. She's losing her one precious hope. She's osing everything she wanted.

He hung up without answering.

"Cammie," Ty whispered as he sped through the darkned streets, ignoring speed limits and indignant drivers like. "I'm so sorry. So, so, sorry." Tenderness roughened is tone. He ached so much, it felt like he needed to cry ut. Biting back the emotion, he lifted a hand from the vheel to gently touch a tress of Cammie's shining hair.

She moaned softly. Her lashes fluttered. Her skin was ce as Ty caressed the back of one limp hand.

"Hold on, my love," he whispered, a catch in his throat. 'We're almost there."

The emergency room was hopping. All manner of broen bones, scraped bodies, and listless victims of some ind of illness or another crowded the waiting room and urrounding hallway. Ty carried Cammie inside and an rderly snagged a wheelchair and helped Ty slip his lovely urden to its depths. Ty followed the orderly who notioned him back to the row of admitting desks where ll seats were taken.

Ty's patience snapped. Never one to handle authority

well, he ignored the rules and strode to the inner roon
in search of Cammie.

"Excuse me!" a thin, tough-faced nurse bit out. "G
back outside!" She pointed in the direction he'd just com

Ty didn't even answer. He moved past her, much to he
shock and fury, and when he found the curtained partitio
which served as Cammie's "room," he shouldered his wa
past a departing nurse.

"Sir, you must leave," she ordered.

"I need to see her."

"Are you her husband?"

"Uh—yes," he lied.

"We need you to fill out the forms. Please . . ." Sh
touched his arm, tried to guide him away from Cammi
who was currently being awakened with some very stron
ammonia-type smelling salts. She groaned and turned he
head away from the noxious odor.

"Please, Mr. Stovall."

Her use of his name brought him back to earth. She'
recognized him, of course. He realized, belatedly, th
causing a scene would only make things a hundred tim
worse. With a feeling of being chastised and useless an
completely at fault all at the same time, Ty retraced hi
steps, his brain sluggish and full of apprehension.

Faces. Blobs of pink color. All turning his way, recogn
tion dawning. He felt claustrophobic, physically sick.

Drawing out his cell phone, he was ordered by anothe
testy member of hospital personnel to take it outside. Th
hospital was a "cell free" zone.

The night was cool, a blessing. With a whispery breez
feathering his skin, Ty first phoned Susannah. Her answe
ing machine listened carefully to his toneless recitation c
the facts. Acting, Cammie had accused him. Well, actin
would get him through now, when all he wanted to do wa
sink down in a huddle and cry.

His next call was to Nanette, who told him calmly an
clearly that there was nothing he could do but just stan
by and be supportive. She would be right there.

Then, staring at the cell phone as if it were an unfamiliar object, he punched out another number without being able to rightly explain why. When his father answered on the first ring, Ty slammed shut the receiver, shocked and horrified at himself. The phone rang right back.

"Caller ID," Samuel bit out before Ty could say more than hello.

"On my cell?" he questioned.

"Just the number, not the caller name. I recognized your number."

Ty suddenly felt like laughing hysterically. "Are you kidding? How did you know it? Did Orren Wesson get you the information, or your buddy, Renquist? You've got all kinds of henchmen, don't you?"

"Why did you call?" Samuel demanded, cutting to the chase. "You sound funny. Something's wrong, isn't it? Where are you?"

"Nowhere, Dad," Ty said, and he hung up and turned the cellular phone off.

Cammie slowly swam up from the depths of unconsciousness. A terrible smell stung her nose. She grimaced and tried to talk. Her tongue refused. It filled her mouth.

The baby.

She jerked awake, tried to sit up, was gently pushed back down by the shoulders. Two strangers in hospital garb smiled at her, one a woman, one a man. "Lie back, please, Ms. Merrill. Wait."

"I'm at a hospital," she realized aloud. "Where's Dr. Crawley?" Her words were a slur, her scared brain recognized dully. Panic filled her eyes.

"I'm Dr. Lenders," the man soothed. "You were unconscious, bleeding. We're checking things out."

"I'm pregnant. How—how do you know my name?"

"Mr. Stovall brought you in. He's filling out the admitting papers."

"Ty brought me?" Vaguely she remembered being in

the empty house. His accusations. A spasm of pain crossed her face and she started to cry.

"Everything's going to be fine," Dr. Lenders assured her, but Cammie knew it wasn't true.

"No," she whispered bitterly, her hands clenching into impotent fists. "No, it's not."

"When Mr. Stovall returns—"

"Don't let him in!" she cried, but it was a bare whisper. She had no strength to scream the feelings rushing through her. "I can't see him. Ever."

Dr. Lenders and the nurse exchanged a glance. With a nod, Dr. Lenders agreed, and Cammie turned her face to the green curtain, locked in her own hellish misery from which there was no escape.

Ty sat in the waiting room, head bent, hands hanging loosely between his knees. Out of his peripheral vision he saw a pair of cowboy boots coming his way. Small feet, slim legs. Nanette.

He lifted his head, the effort almost more than he could bear. Nanette sank down beside him and clasped his left hand, patting it gently. His lips trembled. His nose burned inside. With a tremendous effort he kept himself from turning to the comfort of his mother's arms.

Silence was their companion. Silence apart from the familiar sounds of the hospital: phones buzzing, rubber-soled shoes squeaking, gurneys' wheels jingling as they passed. Finally, Nanette sighed and said, "You're on the news."

Ty groaned. It was the last straw. "How bad is it?" He glanced at her in time to see the end of a grimace. "Tell me," he said to her hesitation.

"Gayle's suicide was rehashed again. They're saying you're unlucky in the fatherhood department. Your first child was killed in the suicide; the second to a miscarriage."

Misery ate at him. And guilt. "I ran away last time," he said. "I'm not leaving now."

"I know."

"Reporters will be here soon," he realized with a start.

"The hospital staff will keep them back. Don't worry."

"Mom . . .?"

She gazed at him tenderly. It wasn't often her son addressed her directly by anything but her name.

"I called my father. I don't know why."

"Did you tell him where you were?"

He shook his head. "I couldn't."

"Well, he probably knows now, so don't be surprised if he shows up here, too."

"I've got to see Cammie."

His plea got to her. Telling him she would see what could be done, Nanette took matters into her own hands. She walked in the direction of the curtained emergency-room bays, encountering no one who opposed her right to be there. Maybe it was her sex, or her age, or her overall sense of serenity, but she discovered Cammie's cubicle just as her gurney was being pulled into the hallway.

"Where are you taking her?" Nanette asked the orderly.

"To another room. This place is too busy. She'll be all right."

"Nanette?" Cammie whispered, hearing her voice. She reached a hand out to her as she passed by. Nanette clasped it, following after the moving gurney.

"Dr. Crawley? My doctor? Is she here yet?"

"I—don't know."

"They've called her. I need her. I'm losing the baby." Her face was white as the sheet covering her, her eyes stretched wide with fear.

"It's going to be all right," Nanette murmured.

"Everyone keeps saying that. It's a lie," Cammie choked. Tears filled her voice as she said, "I'm losing the baby. I'm losing the baby."

"Shhh . . ." Nanette's heart ached. She held on to Cammie's hand and waited until she was settled in bed. "I'll get Ty."

"NO!"

Nanette was shocked by Cammie's vehemence.

"He doesn't want this baby," Cammie said bitterly, a spasm crossed her forehead. "He never wanted it."

"Are you in pain?" Nanette asked, concerned.

"Some. Oh, Nanette . . ." she moaned.

At that moment, a large woman strode in with authority. She wore street clothes, but Cammie's cry of relief alerted Nanette that this must be her doctor.

"They paged me," the woman said.

"Dr. Crawley," Cammie implored. "I'm miscarrying." She was openly crying now and Nanette wanted to cry herself.

The doctor nodded gravely and kindly.

"I think Tyler should know," Nanette murmured.

"Don't bring him here. I can't see him now."

"But, Cammie—"

"No. Please. *Please!*"

"Could you just inform him of the possibility of a miscarriage?" the doctor suggested. "When Cammie's ready, she'll see him."

Nanette nodded and slowly retraced her steps to the waiting room. From Dr. Crawley's demeanor it was clear there was little chance the baby would survive. Cammie was miscarrying.

On leaden feet she returned to the waiting room. She would be the bearer of some very bad news. Only now, the quiet haven was alive with noise and people. Samuel and Cammie's agent—Susannah—and a host of others. Ty stood to one side, looking for all the world like he might take a swing at one of them if they didn't leave him alone. Nanette marched forward, but several burly men in hospital whites reached the crowd first and taut words were exchanged. Seizing the moment, Nanette sidled up to her unhappy son.

"You okay?" she asked, clasping Ty's hand as she came up beside him.

"Where's Cammie?"

"They've—taken her to a room."

"I want to see her."

"Not now."

Ty's eyes searched his mother's worried face. "What's wrong? Is she all right? The baby?"

"Tyler . . ." Nanette pulled him to one side, conscious of the sea of faces turned their way, straining to hear her. "She may have already lost the baby. She doesn't want to see you just yet."

Ty hadn't believed he could feel worse. But now pain exploded inside him. He strode from the mob in the waiting room, moving sightlessly through the emergency room, deaf to all calls in his direction. An automaton, he walked away from the hubbub to a quiet corner where a bench sat in front of a window that looked out on a courtyard where palm trees were uplit amidst hedges of bougainvillea. He pressed his forehead to the panes and closed his eyes.

Cammie, oh, Cammie, forgive me.

It was all his fault. He'd done it. He'd ruined it. He'd thrown away their one chance at happiness because of his own stupid, self-destructive fears. It killed him to think that he might have lost her forever; he'd already lost their child.

Time passed. Lost in his self-recriminations, Ty paid no attention to how long he sat alone. When a hand suddenly dropped on his shoulder, he jerked to attention. Silently wishing the intruder would just go away, he stayed frozen in position.

"Son?" Samuel said softly.

Ty inwardly groaned. His father was all he needed! "I don't want company," Ty muttered between clenched teeth.

"I know that. For what it's worth, I'm sorry. I would have liked a child—for you. I know you think I'm an awful father; I probably am. All those years ago I was jealous of your success when I should have embraced it. That's why I fooled around with Gayle. I never dreamed the consequences would be so great."

Uncertain whether to believe this surprising admission,

Ty didn't move. He'd lost trust in Samuel years before; he wasn't fool enough to believe his father now, just because he was at a low ebb.

Samuel said into the quiet, "I've taken care of the news hounds for now, but there's someone you might want to talk to."

"No," he clipped out.

"It's Camilla's doctor. Dr. Crawley."

That slowly penetrated. Dimly, Ty realized his parents, both Nanette and Samuel, were doing their best to help. He should feel grateful, he thought, but for now, all he felt was numb.

When Samuel touched his arm, indicating the way back, Ty rose on legs that seemed detached from the rest of his body. He walked beside his father, two men who, but for the separation of a generation, were nearly identical. Surreptitious glances slid their way as they passed, from hospital staff and patients alike. The sight of Tyler and Samuel Stovall walking side by side was remarkable.

True to his word, Samuel had scattered the reporters until only Susannah, Nanette, and now Karen Walthers remained. A large woman in street clothes and wire-rimmed glasses stood up and offered Ty her hand. She introduced herself as Dr. Crawley, and suggested Ty follow her to a small office where they could share a modicum of privacy.

"Cammie?" Ty asked as soon as Dr. Crawley shut the door behind her. His voice was hoarse, unrecognizable as his own.

"She's resting comfortably. However, I'm afraid there's no sign of the baby," she said gently.

Ty sank down into a chair, dropping his head into his hands.

"We've put Cammie on an IV and given her a sedative," the doctor explained. "It might be best if she stays the night."

She miscarried.

"Does she—does she know yet?" he asked unevenly.

"Yes."

"May I see her?"

The good doctor's hesitation said it all. Lips twisting, Ty said, "She doesn't want to see me, does she? She blames me."

"She doesn't blame you," Dr. Crawley assured him. "Miscarriage is one of the risks with endometriosis. She knew the chance of carrying full term was slight."

"Endometriosis?" Ty repeated blankly.

The doctor peered at him over the tops of her glasses. "She hasn't talked to you about her condition?" At the slow shake of his head, Dr. Crawley said briskly, "Then let me bring you up to speed, Mr. Stovall. It might help you understand why she feels the way she does . . ."

Blurry outlines. Colors muted by dim light. Cammie lifted one eyelid though it felt held down by weights. *Where am I?* she thought, sensing an unformed ache deep inside herself. Her mind searched for the answer, but even brushing against that truth felt too sore, too raw, so she shied away from digging too hard. Instead, she focused on the room and came to realize she must be in a hospital.

The baby! Memory jolted back sharply.

It's gone.

Whimpering, Cammie wriggled further under the covers, squeezing her eyes shut, slamming the door of her brain on those unpleasant thoughts. She couldn't cope. Not now. Later. Much, much later she would think about her future and what would happen next. With that, she slipped back to welcome oblivion.

Ty wandered the rooms of the house he'd purchased for him and Cammie, wondering if he would ever actually live here. He'd made the purchase the day after Cammie miscarried, the day she left the hospital and returned to her apartment. She hadn't contacted him, and any attempt he'd made in that direction had been met with no response. Once again he'd left messages on her answering machine and with Susannah, but Cammie was unwilling to respond to him.

He bought the house anyway. He liked it. When he realized Cammie wouldn't talk to him and that their life together was very possibly on hold forever, he bought a hefty bottle of scotch and drank himself into a stupor, waking sometime in the depths of the night to feel carpet beneath his fingers as he was stretched out on the floor.

He rolled over and stared through the dimness, feeling wretched. Alcohol hadn't helped. When had it ever? But age and experience had, apparently, since he felt no need to run away and hide this time. Instead, he threw out the extra bottles of liquor and began planning what to do with the rest of his life. He didn't believe it would not include Cammie; he couldn't face a future without her. But he did know that her sadness and loss of belief in him would make for a long, slow recovery.

He just hoped it would be a full one. With his self-destructive days behind him, Ty used this time of solitude productively. He read through scripts and made plans with his agent Susannah, who was very circumspect about any questions he posed regarding Cammie.

So now, here he was. Ten days into his new life without the woman he loved, miserable to the extreme, unable to do anything to correct the wrongs he'd inadvertently heaped on the woman he loved. He'd heard, by default, since Susannah told him nothing about Cammie, that she'd accepted the role on *Cherry Blossom Lane* after all.

The doorbell rang and Ty whipped around, frowning. No one knew he was here, did they?

Cammie!

He ran to the door, flung it open, then nearly slammed it shut again when he encountered Paul Merrill on his porch. "You again!" he spat in disgust.

"Don't slam the door." He held up a hand and a manuscript. "I've got a proposition for you."

"No more manuscripts. No more talk."

"Wait! Wait!" The little weasel actually stuck a foot in the door. "I've tried to talk to Susannah, but she's been completely irrational. If I were you, I'd get another agent! She won't even consider the idea, but I thought you might, given your relationship with Cammie."

Ty thrust his weight on the door, not enough to crush Paul's foot, just enough to give him the idea that he was serious about evicting the man. "How did you know where I was?" he demanded.

"I knew you bought the place. I was going to wait around and see if you showed up, or leave this on your doorstep if I had to. But *voilà!* You were already here."

Ty held tight to the door until Paul's foot began to feel the pinch. With a muffled exclamation, Paul shoved the manuscript through the closing crack, shaking it in front of Ty's nose. Ty read the title and he stopped pushing, more out of bafflement than real interest. It was a teleplay. For *Cherry Blossom Lane.*

"What is this?" he asked suspiciously.

"How about a guest-shot role?" Paul suggested eagerly, his voice muffled behind the heavy planks of the door. "Four episodes. Playing opposite Cammie, as, I think you'll appreciate the irony here, her *brother!*"

"Get lost!"

"Ratings would soar! Don't you see? And from what I gather, you could use an entree into seeing my lovely, stubborn ex again. Think about it. Seriously. And make that agent of yours pay attention to a legitimate offer!"

Paul dropped the manuscript on the foyer floor, his arm disappearing through the crack. Instead of slamming it closed, Ty opened the door wider and watched Paul jump into his car and wave blithely before driving away.

Opportunist. Ty shut the door in disgust. Picking up the script, he warned himself not to read one word. It was a ploy, just another way that Cammie's obnoxious ex had contrived in order to keep himself playing with the big boys.

Ignoring his own advice, Ty folded back the first page and started reading from FADE IN . . .

This dressing room was a bit larger than her previous one. Placing a bright print of a fat ebony cat peering through a spray of huge red flowers on the wall, Cammie stepped back and examined her handiwork. These cubby-holes had no outside view, so one had to make do with whatever they could come up with to brighten the place. The picture was good. It lifted the room's overall mood and Cammie's in the process.

She'd been back a week. The work was welcome. A life-saver, really. Depression had dogged her like a bad smell for far too long. She needed to get over it, once and for all.

Thinking about the baby was still too painful, so Cammie pushed those thoughts aside by indulging in work. She pushed furniture around and fussed with pillows, then she snatched up her script and forced a concentration she didn't feel.

She refused to think about Tyler, too. She was ashamed at the way she'd treated him, but his coldness and accusations had hurt so much, she'd wondered if she would ever be able to take a breath without the resulting pain in her heart. Susannah said he thought she blamed him for losing the baby. Cammie almost called to explain the fallacy of that theory, but Ty beat her to the punch, leaving a series of messages on her phone which were worded so cautiously that she didn't know what to think. It was as if he were afraid to say what he was really thinking, really feeling. Not that she blamed him; she'd pushed him so far away that she knew he wondered what her feelings were.

A darn good question. Oh, she loved him still. She probably always would. But it couldn't be that she was his support and he was never hers. She needed a partner, someone who lifted her up when she was down, someone who listened and consoled and understood.

She didn't need someone whose trust in others was so low that her own motives were always questioned.

A muffled *brrrinnng* sounded. Her cell phone. Inside her purse. Momentarily she debated not answering it. She needed to keep her mind on her script, if possible, and she was afraid her concentration would be shattered—especially if the caller turned out to be Ty. She just wasn't ready to talk to him yet.

But curiosity won. "Hello?" she asked tentatively.

"Hey, hon." Susannah's voice sounded fuzzy and distant. "I've got some—uh—interesting news for you."

"Uh huh?"

"It's about Mr. Stovall, the younger. He's—" The line crackled and spit noise in her ear. Cammie pulled the phone away for a second, then came back to hear Susannah fade in and out with, "*. . . didn't believe it would happen. He's . . . against my advice . . . thought you should know . . . television . . . only four episodes . . . initial meeting today . . . can you believe it? Your brother!*"

"Susannah? Susannah, I can't hear you! Call back." Cammie hung up the phone, then stared at it, willing it to ring. It gave one abortive buzz. She snatched it up, but there was no one there.

A knock on her door. "You're wanted on the set."

Frustrated, and oddly unnerved, Cammie wondered what the heck Susannah had meant about "Mr. Stovall, the younger" in relation to being her brother. *She* sure didn't think of him that way at all, and she was pretty certain the rest of the world didn't, either!

Grabbing her script, she headed through the door to the narrow hallway which led to *Cherry Blossom Lane*'s sound stage. Hurrying, afraid she was already late, she rounded a corner—and came up against a very male chest.

"Sorry," she murmured, then gasped as all her senses registered at once: her ears hearing the tenor of familiar breathing; her nose smelling a musky, masculine scent that sent memory thrumming up the nerves to her brain; her fingers recognizing firm, hard flesh of a man's immovable chest; her eyes, as they lifted upward, soaking in Ty's beloved features like a drowning woman: the devilish arch of his brows, his straight nose, the brackets beside his mouth which varied from discontentment to amusement depending on his mood. And his mood was good right now, she realized, her heart beating a little quicker at the sexy flash of white of his smile.

"Ty," she breathed, afraid to let go, afraid not to.

"Cammie," he beseeched, when she would have pulled away. "Wait. Please let me have a moment. Just let me say what I need to say."

"I'm—I'm late," she stammered, although every part of her wanted to beg her own forgiveness.

"Two minutes."

His hands dropped gently to her shoulders and his gray eyes gazed deeply into her azure ones. Shuddering all over, Cammie silently cursed her weakness, but she was powerless to do more than stare back, her eyes so starved for the sight of him that she could scarcely concentrate.

"How—how did you get in here?" she asked before he could speak. "It practically takes an act of God for anyone's family to show up on the set. Our director's a complete dictator, and he doesn't bend for anyone. Well, except maybe a Stovall, apparently. Still, he tossed out John Cavendish once, and he's got his own series and a string of successful—"

"Shhhh." He placed a finger over her babbling lips. Cammie hushed instantly, undone by the feel of his flesh against her mouth. "They want me to do a guest shot. Four episodes playing the part of your character's brother. I haven't said yes, because I didn't know how you'd feel."

"A guest shot?" she said dazedly. So that was what Susannah had been trying to tell her.

"Cammie, I love you," he said urgently. "I want to be with you. I confess I used this opportunity to see you. I *need* you," he stressed. "Please . . . *please* . . ."

"Oh, Ty . . ."

Hearing her tacit capitulation, his strong arms gathered her close to his chest. She could feel the hard thump of his heart. "My God, I was so scared you would turn away. I'm so sorry for being cruel. I wouldn't let myself believe in you."

"I'm sorry for being too sensitive," Cammie whispered, her voice threaded with tears.

"No, it's not your fault. Darling, we both got caught up in our worst fears." He lifted her chin to gaze into her tear-starred eyes. Her tremulous smile touched his soul. "Never again. We're going to get married. Right away. We're going to tell each other everything and face every problem. I'm never letting you get away from me again!"

She laughed through a sheen of tears. "And we're going to be 'brother and sister' on *Cherry Blossom Lane?*"

"If that's what you want."

"I want to be with you every minute. Every minute," she repeated.

He nodded in joyous agreement. "Cammie, I'd like to go with you the next time you visit Dr. Crawley and see what our options are," Tyler added, stepping into the fire. "I want what you want, and if there's any way we can have children, I'll do whatever I can to help."

Her breath caught. "I don't think that's possible."

"Together, anything's possible," Ty whispered urgently. "Have a little faith, my love. We'll work it all out together."

And then he kissed her, hard, sealing the deal, and Cammie's heart felt as if it would burst with joy. "Together," she whispered.

"Together . . ."

"Ty?"

"Hmmm?"

"Don't ever leave me. I—I know I've pulled away, but it was just that I was hurt and scared."

"I will never leave you," he assured her tenderly.

And Cammie believed in him thoroughly, sensing his total commitment in the power of his strength, the conviction of his voice, the gentle love in his tone. Maybe they could have everything, she dared to finally hope. Maybe someday soon.

EPILOGUE

"Push hard, Cammie," Dr. Crawley ordered suddenly. *"Now!"*

Cammie squeezed her eyes shut and grimaced, straining with all her might. She counted to seven before the urge dissipated and she lay gasping for breath, her hands clutched around the edge of the table.

Ty stood behind her head where she could view his eyes, upside down from hers, gazing at her lovingly from behind his green mask.

"I love you," she mouthed, too tired to project her voice.

She could scarcely believe they'd made it to this point. There had been talk of surgery, several chin-stroking sessions about the condition of her endometriosis, lots of conjecture and worry, then, lo and behold, another positive pregnancy test! Fear had been her first reaction. Contained joy, her second.

But from the get-go, Ty had been upbeat and supportive. "I believe it will happen this time," he told her.

"You're giving me lip service," she'd argued, closing

her ears to her husband's encouragement, afraid to liste
and hope for the impossible.

Ty had gently shaken his head. Smiling at the woma
he loved, he assured her, "No, it's faith. Pure and simple.

She'd been too frightened to believe. She'd carried o
with her role as Donna Jenkins as if nothing were differen
She told no one, not even Susannah, of the possibility.

And in the end, Ty's trust and faith had proved righ
For now, here she was in her twenty-seventh hour of labo
of a very normal—almost boringly so!—full-term preg
nancy.

Oh, little Jeremy was a bit premature, but the Caesaria
everyone had predicted had not been necessary. Cammi
had held on to her baby with a mixture of faith and lov
and now, while her husband lifted her shoulders and th
doctor ordered her to bear down, Cammie listened to th
fast rhythm of her heartbeat and thanked the heaven
above for this beautiful miracle.

"Here he comes!" Dr. Crawley reported happily.

Cammie had been given a local anesthetic, but she coul
still feel the pressure of Jeremy's emerging head.

"He's beautiful," Dr. Crawley said, causing tears to stand i
Cammie's eyes. "Give me one more push for the shoulders.

A baby's wail suddenly pierced the breath-held silenc
Cammie's eyes shot to her husband's, which were susp
ciously damp and transfixed on the slippery little body i
Dr. Crawley's grasp. Cammie followed his gaze.

"Ty . . ." she whispered brokenly.

He kissed her on the lips, through the mask, upsid
down, his gaze tender and filled with love and raptur
Cammie gulped, moved at her husband's emotion.

Her *husband!* Her *son!*

Her family.

"I love you," he told her. "Both of you."

Reaching upward, she held his strong shoulders, lovin
the scent of him, the touch of his beard-roughened chee
against hers. In the end, her every wish had been grante

Someday was today.